Murder for Old Times' Sake

Margarite St. John

Published & distributed by:

Bauer Communications
Fort Wayne, IN
www.reviveworldmedia.com

ISBN 1466450231
Second Edition

Cover design by Angie Underwood, BookCoverPro.com, and Sara Norwood, www.norwoodarts.com.

Coding and page layout by Sara Norwood, www.norwoodarts.com

Library of Congress Control Number: 2012952917

Printed in the United States of America.

Books by Margarite St. John

The Florida Murder Mysteries

Face Off
Monuments to Murder

The Fort Wayne Murder Mysteries

Murder for Old Times' Sake
The Girl with a Curl
Hot as a Firecracker
Agenda for Murder

The Christmas Novel

Postcards from a Tuscan Christmas

Non-Fiction

Finding Mrs. Hyde: Writing Your First Popular Novel

Our Loyal Readers Say About:

Face Off

"I really enjoyed *Face Off*. It is far better than James Patterson, Patricia Cornwell & Stuart Woods I also read over the past few months. I have recommended it to friends!"
- Jamie

"Easy and enjoyable reading. . . .The pace compelled me to read just one more chapter. . . . explosive beginning and end."
- A fan, Marco Island

"Well-written and fast-paced. . . .characters are thoroughly fleshed out. . . surprising and very exciting."
- Anne-Marie

"Interesting characters. . . compelling story line. . . easy comfortable writing style keeps you involved and draws you on. . . I'm left wishing for more!"
- pageturner

"Couldn't put the book down! Extremely well-written . . . suspenseful plot . . . interesting characters. Each chapter ended with a hook, so I couldn't wait to start the next one!"
- Heather

Monuments to Murder

"It took me only two days to read this book. It was funny, disturbing, educational, enlightening, and ended with a good twist. I'm hooked on this author."
- Anne-Marie

"This is the second book from this author that I have read and I absolutely loved it!! Suspenseful, interesting characters with whom it was easy to identify, and a plot that was both intriguing and yet easy to follow. I literally could not put down my Kindle for 2 days until I finished it! I would say that this author has exactly what it takes to please the suspense novel fan and keep them coming back for more! Can't wait to read her next novel."
- Heather

Murder for Old Times' Sake

"The characters are very interesting, the story compelling, and the who-done-it suspense kept me reading to the funny and fitting end. The author fleshes out the good guys, bad guys, and the somewhere in-betweens, as people the reader can sympathize with and understand their motivations and mindsets. I am looking forward to the fourth book."
- Anne-Marie

"Third book from this author that I have read and just a wonderful suspense novel all the way around! Very interesting characters combine with an exiting plot to keep the reader coming back for more. Details are woven in carefully giving the reader the sense that they "are there" as things are happening. Just loved it!"
- Heather

The Girl with a Curl

"A favorite author of mine. This latest novel of hers won't disappoint."
- Heather

"I enjoyed the perspectives of each character.... The ending was a complete surprise."
- Anne-Marie

"A fantastic fifth murder mystery by this author. I could not put this down and I had no idea who the murderer was until the very end. I found the business with the tarot cards fascinating ... A lot of great research.... There were laugh out loud parts.... I highly recommend this book."

-Anne-Marie

Hot as a Firecracker

"A fantastic fifth murder mystery by this author. I could not put this down and I had no idea who the murderer was until the very end. I found the business with the tarot cards fascinating ... A lot of great research.... There were laugh out loud parts.... I highly recommend this book."
-Anne-Marie

Postcards from a Tuscan Christmas

"I loved this Christmas story, its romance, intrigue, and beautiful Tuscan setting. Tales of redemption ... illustrate the meaning of Christmas."
- Anne-Marie

Table of Contents

Part One

Part Two

Part One

"There are moments when everything goes well;
don't be frightened, it won't last."
Jules Renard

There is a way that seems right to a man,
but in the end it leads to death.
Proverbs 14: 12

Prologue

Bruno Makes a Hit

Sunday, July 12, 2009

On a hot Sunday morning in July, Will Berry and his companion Bruno, a seven-year-old German Shepherd once employed as a K-9 officer, watched the sunrise from their cabin on the northern shore of Lake Michigan. Though Will sat in a rocking chair and Bruno lay on the porch, both kept their eyes on the Lake and both drank coffee -- extra cream in Bruno's. They discussed the day, Bruno responding with cocked ears and head tilts.

Then while Will read the *The St. Ignace News* and *Mackinac Island Town Crier*, Bruno thoroughly investigated the yard for wild intruders. He sniffed and peed and occasionally pawed the ground where he detected the scent of an animal that had dared to enter the property the night before without his permission. Failing to find a creature he could run off into the woods and resigning himself to a long wait, expressed with an explosive exhalation of coffee breath, Bruno lay down at the head of the steps to the beach to wait for his master.

Finally, after reading about the archaeological finds at Colonial Michilimackinac and the stone skipping contest at Windermere Point and then completing a crossword puzzle, Will left the porch and presented Bruno with his twenty-foot lead.

They had strolled only half a mile along the beach when Bruno bolted ahead and partway up a bank, very excited. He returned to Will, looked him straight in the eye, barked, and placed his right paw on Will's knee. Then he turned to run off again and returned, repeating the alerting behavior. Will unhooked the lead and said, "Show me." Bruno ran up the bank through a thicket. Will found it hard to follow through the brush and vines, but when Bruno halted and assumed the "stay" mode, Will saw what his well-trained companion had found.

Just visible under a mass of wet leaves and brush, in a natural hollow in the bank, was the spinal column of a human with some ribs and flesh still attached. A portion of a leg lay a few yards farther up the bank. More unidentifiable flesh lay scattered about, the remains marked by swarms of flies. From the corner of his eye Will spotted a delicate piece of silky cloth caught on the branch of a dwarf evergreen and, as he surveyed the area, a strip of duller cloth on a higher branch of a pine tree, shredded but with a few buttons still attached. The rank smell of bear and the sweet smell of human decomposition evoked Will's gag reflex, though Bruno showed no signs of distaste.

Fearing the bear might be gazing at them a few yards away from the cache of human flesh, Will hastily called Bruno to retreat. They then trotted back to their cabin so that Will could phone the police.

1

Exclusive Club

Saturday, January 17, 2009

Alexandra "Lexie" Royce was a publicist's dream. She was beautiful, single again, and though not yet forty, a member of the very exclusive club of female multi-millionaires. She became so famous after being included in *Fortune's* list of the 40 Under 40 richest people in the country, she'd been interviewed by Oprah, lampooned on *Saturday Night Live,* and featured in a *Vogue* spread proving women entrepreneurs could be reduced to the same level of superficiality as socialites, actresses, and models.

As a consequence of her much-publicized new wealth, the whole world was knocking at her door. She'd had to hire a sizable staff, supervised by her old high school friend Jean Arnold, just to sort through the solicitations from charities, invitations to make speeches, inquiries about sitting on boards of this and that, claims from bogus relatives and friends, feelers from head-hunters, offers from cable networks to appear on business shows, pleas from would-be entrepreneurs for a "little" loan to get started, proposals from strange men of all ages and conditions, treatments for self-help books and videos, even a tickler from *Playboy* for a lingerie shoot.

But at the very bottom of her soul, in her darkest moments, Lexie Royce felt like a fraud. She was typically described as a look-alike for Katherine Heigl, but she wasn't born that way. Her beauty had been enhanced by plastic surgery to straighten her nose, enhance her chin, and remove a particularly nasty mole from her neck; veneers to whiten her teeth; liposuction on her hips; and makeup lessons from an artist who once worked for Bobbi Brown. Maintenance required a regimen of massages, facials, manicures, pedicures, highlighting, blowouts, eyebrow-shaping, and workouts with her own personal trainer. Only she knew that when she woke in the morning, she looked as plain and frowsy as anybody else, expelling the same morning breath, trying to recall the same bad dreams, in need of the same strong coffee.

Except for her hapless half-brother, Rolland, who was still running the fourth-generation family scrap business in Fort Wayne, Indiana, she was now alone in the world. Thus, whenever she was described as one of the most eligible women in the country -- as she just had been in *Fort Wayne Monthly* -- she winced. "Most eligible" sounded glamorous, but at its heart it simply meant "most alone and unattached." She had never expected to be divorced at thirty-three. Hadn't she been the most popular girl in high school, the most datable sister in her college sorority? Then why, having had her pick of suitors, had she married a man as volatile and jealous as the dashing Ferrell Hawke, a man she was now deathly afraid of? Because of him, she kept a Smith & Wesson point-and-shoot beside her bed in the 1930s mansion on Forest Park Boulevard where she now lived.

In no part of her life did she feel more like a fraud than

business. She wasn't quite the self-made millionaire her press reports claimed. If her father, grandfather, and great-grandfather hadn't owned and operated Summit City Metals and Scrapyard for almost a century, she'd never have known how to start Junk in the Trunk, her junk-removal business, or Without a Shred, her shredder business. Nor would she have had the capital to get started or the contacts to make the businesses work from day one.

True enough, her success hadn't been all a gift. She worked like a dog and lived lean. She studied every detail of the waste business, enduring both her father's harsh criticisms as she made mistakes and his grudging approval as she built an empire that exceeded his. She weathered threats from union organizers and extortion from "green" advocates. She learned to negotiate with government officials who'd never prepared a business plan or met a payroll and often hated the very industries that paid their salaries. She deferred the blessings of motherhood, skipped vacations and parties, and lost many nights of sleep. Worst of all, she failed to notice her husband's worsening bipolar disorder -- a diagnosis she suspected, from direct observation, was little more than a clinical euphemism for bad character marked by extreme moodiness and occasional violence.

But now she was resting on her laurels: a hundred million of them after taxes and lawyers' fees. A few years after franchising her businesses nationwide, she sold everything to a multi-national waste-hauling operation just before the crash of '08. Her success meant she was inundated with pleas to speak at business conferences. Now here she was, seated at a speakers' table in the ballroom of the Conrad Hotel in Indianapolis, part of a panel of "experts." Trying to look both warm-hearted and humbly wise, she gazed out at an audience of a hundred women, all would-be entrepreneurs.

Though she had a natural talent for public speaking, the experience made her deeply uncomfortable. She couldn't translate her success into someone else's. The amount of good fortune in one woman's life -- in her case, being born with brains and ambition in a capitalist country with a constitution that protected private property, having a wealthy and supportive family, getting a good education, finding a business she was passionate about, selling at the high point of a volatile market -- simply couldn't be replicated in another's, no matter what high-sounding platitudes came out of her mouth. Her discomfort was so great that she vowed never to accept another speaking assignment.

Some women, of course, saw through the platitudes. The question that was just thrown at her proved that. It came from one of the members of the audience sitting in the front row, a worn-looking thirty-something woman with frizzy hair, wearing a shapeless cardigan and thick-framed eyeglasses. She clearly wasn't an admirer. "So, Miss Royce, if we don't have a family to invest in us, if we don't have someone to teach us the business, if we don't have time to make mistakes or let the business grow organically" -- emphasizing the unfamiliar and suspiciously trendy word -- "how do you suggest we get started?"

The woman's tone was the kind Lexie had dubbed "the Uriah Heep whine," an unsavory mixture of exaggerated respect and ill-concealed resentment. Before Lexie could formulate an answer that was both hopeful and honest, the moderator, a woman famous only for organizing conferences like this one, asked the woman to stand and state her name and the business she wanted to be in.

"Sorry. Forgot about that." As she got to her feet, the skeptic laid her hand on her heart as if about to recite the pledge of allegiance. "I'm Myrtle Lodger, from a little suburb outside of Cincinnati." She turned to look at the other hundred women around the room before again facing the panel. "I'm not in any business yet. I want to start a pre-school in my garage. My husband left me with three little kids and no savings . . . another woman, you know, old story . . . so I've got to find a way to support them. I never completed college, I lost my job, I have no money, so . . . ."

Unmoved, the moderator cut her off and turned to Lexie. "What's the answer to that, Miss Royce?"

Lexie hesitated, adjusting the microphone and shifting in her seat to stall for time. "The answer, I'm afraid, is first things first, and the first thing is money. There are other sources besides family -- banks, for example . . . ."

Her answer was interrupted by scattered laughter. Everybody knew the banks weren't lending even to the most credit-worthy borrowers.

"I know, I know, it's tough out there, Mrs. Lodger. But whatever investors you find, such as friends or family . . . whoever they are, if they aren't just making a gift, they'll want to be sure they're making a sound investment so they'll get a decent return on their money. Therefore . . . ." She shifted in her seat again. "The next questions out of their mouths will be what experience you have with pre-schools, what credentials you have for teaching, what you know about running a business."

The answer, just as she anticipated, was none. Fortunately, the panel only had a few minutes left, and Lexie's response was mercifully cut short by the moderator, who adjourned the panel, complimented the staff of the Conrad Hotel, thanked the audience for its enthusiastic participation, and called for a round of applause for the panelists. When the scattered clapping ended and a hundred women were sliding back their chairs, the moderator, straining to be heard, told them to stay hopeful and win with Women Power. Lexie was embarrassed.

Avoiding Myrtle Lodger's sad, angry eyes and a clutch of stragglers eagerly approaching the moderator, Lexie scurried out through a curtain at the back and bolted down the long, curving stairway to Tastings, the wine bar where she was meeting old friends from Fort Wayne who now lived in Indianapolis. One of them was Linda Adler. Though her life had been marked by tragedy -- the murder of her sister, the accidental death of her first child, the failure of her husband's family's restaurant -- she was always upbeat.

As Lexie entered the bar, she saw that her friends had pulled two bar tables together and were laughing heartily at something. Linda, who had a glass of rosé in front of her, spotted Lexie first. She hopped down from her stool and ran to her friend. "Xandra, great to see you!" she exclaimed, hugging Lexie. Throwing her head back for a searching look, she abruptly changed her tone. "Why do you look like that?"

Lexie smiled faintly. "Xandra. Only my high school friends call me that. But I go by Lexie now." Though her given name was Alexandra, she had many nicknames, each marking a milestone in her life: Ally when she was a toddler, the name she called herself; Xandra, the name she gave herself in high school because nobody knew how to spell or pronounce it; and Lexie, the name she chose in college because it seemed grown-up and was easy to spell. "What do I look like?"

"Spooked. Here, come over to the table. Your mascara's smudged." She wet her napkin and dabbed at Lexie's face. Then she signaled the waitress for a glass of wine for Lexie and told her husband, Tad, to pull up another stool. "You look like you've been to a funeral."

After greetings had been exchanged, Linda renewed her inquisition. "So what happened up there?"

"Oh, my God, guys, I can't do this any more. The stories I hear at these conferences are heartbreaking. Remember that depressing Thirties novel we read as juniors, *Miss Lonelyhearts,* wasn't it?" Several of her friends nodded. "The author was West -- Something West -- as I remember."

"Nathanael."

"Who knew you were so smart, Linda?" The table exploded with laughter: Linda had been the valedictorian of their class. "Anyway, everybody had a sad story and the advice columnist couldn't do a thing about it. I just encountered that situation today. The women who sign up for these conferences are so pathetically eager for pearls of wisdom, a hint to make them fabulously rich, it breaks your heart. But for every woman who's going to make it, a hundred are bound to fail." She told her friends the story of Myrtle Lodger.

Linda, who knew many Myrtle Lodgers -- was afraid she might be one herself -- didn't want to hear any more. "Well, drink up. We have a surprise for you."

"I hate surprises."

"We know you do," Jessica Singer chimed in, flipping her long blond hair that hung in loose waves to the middle of her back. At thirty-three, she still looked like a pre-Raphaelite model. "That's why we like them."

"I volunteered to chair our fifteenth reunion." Linda leaned back, a triumphant look on her face.

"Fifteenth . . .?"

"Carroll High School." Linda waved her hand across Lexie's face. "I know you remember high school. You just mentioned a book we read as juniors. Tennis tournaments and football games? Streaking our hair with neon colors? Skinny-dipping in Jessica's pool? Drinking in our parents' basements?" More laughter, a few groans.

"Friends, I remember it well," Tad intoned. "1994, the year the rest of you graduated, the year I was sprung from the prison of weekly detention." Everyone knew he hated school and couldn't wait to work in the family business, a high-end seafood restaurant simply called Adler's on Broadway. Family strife, a deteriorating neighborhood, and a bad economy had finally done it in. He was now managing the food service for Indiana University Hospital. Linda wanted another job as a public school administrator but, having taken a placeholder job at Starbucks, was now managing its busiest coffee shop in Indianapolis and didn't have the time or gumption to look for something else.

"Well," Lexie said, directing herself to Linda, "I guess if we thought about it we could have anticipated a fifteenth reunion, and you're the natural chairman, so I don't get what the surprise is supposed to be."

"The surprise is Steve-o Wright."

Lexie's heart fluttered. Sterling Steven Wright, her high school sweetheart, in those innocent days nicknamed Steve-o. He was good-looking in the sandy-haired way of the Vikings, smart, amusing well-mannered, always affable. In those days, he was also poor and never dressed in the style of the moment. Though he was an excellent baseball pitcher and therefore popular with the right crowd, one of his eyeteeth was snaggly and his ears stuck out, defects she couldn't get past. They'd broken up the summer before college. He was ready to get married, or at least make a binding commitment before they went their separate ways to college, she to Purdue, he to Butler on an athletic scholarship. But she wasn't.

Though she recognized what a singularly good guy Steve was, she couldn't help fantasizing that a more worldly man might be waiting for her in the sophisticated, multi-cultural milieu of Purdue. And indeed there was, for that's where she met the exotic Ferrell Hawke, a teaching assistant working on an advanced degree in engineering. He was attractive in all the ways important to an eighteen-year-old girl from Fort Wayne. Because he was already twenty-four and had a job, he seemed more like a man than the guys her age. He spoke with an engaging British accent that made him seem super-intelligent. His self-deprecating humor and boyish shock of hair concealed an outsized ego. When he told her in confidence that he would have been the eighth Baron of Hawkemere near Chipping Barnet if a century earlier the Whigs hadn't taxed the aristocracy right out of hearth and home, Lexie was hooked.

They were married a week after her graduation. Unfortunately, it took only another few weeks to grasp the seriousness of her mistake. Her regret at marrying the putative eighth Baron of Hawkemere had nothing to do, however, with Steve or any other old boyfriend who might have proved a better mate. Her regret was rooted solidly in

Ferrell's volatile personality. The experience of marriage and divorce had been so searing, she wasn't sure she ever wanted to marry again. Still, if she ever did, Steve Wright was worth thinking about.

She looked down at her empty glass to hide the interest in her eyes. "What about Steve?"

"He's joining us for dinner."

"He's here? In Indy?"

Tad explained. "There's a builders' trade show at the Indiana Convention Center on South Capitol, practically around the corner. He came down for it. He's building that big development off of Tonkel Road, you know."

"Not a good time for developing property, I'd say," Ed observed.

Lexie wasn't interested just then in the real estate market. "Is his wife here too?"

"You didn't hear?" Jessica asked. "They're divorced. Been that way for a couple of years." She patted the hand of her husband, Ed, a plump pediatrician who, despite his profession, was desperate for a cigarette. "Thank God, some of us are still hanging in there."

"Jess!" her husband admonished, nodding discreetly in Lexie's direction.

"Oh, sorry, Lexie." She caught herself. "I didn't mean anything about your divorce."

"No apology needed, Jess. I wish it didn't have to happen, but I'm glad to be done with it. Ferrell got so crazy I was scared out of my mind." *Still am, if you want the whole truth.* "And you can't imagine how glad I am it occurred before I franchised my businesses and started making real money. As it was, the fight over assets was hellish."

"How's that old British twit doing? Or what's he doing?" Tad asked. Though he'd met Ferrell only a couple of times, he'd never liked the smug son-of-a-bitch.

"I let him keep the cabin on Lake James, but I believe he's living in a townhouse near the IPFW campus. He's an associate professor now. One of my former neighbors sent me an e-mail recently, saying she'd seen him romancing some young chick wearing what looked like an engagement ring, so maybe he's on his way to remarrying. I can dream, can't I?" Lexie grabbed a wine list to find something other than the rosé Linda had ordered for her -- and to change the subject. Thinking about Ferrell put her in a funk. "So where are we eating tonight?"

"The Capital Grille, so we don't have to go outside in this weather." Tad nodded in the direction of the hotel lobby, which was the only real estate they had to cross to get to the restaurant. "I've gotten a part-time gig as a food critic for *The Indianapolis Star.* I'll be ordering seafood, but you'll be doing me a favor if you all order something different so I can assess the full range of their" -- he made quotes in the air -- "culinary talents."

"Anyway, Lexie, back to the reunion," Linda said. "I'm the chair with exactly no money whatsoever, so what should we do about that? How do we pay for a big party?"

"Charge a big enough fee to cover our expenses," Jessica said in her matter-of-fact way, as if her pronouncement solved everything.

"But how do I project the amount of money we'll need?" Linda protested. "What's a big enough fee without being too big? Don't I have to plan stuff *before* I know how much money we'll take in?" She turned to Lexie. "You must know how to do that, figuring out what to charge customers."

Am I being asked to underwrite the reunion? "Let me think about it, Linda. Tell me what you have in mind."

At that point, Ed stepped out to have a cigarette, leaving them to chatter about dates, themes, and venues. When he returned, he shook himself and announced it was snowing, the wind blowing like the hounds of hell, probably working up to a bitchin' blizzard.

Two seconds later Linda hopped off her stool again and ran to greet the tall man standing in the doorway, brushing snow out of his sandy hair.

2

A Smoking Wreck

Saturday, January 17, 2009

Even though they both still lived in Fort Wayne, Lexie hadn't talked to Steve since high school. She'd seen his name in the papers occasionally, mainly in connection with property development, and five years ago she spotted him across the crowded lobby of the Embassy Theatre at Christmas. Both were still married then. When she caught his eye, he looked away. The coldness made her sad.

But something must have changed since then. When Steve entered Tastings, he hugged her without a hint of reserve or self-consciousness. Before returning her to the table, he held her at arm's length so he could get a good look. "My God, Lexie, you're beautiful."

"And you're handsomer than ever, Steve-o. Age looks good on you."

They weren't just empty words. He was wearing an expensive lambskin leather jacket in a coppery color a little darker than his hair. He had filled out and grown taller since high school, now standing almost six feet and weighing at least twenty pounds more than when he played baseball. His hair was cut short, almost military-short. His face was squarer, his shoulders broader, his hairline just a little higher than she remembered. But his nose was still boyishly freckled and his dark brown eyes still sparkled when he laughed. Lexie smiled to herself as she returned to her seat. She could tell he'd had a little work done too, his ears pinned back, his snaggle-tooth capped. Their whole generation seemed bent on keeping plastic surgeons and orthodontists in Ferraris and Gulfstreams.

After Steve announced the next round was on him and everybody had ordered, he winked at Lexie. "By the way, I caught your gig last week on Varney and Company. You made sense about how disastrous one-party politics is likely to be for our economy. So good going, girl. Fort Wayne's proud of you."

The conversation quickly turned to the inauguration, in three days' time, of Barack Obama. No one admitted to voting for him except Linda, who came from a blue-collar family and favored unions. Even Ed Singer, who'd grown up in a wealthy Chicago suburb where everyone was Jewish and liberal, worried that the Illinois Senator would import machine politics from Chicago to D.C. He'd held his nose and voted for McCain as the lesser of two evils. Jessica, an ardent Christian -- made all the more ardent by being married to a Jew whom she was gently but eternally in the process of converting -- criticized the President-Elect's responses to Pastor Rick Warren. Both Lexie and Steve expressed their worries about a president who'd never been an executive. Linda, the peacemaker, said she planned to watch the inauguration because she was always moved by how smoothly power changed hands in the United States.

It was a good note on which to end a discussion of politics and the economy. At dinner, seated at a big round table at the back of The Capital Grille, they mostly caught up on their lives, then switched to food, vacations, and where they'd ideally like to live.

"Tiberias, maybe," Ed said. "Jess and I were in Israel last year for about three weeks. I like the archaeological remains, the turbulent history, the Sea of Galilee, everything."

"Be honest, Ed. Would you really move there?" Linda asked. "I've never been to Israel, but speaking of a turbulent history, it just seems to be the center of the world's troubles."

"Yes and no. If I could go back to the homeland without being blown up by a Palestinian, I would. Indianapolis, however, is safer . . . well, marginally safer . . . so I think we're staying here, at least until we retire."

Steve turned to Lexie. "What about you? Isn't Fort Wayne a little provincial now that you're rich and famous?"

Lexie didn't have to think for a second about that. "Good heavens, no. I like visiting New York and D.C., but the traffic, the congestion, the noise, the pushing and shoving on the street -- the crime!"

"You don't think about moving south to warmer weather?"

"I do. The Gulf Coast of Mississippi, maybe. But just to have a second home for the winter months, not all year long."

"I hear you bought a mansion on Forest Park Boulevard."

Lexie sighed. "I did. I'm not sure whether it was a mistake or not. About a year ago I bought a house built in 1930 by an industrialist who somehow still had enough money after the stock market crash to build his dream house. It's beautiful -- really it is -- in the style of Palladian architecture, I'm told. But it's falling down around my head. If I could just get it into shape, I'd be perfectly happy to have Fort Wayne as my home base."

"What have you done to it?" Jessica asked, angling for a tasteful way to offer her interior decorating services. She owned the most exclusive home goods boutique in nearby Carmel.

"Beth at Wild Hare was helping me decorate, but I gradually realized that was wasted energy. The lights flicker. The furnace went out a month ago, and I think the water heater is on its last legs. There's no water pressure. Every last bit of the structure needs works, so I'm afraid I have to bite the bullet and go for a gut job."

"Well, aren't you the lucky one?" Jessica asked. "Sitting right beside Steve the builder."

"Like Tom Builder in *Pillars of the Earth*?" Steve turned to Lexie. "I don't know who's the lucky one, but maybe I can take a look. In a good real estate market, my crew doesn't do home renovations, but this isn't a good market, so I'm free if you want me. We can at least put a plan and an estimate together."

Lexie was struck by the underlying message. He was free. They could put a plan together. Did she want him? She wasn't prepared to answer him directly, so she asked a question that she hadn't thought about in years and probably would never ask in private because then he'd know it wasn't merely a way to keep the conversation going. "When we were in high school, Steve-o, you said you were going to farm. So how did you get into construction?"

"A long story, but I'll try to keep it short. I didn't have the money to buy or lease a farm, but, remember, my mother's people, the Yoders, are Amish. I spent every summer on their farm. There was nothing I didn't learn -- harnessing horses, plowing fields, repairing machinery, and raising barns. Most of all I learned to work long hours, measure carefully, hone my skills. I liked raising barns the best, so I majored in construction management at Butler. Since I was related to a whole crew of young Amish second cousins who knew more about construction than I did and wanted work after I graduated from college, I had a way to get started with a small crew willing to work for peanuts. For several years, we did the small stuff, mostly screened porches and three-season rooms."

I wish you'd told me that when we talked about marriage, Lexie thought. *I wasn't ready to marry a farmer, but an ambitious guy with his own construction company was a whole other kettle of fish.* "I don't mean to pry, but you still had to have some money even to put a modest construction crew together," Lexie said.

Steve looked thoughtful. "Any of you remember my uncle Ben?"

Tad nodded. "He had the vacuum-service shop off of Dupont."

"That was Ben Wright, the vacuum man. Eccentric but very kind. His wife died young and he never remarried. He died just before we graduated and left me and my older brother some money. Bob Passwatter was the trustee. With the help of an athletic scholarship, my share was enough to pay for four years' of college and then start a little construction business. In those days, even a guy like me could get a bank loan."

"Bob Passwatter?" Lexie exclaimed. "You're kidding.

He's my investment advisor too -- Rolland's as well -- an inheritance from Dad."

Lexie almost missed the shadow that passed across Steve's face at the mention of Bob Passwatter, but she couldn't ask about it because suddenly Jessica pointed toward the windows on Washington Street. "Am I seeing what I think I'm seeing? A whole bunch of police cars with their lights flashing. A firetruck too, I think. What do you suppose is going on?" She sniffed the air. "Anybody smell smoke?"

At that very moment, a handsome young black man trotted toward their table, a worried look on his face. "Is there a Mrs. Royce here?" He was holding a claim check.

"I'm *Miss* Royce," Lexie said, pointing to her chest.

"You drive a black Lincoln Town Car, ma'am?"

"I do."

"You're registered at the hotel?"

"I was. I checked out at noon."

"Sorry to interrupt like this, but could I talk to you a minute?"

"Here?"

He cocked his head deferentially. "Maybe you'd come to the lobby with me."

Lexie looked at her friends, her face tense. "We haven't gotten dessert yet."

"Ma'am, I hate to say so, but it's urgent."

"Okay, okay." She excused herself and followed the young man to the lobby of the hotel, where several policemen were waiting. Their faces gave nothing away. "What's going on?" she asked, suddenly fearful. She had no idea why they were there.

The policemen introduced themselves and asked to see

her driver's license. She couldn't believe the story they told her. Her car had been found in flames in the garage. Not to worry, the fire was out now. Hers was the only car to be damaged, but it was completely undriveable, a smoking wreck, really. They suspected it had been deliberately vandalized. In any case, they needed to question her, see some more papers, and she in turn might want to see the car for herself and talk to the hotel about insurance.

When Lexie and a policeman got to the garage floor where her car was parked, she stared at it in horror. The word "c o w" was etched across the hood. The car was still smoking.

"What am I seeing?" Lexie asked.

"Looks like somebody used acid to make his sentiments known before torching it."

"So my car wasn't hit at random then, was it?"

"Doesn't look like it."

After Lexie reentered the hotel lobby, she glanced out the windows to Washington Street. The snow had let up a little but it was still whirling like dervishes in little eddies up and down the sidewalk. How was she going to get home? Suddenly, Steve was at her elbow. "Everything all right?"

"No," she said. "Everything's not all right. It's a damn mess. I need to sit down." As she started to tell him what the police had told her and what she'd seen for herself, the hotel manager, wearing a badge that read "R. Courtney," strode up, saying he was sorry to hear what had happened to her car. Though the valet service and garage were owned by different entities and the hotel therefore wasn't responsible, he wanted to make right what he could, so the hotel would comp her and her husband's room for the night.

She smiled at Steve. "That's awkward."

"I can get my own room, of course, if they aren't sold out in this weather, but I vote for heading out. My Expedition has snow tires and I've even got chains if we need them. I've driven in weather like this all my life and never had an accident. What do you say?"

She glanced again at the storm raging outside. She hated traveling in bad weather, but she wanted to get away from the scene of the disaster, out of the orbit of the madman she suspected had torched her new car. She wanted to sleep in her own bed with her gun resting a comfortable few inches away. She nodded at Steve, then looked up at R. Courtney. "Thank you, but I think we'll pass."

As the hotel manager walked away, Steve asked if she had any idea what might have happened to her car. She looked around before whispering, "My ex-husband. I'd bet on it."

"You think he's that crazy?"

"I do. And who else would write 'cow' when he meant 'bitch?'"

An hour later, after saying goodbye to their friends, Steven and Lexie were on I-69, slowly making their way in the Expedition back to Fort Wayne in a howling blizzard.

3

A Howling Blizzard

Saturday - Sunday, Jan. 17 - 18, 2009

There's nothing like shared adversity to bring people closer. And shared adversity is what Steve and Lexie got on the way back to Fort Wayne.

The first thing out of Lexie's mouth when they got to the Interstate was, "I just realized I left the table without paying my share of the bill. Who paid?"

Steve chuckled. "You had bigger things to worry about."

"No, I'm serious."

"We split it three ways. I offered to pay the whole thing, as did Ed, but I got the impression that Tad was going to be reimbursed by the paper and for some reason he preferred the reimbursement to a freebie from a friend."

"So who paid my share?"

He glanced at her, giving her a quizzical smile. "I did. We divided it three ways, remember? Three couples."

"That's sweet of you, but we aren't really a couple now, are we? So what do I owe you?"

"Lexie, what are you thinking? I'm not poor, and we may not be a couple now, but we're old friends." He glanced at her, but only for a moment. The road took all his concentration. "Sometime you can buy me dinner if that would make you feel better."

She didn't want to admit even to herself how good that would make her feel. She felt more chemistry with him now than she had as a teen-aged girl. "I think that's a bargain. The prices in Fort Wayne restaurants are half those at The Capital Grille."

"And the food is just as good -- better, in my untutored opinion. What did you think of those truffle-oil fries?"

She wrinkled her nose. "Probably the same as you did. So, how about Club Soda this weekend?"

Steve kept his eyes on the road. "Sounds good but I need to check my calendar. Mind if get back to you on that?"

"Of course not," she said, a little taken aback. She'd expected him to accept enthusiastically, since he was the one to suggest dinner. Perhaps he had a girlfriend he was checking with. She hadn't thought of that.

The blizzard was worsening. The whirling snow was falling so fast the wipers couldn't keep up. Drifted in some places, packed hard in others, the snow obscured the painted lines and the shoulders. Only by following in the tracks of the traffic up ahead could Steve determine where his lane was. The wind was ferocious, especially on the overpasses. Every once in a while, they hit a patch of black ice, but Steve knew how to steer into a slide. Staying in the right lane, he kept his speed less than forty, but other drivers didn't. Semi-trucks and a few cars passed them at dangerous speeds.

"If it weren't for other drivers . . . ." Lexie said.

"Good God, man," Steve exclaimed to his side mirror. "Sorry, didn't mean to interrupt, Lexie." A black Jeep

Cherokee was passing them as if they were racing.

"We're probably thinking the same thing. You're a great driver, always were, but I'm scared out of my mind by everybody else."

"I hope you've taken some Valium, because the road's full of cowboys tonight."

"I don't have any Valium, but I'll put your mind at ease by assuring you I'm not going to volunteer to drive even ten miles of this trip. I'll just sit here, tense and nervous, sometimes pushing my foot on an imaginary brake, sometimes grabbing the armrest, sometimes jerking like a spastic. I'll try not to scream."

"Okay with me . . . about not volunteering to drive, I mean. I wouldn't accept help driving even on a good day." When she air-punched his arm, he hastened to explain. "That's not a comment on your driving -- though you were a little spacey if I remember right. Remember that time you backed into a streetlight?"

"Oh, for heaven's sake. That was at least fifteen years ago and I haven't backed into anything since. Well, once, I guess. I backed out of my garage into Phyllis' car. I just forgot she was parked in the driveway."

"Phyllis Whitlow. I haven't thought about her in years. She still work for you?"

"She does. Another inheritance from my parents. Her son, Drago, is Rolland's chauffeur."

"Rolland has that much money, he has someone drive him around?"

"He and I both have interests in the Scrapyard -- as does Matilda while she lives -- but Rolland also gets a salary. A big one, plus all kinds of goodies, like a company-owned car.

He isn't married, doesn't have any kids, so he spends his loot on luxuries and hobbies."

"Well, to finish my thought about driving, in my world, when a man and woman are in a car, the man drives, the woman works the maps, talks to him so he doesn't fall asleep, lights his cigarette."

"You still smoke, Steve?"

"I do when I'm under pressure. Reach into the glove compartment, please, and light one for me."

"Mind if I bum one? It might help me relax."

"Have at it. Makes things more companionable."

She put the lit cigarette into his hand so he didn't have to take his eyes off the road. "Thanks," he said. "You ever wonder how many people are secret smokers?"

"Every party I ever go to, every conference I speak at, about a third of the people end up on the sidewalk or a patio, puffing away. But you changed the subject, my man, about who gets to drive. I like to drive, and I'm not a bit spacey."

"I don't mean you shouldn't drive yourself anywhere you want. This isn't Saudi Arabia, thank God. Our country would come to a dead stop if women didn't drive, and they'd make life hell for us men." He laughed to show her he meant no insult. "I just mean a man should do the work of driving when he's got a woman with him. Sort of a chivalry thing, in my mind."

At that moment, an eighteen-wheeler passed them on an overpass, then at the bottom began sliding and fish-tailing, finally jack-knifing into the median at a high rate of speed. The truck was stopped by an incline and big snow drifts before it reached the south-bound lanes, tipped at a precarious angle, its lights still on. It wasn't going anywhere until morning.

"Fool!" Steve exclaimed. "Sometimes I wish I had a bullhorn mounted on the roof so I could let bad drivers know what I think."

Lexie laughed. "Plus a big bucket on the front to scoop up the errant cars and toss them out of the way."

"Woman, we think alike."

They drove in silence awhile. Finally, Steve asked the question that was on his mind. "Why do you think your ex-husband torched your car?"

She sighed. "He's mean. Sometimes he's violent. He hired a lawyer who's threatening to re-open the divorce settlement now that I sold the businesses for so much money. I think he's trying to scare me."

"Are there any grounds for reopening a divorce settlement?"

"Ferrell claims I defrauded him, concealed the real value of my assets, so if that were true -- which it isn't -- he might have grounds."

"Has he threatened you before?"

She took another deep breath. "About a year before I moved out, he started slamming me up against a wall when he was really angry, sometimes bruising my arms and torso by just grabbing me and not letting go, his face inches from mine, eyes wild, screaming like a madman. Finally, after a party where he was sure I'd flirted with another guy, he choked me. That time, I really thought I might die. You won't be surprised to learn that almost being choked to death was the pivotal moment. After he left for work that morning, I packed up a few things, got into my car, checked into a motel, and never went back."

"Son-of-a-bitch," Steve muttered under his breath. "Did you file a police report?"

"I thought about it, but I didn't."

"Why?"

"I didn't want him to have a record. I wanted to be sure he could keep his job. And I figured I could take care of myself by leaving and getting a gun."

"He got better treatment than he deserved."

"Since then, all the threats have been cowardly -- heavy breathing on phone calls, threatening letters, hiring a lawyer to issue yet more threats. A couple times I've spotted him sitting in his car in front of my house. But nothing as violent as setting my car on fire."

"So, since the fire doesn't sound like something he'd do, we don't know for sure it *was* him."

"No, we don't. I'll keep my mind open."

Without taking his eyes from the road, Steve suddenly pointed past her to the shoulder on the right. "There's that damn black Jeep Cherokee. I hope the driver isn't hurt, but I can't help thinking the lunatic deserves what he got."

The Jeep had plowed into a deep ditch. Its lights were still on and the driver was gunning the motor, rocking the vehicle, trying to get back on the road but only plowing deeper ruts.

"I hope he stays there," Steve said.

"He might freeze to death."

"He can report the accident, call a tow truck." He smiled at her. "Think positively, Lexie. One less idiot on the road, at least for a few hours."

What neither of them could know was that they had just

passed the idiot who torched Lexie's Town Car.

4

The Idiot

Sunday, January 18, 2009

Drago Bott was the guy in the Jeep Cherokee, but he wasn't an idiot. He wasn't crazy either, though his friends sometimes thought so. He just liked mayhem. Doing bad things in secret made him feel good.

If he hadn't been so high on adrenaline when he fishtailed into the ditch, he would have stopped trying to gun his way out before he was in so deep only a tow truck could get him out. Through his driver's side window, rolled up tight, he yelled at the passing motorists creeping along at thirty miles an hour, furious that they wouldn't stop to help. *Pussy-wussies. Girly-men. Pantywaists. Fags.* He stopped only when his vocabulary fell off the cliff and the window fogged up.

Fortunately, his cell phone was still working. Though it was well after midnight, he speed-dialed Rolland. "Rolie, I'm in a ditch somewhere north of Anderson."

"So why you calling me? You know I'm in Vegas."

Drago could hear ice cubes clinking, Rolland loudly slurping his drink. Rolland Royce had worse manners than anybody else he knew. He slurped his drinks and smiled too big. He talked loudly. His lips were always wet. When Rolland was out of earshot, Drago entertained his friends by dissing his boss. *Money don't make a man cool. Now, take P. Diddy, he's got money and he's cool. The trick is, he never smiles.* Imitating his hero, Drago barely moved his mouth when he talked, spoke softly, never smiled big, stared people down.

He didn't even smile at his own wedding. He knew his buddies thought he was a fool, marrying a plump girl with streaked blond hair. In fact, they were astonished he got married at all because he claimed to hate women -- all except his mother, who worked as housekeeper for Rolland's sister. He didn't like most men much either. His father had beaten him so unmercifully that at age six he'd been hospitalized for a concussion, a bruised liver, and broken ribs. Faced with criminal charges, his father had hoofed it out of Fort Wayne, never to be heard from again. It was Drago's life mission someday to find the son-of-a-bitch and beat him to death.

But he couldn't hate all men and women and still live. His association with Rolland was the best thing that ever happened to him. It gave him an outlet for the violence raging inside and it paid well. Rolland needed someone with muscle and spine, since he had none himself, and Drago was all too happy to be both. If Drago hadn't worked for Rolie Royce -- who was nicknamed for his shape and the car he rode in like a pasha -- he'd have hated the man. Though Rolie was one lucky bastard, he didn't seem to know it. He thought he'd earned the easy life he led. Rolie might be clueless about life, but Drago wasn't. He bored his buddies saying, *There ain't no justice in this world. Know that.*

Rolie, the undeserving fool, had inherited Summit City Metals and Scrapyard -- well, a partial interest anyway, which he shared with his mother and sister -- and the job of running it, but he rarely showed up at work or did anything useful when he got there. If it weren't for Nate Grabbendorf, the nasty old fart who'd been second-in-command for thirty-five years and knew as much about scrap as old man Royce had, the place would have gone down the toilet. And if it weren't for Drago Bott's street contacts and collection methods, Rolie couldn't have kept dealing weed without getting arrested or killed, a profitable sideline started in high school when his father cut off his allowance.

"Why you still out there in the desert, Rolie? The gadget show ended a week ago, you said."

"International Consumer Electronics Show to you. It *did* end a week ago, but I got lucky at the craps table and I'm riding the wave. Besides, I met somebody."

Somebody like a 'ho? Drago wondered, but not out loud. "You got business here, brother. You neglect your shit, somebody's gonna be steppin' in it."

"But not you. You're my man. So . . . how'd things go? No essay, keep it short."

"Done. The car's totaled. I wrote 'cow' on the hood with acid."

"Good."

"Why that word?"

"So she'll think Ferrell did it. That's the word he would use. Anything else I should know about?"

"She left with some dude, didn't see where they went."

"Who was the dude?"

"I think I saw him once at the Yard but didn't get a

name."

"You cover your tracks?"

"Like the Phantom Flyer. Lots of cops around, though. One of them, a brother with his hand on his holster, even looked at me, I'm standing outside the hotel. One homeboy to another, you know? I pretended I was waiting for my car to be brought to me, but he thought I was a car-hiker, asked me what I knew. I said nothing, I was a visitor, just like him." Drago laughed at his own cleverness. He despised all men in authority, but thought black men were the worst. Was it Uncle Tom or Jim Crow they were called? He wasn't sure. He just knew he resented them.

Sometimes, though, he wondered if people thought that's what he was, a race traitor. He looked more white than black, not much darker than Rolie. His whole life had been lived with his white mother and grandmother. He didn't even know his dad's people. He'd grown up in Huntertown, attended mostly white schools, had few black friends. He affected the tight jeans and jackets of urban cowboys rather than baggy ghetto clothes. He was too short to play basketball, and though he ran track, he was never a star, so in school he'd had very little of the cachet of being black. He was even a good student when he applied himself. Sometimes he pretended to be Brazilian. When the black kids at Carroll had taunted him about trying to be white, he shot back that he was a man of the world, something they'd never understand. He nevertheless studied the mannerisms and language of rap artists so that when he went to the 'hood on drug business for Rolie, he could hold his own.

Now, he was Rolie's chauffeur and chief enforcer, and he was married to a white girl. He knew he was supposed to care about being black, but he just didn't. Skin color was of no more importance to him than to Rolie. Both of them cared only about green, the color of money. Drago would make a living any way he could, with anybody that gave him a chance. True, he admired Al Sharpton and Jesse Jackson making a living off of race, but that's all he admired them for -- living off of righteous anger and big words. That was a good trick, being a professional black man, but it wasn't how he rolled.

"So, Drago," Rolie said, finally breaking the silence. "Go buy yourself that Sony 46-inch flat screen you've been drooling over. Get some speakers for it. You should see what Bose is doing these days. I'm bringing brochures home."

"I'm not thinking about no TV right now. I'm freezing to death here. The wind's shakin' my ride so hard I can't get the door open."

"Call a tow truck, Drago. You got my credit card, your phone's working, do what you have to do. I can't talk now."

Drago heard women's voices in the background. *So it's a bunch of 'ho's who've kept you an extra week in the desert, you old turd. Doing what? Drinking, showing off your new gadgets, pretending you like doin' the nasty, you're not too fat to do it, you'll get on it any minute?* Drago laughed.

"On it." He was so witty. He'd tell Lucy soon as he got home. She'd laugh as if he were as clever as Chris Rock; then, because he was so hot, she'd do a little something special, make him feel good. After they got out of bed, she'd hand him whatever wad of Benjamins she'd slipped out of the till at her parents' liquor store, and he in turn would peel off a couple of bills for her, tell her in a condescending voice to treat herself to a chocolate float at DeBrand's or a new dress at Steinmart.

He relished the fact that the Flowers had no idea they were supporting the man they thought wasn't good enough for their sweet Lucinda Rose. As an equal-opportunity con-man, deceiving the Flowers was another of Drago's triumphs, for just as he scorned the pathetic sods who bought drugs from him, which he never touched himself, he equally scorned Lucy's parents, who foolishly trusted their precious daughter. All of them were fools -- everyone in the world. They deserved to be ripped off.

The only unexpected thing about his opportunistic marriage was that he'd come to like Lucy. She was uncritical, never asked difficult questions, made his life easy. She was pretty and silly. She adored him. She cooked for him. She let him have the remote. Though she talked too much, he'd learned to tune her out.

The only time he'd hit her was one evening when he was drinking, complaining about his brutal father, making vague plans to find the son-of-a-bitch and punch his guts out. Lucy asked him why his mother hadn't protected him. Shouldn't he be just as mad at her? He stared at his silly wife in disbelief, dissing his mother like that. He hit her before he could stop himself. Afterward, for the first time in his life, he was ashamed at what he'd done. And he was paying for it. Now, when he tried to talk to Lucy about his childhood, she covered her ears and made taunting sing-song noises to block out his words.

Drago wasn't ready to end the conversation with his boss. He didn't like being alone in a ditch in the middle of nowhere, his feet and hands freezing, unable to see out the frosted-up windows, rocking in the wind gusts. "Tell me,

Rolie, what was the point of torching the Town Car?"

"You're talking too much." Drago heard his boss do some more slurping. "Like I said, call a tow truck and stop bothering me." There was a long pause. A woman laughed in the background. "I'll be back Tuesday. Ask Trude for my schedule, pick me up at the airport. And don't make me wait."

It took Drago another hour and a half, with the help of a tow truck, to get out of the ditch. Back on the road, heading north to Fort Wayne, he drove his Jeep like a stock car, as if he'd learned nothing. Too prideful to drive like a pussy, intent on staying in the left lane so he could pass everybody, he twice more careened off the road but fortunately without getting stuck for long. It was just getting light when, mad as hell, he finally reached home.

5

In My Dreams

Sunday, January 18, 2009

On Sunday, Lexie met her friend Jean Arnold at Biaggi's after services at The Chapel on West Hamilton. Already ensconced in a round booth in the bar, Jean was deep in *The New York Times* travel section, a half-empty glass of chardonnay in front of her. An inveterate traveler and long-time subscriber to *Travel + Leisure*, Jean was perpetually planning her next vacation. Though she dreamed about Europe, insisting she would someday see England, the home of her ancestors, she somehow always ended up in the Caribbean, alone, in a modest hotel with a good beach, planning a trip to London.

After Lexie ordered a Prosecco and both had ordered Seaside Benedicts, they talked a few minutes about Jean's latest hairdo, a flippy, textured bob in an unnatural shade of red.

"Your highlights always looks so good," Jean said.

"You've got to try In Touch Salon, Jean. See if Cindy, the owner, will take you."

"You don't like my new do?"

"The cut's good, but I don't think the color does as much for you as it should."

"I'll think about it."

After some more small talk, Lexie told Jean about how her car had been torched in Indianapolis.

"Well, tell me more, but first let's toast the end of the blizzard." Smacking her lips, Jean set her glass down. "Did I just hear you right? Your car was torched?"

"Burned to a crisp. Whoever did it etched the word 'cow' on the hood. Fortunately, though I'd checked out, I hadn't put my bags in it yet."

"So how'd you get back to Fort Wayne?"

"Steve-o drove me home last night. Remember him?"

A flash of anger crossed Jean's face so fast Lexie might have missed it if she'd blinked. She was a little taken aback. "What was that look?"

Jean widened her lovely gray eyes in exaggerated innocence. "What look?"

Lexie shook her head. "Never mind." *I must be imagining things.* "Anyway, Linda invited Steve to join us for dinner. It was a good thing he was there or I'd have had to stay overnight and rent a car this morning, which I most assuredly didn't want to do."

"His girlfriend wasn't with him?"

"I didn't know he had one." *So that's why he has to check his weekend calendar.* "He never mentioned her."

"She's Vicki Grinderman, Judge Grinderman's daughter. Very pretty. Looks a little like you. She's a paralegal he met when he got divorced." Jean sipped her wine. "So, what was Steve doing in Indianapolis?"

"Attending a builders' show at the Convention Center."

She made a contemptuous sound. "He's wasting his time. Nobody's building anything in this downturn. In fact, I hear his new development is on hold. You know that one off Tonkel Road. Tonkel Towne or whatever he calls it." Her tone was sarcastic.

Lexie laughed. "Tonkel Towne. Sounds sort of honky-tonk. I don't think so."

Jean softened her tone. "You're right. But it's something pretentious." She snapped her fingers. "Elysian Fields. Nobody will know how to pronounce it or what it means."

"Do *you* know what it means?"

"The final resting place of the souls of the heroic and the virtuous. Greek mythology."

"You know that off the top of your head, Jean?"

"No. I looked it up in Wikipedia when I saw the article about him in the paper."

"I'm impressed. I'd never have bothered to look it up, even if I'd seen the article you're talking about."

"Too important now to read *The Journal Gazette*, are you?" Jean hastily looked away when she caught Lexie's expression. "Just kidding."

Her friend's laugh sounded a little fake to Lexie. What was going on? First, a dark look when Steve was mentioned, then ridicule of Steve's Tonkel Road development, finally a little dig about Lexie's supposed self-importance. "Something on your mind, Jean?"

"No."

"You don't sound convincing."

"Nothing's on my mind. Believe me. So, do you know how your car caught on fire?"

"It must have been set on fire. It was new, so I'm pretty

sure it didn't set itself ablaze, and I can only imagine one person in the world who'd want to destroy it and leave me stranded more than a hundred miles from home. Furthermore, there's only one man I know who would use the word 'cow' instead of 'bitch.'"

"Who?" She sipped her wine. "Oh. Ferrell-the-ferrett."

Lexie laughed. "Why do you call him that?"

"Sneaky devil. You think you've broomed him out of your house, he's hiding under the buffet." She ran her hand through her hair. "Hate to tell you this, but his lawyer just demanded you repair the screens on the cabin at Lake James. Claims you lied about their condition."

"He did his own home inspection, didn't he?"

"I'll have to look at the papers again, but I don't think so."

"Well, he'd been there often enough when we were still married, he should have known what he was getting. Did he copy Marty on the demand?" Marty Solomon was her divorce lawyer.

"Yes. I'll talk to him tomorrow." Jean sipped her wine. "So, how'd the speech go in Indy?"

"Terrible. Decline all speaking engagements from now on."

"That bad?"

"Heart-breaking crowd. One of the panelists kept talking about determination, will-power, believing in yourself -- all the meaningless clichés you can think of. You could smell the bewilderment in the room. I, on the other hand, talked about capital, investors, business plans, experience -- all the stuff that's just as meaningless if they're beyond your reach."

"And what could be smelled in the room when you

talked?"

Lexie laughed. "Touché." She thought a minute. "Discouragement. Worry."

"I sympathize with them. I had dreams once myself."

"Of what?"

"Going to Hollywood."

"Really? Doing plays at the Civic Theatre isn't enough? You get great reviews. People know your name."

Jean made a face. "No money, though. Outside of Allen County, nobody knows my name."

"But you're going to be Miss Nancy in *Curtains* at the Civic Theatre. Doesn't that start in July?"

"It does, for a couple of weeks, but I'm just the understudy. And I'm still going to be working for you."

Lexie looked thoughtful. "You make that sound so awful."

"You mind if I check the dessert menu?"

"Don't mind at all, Jean. But don't change the subject. You're starting to scare me."

"If I order the white chocolate bread pudding, should I ask for two spoons?"

"Sure."

Jean folded and refolded her napkin. "I don't mean to complain. I like my job, I like working for you. But . . . ."

"But what?"

"I just thought my life would be better at this age than it is. I thought I'd be married to someone like Steve. If I wasn't a big star, at least I'd be landing bit parts -- meaty character parts, you know -- in movies, or even just TV shows. I thought I'd have enough money not to worry. I'd be living somewhere warm and exotic. I'd have at least two kids."

Lexie heard nothing after "someone like Steve." "Did you say you'd be married to someone like Steve?"

"Did I say that?" Jean slid the bread pudding to a position equidistant between them. "Here, have some."

"Back to Steve."

Jean frowned. "Did I ever tell you I dated Steve when you threw him over? Well . . ." she said, her voice trailing off, "not dated exactly."

"No."

"I visited my brother at Butler, saw Steve at a party. I got a little drunk. I think I made out with him."

"What happened?"

"I'm not sure what happened."

"I mean afterward."

"We never spoke again." *I called him, left a lot of messages, but he never called back.*

"Do you still have feelings for him?"

"No. Well . . . yes, in a way. I still see him in my dreams."

"Why didn't you ever talk to him, see if he just needed a little nudging to feel the same way you did?"

"Too shy," she lied.

"Well, I might be seeing more of him, Jean, unless he's really involved with Miss Grinderman. If that happens, I hope it doesn't cause problems between us. If it does, the workplace could become bloody awkward."

Jean sighed. "I need my job, so I give you my word. There'll be no problems." She straightened her shoulders, lifted her chin. "Besides, you know, Dwight's still hanging around. Good old Dwight."

Lexie pictured good old Dwight, a nurse who worked the night shift in Dupont North's emergency room. He was a nice enough guy, a little short, a little bald, always joking, but if he ever had any ambition to move out of the bungalow he shared with his brothers -- the "snake ranch," as they called it -- he gave no sign. "Do you two ever talk about marriage?"

"We do. But that's all we do -- talk about it. Unless I learn to like football, he says, nothing's going to happen."

"Well, then, Jean, I suggest learning to like football."

Jean laughed, a little shakily. "Unfortunately, I hate all sports. But at least he's promised to go to London with me if I agree to go with him to the Super Bowl."

"How bad would that be?"

"Mmmm."

"Well, look on the bright side, Jean. Count your blessings. You have a good job," *at a superb salary for Fort Wayne, if I do say so myself,* "dramatic talent, and an easy-going boyfriend who'll do anything for you . . . well, almost anything. And you can travel if you want to."

"But I don't have somebody like Steve."

Well, I don't either, Jean. Not yet anyway.

Lexie was uneasy as she headed home after lunch. If she let Steve back into her life -- assuming he wanted back in -- she might experience tension with Jean at work. She didn't need that right now. She had enough other challenges -- challenges money couldn't solve. That was one of the stunning revelations about accumulating a lot of money. It was very good to have a solid fortune you'd earned yourself, but by itself it didn't cure loneliness, mend relationships, or make a person wiser.

And sometimes, because money made so many things easier, it blinded a woman to the dangers around her.

6

Elysian Fields

Sunday, January 18, 2009

After listening to a sermon by Pastor Luther Whitfield at the New Covenant Worship Center -- a sermon about the five ways to show God's love to people at their breaking point -- Phyllis Whitlow and her older sister Ruth Newsome drove up Tonkel Road north of Union Chapel until they reached a brick column marking a narrow paved lane running east from Tonkel. The column was inset with a large square stone in which the name *Elysian Fields* was carved. She turned onto the lane, which for a few yards was swept almost bare of snow by the winds. When she reached a big snow drift blocking her way, she stopped without turning off the engine. She didn't want to get stuck.

Phyllis looked around. There was no longer any heavy equipment in sight, though a stubby little construction trailer still sat a few yards to the north. The side panel read *Wright Construction Co., Inc. Construction Done Right* in bright red script. Though snow covered the ground a foot deep, she knew a few acres, formerly planted in corn, had already been graded, but a little grove of trees in the southeast corner looked as it always had. She'd been relieved to hear that the worsening economy had stopped the development in its tracks.

"Doesn't look like Carver's Grove has been touched, does it?" Ruth asked.

Directing Ruth to hand her the binoculars from the glove compartment, Phyllis adjusted them until she could see the grove up close. It had no name other than the one Phyllis and Ruth had given it. She focused on the tall oak soaring above the scrubby pines, cottonwoods, and black willow. A big crow's nest was visible in the topmost branches of the oak tree. Then she swept the ground for any signs of a disturbance. "I can't tell. Too much snow."

Ruth took the binoculars and had a look for herself. "You find out yet if the grove'll be left standing?"

"No. How do you find out something like that?"

Ruth considered the problem. "Come out here when construction starts again, pretend you're interested in buying a lot, want to know if the trees will be preserved. Act like one of those nut jobs who never want a tree cut down."

Phyllis looked at her sister with admiration. "I'll do that. What do you think 'Elysian Fields' means?"

"No idea."

Phyllis suddenly slapped the steering wheel. "But what if they tell me what I don't want to hear -- they're going to take all the trees down, grove too, churn stuff up?"

"Got me."

"When we buried him out here, I didn't think he'd ever be disturbed."

"He's probably just bones now," Ruth said. "Maybe nobody'll notice. Or think they found a dead horse or something."

"The wrong end of the horse, more like." They giggled.

"Black humor," Ruth said. They giggled again at their unconscious play on words.

Nervously turning the wheel like a child playing at driving, Phyllis continued, "Carver wasn't much more than skin and bones when he was alive. If the wiry little son-of-a-gun had weighed any more than he did, we couldn't have carried him out there."

"Good thing he got to be a cook in the Navy. He wasn't big enough for wrestling heavy machinery."

"I don't know about that. He was awfully strong."

"He was a chef named Carver. Carver Bott. I always thought it was strange how his name fit his job."

Phyllis laughed. "That was nothing more than coincidence. He was named for George Washington Carver, Ruth."

"Didn't know that." Ruth looked at her sister. "I'm glad you changed your name back to Whitlow. Phyllis Bott never sounded right to me."

"Me either."

"Speaking of names, if you were going to go to the trouble of naming your son Pendragon, why don't you ever call him that?"

"Too long. I never had a nickname, nor did Carver. I wanted my son to have a big name that sounded masculine and important but could be shortened to something unusual. I like Pendragon because it's an old name meaning a chief, a king, a head dragon. But of course it had to be shortened so it wasn't too big for a little boy to carry around."

Ruth had her own views of whether the nickname

Drago was less burdensome than the given name. "Pendragon wasn't in the book of Christian baby names, I'm assuming."

"No. But it was in the tales of King Arthur, which I was enchanted with in middle school. I read the King Arthur stories to Drago when he was little so he'd know where his name came from and could be proud of it."

"Speaking of Carver -- that night we buried him?" Ruth shivered. "That was a night I'll never forget. I'd never dug a grave in my life. Hope I never have to do it again." Ruth replaced the binoculars in the glove compartment.

"Amen to that. I really did think that one day he was going to kill Drago."

"Don't count on me to come out here and dig him up, by the way."

"No worry there. I'll just have to deal with whatever happens."

"When you told me you'd shot Carver, I was shocked. I didn't even know you had a gun."

"I didn't, Ruth. It was Carver's. He threatened me with it more than once, but until that night, I'd never picked it up, much less fired it. Now I go to H&H's firing range twice a year. I'll never depend on luck again."

"Come to think of it, I never saw that gun afterward. Was it is in his pocket or something when we put him in the ground?"

"No. I threw it in the St. Joe River the next morning on my way to work."

"The cops never talked to you, did they?"

"Well, they did, but they asked questions about where he'd gone, why he skipped bail and didn't show up to court. They didn't suspect he was dead. And since I was the one on the hook for his skipping bail, having pledged the house, I didn't appear to have any motive to harm him. Thank God, you helped me get rid of his old Mustang."

"Driving it to Jackson and leaving it a few blocks from the prison was brilliant. As if Carver would ever have gone anywhere near that hellhole on his own." Ruth shifted a little. "You ever ask yourself why you married him in the first place?"

"I was waiting tables at Pete's on Calhoun, he was the bar cook. We took our breaks together. I was eighteen, he was older, very manly. He seemed so much wiser, more experienced, than the boys I'd dated. He was good-looking too, funny, told me great stories about a life I'd only read about. I liked him. So . . . ." She paused. "So one thing led to another."

"Still . . . ."

"He wasn't drinking in those days, Ruth. Since we both worked in a bar, surrounded by temptation, I assumed he didn't drink at all -- and he didn't the first few years we were married. He was a good man when he wasn't drinking."

"Why take on the problems of a mixed marriage?"

"I didn't think there would be a lot of problems other than Mom and Pop. I thought the idea that we're all children of God, that the civil rights movement had changed things, meant people didn't see race any more."

"You were wrong."

"I was wrong."

"Carver didn't look very happy when you got pregnant. He looked like he'd been pole-axed."

"No, but he stepped up to the plate and married me, didn't he? I took that as a good sign. And he seemed happy enough to be a father when Drago was born. I took that as another good sign. He always had a job, even in his worst days . . . ."

Ruth was growing a little impatient. "But you knew when you worked at Pete's he'd been in prison, didn't you?"

"I did. I give you that."

"Didn't that give you pause?"

"Not really. I was idealistic in those days, in my missionary phase. I thought I could help a good man who'd gone wrong make a better life. He even went to church with me. Sometimes."

"How many women get in trouble thinking that way, do you suppose? They're going to change a man just by loving him."

"Millions."

"Their thinking is so confused. 'My man is basically good -- yet he's bad enough he has to be made better, and I'm the woman to do it.'" Ruth snorted her contempt. "Only God can transform a life."

Phyllis was less concerned with the past than the future, and the mention of God triggered her fear. "You think I'll go to Hell for what I did?"

Ruth took a moment to reply. She'd ragged on her sister enough. "I don't think so. You did what you had to do. And you're sorry, aren't you?"

Phyllis slowly backed out onto Tonkel Road, then headed south to Dupont so they could eat breakfast at Bob Evans, where Ruth's youngest daughter, Janet, waited tables. She always slipped them something extra, sometimes even pie.

They'd almost reached Dupont before Phyllis finally

answered. "You want the truth? I'm not all that sorry. Sure, I miss the good times, don't like living alone. But I had to save Drago any way I could."

"Does he have any idea what you did to save him?"

"Good heavens, Ruth, no. Drago doesn't know a thing. He still thinks it's his duty to find Carver and beat him to death."

They laughed again. Sometimes dark humor was the only thing that made the bad times bearable.

7

Luxor

Sunday, January 18, 2009

Late Sunday afternoon, Rolland Royce stepped reluctantly into the "inclinator" at the Luxor hotel in Las Vegas. The 39-degree angle of the pyramid and thus the elevator's angled descent made him sick even when he wasn't hung over. Afraid he'd barf on the way down to the main floor, he closed his eyes and tried to think about something else.

But he didn't want to think about just anything. He certainly didn't want to think about what happened after the call from Drago. He'd been drinking when the little shit called. Afterwards, he continued drinking way too much Knob Creek, diluted only slightly with a couple of ice cubes. The two women, whose names he thought were Minx and Jinx or something like that, were a little older than he expected, but they'd made him feel good, the way he liked, doing no work himself. Basically, in the sack, he was a wide receiver, women were the running backs. Then, while he thought they were still in the room with him, he blacked out. He couldn't even remember dreaming anything.

When he woke up mid-afternoon on Sunday, he was alone. His head felt like it was in a vise. He couldn't focus his eyes to see what time it was. His stomach was simultaneously empty and overflowing with acid. Crawling to the bathroom, he felt weak as a baby. Finally, he had the strength to order room service, coffee strong and black, some pastries to settle his stomach, a Bloody Mary (the hair of the dog), and Pepto-Bismol if they had it.

He tried to remember what Drago called about. The car had been torched. He was sure he remembered that. Drago hadn't been arrested, was on his way home, stuck in a ditch somewhere. Picturing Drago driving in a blizzard made him laugh -- weakly, to be sure, but still he laughed. If he had to fend for himself in a hostile world, so could Drago. Now he had to take the next step, make sure he could keep track of Lexie's every move.

Threatening his half-sister gave him no pause at all. His dad had always loved her best, lending her money to get started in business while at the same time cutting off his allowance. She got A's in school without, so far as he could see, studying much. She didn't break rules. She was popular at school. She kept her distance from her step-mother -- Rolland's mother -- without being disrespectful. If there was any kind of woman Rolland despised, it was a goody two-shoes, and that was Lexie.

Around four o'clock he finally felt steady enough to get dressed. When he grabbed his wallet, it felt flat. Alarmed, he peered inside. His credit cards and driver's license were in place, but the cash was gone. He'd had about ten thousand in large-denomination bills when he left the craps table and cashed out his chips. Thank the gods of gambling he'd taken most of his winnings as a house credit. He stared at the empty pocket in his wallet in disbelief. Then he looked wildly around as if Minx and Jinx might be hiding somewhere in the suite. He'd kill them if he could find them.

Women! How hateful and selfish they were.

He thought about calling hotel security or even the police, but he instantly thought better of that impulse. How would he explain the circumstances so he looked good, like the respectable businessman, the much-admired whale he imagined himself to be? What if they searched the room, found the little stash of pot he hadn't yet smoked? At that thought, he whirled to look at the bed. He walked over and lifted the mattress. He couldn't believe his eyes. No stash.

He walked back to the dresser. His gold cufflinks were gone too. He checked his briefcase, breathing a sigh of relief when he saw that his airline tickets, iPhone, and BlackBerry were still there.

Furious, he walked over to the canted window, as close as he could get to it, and stared out at the neon skyline. He knew he needed to change his life, big time. No more strange women. No more gambling. He'd been lucky, but he'd been wagering way too much money. Maybe he should get out of the pot business too. The new drug gangs in Fort Wayne were making it way too dangerous, and meth was overtaking pot anyway. The Scrapyard still made a profit, but nothing like what it was in his dad's day. When he got back to Fort Wayne, he'd start learning the business, put a little fear into Grabbendorf, who was way too big for his britches.

But Rolland could never stay on a subject long. Self-criticism was depressing. Introspection was for girls.

So, since he wasn't going home until Tuesday, he decided

to make the best of it. He'd never seen the Cirque du Soleil show with Criss Angel or Fantasy, the topless revue that was so famous. Maybe it was time. Though he despised slot machines as old-lady entertainment, he'd linger in the atrium, spend a few minutes with the slots before the show, a way to ease his need to gamble without risking too much. His appetite was back too, so a good steak dinner was in order. Some shop would surely have gold cuff links. Maybe, at some point, he'd even sit by the pool, see what happened.

Comforting himself with the high-minded resolutions he'd just made and feeling almost sober, Rolland decided to put away his worries and get some cash. Then he'd saunter forth to enjoy the enticements that Las Vegas so generously offered, like desserts on a buffet.

8

Yonja

Monday, January 19, 2009

Early Monday morning, Ferrell Hawke trotted, breathless, to Kettler Hall on the campus of Indiana University-Purdue in Fort Wayne. He was calming down but still riled up enough that he could hardly focus his mind on Statics, the course he taught to pre-engineering sophomores who would have to transfer to Purdue at Lafayette to get their engineering degree. He was riled up because his girlfriend, Tiffany, was never satisfied, no matter what he did for her.

Earlier that morning, when he opened the coat closet to grab his microfiber, down-filled, synthetically insulated, hooded winter jacket that looked like crap but kept him from freezing to death on his half-mile walk, he noticed a brand new fur coat hanging at the far end of the rod, pushed back a little as if to hide it. He pulled it out and examined it. Was it mink? He thought it might be. The label read "Pappas Furs." He knew about Pappas Furs because Lexie had been a steady customer. She'd had her mother's opera-length mink refashioned into a reversible jacket. She'd purchased several more expensive fur jackets that she called "casual furs." He hadn't cared about the bills in those days because Lexie paid them, but now he was worried -- and furious. Staring at the jacket, something inside caught his eye. He took a closer look. The name *Tiffany J. Chow* was embroidered in gold thread near the bottom of the lining.

"Tiffany," he yelled without turning around.

No answer.

He turned to project his voice up the stairwell. "Tiffany," he yelled louder.

The silence was deafening. Still holding the wooden hanger on which the coat was draped, he marched upstairs to their bedroom. All he could see on the bed was a lumpy comforter, deformed by a vaguely human shape. He roughly picked up the comforter and threw it to the side. Tiffany didn't move. The silk pajama top she was wearing -- his best monogrammed pajama top, damn it, an intimate gesture he had come to resent -- was hiked up, exposing her lovely round, undimpled ass. For a few seconds, he was tempted to throw the coat aside and catch a quick one. But he was already five minutes late, and he needed the job. It was so much easier being a professor than one more unappreciated civil engineer working sixty hours a week in a big shop that didn't seem to find his accent charming.

He made his voice soft and threatening. "Tiffany. You can bloody well stop pretending you're asleep. What's this coat doing in the closet? Where'd it come from?"

Still, she didn't move. He roughly pushed her shoulder. "Get up now or you're going to wish you had."

She twisted the upper half of her body so she could look at him through one sleep-filled, almond-shaped eye. "Stop." She put her hand on the shoulder he'd gripped. "You're hurting me."

He shook the coat. "What's this?"

She rolled over on her back. "Stop it, Yonja," she whispered. At least that's what it sounded like to Ferrell. He'd learned from her parents that her pet name for him was *yuān jia*, which in Mandarin meant a lover one always goes back to despite quarrels. He also learned she didn't speak Mandarin fluently at all. She just liked to use the occasional random Chinese word to keep him off balance, make him feel like an ugly Englishman who was too lazy to learn any language other than his own. He could never be sure whether she was complimenting or insulting him. He couldn't even be sure she wasn't just talking nonsense out of her ass.

Tiffany liked being Chinese when it suited her, American when it didn't. Her given name, he'd learned, was Chen Chow but she adopted "Tiffany Jean" in high school. She spoke perfect English but now and then threw in a sing-song phrase that might or might not be Chinese, sometimes even affecting a British accent, as if mocking him. She was extremely intelligent, but adopted the manners of a seductive princess when she wanted something.

Tiffany was so intriguing, so mercurial, so beautiful, so eager to be in his life, Ferrell had no defense against her when she took advantage of his office hours to beg for help with the application of Newton's first law to a bridge she was designing as part of a team of architectural engineers. As it turned out, there was neither a bridge nor an engineering team, and she knew Newton's first law as well as he did, but by the time he figured that out, his sanity had slipped away.

In those heady days, he was still in the throes of his ugly divorce from Lexie. He was taking his Tegretol exactly as prescribed and therefore pretty much on an even emotional keel. But he was very lonely. At night in his townhouse, he rented every Chinese film he could find. The best, he thought, was *Raise the Red Lantern,* starring Gong Li as Songlian, a young girl forced into becoming the Fourth Mistress of a wealthy older man; eventually, after many tragedies and intrigues, she finds life so fruitless she goes insane. It was a film the Chinese censors had approved, then banned for awhile when they realized it was a subtle critique of an authoritarian government. When a student looking like Gong Li wafted into his office, he was transported into a fantasy world. The script in his head had become flesh.

In only a matter of weeks after that first office visit, Tiffany had moved into the two-bedroom townhouse he bought near the campus. She pretended to like it at first but now complained daily -- hourly on weekends -- about how small it was, though it was too big for her to clean. They needed a deck and a pool, not just a postage-stamp patio where the barbecue grill was parked. A cleaning lady was a must. The cabin on Lake James was okay, but she dreamed of a house in Florida. She didn't want him to watch football. She wanted more clothes. She needed a loan to pay her tuition. She urged him to invest in Chow Chow, her parents' take-out restaurant in a strip mall on Dupont so they could take the vacant space next to them, create an eat-in area, maybe even a bar. Taking care of her family was her sacred duty and therefore his as well. Didn't he know that?

They didn't argue all the time, of course, and there were things she liked about her Yonja. He had a prestigious degree and a comfortable job. He was handsome, strong, and intelligent. He looked like the British aristocracy he claimed to be. He drove a year-old, pre-owned Aston Martin convertible she loved, borrowing it every chance she got. Before she walked into his office, she knew through her sister, Xiu-Xiu Chow, that he'd gotten millions from the cow that had been his wife and had invested a million of it with Passwatter. Because Ferrell supported her, she no longer had to work at the family restaurant or pay her own bills.

And there was plenty he liked about her as well. She was young and exotic. People thought she was a movie star. On campus, they pretended to be nothing but acquaintances so he wouldn't get fired, but elsewhere she acted like an adoring wife. Her obvious intelligence was a point of pride. She was open to sex anytime, anywhere, never ever begging off because of fatigue or a headache.

But the fur coat still infuriated him, mostly because the only way to keep up with her spendthrift ways was to start depleting his secret investment account, which he didn't want to do. He'd fought hard for the divorce settlement. He'd hired Bob Passwatter as his investment advisor on the strength of Bob's promise of a steady ten percent return. If he couldn't get Tiffany's spending under control, he'd be back to living from paycheck to paycheck or invading his nest egg. He'd tried to talk to his Chinese princess about her extravagance a million times, but after she agreed to whatever demands he made and he thought they'd finally had a meeting of the minds, she did what she wanted anyway. Her credit card bills told the tale of her perfidy.

By the time he left the townhouse, he felt a little better. She promised to pay him back once she completed her master's and got a job. The kiss sealed her promise, making it almost impossible to walk to work without getting arrested for indecency. Still, he was seething with suspicion. If she didn't keep her promise this time, he would have to admit he was a fool.

9

Pancakes for Breakfast

Monday, January 19, 2009

On Monday morning, Lexie called her brother on his cell to ask him to accompany her to various auto dealerships. She needed to buy a new car and wanted some male support. It was dispiriting but true that even in 2009 female buyers were treated by most car salesmen with condescension, the emphasis on color and the quality of leather seats rather than horsepower, fuel efficiency, and resale value. There was no answer. She called the Scrapyard. Trude told her Rolland wouldn't be back from Las Vegas until late Tuesday.

So Lexie decided to make a surprise visit to the Scrapyard. She hadn't been there for months. Through Bob Passwatter, Rolland had proposed that she lend about five million dollars to the business for installation of a copper smelter. The Scrapyard's credit line had been cut to the bone, and no new bank loans were currently available. Rolland's proposal had been drawn up when copper prices soared at the beginning of the previous year, but in the last quarter of 2008 the price had dropped precipitously. She couldn't determine from the papers she was given how a copper smelter made financial sense at this moment. And she couldn't determine how she'd get paid back.

Nate Grabbendorf, as always, was brusque and uncommunicative. Given his salary, Lexie wondered why he never replaced the incisors that were missing on the left side of his mouth. What was so difficult about clipping nose hairs? shaving every day? cleaning his steel-toed workboots? Nate wasn't an especially ugly man, but he needed a lot of grooming. Still, he never missed work and knew the business inside out. He kept the Yard running without much help from Rolland.

Before she entered the office, she spent a half hour scrutinizing the trucks entering the shed, curious about what scrap was being offered. There were a few semis loaded with wrecked cars, but most of the vehicles driven into the Yard were old beat-up pickups. She recognized a few of the drivers, a United Nations rabble of men who spent their days scouring alleys and abandoned properties looking for valuable metal. So far as she could see, there were the usual heaps of industrial scrap from demolition sites, such as rebar, railroad signal lines, and grounding bars from electric substations, and used appliances from national hardware chains. But, as always, she was suspicious of the pickups loaded with copper wire, manhole covers, street signs, catalytic converters, and large air conditioners. She'd have to check with her friend Dave Powers at the police department about theft reports. If she was going to be a volunteer consultant to the Indianapolis Metal Theft Project, which had been started in 2008, the Royce family operation had to be clean.

When she finally entered the office, Nate Grabbendorf wasn't there. Trude said he was taking care of a problem at the compactor.

"I'd like to see the records, Trude, about the scrap that's been bought."

"For how long?"

"Say, the last six months."

"Did Nate say it's okay?"

Lexie suppressed her irritation. "I haven't seen Nate, but you know I don't need his permission."

Trude scowled. A stocky woman in her fifties who had never married, Trude had started with Summit City Metals and Scrapyard a few weeks after she graduated from high school. In her mind, the Scrapyard was sacred ground. In the flu season, when yard workers were laid up, she worked outside as needed, but the office was her private sanctuary.

She had respected Isaac Royce as if he were a benevolent monarch, and she had loved him as well. He was a demanding and temperamental boss, but he was the most intelligent man she'd ever met and he was more than fair to her. Her grief when he died was real and lasting. She didn't respect Nate Grabbendorf in the same way, but she was careful to act as if she did so she could keep the little perks Isaac had bestowed on her without ever letting Nate know exactly what they were. And she hotly resented both Alexandra and Rolland when they came around, so young and spoiled, interfering in her business as if she didn't know it better than they did.

"I don't understand these records," Lexie said after a few minutes. "Is there a key to the initials? Doesn't somebody enter the license plates, check identification?"

"Yes."

"Yes, what?"

"There is a key in another record, and we do check

license plates and identification."

"That's the record I want to see."

At that moment, Nate stomped into the office. As usual, he had a two-day stubble and a toothpick rolled in the side of his mouth. "What's going on here?"

Trude pointed to the report on the desk. "Miss Royce is looking at our records."

"Well, Miss, I wonder if you'd excuse us today." He looked at Trude. "Call the police. There's a body in one of the cars we compacted."

Lexie gasped. "You're not serious."

"I'm always serious."

"Who is it?"

"Now, ma'am, that's what we're going to find out."

"Is the person alive?"

Nate snorted. "Not very likely. From what I can see, he's about the thickness of a pancake."

"How'd the body get in the car?"

Nate ignored Lexie, turning his attention to Trude. "I told Rex to shut down the compactor. Tell Mike to make sure he does. Put the compactor crew to work in the paper shed. I don't want them wasting their time. The truck's coming at two, and the cardboard needs to be bundled before we ship it out."

Just before he left the office, Nate turned back to Lexie. "We'd like to help you out today, but it's going to get a little hectic around here. . . unless, of course, you want to be here when the cops come. But I don't think you'd be much help since you don't seem to know who's dead. Right?"

"Right," Lexie said, feeling like a schoolgirl who'd been dismissed from study hall for whispering too much.

10

A Hard Bargain

Monday, January 19, 2009

About a block outside the gate of the Scrapyard, Lexie spotted Drago's black Jeep Cherokee approaching. She honked, signaling him to pause.

Drago rolled down his window and leaned out. At the sight of her, he'd have smiled if he wasn't in his P. Diddy persona. Against his better instincts, he liked his mother's employer, even though she was rich and beautiful and, like Rolie, had it all. Unlike Rolie, she was always nice, never acted uppity. On nothing more than his word, she loaned him the downpayment on his first car the day after he got his driver's license seven years ago. He'd never forget that. "What's up, Mizz Royce?"

She pointed over her shoulder. "They just found a body in a crushed car."

He looked straight ahead for a second. Had Junebug put the guy on the floor between the front and back seats, covered it with a tarp, the way Drago had instructed, or not? Apparently not. "How'd they find a body, the car was already crushed?"

"I don't know." She spotted two patrol cars approaching with their lights flashing. "You're going to have to pull over, but would you mind waiting a second?"

Drago looked in his rear view mirror. "I'll be right over." After he pulled onto the shoulder, he cut the motor and, after the patrol cars had passed, walked over to her car. He slapped her door. "Pretty lady like you shouldn't be driving an old wreck like this."

"Drago. It's not a wreck."

"An old Honda Civic ain't no car for a lady like you, know that. So where's the Town Car?"

"That's what I wanted to talk to you about. It was torched Saturday night in Indianapolis."

Drago composed his face. Why did she want to talk to him about it? What did she know, or what had she guessed? Long ago, he'd learned the value of silence, so he waited to hear what she'd say next.

"I need to buy a new car, but Rolie isn't back yet, I guess."

"He's coming back tomorrow."

"That's what Trude said." She stared for a few seconds at his Jeep. It looked just like the one she and Steve saw in a ditch north of Anderson. "You didn't happen to be in Indianapolis Saturday night, did you?" She laughed.

He cocked his head, waiting to hear more.

"Just kidding. You're too good a driver to land in the ditch the way that guy did. Anyway, what I wanted to ask you was whether you happen to be free to go with me to a few car dealerships? It helps to have a man along, you know." She looked behind her. "Or did you want to find out what's going on at the Yard?"

He too looked at the Yard. Best to stay away. "They're closing the gate anyway, and I've got nothin' to do till Rolie gets back. Where we going?"

"I thought I'd look at MINI-Coopers, maybe a convertible. Something different."

"Tell you what. Let's put your car in the Jefferson Pointe parking lot, then I'll motor you around anywhere you want to go."

The surprise of the day to Lexie was just how good a bargainer Drago was. Their first stop -- and, as it turned out only stop -- was a small but elegant dealership called The British Embassy, where Rolie bought his Rolls Royces and had them serviced. Drago acted like an old friend when he introduced Lexie to Miles Webber, the sales manager. After a few minutes of chitchat about her relationship to Rolland and the "accident" with her Town Car in Indianapolis, Miles said he was honored by their presence and would personally take care of Lexie rather than assigning her to a salesman. A little man wearing a badge reading "Eddie Rohrer," who'd come up to them during the introductions, backed away, looking rather sad.

Out in the lot, Miles did his best to interest Lexie in a Rolls, or even a Bentley Flying Spur, a bargain at less than $200,000, but she couldn't be distracted from the MINIs. She watched with amusement as Drago strutted around, opening hoods and kicking tires, making deprecatory remarks about every car they looked at. He was swinging his shoulders, doing the ghetto walk he affected when he was proving some point or other. With his handsome, pouty face, he looked like a model for a Guess ad in his black lambskin jacket, designer jeans, and snakeskin cowboy boots.

Finally, she returned to the red convertible with the black leather interior that had taken over her brain. Miles readily agreed to let them take it for a spin west on Illinois Road to the junction with I-69 and then back. "What do you think, Drago?"

"Very cool. Top down's the only way to go, but you'll have to wait for Spring, I guess. Anyway, it'll get you a lot of attention."

"I'm not sure I want a lot of attention."

"Pretty lady like you don't need no stinkin' red convertible to get attention. You could drive a Jeep like me and men'll be running off the road, picturing stuff in their heads. So buy what you want."

When they returned to the showroom, Miles had them take a seat in one of the cubicles and excused himself to prepare some paperwork in his office. When he returned, he handed her a paper naming a price, saying it was a special number in honor of Rolland. It wasn't bad, but Drago had other ideas. He picked up the paper, looking at the quote for a long minute and making dismissive noises. Then he looked up at Miles and said maybe they could talk, just the two of them, in Miles' office. When Lexie rose to follow them, Drago patted her shoulder, giving it just the tiniest push so she'd sit down again. "Mizz Royce, we'll be right back. This is guy stuff. Know that."

When Drago and Miles returned with the papers, Lexie couldn't believe the new number she saw, a price thousands of dollars less than the original offer, allegedly hundreds below dealer cost.

She handed the paper back to Miles. "Is this real? You mean it?"

Drago spoke before Miles could say a word. "It's real, if you still want the car."

She did. Miles said it would be ready on Tuesday. Drago volunteered to come get it and drive it to Forest Park Boulevard so she wouldn't be inconvenienced.

When Miles excused himself again, Drago congratulated her on her new ride. "You happy, Mizz Royce? This ain't the ride I'd have bought, but so long as you're happy . . . ."

"I'm happy, Drago. And in shock. You must drive a hard bargain."

"Ain't so hard when you know what you're doing."

"I take it you know Miles Webber from servicing Rolland's car."

"That and more. We run into each other, time to time." *When he's buying drugs.*

"You're friends?"

"Wouldn't go that far."

"You just happen to know a guy who isn't exactly your friend yet you drive that hard a bargain with him? Maybe you ought to be running Summit City Metals."

He smiled deferentially. "I'm happy where I am. I got the best job in the world."

"You saved me so much money, Drago, using half a day to help me, would you be insulted if I gave you a little something for your time? How about five hundred? Get yourself another pair of those special boots."

Drago wrestled with his pride and greed for a split second. His boots cost three times the amount she was offering, and he wanted to tell her that but knew it was stupid. Still, five hundred was nothing to sneeze at. In other circumstances, he'd have accepted her offer. "Another time, Mizz Royce. It was my pleasure. Now let's get you back to that old Honda that's seen better days."

Drago took the long view. Sometimes it was good for certain special people to owe you. His gesture of good will had the added benefit of diminishing his guilt about the car he torched in Indianapolis and the device Rolie wanted him to install on the new MINI-Cooper before he delivered it to her the next day.

11

Everything a Man Should Be

Monday, January 19, 2009

Robert Thurman Passwatter was everything a man should be. Though he was enrobed in dignity, he allowed his wife and a few select friends to call him Bob. At sixty-one, he had the body of an athlete. He was a very smart financial advisor with a super-exclusive clientele who could invest a million at a crack without flinching. People trusted him.

His résumé was impressive. An ardent servant in the vineyards of the Lord, he was the past president of the Board of Deacons and the current Treasurer of the Three Rivers Congregation of the New Covenant, a non-denominational church with several thousand members, many of whom were as wealthy as he was. He did not tithe, strictly speaking, informing his fellow deacons and officers that the dividends he produced for the church on its investments and the financial reports he prepared *gratis,* by all rights, should be factored into his annual contribution. Besides, he was very charitable. Thanks to the one percent mandatory deduction from all his employees' paychecks, Passwatter Global Investments was always the biggest contributor to his favorite charity, The United Way. The publicity from that annual feat had made him famous. He served on numerous prestigious community boards, where his fundraising abilities were highly valued.

His personal life was the envy of his friends. He had an intelligent wife, two sons who were both successful businessmen, and a six-year-old granddaughter he adored. Twenty years ago he'd built a mansion in Sycamore Hills and now was building his dream "cottage" in Pass Christian on Mississippi's Gulf Coast. Having chosen the location for its name, he and Clarissa were still debating what to call the home to which they would someday retire, but the puns on Passwatter and Pass Christian set their brains on fire. Every Fourth of July, every Halloween, and every week between Christmas and New Year's, he and Clarissa celebrated at their eight-thousand-square-feet Adirondack home with its seventy-foot porch on Lake Michigan in the Upper Peninsula of Michigan. Called Eagle Pass Lodge, the log structure was so special that in 2007 it had appeared on the cover of *Log Home Living*. He played golf passably well, though not as well as he claimed.

The day he turned sixty, he started writing his memoirs but found it was slow going, far more work than he'd anticipated. He knew people were supposed to spill their guts in a memoir, but he couldn't bring himself to do that. He wanted to tell only the good bits. Clarissa, however, who after much urging had finally read a draft of the first couple of chapters, said he'd have to get creative if he really wanted people to read six hundred pages of a saintly life. He thanked her for the compliment.

He was educated too, a proud graduate of Columbia

University in New York City, where forty years earlier he'd met his wife, an equally proud graduate of Barnard College. He wore his huge class ring with pride.

His suite of offices on the eighteenth floor of the prestigious Lincoln Tower reflected Bob's success and refined taste. Audubon prints and framed *New Yorker* magazine covers embellished the walls. Persian rugs enlivened the walnut floors. Fresh flowers were always on display. His magnificent collection of Russian icons and his wife's Lladró figurines, displayed in various mahogany cabinets, lent an air of elegance.

Every morning that Bob Passwatter strolled into his offices, he congratulated himself on the tidy, prosperous little world he had created. Everything was clean and neat, everything in its place. All his employees were required to keep their cubicles in perfect order, no personal items displayed. He insisted on a strict dress code, so everyone from the receptionist to the mailroom boy looked like a market analyst. No one, not even his executive assistant, referred to him as Bob. He was always Mr. Passwatter, a sign of their deep respect.

By the time he graduated from Columbia, he had come to feel there was no other city in the world as sophisticated as New York. Every other part of America was déclassé, especially the Midwest, most especially Fort Wayne, his hometown. His father, however, had different ideas. He'd sold his farm chemical conglomerate to ADM, and if Bobbie, as he was then known, wanted the capital to start his own business, then he'd have to return to Indiana. Les Passwatter reminded his arrogant son that in Fort Wayne there were more millionaires relative to the modest population than anywhere else in the country, so if he needed investors, there was no better place to get started. Bob reluctantly acceded to his father's wishes. He had no high-value contacts in New York, anyway, where he'd always been regarded as a rube by his prep-school classmates. He had no money of his own. New York rents were high and the office spaces ugly. The apartment he and Clarissa shared in Manhattan was the size of his mother's closet in Fort Wayne but without the amenities, like reliable heat and an absence of cockroaches. So, after many hot arguments with Clarissa, who wanted to give the East Coast a chance, they moved back to where they started.

The first work of art Bob bought after he opened his office in the Lincoln Tower was Saul Steinberg's famous *New Yorker* cover from March 29, 1976, depicting the Manhattanite's provincial mental geography whereby the land mass west of the Hudson was just a featureless rectangle ending at the Pacific. For years, every time Bob looked at that cover, he sighed. Why, oh why, did God see fit to place him in the featureless rectangle separating the oceans? To be sure, his light shown brightly in the provinces, but he knew it would have been glorious, like the powerful beacon of a lighthouse, had he been born on the Upper East Side of Manhattan.

On Monday morning, he was composing a note for *Columbia Magazine* to update his classmates on his triumphs. Every time he read the alumni notes, his stomach knotted up with envy. On the cover was Bernie Katz, wearing a Savile Row suit and posed in a massive leather chair, as if he were the president of the world; he had just pledged $100 million to the business school. Richard Jensen Petersson, pictured smiling with a very serious President-Elect, was said to be in line for the ambassadorship to Sweden. Sheldon Goldfinger, riding an elephant and still wearing a headband like the hippie he'd always been, was just back from three years in India, where for *National Geographic* he documented the appalling diminution in the tiger population. Chesney Dudley Smith III, now a full professor at Yale, had just been awarded a hefty grant to study the connection between Irish and Indian poetry in the Twentieth Century. His own self-published tome of poetry, reflecting the influences of New Age and Pre-Raphaelite bards, had been well received by the literati. Lyle Turbine, a consultant representing an international coalition of green industries before the United Nations Commission for Social Development, was performing the kind of service "our fevered, over-populated planet desperately needs."

Robert Thurman Passwatter wished he too could astound his classmates in the same vein. But even if he could name some of his wealthiest clients or reveal what his income was, which he would never do because his ethics were of the highest order, they wouldn't be impressed. He couldn't help it, he'd begun to resent Clarissa for making him return to Fort Wayne. Sometimes his conscience pricked him when his thoughts twisted in that direction, for he knew he was the one who insisted on leaving the Big Apple for Johnny Appleseed, but still the hot tar pit at the bottom of his soul belched sulfur toward his mate. But for her, he'd be living in New York City, the trusted advisor of heads of state. Had he not gotten romantically entangled at such a young age, he might have become the man who set the pages of *Columbia Magazine* on fire.

Lost in thought, he doodled for awhile. Perhaps he'd

compose some self-deprecating, witty note about writing his memoirs, running 10Ks when he had the time, flushing with embarrassment when he spotted his own face on a billboard announcing his generous contribution to The United Way, and the difficulty of managing his various vacation homes.

He was still writing draft after draft when Xiu-Xiu Chow, his efficient and beautiful executive assistant, knocked on his closed door and without waiting for an answer entered his sanctuary. He quickly slapped *The Wall Street Journal* over the legal pad in front of him. "Timothy Schelling is here to see you."

"Tell me again why he's here."

"He wants you to handle his investments."

Bob stood, ready to greet the man.

"Would you mind, Mr. Passwatter, if I leave at one? My mother has a chemo appointment at Lutheran and she doesn't have anyone to drive her there today."

"How long will you be gone?"

"It's going to take all afternoon, so if you don't mind I won't return today." She assured him she would make up the time before the weekend.

Bob prided himself on the flexibility he accorded his executive assistant. He was a generous and thoughtful employer. All his employees loved him. He smelled love every time he entered the imposing front door of the suite. "Of course, Miss Chow."

She laid a piece of paper on his desk. "Here is your schedule for the rest of the day as well as tomorrow morning. Chelsea will be right outside if you need anything. I've made sure she can take care of any emergency that arises, and of course you can reach me on my cell if you really have to."

Bob watched in fascination as Xiu-Xiu Chow turned to leave his office. She was expensively dressed, her silky hair cleverly cut to look both professional and inviting. He loved her slender hands, the long oval nails polished without a chip. He was especially pleased she was Chinese; the idea of diversity was very appealing to a modern religious man -- a man of the world even if he was stuck in Steinberg's featureless land mass.

Xiu-Xiu floated out of his office, trailing just the wisp of a perfume evocative of an opium den, though of course he'd never been in one and assumed she hadn't been in one either. Among certain male friends on the golf course, he humorously referred to Xiu-Xiu as his office wife, while at the same time letting them know without words that he would always keep the relationship chaste, as befitted a church deacon, despite the temptations she offered daily. He never, ever confessed that once he'd hinted to her about meeting after work. She'd pretended not to understand and neither of them had ever referred to the incident again.

Bob spent the next hour gently persuading Timothy Schelling not to invest his money with Passwatter Global Investments until he'd taken the time to be sure he was wholly committed to the enterprise of a lifetime. The terms of becoming a Passwatter client were stringent: at least a million dollars up front, no withdrawals of principal for seven years, complete trust in the Passwatter expertise. "Amateurs don't take the long view, but I do." The reward was a steady ten percent dividend, no matter how the market fluctuated. "Be forewarned: I don't take calls from frantic investors when the bottom drops out, you understand. A waste of my time. And there are no exceptions to the rule on withdrawals of principal."

Somehow, instinctively, with no training at all, he knew how important it was to play hard to get, like a coy schoolgirl. It was the cleverest way he'd ever found to make people so eager to invest with him, so trusting, that they were honored just to get in the door.

Robert Thurman Passwatter, financial genius, was a legend in his own time.

12

Lingerie Run

Monday, January 19, 2009

Xiu-Xiu hated H&M like poison, but Tiffany loved it. On Monday afternoon, it took almost three hours before Tiffany finished sorting through the racks, trying on mountains of clothes, comparing each outfit to pictures she'd torn out of her favorite fashion magazines. Her style was a mixture all her own of couture, bohemian, vintage, grunge, hippie, and Asian. What help the fashion magazines provided was beyond Xiu-Xiu. She couldn't see any resemblance between the *Vogue* and *Bazaar* spreads Tiffany was so enamored with and the heap of garments that the frazzled clerk finally folded into bag after bag.

They then spent an hour in Macy's, where Tiffany tried on dozens of rings, finally selecting a massive square-cut amethyst that dwarfed her hand. Both of them bought perfume and lingerie, and Xiu Xiu treated herself to scented candles and new boots.

When they were finally sipping strawberry lemonades and debating appetizers in a booth at Red Robin, Xiu-Xiu asked her little sister how she proposed to pay for all the stuff she'd just bought.

Tiffany's face was instantly defiant. "I could ask you the same question."

"I work, Tiffany." Her tone was sharper than she intended. Tone it down, she told herself, or Tiffany might make a scene. "I earn my own money, and I have a budget. You don't work, and so far as I can see you don't have a budget. You just buy whatever takes your fancy."

"I put it on Yonja's credit card, of course."

"The Hawk never complains?"

Tiffany laughed. "All the time. In fact, I promised this morning not to buy another thing until I got a job."

"Promises don't mean anything, I take it."

Tiffany tossed her head, like a horse chafing at the bit. She wasn't responding to that jab.

"So what's the Hawk going to do when he gets the bill and finds out you broke your promise?"

Tiffany studied her new ring. "Have you ever seen an amethyst this dark and this big?"

"Focus, girl. What's he going to do?"

She looked away. "Throw another fit, I suppose. Who cares?"

Suddenly, Xiu-Xiu's cell phone trilled. "Excuse me," she said when she saw her boss' name on the screen. "Yes, Mr. Passwatter."

"Are you still at Lutheran?"

Xiu-Xiu closed her eyes. "Yes. I'll be here at least until five. Do you need something?"

"It'll wait until tomorrow. How's your mother doing?"

"She's bearing up. Thanks for asking."

"Sorry to bother you. See you tomorrow."

Xiu-Xiu put her phone away. "Sometimes I feel like a slave." She sighed. "Anyway, back to the subject. Where'd you get that fur coat you're wearing?"

"Yonja, of course." She pulled the collar toward her so she could stroke it. "He likes to see me looking rich."

"Really?"

"No." She pouted. "He's cheap."

"Perhaps you should think about what you're doing, Tiffany. If he kicks you out, who's going to pay your tuition? Your rent?"

"Forget about the tuition. I'm not registered this semester."

Xiu-Xiu was shocked. "Does the Hawk know that?"

"No. He gave me a check, I pretended to pay for my courses in the business department. Then I spent the money."

"He hasn't noticed you're not going to class? That you're not on campus?"

"He has to pretend we don't know each other anyway, so he isn't likely to check with the registrar or the head of the business department, and, besides, I do show up now and then at his office, just to keep up the pretense."

"So are you ever going to complete your master's in business?"

Tiffany shrugged. "I'm bored with the whole idea of being an engineer. Maybe someday I'll get serious about it, but if Yonja throws me out, I'll just get an engineering job. I have enough education for that."

"I guess you haven't noticed there are no jobs now. If he kicks you out, you're up a creek."

Tiffany suddenly pulled up the sleeve on her sweater.

"See this bruise? Getting kicked out wouldn't be the worst thing that ever happened to me."

"He hits you?"

"Once. Twice. Sometimes he pulls my hair or squeezes my shoulders really hard."

"What are you thinking, Tiffany? Get out of there now."

"Not yet. Not until I get what's coming to me. Battle pay, you might say. That's what I want to talk to you about."

"Me? I'm not lending you another dime. *Mah mah* and *bah bah* won't either. And you're not moving in with me again."

Tiffany waved her hand dismissively. "I don't need any of you for that. Yonja has millions."

"But you don't."

"I could." She smiled at her older sister. "And you can help."

Xiu-Xiu suddenly had a feeling she knew where this was going. "Don't say another word."

"Oh, but you're going to listen, *jie jie*. You know what you did, I know what you did, but *mah mah* and *bah bah* don't."

Xiu-Xiu stared into space, temporarily lost in thought about a subject she hated. She was so remorseful at having had an abortion her parents knew nothing about that she'd avoided romantic entanglements ever since. Her limit was three dates, then a breakup before she had to confront the question of bedroom intimacy. "I took an afternoon off for this?"

"I want to see a statement of Yonja's account. I want to know how I can get some of his millions. Unless, of course, you want to give me some of that loot you're collecting from

Passwatter."

"The only *loot* I get is my salary, and I work like a dog for that." She decided not to mention the hefty bonus she got every Christmas. "If you want to see Ferrell's account papers, you might try looking through that townhouse of his. As you're always complaining, it's small enough it shouldn't be that hard to find a file."

"You think I'm not smart enough to think of that? I've looked everywhere. I've turned his little office upside down. He must have the papers sent to his campus office or something. You get me the papers and get the dividends redirected, I'll give you a percentage of whatever I get my hands on."

"The only money you could get your hands on would be quarterly dividends, and for our clients the dividends are either reinvested in their Passwatter accounts or directly deposited to a bank account somewhere else."

"I'll open a bank account for myself; you do the paperwork so the dividends go to me instead of Yonja. Use numbers, no names or anything. It could be years before he figures out what's what."

"That's not possible."

"I don't believe it. We'll call your cut an administrative fee or something. I'll pay it under the table so you don't get taxed."

"You don't know what you're asking, Tiffany. I could lose my job and we could both go to jail."

"Your boss loves you. Ask him to arrange it so your fingerprints are nowhere to be found."

Xiu-Xiu gazed with wonder at her devious sister. "Why don't you ask him that favor yourself?"

"Because he doesn't know me. He doesn't love me."

"You make that proposal to Mr. Passwatter, you'll be in the arms of a cop before you know it. He's so honest he doesn't even cheat on his own expense report. I know that first-hand."

"Where's your loyalty?"

"*My* loyalty? Where's yours?"

"Think about it, *jie jie*. It's not fair, me being this poor, always having to sneak around just to put clothes on my body, a few rings on my fingers. If I had a little money, I'd pay for this snack instead of you always having to do it." She gazed again at her beautiful ring. "Why shouldn't I have as much as you do?"

Xiu-Xiu laughed grimly. "Because your Mandarin is atrocious. You might work on your phonology."

Tiffany threw her napkin at Xiu-Xiu. She was suddenly amused. "It's good enough it makes Yonja crazy." Her stiff-necked, straight-laced sister was so intractable, she decided to change course temporarily, entertaining her with an account of the morning's confrontation with Yonja.

Before they left the restaurant, they each tried out the perfume the other one had bought. They chattered about inconsequential things. In the parking lot, Tiffany hugged her big sister. "Forget what I said in there about Yonja's account. I don't know what gets into me sometimes. Are we good?"

"We're good, Tiffany. But if the professor hits you again, get out of there. Hear me?"

Tiffany shook her head, laughing. "I'll think about it. But, remember, I'm a survivor."

★★★★★

When Xiu-Xiu returned to her Old Fort apartment on the river, she fed her blue Persian, Miss Lila, poured herself a glass of wine, lit one of her new scented candles, and turned on the local news. After putting a Stouffer's spinach soufflé in the microwave, she went to her bedroom to put her purchases away. When she opened her lingerie drawer, she couldn't believe her eyes. It was empty except for a blue satin sachet. She ran her hands around the drawer as if her treasures might still be there but had suddenly become invisible. Wondering if she'd done some crazy thing, like switching things around in her sleep, she jerked open all the other drawers in her dresser, but there was no lingerie to be seen. She stared in shock at the dresser, then the rest of the room. At least twenty sets of the most expensive lingerie she could find -- Ell & Cee, Myla, La Perla, Agent Provocateur, Felina -- had disappeared.

She sat down on the bed. If Tiffany was still living with her, she'd know where to look, but Tiffany was living with the Hawk and she knew where her sister had been all afternoon. The only persons who had her key were her parents. In a panic, she stood up and ran to the front door. There were no signs that the door had been jimmied or the deadbolt tampered with. She squinted through the peep hole in case the thief was inexplicably standing on the other side of the door, but saw only an empty hallway. She tested the lock again and then fastened the chain.

She made a frantic tour of the apartment. What else was missing? Didn't thieves usually go for electronics? But her computer, iPad, TVs, and DVD player were present. The little safe in her bedroom closet was locked. The file cabinet in her office did not appear to have been opened, and the modest emergency stash of currency she kept there was in its place. There was no jewelry missing from her bedroom.

A thief who specialized in lingerie! How creepy was that? She was so freaked out it took a half hour before she could be sure she was composed enough to seek help.

Reluctantly, she sat down, pulled Miss Lila onto her lap, and called the police.

13

Security Tape

Friday, January 23, 2009

Dave Powers ran and re-ran the security tape from the Conrad Hotel garage in Indianapolis. Lexie stared at the computer screen, puzzled by what she saw. When she gave the signal, Dave stopped the dark, grainy tape so she could study the figure as he entered the third floor of the garage at 8:17 pm on Saturday, January 17, 2009.

She looked at her old friend from high school, the first black quarterback of the Carroll Chargers, now working in the property section of the Investigative Bureau of the Fort Wayne Police Department. He told her the Indianapolis police sent Fort Wayne the tape as a favor.

"What am I seeing here, Detective?"

"For old times' sake, call me Dave, okay? I think we're looking at an old white man, don't you?"

"I'm confused. The face looks old, what I can see of it, but notice how the guy walks. A lot of spring in his step."

"I noticed that too. But maybe he's a fitness buff." He enlarged the image. The man kept his head down, a billcap hiding the upper half of his face, as if he was aware of security cameras.

"Can anybody read the logo on his cap?"

"One of our patrolman who saw this said it looks like a vintage Colts cap. It's a dark color, and that patch looks sewn on, but the resolution isn't good enough to read the logo or writing." He touched the screen. "That curve looks like part of a horseshoe, doesn't it?"

"I can't tell. You don't think he's wearing a mask, do you?"

"Could be, I suppose, but if he is, it's a damn good one."

"What's that he's carrying?"

"Looks like a gasoline can. You'll notice he's wearing gloves."

"Looks like he's wearing a trench coat too, very light colored for a man's coat. I wish I could see his hair or his shoes or something. Could you back that up again, let me see him walk?"

They both studied the moving image again. Unfortunately, the camera lost the man a few seconds after he came out of the stairs, yards before he could have reached her Town Car. "Are you sure this is the guy who torched my car?"

"Not a hundred percent, but given the time the fire was detected and the look of the other figures the camera picked up over a twenty-minute period, our counterparts in Indy think he's our best bet. We don't have any reason to disagree."

"But the attack on my car looks like a personal attack on a woman, specifically me. Why me, Dave? I don't know anybody in Indianapolis who'd pick me out for special vandalism."

"He doesn't have to live there, you know."

Lexie squinted at the tape, which had been paused on the man as he emerged from the stairway. "Is there any way to tell how tall the guy is?"

"Not without calling some experts in, do some geometric calculations using shadows and angles. Why'd you ask?"

"Just between you and me, the only guy I know who'd want to write 'cow' on the hood and set my car on fire is my very British ex-husband, but he's a little over six feet and the guy on the tape looks shorter than that, doesn't he?"

"That's my guess."

"I suppose Ferrell could have hired someone in Indianapolis to do his dirty work."

"It isn't that easy for an ordinary citizen to find a thug for that kind of work. Unless he's not an ordinary citizen."

"He's pretty ordinary, at least in those terms. He's a professor at IPFW."

"Does he have any connections to organized crime that you know of?"

"No."

After a long silence, Dave sat back in his chair. "If we're going to get more movement on this, Lexie, we'll have to give our brothers in the capital more than your suspicions. They've got so many arsons and murders to deal with these days, a car fire doesn't get the headlines. And I'm sure you understand it's outside our jurisdiction, so this is about as much a favor as we can do for you."

"I understand that, but unless I can somehow be satisfied the crime wasn't personal -- and I don't see how I can -- I'm going to be looking over my shoulder. It makes me nervous."

"Not trying to pry into your personal life or anything,

but are you living alone these days?"

Lexie nodded. "In a big old house on Forest Park Boulevard."

"Nobody to protect you, then." He looked thoughtful. "Until there's a threat of real harm directed to you, there's not much more we can do. But, if something happens that alarms you, call me personally, day or night. I'll see what I can do."

"I also wanted to talk to you, Dave, about the kind of scrap we're seeing at the Yard."

"And how about the body we found there on Monday? Nate Grabbendorf didn't seem all that concerned, but maybe you want to hear about it."

"He complained about the Yard being shut down for half a day, so I've heard that much."

They talked awhile about both subjects. When she left, she knew little more than what she suspected all along: Because of the bad economy and the price of metal, thefts of street signs, manhole covers, and home air conditioners were sharply on the rise. And until DNA testing was done, the body in the crushed car couldn't be positively identified, though the cops had discovered who the car belonged to and suspected the registered owner, a well-known drug dealer, was the victim.

An hour later, when she reached her darling new car, Lexie sat with the motor running a few minutes, letting the grainy security tape run through her mind again. Something about the old white guy in the trench coat seemed familiar.

14

Fizzle at Club Soda

Friday, January 23, 2009

When Lexie reached Club Soda at a little before eight, she found the front room on Superior already crowded and a blues trio warming up. She hadn't been to a downtown eatery for awhile, but she always admired Club Soda's brick walls and hardwood floors, the lofty feel of an old industrial building. She eyed the bar, ready for a really good martini. Club Soda was famous for its martinis.

To her horror, she spotted Jean and Dwight squeezed into two chairs at the bar. Jean had her back turned so she didn't see Lexie. Really! Lexie frowned as the hostess took her coat. Since Jean had made the reservation for her and knew Lexie was taking Steve to dinner, she should have had better manners than to show up at the same restaurant. Hoping to avoid an awkward meeting, Lexie told the hostess she'd prefer to slip into the adjoining room, where she'd wait for the man she was meeting near the back door to the parking lot. Perhaps, when a table was available, they could eat upstairs instead of in the bar area.

Five minutes later, Lexie spotted Steve as he made his

way toward her, stopping at several tables first to greet people he knew. When they were seated upstairs and had both ordered martinis, she congratulated him on being recognized like a rock star.

"I know a lot of people, that's true, but I think you're the rock star, Lexie. For that very reason, though lots of people recognize you, they're afraid to approach you."

"You've lost me."

"Your star has risen so high, you probably seem unapproachable. Sort of like the Queen of England."

She studied his face for signs he was mocking her. "Well, I can't imagine that's true. The Queen's car doesn't regularly get set on fire, I'm guessing. And the sales manager at The British Embassy didn't know me from a bag lady. If it hadn't been for Drago, I'd have gotten as bad a deal on my new car as anybody else." She sipped her Lemontini. "My mistake, I think, is that while I was building my businesses, I didn't take enough time away from the office to keep up friendships. Or else the only things my old friends remember about me is that time I backed into the streetlight and the nastiness of my divorce."

"That part about the streetlight may be the truth. It's what I like most about growing up in a small city. People know you too well to put you on a pedestal. I'm sure the people who grow up with a guy who becomes president of the United States think it's a fluke a klutz like him rose so high. They remember when he fell through the ice or lost a critical game or did some other amazingly stupid thing."

Puzzled by his inconsistency -- she was a rock star too important to approach but couldn't possibly be put on a pedestal because once upon a time she'd backed into a streetlight -- she glanced at the menu. "Want to share an appetizer?"

"Anything but the Sesame Sashimi. I've never warmed up to raw fish."

"How about the Ring of Fire then? Spicy shrimp."

"Perfect. I don't know how it happened, but I've grown to like very spicy food."

After she placed the order, she asked, "Are you still interested in helping me put a plan together to rehab my house?"

"Sure. I can come by next week if that suits you."

They talked awhile about what she had in mind and, consulting their BlackBerrys, decided on the following Tuesday for him to tour the house.

After they'd ordered their entrées, Lexie finally got up the courage to ask the question uppermost in her mind. "Just so I know where things stand between us, are you seeing anybody these days?"

"I could ask the same thing of you."

She laughed. "I asked first, Steve."

"So you did. I've been dating a local girl for awhile."

"Is it serious?"

He briefly looked away. "Serious enough I take her out on Saturday nights. But I'm not in love, if that's what you're asking. No marriage plans. How about you?"

She shook her head. "I haven't dated at all since the divorce."

"What's on your mind, Lexie?"

Humbling herself was an unfamiliar emotion. "I made a mistake all those years ago."

"Did you?" His face clouded over and his voice was

cool. “What mistake would that be?”

Lexie suddenly felt like a schoolgirl facing a test she hadn’t studied for. “I didn’t know what I had.”

“Why not?”

“I’m not sure,” she said, eager to find a face-saving excuse. “A schoolgirl with no basis of comparison, who didn’t know the world. I didn’t appreciate what a good man you are.”

“Because I was poor and awkward?” He placed his hands on either side of his head like wings. “Because my ears stuck out?”

Lexie was rapidly losing her appetite. “No. Because I thought you were going to farm and I didn’t want to live on a farm.”

He stared at her, letting the awkward silence grow. “If you love somebody, does that really matter?”

“I was young, Steve. I thought it did.”

“I’d have lived in a gravel pit with you.”

She looked away.

“You led me on, Lexie. We’d dated so long I thought you were as committed as I was.”

“But you never said anything. Neither of us did. We never talked about marriage or even getting engaged until one night you said something about not dating anyone else when we went off to college.”

“I thought we had an understanding,” he said stubbornly.

“I think I’ve just made another mistake, even trying to talk about it.”

Steve’s face softened. “I hope I’m not that much of an ass. It’s brave of you even to bring up the past. But you must know there are some old hurts that are still pretty raw.”

“Do you think there’s any possibility they could be

healed?"

"I don't have a crystal ball, Lexie. But I tell you what. We'll take it one day at a time."

After their food was served, they talked about safe, everyday subjects -- her new car, his plans for the stalled Tonkel Road development, the grainy security tape she'd just viewed at police headquarters, the high-school reunion neither was enthusiastic about. The waiter had just cleared their table when Jean suddenly appeared, face flushed, her walk unsteady, excited about something. Without an invitation, she plopped down on the banquette Lexie was occupying.

"Dwight just went home in a snit. I'm all alone, so if you don't mind, I'll sit with you. You eat already?" She smiled broadly at Steve.

"What do you mean, Dwight went home in a snit?" Lexie asked.

"We broke up."

"Over what?"

"Football." She raised her arm and yelled at a passing waitress. "Over here! Dirty martini! Make it a double."

Lexie put her hand on Jean's arm. "Calm down. You're making a scene."

Jean turned her face to Lexie. Her eyes were watery. "Calm down? *Calm down*? Have a heart. If you can find it under that fancy jacket." She turned to Steve. "Remember that time at Butler we made out? Whyn't you ever call me again?"

Steve looked as if he'd been sucker-punched. Diners were staring, some laughing, some chattering in whispers. "Lower your voice, Jean."

"Why?" she asked, louder than ever. "You embarrassed? You should be, leading a girl on like that."

"Why don't you go home?"

"Because I don't want to. I'm not finished. Why didn't you call me, Steve-o? I could have made you happy. I could still make you happy. Happier than Lexie ever will." She turned to her friend. "Not that you're a witch or anything. Don't mean that. Good boss." She patted Lexie's arm as if patting a dog. "I love my job but . . . ."

Steve slid his chair back. "I'm going to take you downstairs. I'll call you a taxi."

Jean began to cry. "Can't afford a taxi."

On what I pay you? You could order a limo and not notice. "I'll pay for it," Lexie said to Steve.

"If you leave me alone, I'll kill myself. I swear I'll kill myself."

"I'm calling Dwight to tell him to pick you up. Give me your cell phone. Is he on speed dial?"

"Not Dwight."

"You want us to call the cops, have them take you somewhere you can sober up?" Steve asked.

Jean, shaking her head, handed Lexie her purse. "In there. Phone's in there."

Lexie called Dwight, who agreed to return for Jean. Steve took her downstairs and waited with her on the sidewalk, where the cold fresh air did nothing to restore her sobriety. Despite having a hard time staying upright and uttering a coherent sentence, she was still trying to seduce Steve when Dwight arrived.

A half hour later, having seen Jean safely installed in Dwight's Kia, Steve returned to the table. Lexie said she'd paid the bill and was ready to leave if he was. He was. Though they didn't make another date, Steve walked her to her car, saying he'd see her on Tuesday if that was still on. It was. They parted without a hug or a peck on the cheek or even a handshake.

15

I've Done Worse

Friday, January 23, 2009

January 23 was Phyllis Whitlow's forty-third birthday. As her only son did every year on that occasion, Drago drove, without Lucy, to his mother's house in Huntertown. He could have walked the few blocks from his house, but he never walked anywhere if he could drive. He and his mother moved to Huntertown when he was six and he'd never left. It was a very small village lining Highway 3 north of Carroll Road. Though the population was mostly white, Drago had experienced little racial hostility growing up. In fact, he'd been something of a novelty when he was little; now he was a fixture.

Drago needed a night alone with his mother from time to time, and Lucy, whose relationship with her mother-in-law was still in its early stage of wary politeness, never objected. Besides, whenever Drago said he'd be home late, no matter what the reason, she went out with her girlfriends from high school. Tonight they were at Piere's on St. Joe Road.

Phyllis was the only person in the world Drago could

truly confide in. The confidences he made to his wife were hedged around with evasions, exculpations, and half-truths, or, if the story required, heroic exaggerations. But he didn't have to edit what he told his mother. Phyllis listened to everything he had to say with love in her eyes. Though she sometimes counseled a different course than the one he was inclined to take, she never judged him. If he'd been caught red-handed robbing the United States Mint, she'd have argued that it wasn't him, he didn't do it, he didn't mean to do it, somebody made him do it, and he'd never do it again. Her boy was perfect. She had convinced herself that his handsome face was the accurate manifestation of a good soul within. To her, the blending of the blood of Europe and Africa signaled a new era of harmony and love.

Drago's old home was nothing special. Clad in faded yellow clapboard, Phyllis' Cape Cod bungalow had been built in the late Forties and then added onto a couple of times to bump out the kitchen, tack on a side porch, and attach a garage. His grandmother Ethel Whitlow, who had opposed her daughter's marriage to a black man but unabashedly adored her grandson, had lived with them until she died from a fall when he was sixteen.

Though the house possessed no architectural distinction and, despite the additions, was small and outdated, it held good memories and Drago was therefore very fond of it. Once he and his mother moved to the north side of Fort Wayne and his father seemed to be gone for good, he could relax. He felt safe in the little yellow bungalow. His bedroom on the second floor, distinguished by a ceiling that sloped so sharply no one could stand up on the south wall, looked exactly as it had the day he graduated from high school and went to work for Rolie. His collections of matchbox cars and baseball caps were displayed just as he had arranged them. The walls, partially covered with *Star Trek* posters, were still the bright shade of blue he demanded when he was eleven.

He noticed when he parked in the driveway that it was in need of repair and a shutter on a side window was sagging. The lawn needed resodding. He wished he was handy with tools, but he wasn't and he had no interest in learning.

Walking around to the passenger side of his Jeep, he carefully removed the vintage Colts billcap from the back seat and put it on his head backward Then, from the front seat, he retrieved the gifts he'd brought for his mother. A frown momentarily creased his forehead, for he hated carrying anything, especially an ungainly bunch of stuff. It looked undignified and unmanly. Only women carried things. But Friday evening, as he approached the door to his mother's garage, he was juggling a cello-wrapped bunch of roses from Walmart, a box of Russell Stover chocolates, a small box holding a Walmart gift card, a wadded up trench coat, and a paper bag full of trash. Though his walk was as jaunty as always, the load of crap he was carrying meant he couldn't swing his shoulders the way he liked.

Phyllis watched him from the kitchen window with concern. Something about his face betrayed a heavy conscience.

The smell of Amish chicken and noodles suffused the house. Drago smiled, as he dropped the paper bag into the kitchen garbage can and walked over to hug his mother at the stove. Chicken and noodles with homemade yeast rolls was his favorite meal, especially welcome on a cold night. Lucy wasn't a bad cook but she refused to follow any of her mother-in-law's recipes, so if Drago wanted a home-cooked meal that evoked the best memories of a childhood that started out badly but ended fairly well, he had to go home to Mom.

After they'd eaten hot apple pie with vanilla ice cream, which they both agreed was better than any birthday cake, and Phyllis had cleared the table, she sat down and reached out to touch his arm. "What's on your mind, son? You seem a little subdued."

He demurred at first, but Phyllis persisted. She pushed the vase of roses further to the side of the table and offered the open box of chocolates to her son. He didn't even look at them. "Everything okay with Lucy?"

"Yeah. She's always the same."

"She still on that Atkins diet?"

He laughed. "I don't know, but probably not. I don't think Pepperidge Farm Milanos and Ben and Jerry's Peanut Brittle are low-carb, do you?"

Phyllis laughed too. "No. She has a sweet tooth, that girl." She paused. "And everything's okay with Rolie?"

"Again, same as always. Somebody should send him to charm school, though." He recounted his phone conversation with Rolie the night he returned from Indianapolis.

"What were you doing in Indianapolis last week?"

"Taking care of Rolie's business."

"What business was that?"

He nodded in the direction of the trench coat he'd thrown on a chair. "Bad business. Get that coat cleaned before you put it back. Has Mizz Royce missed it?"

Phyllis shook her head. "If she'd looked for it, I'd have told her it was at the cleaners and there was a delay in getting it back. Did the coat make a trip to Indianapolis?"

"Yeah, but you don't want to know. Mind if I smoke a cigar?"

"Not at all. Let me get your special ashtray." When she returned, she folded her arms and leaned on the arm of the chair. "Now tell me what's on your mind."

"I hit Lucy."

If there was a sin that riled Phyllis, it was a man hitting a woman, but she wasn't ready to believe the worst of her son. "You didn't."

"I did."

"What'd she do to you?"

"Nothing."

"Oh, come on, Drago. She must have done something."

"I told her about my dad putting me in the hospital. When I said I hated him so much I wanted to find him and kill him, she asked why you hadn't protected me. Shouldn't I be as mad at you as at him? she asked."

Phyllis fell silent, wrestling with the desire to tell him what she'd done to protect him without implicating herself in murder. "She hasn't stood in my shoes."

"I know. Nobody has. That's why she set me off, saying that."

"Are you sorry?"

"Very. I lost my cool. I looked weak."

"She isn't the girl I'd have chosen for you, Drago, but if I've taught you anything, it's that you can't abuse your wife, no matter what she says or does. Stay cool. Just walk away. Go for a run."

"Wish I could be like you. I never seen you lose your temper."

That's because you were in the hospital when I did, my boy, the one time I lost it all the way to the moon and back. "Language, Drago. 'I have never seen.' You know better."

"If I spoke that way on the street, I'd be shot on sight. Anyway, where do you think Dad is? Any idea?"

"Why are you still thinking about him? He's gone. Let's hope he stays gone."

"Because someday I *am* going to find him. Know that."

"And do something that'll land you in jail for the rest of your life?" She shook her head. "Not worth it, son."

"Rolie's up to something, you know."

"What?" Phyllis was confused by the abrupt change of subject. "What's Rolie got to do with Carver?"

"Nothing. He's just all up in my head. Mizz Royce bought a new car Monday. I helped her negotiate the price." He looked proud.

"Rolie told you to help her?"

"Nah, that was an accident, me meeting her like that just when she was about to start looking. She wanted a man with her. But when I called Rolie from the dealer's lot, tell him what was up, he ordered me to install a tracking device on it." He nodded in the direction of the trench coat. "Might as well come clean about the whole thing. He had me go to Indy to torch her Lincoln, which I did. I wore the coat, a hat and mask, gloves, rubber boots, the whole shebang."

"What'd you do with the mask and stuff?"

"That's the sack I stuck in your garbage can when I came in. I kept the hat, though. It's too valuable to throw away. Anyway, I guess he knew by trashing the car she already had, she'd have to buy a new car so he could put a transmitter on it."

"He could have done that to the Lincoln."

Drago looked chagrined. "You're right. What's he up to, you think?"

"Meanness. He's been mean to his sister ever since he was old enough to lift a stick. He was jealous from day one. He used to break her dolls, hide her jewelry, burn holes in her clothes. One time he snuck up behind her and brained her with a broken broom handle. She got a concussion that time, had to have staples in her scalp. If her step-mother hadn't 'fessed up about what she saw, nobody'd have known who did it."

"I don't mind doing bad things, time to time. It's in my nature. But I really don't like going after a lady never done me any harm. She's even nice to me, you know."

"Putting a transmitter in her new car isn't such a terrible thing, is it?"

"Depends on what he does with it."

"Maybe he just wants to be sure if his sister has an accident, he knows where to find her."

"Mean Man is suddenly nice to his sister?"

"No, you're right, son. So what do you think his purpose is?"

"Not sure. All I can do, keep my eyes and ears open." He stubbed out his cigar. "Mom, is it a sin to kill a man?"

Phyllis went pale. "Why are you asking that, for heaven's sake?"

"Because that's what I did a week ago. A dealer, a muscle-bound guy with a real bad temper, thinks he owns the East Side. One of those Bosnian immigrants, you know. They like to fight. I ran into him, he pulled his gun."

"He took a shot at you?"

"No. But I thought he was going to. He'd have killed me if he'd gotten the chance."

"You killed him?"

Drago nodded. "Deader'n a doornail. Told my guys to put him in the back of his car, cover him with a tarp we found in his garage, have it towed to the Yard, where it was crushed."

"It was self-defense, wasn't it?"

"Guess you could say that."

"So nobody knows but you and me."

"Well, a few others. Plus a guy at the Yard spotted the body, so now the cops know too."

"Are you in trouble?"

"No. Not with the cops. Don't expect to be. Trail's too twisty, been swept clean. But the Bosnian's gang isn't likely to take it easy on us."

"I hate the drug business."

"Pot's not that bad, you ask me."

"You don't smoke it, do you?"

"No. Tried it once or twice, but it gives me the mother of all headaches. Besides, I gotta keep my head straight in this business, since Rolie's got his up his ass half the time. A lot of money's at stake, you know. Rolie played it right, it'd be bigger business than scrap metal."

"But it's a dangerous business. Whyn't you sell cars or something? You'd be good at it."

He laughed. "Work somewhere some ugly dude tells me what to do all day, when to get to work, when to leave, what to wear, what to say? No." He paused. "But you always talkin' about God, I'm just curious. Did I do wrong?"

"I've done worse."

Drago laughed for the second time that evening, this time with genuine humor. "Tell me another story, Mom. Nobody's done worse than I have. 'Cept maybe Rolie."

For the time being, Phyllis left it at that.

16

Panty Raider

Saturday, January 24, 2009

On Saturday, Lexie arrived at the Clubhouse at Sycamore Hills Golf Club just before noon, when the festivities were to start. She greeted her step-mother, Matilda Royce, with the Hollywood air kisses that now seemed to be hard-wired into all upper-class women.

Matilda looked every inch of the aristocracy she believed she had risen to when she married Isaac Royce, the Scrapyard King. Her St. John black knit suit had been tailored to fit her frame, bosomy on top, a little paunchy in the middle, and flat as a board in back. Her 12 mm Mikimoto cultured pearl necklace sparkled with an off-center diamond closure. She had replaced the small marquise diamond in her engagement ring with a seven-carat heart-shaped diamond, which she wore on her freckled right hand. The only signs that she wasn't quite up with the times were her over-highlighted blond hair, air-blown and stiff as a fibrous helmet, and the black sheer hosiery she wore even with strappy stilettos.

When Isaac died of a massive heart attack four years earlier, Matilda wasted no time moving from the five-bedroom Craftsman in Pine Valley where Lexie had grown up to an ornate *faux* Queen Anne in Sycamore Hills. Her excuse was that the memories in Pine Valley were so painful she needed a fresh start, but Lexie suspected the real reason was to have a more impressive address and to be near the Jack Nicklaus golf course, where Matilda had always spent most of her summers anyway. At 59, Matilda was still an avid golfer. Shopping at the Indianapolis Fashion Mall was her second hobby.

The bridal shower was for Doreen Soren, Matilda Royce's niece, who at 37 was getting married for the first time -- to a social worker. Lexie had met the bride-to-be a number of times in her role as the leader of a citizens group attempting to shut down Summit City Metals and Scrapyard on the grounds that it was an eyesore, truck traffic and noise damaged the neighborhood, and the runoff of stormwater contaminated the river system. Once, after a particularly contentious public meeting about a proposed expansion, she cornered Doreen in the parking lot, well away from everyone else.

"We provide a service the public needs, Doreen."

"We wouldn't need it if our culture wasn't so materialistic."

Well, you dingbat, neither one of us can remedy that. "The Scrapyard pays a lot of taxes."

"But not enough to make up for the water pollution and dust you cause."

"We treat all our runoff and the Yard is paved. What more can you ask? And think about it: aren't we doing the very thing you want, recycling stuff that has another use?"

Doreen waved her bottle of water. "The Yard is a nuisance, and aesthetically, it's ugly."

"Ugly? I suppose it is, but the Yard isn't a nuisance. It's as clean as we can make it -- at great expense, I might add. But in any case many of the people we employ would otherwise be on welfare."

"But you ruined their neighborhood."

Lexie wanted to scream. "The Scrapyard was built a hundred years ago in the middle of nowhere. It was our neighborhood first. Then the people moved to us."

Doreen bristled. "For sure, the people who live here don't need another auto crusher."

Lexie pointed at Doreen's Prius, the back bumper of which was adorned with a sticker commanding **HONOR YOUR MOTHER (EARTH)**. "Where do you expect that car of yours to go when its life is over? A museum?"

Doreen gave her a smug smile. "That's an idea. That's where you should be. We're all socialists now, you know. Your day of cheating the people and getting rich on their backs is over."

Lexie, the businesswoman who was proud of the family business, was stung to the core. "I employ people. I give them jobs. Scavengers make a living from us. Householders get a little money for their old electronics. How does that amount to cheating them?"

"If you're so charitable, why don't you just divide up your millions among them? Why make them work at all? You can afford it." She sneered. "I suspect you could live on a few million if you really tried. If I were you, that's what I would do."

At that, Lexie threw up her hands and walked away. It was unseemly to argue in public, and she was afraid of saying something she'd regret. Besides, she was feeling beleagured:

everyone, even strangers, wanted her money.

After that, neither woman could bear the sight of the other.

Nevertheless, though Lexie had little use for Doreen Soren, she felt a duty to honor her father's widow, so here she was, bearing an earth-friendly, sustainable gift: queen-size, 400-count, bamboo-fiber sheets in natural Sahara-desert tan, exactly as listed on Doreen's registry. No animals or even cotton bolls had been sacrificed in their manufacture. The sheets were so dreary Lexie couldn't look at them long enough to wrap them herself, which she wasn't supposed to do anyway, for the "recycled" invitation had requested that all gifts be left unwrapped or wrapped in reused grocery bag paper in the name of being good to Gaia. So Lexie, with malice aforethought, deliberately ordered the store to wrap the sheets in stiff, shiny, metallic turquoise paper, tied with flocked pink ribbons and embellished with all the silver fronds, flowers, and bells it possessed. After placing her package in the middle of the gift table, Lexie stepped back to admire her offering, a gaudy bit of jetsam in a sea of monochrome flotsam.

Stepping back, she bumped right into Matilda.

"My dear," Matilda said jokingly as she grabbed Lexie's shoulders and nodded in the direction of the turquoise package, "I see you didn't read the invitation."

"Oh, I did." Lexie turned, smiling mischievously. "I read it very carefully, Matilda. Inside are the ugliest sheets you've ever seen, exactly the ones Doreen wants. Anyone who sleeps on them is guaranteed nightmares about the loss of the rain forest and the melting of the ice caps."

Matilda laughed. "You're braver than the rest of us then."

"No champagne either? I assume that serving bubbly would be an extravagant use of scarce resources."

"Well, I did find some gumption on that subject. Doreen and some of her friends are having sparkling grape juice, but for the rest of us . . . . here's a waiter now. Have a glass of the good stuff."

Lexie snagged a flute, and after tasting it, asked "Cristal or Dom?"

"Dom."

"Well, good going, Matilda. You always give great parties."

"I appreciate that, Lexie. Doreen wanted me to screen some little short film she's fond of about global warming, instead of playing a silly game, but I put my foot down about that too."

"So what are we eating? I know it'll be good."

"She wanted vegetarian, but I insisted on salmon. We fought for a month about what kind of salmon, farmed or wild, would be acceptable."

"And?"

"Wild Alaskan Salmon. I still don't understand why. Something about Greenpeace. I guess Greenpeace thinks all salmon farming is bad."

"So, how's Rolie doing?" Lexie asked.

"I was going to ask you that. I haven't heard from him in a couple of weeks."

"He was in Las Vegas the last time I tried to reach him."

"Let's not talk business for more than a second, but have you considered his request for a loan or some addition to capital? The Scrapyard's profits are way down, you know, and if he can get some new machinery put in there, we could all start living well again."

You look like you're living pretty well, Matilda, for never having earned a dollar in your life. Am I being asked once more to share my wealth with greedy relatives? Pushing her resentment to the back of her head, Lexie kept her voice neutral. "I have an appointment to talk with Bob Passwatter about it next week." She looked around the room. "So where am I sitting?"

"With Doreen's mother and two of her cousins."

Doreen's mother was Abigail Soren, Matilda's older sister. The two women physically resembled each other enough to be tagged as sisters, but they shared almost nothing in the way of personality or manners. Though Lexie had only met Abigail once, once was enough. "Really? What did I do to deserve that . . . that honor?"

Matilda uncharacteristically looked a little ashamed. "You're so sparkling, my dear, I know you'll keep the table lively. I wish I had one of you at every table. But at least my friend Grace will be right beside you. She's a hoot, you know."

Grace Venable was indeed a hoot. At 63, she was taking salsa lessons and had booked a trip to Argentina with her young dance instructor to practice the art of the tango -- in the sheets as well as out, if she got lucky, she said. In her youth she had written erotic romances for Harlequin under a pen name and then married an old, rich, very sick man who was big in the publishing business in New York City. After a few grueling years, he had left her a happy, prosperous widow, after which she wrote no more romances but instead lived them on six-month cruises all over the world. She told many slightly cruel anecdotes about her one and only husband and some funny stories about the publishing biz.

"Did you ever think about marrying again?" one of the women asked.

"Oh, sure, for about a tenth of a second," Grace joked. "But I like my independence. I never have to negotiate any more, you know. If I want to go take tango lessons in Argentina, I go. If I want to buy another Jil Sander suit, I buy it. No questions asked."

Doreen's mother, who was dressed like an unimaginative gypsy, shot her a censorious look. "That isn't all marriage is, you know."

Grace, who had no interest in a serious conversation and was immune to censorious looks, quickly changed the subject to a startling crime wave in Sycamore Hills. "You've all heard about the Panty Raider?"

Doreen's mother frowned. "Pantry Raider. Did I hear you right?"

Grace took pleasure in that frown. "LaPerla, Abigail, not pearl onions. Pant-y, not pant-ry. Every week for the last couple of months some woman comes homes to find her lingerie drawer missing some key items."

"Women here, where you live?"

"Right here, in this glorious subdivision," Grace said triumphantly, as if Sycamore Hills were inordinately proud of its distinction.

"Are there signs of a break-in?"

"To my knowledge, never. A patio door is left unlocked, a window cracked, a garage door open -- that's the way he's thought to get in. Unless somehow he's managed to get hold of everybody's key."

"Is there a theme?" Lexie asked.

Grace guffawed. "Women's delicates. He steals matching sets of panties and bras. No color or brand preference, no particular size, according to the ladies I know, but the bra and panties have to match. So that's the theme -- matching lingerie. Imagine! A thief who's a lingerie snob."

Lexie giggled. "Do you think he goes home and wears the stuff?"

Everyone but Abigail laughed at that image, and all of them had an opinion, mostly affirmative.

"By theme, Grace, I meant some tie among the women who are his victims. They're all teenagers or older widows or working women or something?" Lexie paused. "We're assuming it's a man doing the dirty deed, I suppose."

"These days you never know, but I assume it's a man. If the police have spotted any connection among the victims, they haven't said. I happen to know, however, that the victims in Sycamore Hills are all women who live alone."

"And no lingerie thefts elsewhere?"

"That I don't know."

"Do the police have any theories about who the thief is?"

"None that I've heard."

"Has anybody spotted him?"

Grace shook her head. "The rumor is that it's some guy who knows the neighborhood, a man nobody would notice. Maybe a postman, a FedEx truck driver, a landscaper, a teenager regularly walking home from the school bus, a guy who jogs every day or rides a mountain bike. A man nobody notices because they expect to see him and think he belongs in the neighborhood. But that's just a wild guess."

"What do you think?" Lexie asked. "Who do you

think it is? You have lots of experience with villains -- from your fiction, I mean." She patted Grace's arm to prove she wasn't referring to the old dead husband or the young dance instructor or any other men in her free-wheeling, eccentric life. "So who is it?"

"I'm torn." Though Grace's eyes still sparkled with humor, she sounded serious. "Is it somebody who looks so normal nobody would suspect him of a sick fetish, or is it somebody who looks crazy? I don't know."

Doreen's mother spoke up. "Men like that are dangerous, aren't they? At first, they just steal . . . well, they just steal underwear, but then they start . . . you know . . . ." She lowered her voice to a whisper. "Raping and killing."

"You do have an imagination, don't you, Abigail?" Grace cackled. "I wouldn't have guessed that."

Catching an angry look on Abigail's face, Lexie did her best to defuse the bomb Grace had just thrown. "Tell us, Grace, you know so much about the Panty Raider, have you been a victim yet?"

Grace laughed. "I pray to be a victim just so I have a good story to tell at parties like this. Don't we all want our friends to think we wear gorgeous lingerie that men fantasize about getting into?" Catching Abigail's look, she quickly corrected herself. "I mean stealing, of course. But since I always set my alarm when I leave the house, I guess I'm not all that sincere about having my home broken into."

"Well," Lexie mused, suddenly unable to remember whether she'd set her house alarm, "I was thinking about selling the house on Forest Park and moving here just so I could avoid the massive rehab work I have to do, but I guess I should wait until the thief is caught."

17

Head of Steam

Saturday, January 24, 2009

On Saturday, halfway through his run down Forest Park Boulevard in an old historic district where he knew Lexie lived, Ferrell Hawke checked his watch. It was just after one. He was wearing his warmest Ronhill running gear ordered from the UK, a fact he made sure his friends knew. In his mind, the United States would never be anything but a rogue, somewhat demented colony with an inferior quality of life.

Though he really wasn't much of a runner, having barely finished the 5k Mastodon Stomp at IPFW the year before, Ferrell looked every inch the athlete. Maybe if he quit smoking a pipe and drinking half a pint of scotch every night, he wouldn't get out of breath so quickly. Working out a little wouldn't hurt either. His membership in Summit City Fitness was seriously underused.

On Saturday afternoon, he was jogging faster than usual, propelled down Forest Park Boulevard by a mighty head of steam. The fuel burning at the bottom of his soul like sterno gel was anger that burned and burned without ever being consumed. He'd been born angry, and the life he'd been allotted had done nothing to mellow him. The gods of spite and jealousy dogged his every step.

It had been that way forever. Despite the skeptical reception he experienced in his adopted country, he really had been born into the British aristocracy, just as he claimed. If his grandfather hadn't lived like a king in exile, heedless of the insufficiency of his fortune to support the offspring he'd produced legitimately and otherwise, some family money might have remained to underwrite the next generation. And if his handsome, amiable father weren't such a feckless solicitor, overpaying his assistants and under-collecting from his clients, the Hawkes might at least have lived an upper-middle-class life.

But they hadn't. The five Hawkes had occupied a terrace house far too small for comfort, overstuffed with the unlovely, uncomfortable antiques his mother took great pride in. She couldn't cook worth a damn, and his father never owned a car. Wearing second-hand designer-label clothes his mother sniffed out at church jumbles, Ferrell and his brothers had been forced to go to school with all the louts and guttersnipes they'd been bred to despise as their social inferiors. Every last mental picture he had of his London past was archived in the sepia-toned part of his memory bank.

Then came the misfortune of marrying the workaholic, self-absorbed Lexie. He could have married anybody, but, no, he had to marry a girl who was single-mindedly intent on making a name for herself and a fortune to go with it. Worse, a girl from Fort Wayne, an undistinguished city that sat on a featureless prairie enclosed within a dome of gray clouds, where he now found himself stuck like a horse with its head caught in a barbed wire fence.

He thought he'd outsmarted Lexie in the divorce. He'd taken the Lake James "cabin" subject to the mortgage, on the assumption that lake property would appreciate more than any other, but it was now under water, so to speak, and needed extensive upgrades to suit Tiffany. Instead of cash, he took his spoils in Potash and Monsanto stock, which at the time had a higher stock value than the cash he'd been offered, but last year in October their stock prices had crashed, leaving him with less than half the nest egg he'd started out with. Then he'd taken half of what was left after that debacle and invested it himself in copper, pork bellies, soybeans, and other commodities. Knowing nothing about the commodities market, he'd lost all that money too, and but for a fortuitous stop order, would have lost more than his original investment.

The remaining money, a shade more than a million, he'd reluctantly invested with Passwatter Global Investments. Despite Bob's reputation as the local financial genius, he was reluctant to invest with him because he distrusted everyone associated with Lexie. Still, anybody who was anybody had to invest with Passwatter. It was a status symbol an academic like him couldn't live without. And, since getting on the inside wasn't easy, he knew it was a good thing, like being admitted to a country club he couldn't afford. Just as Ferrell's friends had warned, Passwatter had put him off for months before allowing him the privilege of becoming part of the global "family," where all his clients were "citizens of the world."

The euphoria of being part of the smart crowd lasted only a day. Once he'd been admitted to Bob's family of global citizens, Ferrell was immediately afflicted with second thoughts. A ten percent return was rather paltry, wasn't it, given Passwatter's reputation as the high-flying master of the universe? The seven-year restriction on withdrawals of principal was a form of slavery. But in his cooler moments, he grudgingly rationalized that ten percent was a better return than he could manage on his own, and being forced to leave his money alone for seven years was probably a good thing.

But the restrictions grated on his nerves. Restrictions of any kind grated on his nerves. And lately the fact that he couldn't get at his own money had become positively infuriating.

He'd been able to live just fine on his academic salary until Tiffany came along, but now he couldn't. Her credit card bills averaged over five thousand a month. She wanted to buy a big house, she nagged for a cute car of her own, she begged to be taken to New York City to attend Broadway shows on her birthday, and she longed to spend the summer in the Caribbean. She demanded that he purchase life insurance, naming her as the sole beneficiary, so as a matter of fairness, he purchased insurance on her too, meaning he was paying double premiums. She touted the benefits of a substantial investment in her parents' take-out shop. Once in awhile she mused about how he might want to stake her to a boutique in Covington Plaza, where she'd seen the ideal empty space. Wouldn't it be great if she owned a successful shop where the richest Summit City women shopped?

But, so long as Tiffany continued to spend money the way she did, Ferrell knew he could never save enough from his salary to do any of the things she wanted. Something had to give.

He needed to talk to Lexie. Maybe if he groveled a little, she'd acknowledge that, as a matter of decency and morality, she owed him some of the obscene profit she made from the sale of her businesses after they were divorced. Surely she could see that, for old times' sake, she owed him a little slice of the enormous money pie Fortune had handed to her. He'd been at her side all the while she made a success of herself. If he had a dollar for every time some wanker had referred to him as Mr. Royce, he'd be rich. That must count for something. Besides, Lexie had so much money now, she'd never miss a few million. How much was any one woman entitled to?

As he neared her house, he slowed down, both because his legs were starting to ache and because he wanted to take a good look at the mansion she now lived in. Distaste for the Palladian architecture that filled his field of vision pinched his frost-bitten cheeks, his chapped lips, his wary eyes. Lexie fancied modern things. What in hell had overcome her good sense long enough for her to buy a period piece like that? Why did she deserve a bloody mansion all for herself? Would Tiffany like it?

Once he reached the end of the block, he turned around. He would go back, run up Lexie's walkway, ring the bell, see if she was home. Since Phyllis' car was not in the driveway and Saturday was normally her day off anyway, Lexie would be alone. Maybe she'd even be sitting in the dark, regretting the divorce, ready to ask his forgiveness or do anything he wanted to ease her conscience at having kept her millions to herself. He might as well have the talk with her now rather than putting it off and maybe losing his courage. Never let a head of steam go to waste.

After five minutes of ringing the bell and a quick peer into the glass panels beside the heavy front door, he decided the house must be empty. He trotted around to the back, where, knowing Lexie, he might find an unlocked door.

★ ★ ★ ★ ★

Lexie didn't have to move to another part of town to be a victim of the Panty Raider. That night, as she was getting dressed to go to dinner with some friends, she discovered that her lingerie drawer had been cleaned out. After a few moments' of hesitation, she called Dave Powers.

18

Don't Shoot the Messenger

Sunday, January 25, 2009

Lexie knew that Sunday breakfast at Biaggi's with Jean might be awkward. Normally Lexie would have a lot to tell Jean -- about her new car, the trench-coated figure on the grainy security tape from Indianapolis, the bridal shower with a political cause, the Panty Raider, and her own empty lingerie drawer. But the embarrassing scene at Club Soda was now the 800-pound gorilla in the room.

Though Lexie spent a few hours every day at the office in the Lincoln Tower where Jean oversaw the handling of the flood of inquiries and pleas directed to Alexandra Royce, Potential Benefactress and Easy Mark, they restricted their conversation, as a matter of policy, to business. Sunday lunch was where they caught up on their personal lives.

But the semi-circle booth in the bar, where they typically sat, was not occupied by Jean when Lexie arrived. Dwight was sitting there, nursing a glass of water, his eyes switching from the lobby door to an overhead television featuring a football game. He stood up and greeted Lexie with a handshake and a big smile.

"What a surprise!" Lexie said. "Where's Jean? Is she coming?"

Dwight waited until they'd settled themselves to answer. "That's what I wanted to talk to you about."

"Is she okay?"

He laughed. "As okay as any other drunk after a night of crying and puking, I suppose. For me, it was like being back in the emergency room, making sure she stayed on her side so she wouldn't choke to death on her own vomit."

"Dwight! She's not a drunk."

"Do you drink an entire bottle of wine every night, Lexie?"

"No." The question took a second to register. "But she does, is that what you're telling me?"

"That's what I'm telling you." Despite the seriousness of the subject, his eyes were merry. "Her bar bill is always bigger than her food bill. For how many boyfriends is that a bragging right?"

"I didn't know that. Gosh, I didn't even suspect it . . . . So, she's still at home, sobering up?"

They were interrupted by a waiter Lexie didn't recognize. He placed some bread and olive oil on the table and asked if they'd dined there before. The question always irritated Lexie. She'd dined there every Sunday for years. Didn't anyone ever notice? Glancing apologetically at Dwight, who stuck with water, and feeling self-conscious about imbibing alcohol given the problems Jean was having, Lexie nevertheless ordered her usual glass of Prosecco.

Once the waiter had left, Dwight resumed. "That's the real reason I'm here. I talked Jean into checking herself into Hazelden to dry out. She's still at home, but I'll take her there tomorrow if you agree. We're going to drive to Minnesota, make a trip of it, save the air fare."

"Of course, but why do you need my agreement?"

"She doesn't want to lose her job, but if she goes to a treatment center, she's going to have to be there at least a couple of weeks, maybe longer. She's scared to death you'll fire her."

Lexie, who'd been thinking of doing that very thing, realized she had to back off lest she appear to be kicking an old friend while she was down. "Of course I won't fire her . . . . She has some vacation weeks coming, if I'm not mistaken."

Dwight cleared his throat. "She's hoping to keep her vacation days."

Lexie was stunned. "Really? Jean doesn't want to be fired for taking an open-ended sobriety leave *and* doesn't want to lose her vacation time either. She wants it all. Do I understand that right?"

To his credit, Dwight looked embarrassed. "That's what she told me. She's booked two weeks in London in September. Paid for our plane tickets, put a deposit on a bed-and-breakfast in Kensington, even booked a tour of the Tower of London. First thing when we arrive, we're taking a ride on the Eye so we get the panoramic view of the city. She's got a whole notebook of brochures and stuff. Every day is planned down to the last minute. I'm going to have to start walking just to get in shape."

"I didn't know she already made so many commitments for London. Last week she sounded like she was just thinking about it."

"She's thinking about it, all right. That's all she thinks

about."

Well, not quite, if you only knew. She thinks about Steve Wright quite a lot. "You're going with her? I thought you'd broken up."

"We break up all the time, but it never sticks." He laughed as if constant breakups and reunions were a normal, amusing fact of life. "It'll be that way till I die, probably."

"Well, I'll have to think about her vacation days. I won't fire her for going to Hazelden for however long she needs to be there, I assure you of that. But I'll have to think about the rest. If I give her leave to go to London in September, will she be paid or not? We've been friends forever, and she's a good assistant, but business is business and I need an assistant I can count on." *Especially given what I pay her.* "Fair enough?"

Dwight rolled his head around as if loosening his neck muscles instead of evading a definite answer to the question of fairness, then put his hands in the air. "Just don't shoot the messenger, okay? Not till after I've eaten. I've got my eye on the osso bucco." He looked up at the waiter who had just approached. "Lunch is on me."

19

Fatherly Advice

Wednesday, January 28, 2009

On Wednesday, Lexie took the elevator from her seventh floor office to Bob Passwatter's on the eighteenth. Bob was like a second father to her. She needed his advice. And she needed to give him an answer on Rolie's proposal.

"Alexandra, so good to see you," he said, moving from behind his desk to greet her with a hug. "How's my favorite lady in the world?"

"A little lost at the moment, Bob."

"You? I don't believe it."

"I think I'm being stalked, I hate the house I bought, there's no man in my life, Jean's giving me trouble, I'm conflicted about Rolie's request for money, and I need something productive to do."

"Good Lord. That's quite a list. Where do we start?"

"Well, let's start with the house. I had Steve Wright take a look at it yesterday."

"Hold it right there. Why Steve?"

Lexie gave him a puzzled look. "Why not Steve? He's an old friend and a successful builder with a great reputation.

Because of the downturn, his crew has some time for renovation."

"I never liked that guy. Something about him."

"What do you mean?"

"Can't put my finger on it."

"Isn't he a client?"

"No. I handled his uncle's trust but once he started making a name for himself, he dropped me like a hot potato. Not like you and Rolie and your step-mother and that ex-husband of yours." He smiled. "Though I'm disappointed you didn't invest all your money with me."

"I know, I know," she said. In fact, ninety percent of her assets were invested elsewhere as a matter of prudence. "But, Bob, it's nothing personal. I just don't believe in putting all my eggs in one basket. Simple as that."

"Well, we'll have to work on that. I want to see you get the best return you can get, and nobody beats me in that department. So what about the house?"

"If I'm going to live there, I need to spend at least a hundred thousand, maybe closer to a quarter of a million. Therefore, I'd like you to set aside that much in an escrow account from which I'll pay Steve as the work progresses."

Bob frowned, steepling his hands. "I don't like to see you depleting your principal."

"By so little?"

"Not in this market. Not on a house that's declining in value. You'll end up spending more than you can get out of it in the next ten years."

"Put it that way, it may not be rational to spend that much money on the house, but I've got to live there. Tell you what, just stop reinvesting my dividends in Passwatter Global

Investments and deposit them in an escrow account at Tower Bank. How about that?"

Bob was still frowning. "I think it'd be better for you if the control stays here. I don't trust anybody else. I'll have Xiu-Xiu get you the paperwork. We'll set up an escrow account if Steve will agree to have his payout transferred to an investment account he sets up here. Everything stays in house and everybody wins."

"I don't know if he'll agree to that. He has to pay for materials and labor, after all. Besides, the investment account you set up for him would be too small under house rules, wouldn't it?"

"For you, I'll make an exception. Talk to him about it. Make him see the light."

"Staying on the subject of money, I don't like Rolie's proposal to have me inject more capital into the family business, or make a loan so he can install a copper smelter."

"Why not? Doesn't he project a big return?"

"I can't see the basis for his projections."

"Well, on that subject, I'll hold my counsel. The consideration, after all, isn't strictly financial. It's a matter of your sacred duty to family. Rolie and Matilda are both living on a lot less than they used to, while you're doing just fine."

"Bob! Is this a guilt trip?"

"If you feel guilty, that's up to you. I'm just pointing out the obvious."

She sighed deeply. "Well, my life is no bed of roses. My car was torched in Indianapolis, as I'm sure you heard, and Saturday night I discovered I was the latest victim of the Panty Raider."

"The who?"

"Some guy who breaks into the houses of single women and steals their lingerie."

"Oh, him. Xiu-Xiu was a victim too."

"Does she live in Sycamore Hills?"

"No. Downtown on the river, in an apartment. Why?"

"Grace Venable told me she thought the Panty Raider was operating in your community."

"I hadn't heard that. But back to you. How did the guy get past your alarm?"

"You know I don't use it. I constantly forget the code, and every time there's a short power outage or the wind blows too hard, the alarm sounds and I can't get it shut off."

"Well, you're going to have to change that. A beautiful woman like you, living alone in the city . . . ." He shook his head. "My fatherly advice is to start using the system you've paid for." He rolled back his desk chair. "You mentioned something about being stalked."

"My car was torched at the hotel where I was giving a speech in Indianapolis, and it seems to have been a personal act rather than something random. Mine was the only one touched, and 'cow' was written in acid on the hood. Then the Panty Raider."

"Since you're not the only victim of the Panty Raider, as you call him, that doesn't sound especially personal, but the car is different. Any idea who that might be?"

"I was thinking Ferrell, the only violent person I know and the only one who'd use the word 'cow' instead of 'bitch.' But the guy in the security tape, which I viewed a few days ago, looks too short to be him."

Bob chuckled. "So, a surfeit of bad men in your life. Have you been making enemies, Alexandra?"

"If I have, I didn't know it."

"Go home and read Proverbs 16: 7."

"What's it say?"

Bob gazed at the ceiling. "'When a man's ways are pleasing to the Lord, he makes even his enemies live at peace with him.'"

"So my ways aren't pleasing to the Lord. It's my fault things are going wrong."

"Look at me. I don't have an enemy in the world." He stood up. "Tell you what. Clarissa and I are starting a Bible study at our house, Wednesday evenings, 6 - 8, snacks and apple juice served. We're studying the Beatitudes."

Lexie stood up too, but she had no idea what to say, she was so insulted.

Bob walked around his desk to give her a hug. "I hate to cut this short, but I've got a new prospect coming in."

"And you're going to talk him out of investing in Passwatter Global Investments, I suppose."

He laughed. "You better believe it. That way, he has to think about it, long and hard. Once he becomes my client, he's grateful, knows he made a wise choice, and my way is made smooth as glass."

Is there a proverb for making your way smooth as glass? she wondered a little testily, but held her tongue, saying only that she'd get back to him about Bible study. She had a busy schedule.

20

Divination

Friday, January 30, 2009

Vicki Grinderman was a New Age priestess. She'd bought dozens of books about New Age transformation, some of which she had actually read except for the boring or difficult bits. Deepak Chopra seemed especially profound because he made no sense. She meditated and practiced yoga. Meditation was very frustrating, for she could never clear her mind, but yoga kept her supple. She religiously poured over daily horoscopes for herself and her closest friends. Oprah Winfrey was her idol for pointing out that there was more than one way to heaven. So freeing! She was enchanted with the notion that she could make up her own religion out of the agreeable bits and pieces of the old ones.

It had only been a few years since she'd been awakened to the Mayan-Nostradamus-Druid prediction that the world as we know it will end on December 21, 2012. The reason was clear to her. For the first time in 26,000 years, the sun would block the earth's view of the center of the Milky Way where the stars in the galaxy were born out of a black hole. When she tried talking to her parents about it, her mother pointed out that the earth was only 6,000 years old, so how could such an alignment ever have happened 26,000 years earlier? Vicki, who had no answer, felt sorry for her clueless Christian mother.

Anyway, the blocking of all that energy by the sun meant something magical had to happen on earth. The idea that a black hole, like a satanic navel, sat at the center of the galaxy, radiating energy and spewing stars, made her brain overheat. How did it do that? What did it mean? It must portend something huge when the earth's view of the black hole was blocked.

She was entranced by two opposing New Age theories. On December 21, 2012, either the globe would be smashed to pieces and everyone would die through physical cataclysm -- asteroid impact, nuclear war, gamma ray burst, mega solar flare, polar shift, catastrophic earthquake, supervolcanic eruption, tsunami, something like that. Or it would be changed for the better. Through some supernatural means, the old materialistic, war-mongering, earth-destroying, jingoistic culture would die and something entirely new would be born: a golden age of higher consciousness, a quantum leap in spirituality, and a new plane of existence.

The idea of higher consciousness was very alluring; sometimes she thought she grasped the concept, but it was like trying to grasp the corner of a blanket of fog. The moment she thought she'd experienced a higher consciousness, she lost the words to describe it -- though magic words rolled continuously through her mind. The phrases galactic alignment, spiritual awakening, golden age, cosmic energy, global peace, and harmonic convergence were like talismans. She stenciled her favorite New Age phrases on pieces of slate she laid throughout the flower bed near her front door.

For Vicki, it was completely natural to anticipate a higher collective consciousness rather than global annihilation. At 26, she was too young to have only three more years of life to look forward to. Whatever happened on December 21, 2012, she didn't plan to die.

She would be spiritually reborn. She knew that. A year ago, at her urging, she and her parents spent two weeks in the Yucatàn peninsula, where the Mayan calendar ending on 12/21/12 was born. While her parents stood around spraying insect repellent on each other and checking boat schedules, she crawled up and down the Mayan ruins of Chichen Itza and Tulum. She listened avidly to dark little men with heavy accents explain what she was seeing. The feathered serpent god Quetzalcoatl fired her imagination. The thought of playing a ball game for keeps where the losers actually died on the June solstice was mesmerizing and scary as hell. But, of course, she would be a winner. A game like that gave life the kick it needed.

Once the Grindermans returned to Cozumel, where her parents insisted on spending the final full week to recover from the horrors of the jungle and its strange ruins, she purchased a silver pendant honoring the serpent god, vowing never to take it off -- though she did when only gold jewelry would do. That was the beginning of her collection of sacred snakes -- all inanimate, of course.

Back at home, she began concocting rituals with incense candles and nonsense chants, crystal ropes draped around her neck, a collection of onyx serpent-god figurines from Mexico lined up on her coffee table. Her best friend, Trent Senser, her gay co-worker who followed her around like a pet dog, was the first to be introduced to her secret rituals, but she had cautiously introduced Cricket, her younger sister, and then some of her more open-minded girlfriends as well.

Now they made a party of it once every month. They were eating slippery chunks of avocado and drinking Bloody Marys in honor of the Mayans, who she regretfully acknowledged to herself ate human hearts and drank blood. Human sacrifice, of course, was sickeningly old-fashioned and unnecessary to reach a higher consciousness. She knew the Mayans didn't listen to Santana either, but she couldn't find any Mayan music at Best Buy, and the sound of Andes flutes just didn't set the right mood.

"Why aren't you out with Steve tonight?" Trent asked, trying to find a comfortable position on the floor. All the pillows in the world couldn't make a hard floor into a soft retreat, but since Vicki's little villa in Le Cavalière lacked enough seating for the nine of them, the floor was where they had their "picnic."

"Saturday night. That's the only time he asks me out."

"But that's good, right?" Cricket asked. "Saturday night means he's serious."

"Of course he's serious. Look at me. If you were a guy, wouldn't you want a piece of this?" She thrust out her chest; she would have done a little burlesque move or two if she'd been standing up.

"Why would I have to be a guy?" one of the girls asked flirtatiously, in the way of modern pansexuals. "When's the palm reader going to get here?"

Fortunately, the palm reader was only twenty minutes late. She was a middle-aged woman who invited her accolytes to call her Mama Bee. She looked like everybody's mother except for the clothes she wore, revealing a lot of décolletage half-obscured by flowing scarves and long necklaces featuring seed pods, silver-nickel bells from India, and African trade beads. Though Mama Bee was Caucasian, she wore her graying hair in cornrows, a narrow tie-dyed chiffon scarf knotted around her forehead.

"I'm not going to sit on the floor, girls. Do you have a card table or something?"

"No," Vicki said, "but I have a TV tray. Will that do?"

Mama Bee frowned. "It'll have to do, I guess. Two chairs, one for me, one for the client. And I need a lamp. I like candlelight as much as the next woman, but I don't want to miss anything."

Once seated, she placed a penlight on the tray and donned half-glasses. Then she gazed at her expectant audience, letting her eyes rest briefly on each face, allowing the tension to build. "First, let me give you a few words about palm reading. It's called chiromency or palmistry by some, but let's just stick with palm reading, which is the art of foretelling the future by studying the lines and mounts of the palm and its overall shape. I can also divine the karmic past. My art is an old one, with its roots in ancient India, where I studied one whole week thirty years ago. Each area of the palm is related to a god or goddess. The left hand is what the gods gave you, the right what you managed to do with it. Any questions?"

Cricket shot her hand in the air. "Are you a prophet?"

"Yes, you could call me that." But Mama Bee had no interest in answering more questions. "Now, let's get to the good stuff." What she really meant was that, as a careful businesswoman, she wanted to spend as little time as she could earning the fee she'd quoted to Miss Grinderman. From the giddy state of her subjects and the half-full pitchers of Bloody Marys she spotted on the floor, she realized, too late, that she could have doubled the quote if only she'd known. Telling her own future, she'd discovered the hard way, was much more challenging than entertaining a roomful of overgrown school girls.

"Before we start, I'm going to ring this bell to summon the spirits that guide me. So close your eyes and think divine thoughts."

Everyone closed their eyes with the intention of summoning the highest thoughts they knew, but before any appeared, Mama Bee clapped her hands and switched on the table lamp. "So, who's first?"

Vicki announced that they'd proceed in alphabetical order by last name but, as the generous, organized hostess she was, she would go last.

Vicki's reading was worth waiting for.

Mama Bee started with the left hand, spending a minute just turning it over, then back, then over again, closing her eyes and rubbing the palm as if she were reading Braille. Using her penlight, with furrowed forehead, she studied the lines on Vicki's left palm. Then she did the same with the right hand. Vicki waited, breathless.

"Okay. You have long fingers and dry skin, a lot of undefined lines, so you have an Air Hand." As the girls and Trent had already learned, a hand could be earth, air, water, or fire. Vicki's was the only air hand in the room.

"Now, for the Heart Line. Ah, you're a romantic. Very much in love at this moment. But you've been in love before, haven't you?"

Vicki nodded.

"All your past lives were marked by love as well, so you're an old hand, so to speak, in the romance department."

"Am I going to get married soon?"

"We'll see. There's an order here, so stay with me. Then the Head Line. You have a great thirst for knowledge, especially of the occult. You want to teach others."

"Which I do. I want to start a New Age boutique. I'll have -- ."

Mama Bee cut her off. "The Life Line indicates a big change is coming in your life, very soon."

"Oh, good!"Vicki exclaimed, sure it meant marriage to Steve Wright.

"2012," Trent interjected. "Isn't that the big change coming to us all?"

"That, of course," Mama Bee said, looking at him over her glasses as if he were a rare white leopard. She hadn't seen a man in one of her readings in years. "2012 is a magic year for everybody. But the change I'm seeing is special to Miss Grinderman."

"Go on,"Vicki said, practically bouncing in her chair.

"The Sun Line and Fate Line, which run parallel to each other, indicate that the big change that's coming involves a man. The Travel Line indicates an unexpected trip to a faraway place."

"My honeymoon. It must mean a honeymoon on St. Kitts, the way I always dreamed."

"I'm not done. The Fate Line indicates an obstacle you'll have to overcome."

"Oh, no."

"Well, let's not despair. There are obstacles in every life.

Let me take a look at the Girdle of Venus." She spent a few seconds inspecting the Girdle of Venus. "Ah, you're good at manipulating people to get what you want. Is that right?"

"I got my parents to go the Yucatàn, which they hated."

"She tricks me into doing half her work," Trent said, chuckling to prove he didn't mind.

"She told me my boyfriend was beneath me, so I threw him over," Cricket said, looking rather sad.

"That's good," Mama Bee said, giving Vicki her most encouraging smile. "Your manipulation of the obstacle -- a circumstance you didn't foresee -- will help you avoid a bad outcome. In fact, it will make you the subject of great fame, just as you were in your past lives." Mama Bee switched off the lamp. "And that, my New Age comrades, concludes the evening."

"But I want to know more," Vicki pouted. "Especially whether I'm getting married."

"Well," Mama Bee said, pretending to consider the matter. Always leave people wanting more. "If you want me to look more deeply into the space-time dimension, I'll need my crystal ball." The mention of the space-time dimension was her best trick. Injecting the air of science into the art of divination made her seem fabulously astute, many notches above the average carnival fortune teller.

"Do you have it with you? The crystal ball, I mean."

"No. That's a different reading" -- *and a bigger fee* -- "altogether. It takes longer, and for me it's very mentally demanding, very draining. The spirits leave me empty afterwards, and it takes days to regenerate my energy. But I'm sure I have an opening soon, if you want to schedule something."

Vicki's friends were excited. A crystal ball party was just what they needed. The palm reader told them how to prepare for an evening with the crystal ball.

Vicki and her friends ended the evening discussing their various fortunes as told by Mama Bee and arguing about whether the "spirits" they were consuming by the pitcher had anything to do with the cosmic spiritual revolution that would occur in 2012.

★ ★ ★ ★ ★

That night, Vicki's sleep was disturbed by a dream she didn't understand. At twilight, in a strange city, she found herself standing on a concrete island in the middle of traffic-choked streets. Along with many other people of both sexes and all races and ages, she was waiting for a trolley. Aside from a few mothers holding babies, the people waiting with her seemed to have no relation to each other, nor even to the dogs that were milling about. She had no idea where the trolley was going, but reluctantly she knew she had to board it.

21

Every Man Says That

Saturday, January 31, 2009

By Saturday night -- date night -- Steve felt as if he'd lived in a fog of confused emotions for days on end. A week ago Friday, at Club Soda, he'd said things to Lexie he now regretted. He'd been harsh. He'd acted as if all the fault for their breakup before college was hers, yet he knew that wasn't true. They were too young in those days to know what mattered in a marriage. He hadn't had a clear idea of what he wanted to make of his life, and for a girl to hitch her wagon to an ox that didn't know where it was going was stupid. Things like the profession a man pursued and where a couple lived did matter. True, he was still smarting from the wound she caused, but did he have to say so? Shouldn't he be mature enough to get past it? He wanted her to ask his forgiveness for the wrongs she'd done to him, but in unguarded moments he acknowledged that he wasn't perfect either. He too needed to seek forgiveness.

On Tuesday, when he toured the Forest Park mansion with Lexie, he wanted to say something to heal the rift. Though she was friendly enough, she never really gave him an opening to say anything personal. She acted, not standofffish, but pleasantly businesslike, as if there were no strain between them. Unsure of where they were going with their friendship -- if they were going anywhere at all -- he left without asking her out again.

And he was unsure of something else as well. What in hell was he doing seeing Vicki, a girl so much younger than himself, a girl he didn't love, though at the beginning he thought love might blossom if he gave it enough time? His aunt had warned him that dating a girl on the rebound from his divorce was a stupid business. He was confusing lust with love, she said, and if he had any sense, he'd date someone his own age. At the time, he was so in need of companionship and intimacy, he couldn't see the truth of that advice, and the fact that a girl as young and pretty as Vicki admired him was irresistible.

But now he was beginning to see that he was making a mess of things. Dating was never casual, especially for women and especially when it continued for several years. Vicki had ideas far different from his own about where their relationship was going. He should have foreseen that. He had to end it soon.

He'd suspected that they were working at cross-purposes for months, but Saturday night at Hartley's he heard enough from Vicki that he couldn't kid himself any more about what she expected to happen, and soon. He was telling her about his plan to spend a week with his buddies in Arizona in late February. They were going to watch the Cleveland Indians in spring training at the Goodyear Ball Park and get in a round of golf every afternoon. Vicki's eyes glazed over.

When he paused, her eyes refocused. "You're not taking

me?"

"It's a guys' getaway." He smiled to soften the blow. "No women allowed. No wives, no girlfriends. That's the rule we've all played by for the last six years. You knew that last year when I went and didn't say a thing."

"I was pretending to understand."

Pretending? "Besides, you'd be bored to death, Vicki. You don't watch baseball or play golf. I know you well enough to know that, don't I?"

"You don't know me well at all if you think it's okay for you to go off with your buddies for a week without me."

"We don't go to strip clubs or nightclubs or do anything our wives and girlfriends wouldn't approve. It's not that kind of getaway."

"I don't care," she pouted. "I thought we were going to spend a week in Cozumel."

Steve was genuinely puzzled. "What made you think that?"

"Because I want to go back there. I must have mentioned it dozens of times. You should see the pyramids, the ball court, the giant serpent. I want to go there on the June solstice when the sunlight intersects . . . ." She couldn't remember what the sunlight was supposed to intersect with, nor even why it mattered. "It's the only way to understand the 2012 prediction."

He was irritated by the reference, which he'd heard too many times. If there was one day on which the world would *not* end, it was December 21, 2012, he was sure of that. Doomsday dates were always wrong.

"I think you should stop worrying about the end of the world."

"I'm not worrying about it. I'm looking forward to it. We're all going to be spiritually transformed. Mama Bee agrees."

"Who's Mama Bee?"

"She's a palm reader. I had her come to the house last night and read my friends' palms. You know what she saw in my hand?"

"What?"

"A big change is coming in my life, a change involving a man and an unexpected trip to a faraway place."

He had an idea of what was coming. "What's that supposed to mean?"

She laughed. "Guess."

"I can't guess," he said stubbornly.

"Don't make me say it, Stevie."

He recoiled at the babyish nickname. It made him sound about ten years old. "I'm not making you say anything, Vicki. I think we should order."

After they'd ordered, walleye for her and a rib-eye for himself, Vicki returned to her theme. "Isn't it time we talk about where we're going? I'm 26, after all. If anybody asks me where I'll be next year, I want to have an answer. And I don't want it to be the same answer as I gave last year."

"And your body clock is ticking, is that it?" He knew he sounded sarcastic.

She looked hurt. "No."

"No?"

"Well, yes. I want a child. But I want a husband first."

"Are you saying you want me as a husband?"

She laughed shakily. "You'll do, Stevie."

"But I told you when we started seeing each other that

I didn't think I'd ever marry again."

"Every man says that," she said dismissively.

"Well, I'm not every man. I meant what I said. I never led you on."

"Oh, but you did. Once we started going out on Saturday night, you gave me the unspoken signal."

"The unspoken signal?"

"When a guy asks a girl out every Saturday night, then he's serious. Someday he's going to give her the ring she's been waiting for her whole life. It's just a matter of time."

"I wish somebody had warned me about that."

They continued talking at cross-purposes, Steve patiently, Vicki petulantly, until they'd finished eating and he'd paid the check. He slid his chair back but she didn't move. Her face was flushed, her eyes red and watery.

"You ready to go, Vicki?"

"So, what's it going to be, Stevie? Are we going to get married or not? I'm not leaving until I get an answer."

"If you want an answer this minute, I'm afraid it isn't what you want to hear."

She was quiet for a few seconds. She looked around the room and then at him. He thought he'd dodged a bullet, but he was wrong. "You asshole!" she suddenly screamed, throwing her glass of water in his face. "You spiritually corrupt piece of shit." She threw her napkin at him. "You unevolved pig. You snake in the grass. You . . . ."

Steve was mortified. The restaurant was small, and he recognized a couple of the other diners, who of course were transfixed by the scene. Nothing he could say or do would end Vicki's tirade. In fact, she continued screaming epithets as she followed him to the car.

All the way to her house, she cried and berated him. She begged him to change his mind. She screamed some more, calling him every bad name she could think of. She hit him in the arm. She reviewed every wrong he'd ever done to her. Again, she begged him to change his mind, make her happy, start down the path of married life. Then she cursed him. "I hope the asteroid makes a direct hit on you, Stevie Wrong."

It was all Steve could do to walk her to her front door and wait until she let herself in. When he heard the lock click, he stood there a minute, debating with himself. He shouldn't leave her alone in such a distraught state. He could hear her sobbing. But unless he gave into her demands about the future, there was nothing palliative for him to say.

So he returned to his car, shaking with the humiliation he'd just endured at Hartley's. He was so consumed with self-loathing for his willful blindness, as well as anger at Vicki's unreasonable expectations, that he had to will himself to calm down before he started the car. Instead of going directly home, his emotions in a turmoil, he found himself driving through the serpentine streets of Le Cavalière, then returning to Vicki's house, where he idled. Lighting a cigarette and composing scripts in his head that would comfort Vicki while letting him off the hook, he kept his eye on the house. All was dark. Finally, when he spotted the flickering light of the television, he pulled away.

22

Perfectly Innocent Fetish

Saturday, January 31, 2009

Once in her house, Vicki was so distraught that she didn't bother to turn on any lights before she threw herself, face down, onto the Indian daybed she used as a sofa. She cried and pounded the pillows the way she had when she was two years old.

But tantrums couldn't last forever, especially when there was no audience and the spangly paillettes on the Indian pillows were cutting into her face. Exhausted and in need of refreshment, she rose and walked to the kitchen, turned on the under-cabinet lights, found a tissue, blew her nose, and then poured the remains of the Bloody Marys from the night before into a large tumbler.

Back in the living room, she turned on the television to a station than ran reruns of *The Nanny*. She liked Fran Drescher so much she'd copied as many of her exaggerated smirks and frowns as she could and would have worn the same colorful, tastelessly skintight clothes if she could have found them. Vicki was in awe of Nanny Fine's skillful manipulation of the clueless Maxwell Sheffield, her widowed, handsome, uptight, very rich boss. If she just watched enough programs and thought about it a lot, Vicki was sure she could learn something useful from Fran about how to handle Steve, who, though he didn't realize it, was madly in love with her. He had to be.

During a commercial break, Vicki rose again to make herself another pitcher of Bloody Marys. Before she reached the kitchen, something caught her eye as she passed the corridor leading to the bedroom wing, where the guest bedroom faced the street and her bedroom faced the backyard. Her bedroom door was closed, but light was seeping under it. She couldn't remember closing the door before she left or leaving a light on. She never did that. Her father, the judge, had drilled into his children the moral importance of not wasting food, water or electricity. Oh, well, she decided, she'd do better next time. Right now, she needed another Bloody Mary and didn't want to miss a minute of Nanny Fine.

So she proceeded to the kitchen, where she mixed a new pitcher of Bloody Marys. On her way back to the living room, as she was passing the corridor again, she thought she heard a noise, a soft thump, from the direction of her bedroom. She cocked her head, unsure of whether she'd really heard something or only imagined it. Then she heard it again. The hair rose on her arms and her spine tingled. Was someone in the house? Surely not. She always locked the doors.

Creeping back to the kitchen, she set her tumbler on the counter and stood there, frozen, trying to decide whether to run out of the house screaming or instead find out what was making the noise. If she was just imagining things and ran outside at ten at night, screaming and disturbing all her neighbors, she'd never live it down.

She tried to recall everything Mama Bee had told her. She had a bright future. A big change involving a man and a faraway trip lay ahead of her. There would be an obstacle, but she'd overcome it. She was so smart she could manipulate anybody. She would be famous.

So what did she really have to fear? Her future had already been written. Powerful gods were on her side.

Maybe it was Steve in the bedroom, surprising her, the way he once did at his home, where he'd lit candles in his bedroom as a surprise. But how did he get in? Suddenly, she realized that in her fury she probably hadn't locked the front door behind her when she slammed it on Steve, but she was unwilling to check it out for fear of what she'd find. It had to be Steve in her bedroom. He must have sneaked in while she was in the kitchen, wanting to make up and surprise her. Perhaps he was ready to propose.

Hoping for the best but not completely convinced it was Steve waiting for her, she crept down the hallway, straining to hear any sounds that might be coming from the room. She stood outside the door, her hand hovering above the knob, picturing exactly where the wall switch was so that once she opened the door, fast and hard, she could immediately flip the switch for the overhead light. Light, she knew from her childhood, scared the monsters away.

She was not prepared, however, for the monster waiting for her on the other side of the door. There was so much to take in she couldn't register everything at once. The man was standing in front of her full-length mirror, wearing her best silk teddy in nude silk with black lace trim and a matching thong from Victoria's Secret. Her lovely garments were stretched beyond recognition. The only other thing he was wearing was his own athletic socks. He was holding a little camera. The clothes he'd worn into the house were scattered across her bed. The squat little crystal lamp on her dresser, draped with a scarf, was softly lit. The lingerie drawer in her dresser, which had been pulled out and set on the floor, was festooned with a jumble of bras and panties.

As she stared at him, he suddenly did a weird little dance. Was it meant to be sexy? So revolting! Though she knew from her father's safety lectures that she should pretend not to recognize him so she could escape with her life if he had violence in mind and would only let her live if he was sure she couldn't identify him, she couldn't manage the deception. She stared in disbelief. Not him! She never in her wildest dreams imagined him to be a pervert. If he hadn't been wearing her lingerie, if he'd been normally dressed, she would have assumed he had some unexpected but still believable reason for appearing at her door, unannounced, late at night.

She couldn't help it -- she fired a fusillade of hysterical questions at the man. "What are you doing in my bedroom? Why are you wearing that? How did you get in?"

The man had to think fast. He'd never been caught in the act before. Caution was his hallmark. He never entered a house that wasn't empty. He chose victims he knew, at least on sight, and he studied their habits enough to estimate accurately how long they'd be gone so he could take his time selecting the lingerie that excited him the most. Because his victims would recognize him if they ever got a look at him, he took the precautions of a second lieutenant leading a platoon into battle.

When Vicki turned to bolt out of the room in the direction of a phone, he sprinted toward her, grabbing her long hair and wrenching her backwards. She stumbled, falling hard to the floor on her back. She'd have screamed if the breath hadn't been knocked out of her. As it was, she gasped out a few, breathy words he could hardly hear. "Please, don't hurt me. I'll swear I don't know you."

He put his hand roughly over her mouth and growled, "Shut up. Do what I say, I'll let you live."

"Just leave. I won't call the cops," she mumbled. When he began to tear her camisole and skirt off, she bit his shoulder and brought her knee up to his groin, at the same time gasping out a few more words. "I want to live. I'll do anything you say."

His shoulder was bleeding but he rolled his pelvis away in time to avoid the blow to the groin. Once he rolled back onto her supine body so that he could control her with his weight, his face was inches from hers. The look of disbelief in her beautiful blue eyes said, *This cannot be happening,* though no words came from her mouth. He had a momentary impulse to laugh. But it was the terror in her eyes that stirred something new in him, something he'd never have predicted. She was young and sexy, afraid and pleading for her life, his to do with as he pleased. All the power was his.

"Please," she whispered. "Anything."

He struck her hard in the temple, then ripped off her bra and panties. As he raped her, he fantasized that her limp body and dilated pupils meant she acquiesced in the act, even enjoyed it.

A few minutes later, as he lay, spent and panting, on top of the girl, he realized with a jolt that he couldn't let her live. She knew who he was, of course. The semen inside her could only be linked to him if she was alive and identified him as her assailant. The bruises on her head and body, the bite mark on his shoulder, would give the lie to his claim of consensual sex.

So he strangled her with her own bra. The minute she started gasping for oxygen, her body began to spasm, lurching so hard he had difficulty staying on top of her, but he was very strong, and in a sense he was fighting for his life as much as she was fighting for hers. Surprised at how many minutes it took for her to die, he marveled at how hard it was to end another person's life. Fascinated by what was happening, he found he couldn't take his eyes off hers as she fought for air and finally lost the battle.

At last, when he was sure from her fixed pupils that she was dead, he rolled off the body and lay there a few minutes, thunderstruck at what he'd just done. He hadn't planned to kill her. If he could have been sure she didn't recognize him, perhaps he could have let her live. After all, he was not a killer. He was just an ordinary man in a bad situation. Perhaps he should start wearing a mask.

He studied her face a few minutes. It was ugly now. Her skin was blotchy, her blank eyes bulging, her purple tongue swollen and protruding. In death, Vicki Grinderman disgusted him. But she was a trophy too. He got to his feet, found his camera, and took several pictures of her corpse from different angles. He already had a collection of photos of himself wearing all kinds of lingerie; he made sure his face was obscured in every picture. Now he had the start of another kind of collection.

But it should never have come to this. He'd never killed

before. All he ever wanted was some lingerie, for God's sake, lingerie for his growing collection. He knew from the Internet he wasn't alone in that interest. Contrary to the views of the unsophisticated critics of sexual freedom, his interest in wearing women's underwear wasn't a fetish, nor was he a cross-dresser. There was nothing wrong with him. Instead, his pleasure in dressing up like a woman was a perfectly innocent hobby, a healthy way for a man to express the age-old, universal desire to be made whole with his female side.

He got up, took off the silky garments that made him feel special and stuffed them with the bra he used as a ligature and Vicki's panties into one pocket of his puffy jacket and his camera into the other. Then he put on his track shoes and dressed in his running clothes, pulling the hood low over his forehead, the drawstring tied very tightly. He left the same way he entered -- through the side door to the garage, where he'd earlier removed a pane of glass and simply twisted the thumb lock to let himself in. The interior door to the house fortunately hadn't been locked.

As he retraced his steps through the girl's snowy backyard to the woods and then the public trail that ran behind Le Cavalière toward the Parkview-YMCA running path across Dupont, where his car was parked, he noticed a light come on in a house he passed but was sure no one could identify him even if they could see him in the dark.

On his way home, he promised himself that he'd never kill again. He wouldn't start a collection of corpse pictures. What he'd done was dreadful and permanent. He'd plan better next time so that murder was never again necessary.

Still, it had given him a rush, a sensation so all-encompassing, so powerful, that it dwarfed every other emotion he'd ever experienced. The godlike power of life and death was like no other.

23

Super Bowl 43

Sunday, February 1, 2009

On the evening of Sunday, February 1, in Autumn Ridge, Steve was comfortably ensconced in his basement media room, enjoying the 43rd Superbowl. He'd invited over his brother Frank and his wife Winnie, plus half a dozen friends and their wives to watch with him. The women had gathered at the bar to talk about Busch Gardens and other tourist attractions in Tampa, where the game was held; the talent and weight problems of Jennifer Hudson, who was going to sing the national anthem; and the relative merits of various recipes for gluten-free appetizers. Their gossip was punctuated by attempts to heat up more appetizers and straighten up the mess the men had made.

Around the corner, a few yards away, the men were lounging on a tan leather sectional, their feet up on a bronze coffee table, watching the game on a high-definition 50-inch flat screen television custom built into the library wall. Drinking beer and smoking cigars, they were amiably arguing about whether it was reasonable for the Pittsburgh Steelers to be favored by seven points over the Arizona Cardinals.

All of Frank's contributions were made in a parody of John Madden's distinctive voice and delivery. By the end of the evening it was unanimously voted that John Madden's presence as a color commentator meant that a traveling circus somewhere in the world was missing a clown.

The call to Steve came during Bruce Springsteen's half-time presentation. He stepped into the adjoining workout room to take it.

"Steve. This is Paul Grinderman."

"Nice to hear from you, Judge."

"Could you put Vicki on the phone?"

"I would if she were here."

"Vicki's not with you?"

"No, she's not. Why?"

"She was supposed to come over for dinner tonight, watch the Super Bowl with us. The whole family's here. But Vicki's not answering her phone. We thought she might be with you. Have you seen her today, or talked to her?"

"No." He winced at the story he would have to tell if the Judge probed any further.

"Did you see her last night, Steve?"

"I did. We had dinner at Hartley's" -- *where we had the mother of all arguments* -- "and I dropped her off" -- *screaming and sobbing like a child denied her favorite toy* -- "at her house."

"Dropped her off?"

"I had to make an early night of it, so I went to the door with her but I didn't go in."

"About what time was that?"

"Around nine, I think."

"Did she say anything about what she had planned for today?"

"Not a word."

"Do you have any ways of contacting her that we might not have?"

"None that I know of."

"Well, if you have any idea where she might be or who she might be with, would you give us a call? Or if you hear from her, let us know right away."

"Sure thing, Judge."

"I don't mean to make a mountain out of a molehill, but we're worried. It's not like Vicki not to text or call us at least once a day."

"I'm sure everything's all right."

"Well, I don't mean to interrupt your evening. You're probably watching the Super Bowl too."

"You bet. I have a bunch of friends over."

"I see the third quarter's almost starting, so I'll let you go. Are you betting on the Steelers or the Cardinals?"

"Steelers. How about you?"

"I always like an underdog, but I'm no fool."

There was an awkward silence. "Well, Judge, let me know when you hear from Vicki."

"I'll do that."

Steve returned to his party, just the tiniest bit worried. Vicki was a bit flaky, but he'd never known her to blow off a date or a party, and she was close to her family. He felt guilty about how they'd left things Saturday night. She might be pouting, proving a point through silence. He knew from his former marriage that when a woman got really angry, sometimes she went mute, using blackout as effectively as an assault rifle.

After his guests left, Steve called Vicki on her cell phone.

He left a message. "Vicki, this is Steve. A few hours ago your father called me, asking where you are. Call him, please. He's worried. Or call me. Just let somebody know where you are and what you're doing."

24

Rancho Salud

Monday, February 2, 2009

Late in the afternoon of Groundhog Day, Lexie and Jessica Singer were sitting side-by-side on lounge chairs at Rancho Salud in the Red Rock country around Sedona, Arizona. Though they'd only arrived on Friday, they were already exhausted, starved, and furious.

Jessica removed her sweaty headband and pulled up the collar on her jacket as the temperature fell. "If I'd known it was going to cost me six thousand dollars to hike four hours a day, practice high-impact yoga two hours and pilates one, endure the most painful deep-muscle massages invented by Auschwitz Gertie, live without coffee, wine, and meat, get up at 5:30 and go to bed at 8:30, all to lose three pounds -- I'd have stayed home. I could have lost that much shopping all day long at Nordstrom's and had something to show for it."

"I don't mind walking," Lexie replied, "but hiking ten miles everyday, all of it uphill, isn't what I bargained for. By the way, how is it we only walk uphill? Isn't there some law of physics that says that's not possible?"

"I thought I'd like yoga, you know? But Downward

Facing Dog is just obscene, don't you think?" Jessica donned her Gucci sunglasses against the rays of the setting sun. "When we're supposed to be meditating in the lotus position -- which hurts like hell, by the way -- all I can think of is wine and a big juicy steak with a loaded baked potato."

"If I get started thinking about food, Jess, I'll drown in my own drool. Oatmeal with almond milk for breakfast is utterly disgusting."

"Yesterday's salad of chickpeas and roasted baby beets would fit in my daughter's dolly teacup, for heaven's sake. I mean it. I'm not kidding. And last night's dinner, if you can call it that, of lentil cake on steamed spinach was even smaller." Jessica shook out her hair. "It was the best appetizer I ever ate. I give you that."

"I literally dream of prime rib."

"How many of the dozen women who are here have vomited repeatedly on the hiking trail, do you think? Ed says they're suffering from low blood sugar levels."

"Half, at least."

Jessica picked up her walkie-talkie and pretended to throw it. "What are pea shoots and tendrils, by the way? That's what were getting tonight with gluten-free banana bread. We're being forcibly detoxified."

"If I get any more detoxified, I'll be a raging maniac."

Jessica pointed one spandex-encased leg at the setting sun. "I'm beginning to like my thighs. So juicy and plump. What about you?"

"I'm ready to bag it and call The Phoenician. What do you think, Jess?"

"It's a deal. You make the arrangements tonight, I'll face down the prison guards tomorrow morning, tell 'em we're out of here."

Lexie shaded her eyes. "The mountains, however, are absolutely gorgeous, especially at sunset. Though, if you ask me, it looks like somebody ran a dump truck through the sky and simply let a load of rocks fall where it would."

Jessica laughed. "Well, at least you see rocks. They look like layer cakes to me; the pink and gold peaks are frosting." Jessica's stomach rumbled. "I definitely see frosting."

They laughed, then drifted to other subjects. "So, you haven't told me yet, Lexie, how the ride back to Fort Wayne was after your car was torched. You and Steve have something going on again?"

"I don't know. It's been fifteen years and one divorce each since we broke up, but he still seems to be angry about it. The ride home from Indianapolis in the blizzard was fun, like old times, but that mood didn't last a week. Besides, he has a girlfriend."

"He does? Who?"

"Judge Grinderman's oldest daughter, Vicki."

"How old is she?"

"I'm not sure. Mid-twenties, I think. He says he's not serious, though they've been dating a couple of years, I hear."

"So . . . ?"

"So, he's going to do some work on the house I bought last year, if I can get an escrow set up. At least we'll see each other from time to time and have something to talk about. But so far that's all Steve's doing for me."

"Does that disappoint you?"

Lexie considered her answer. "It does. More than I would have guessed. Did you know, by the way, that Jean still has a thing for Steve?"

"I didn't know she ever did."

"Neither did I till she spilled the beans a few weeks ago." Lexie told her friend about Jean's confession at Biaggi's, then the drunken scene at Club Soda, and finally Jean's retreat to Hazelden and her plans for a two-week London vacation in the Fall. "I'm paying her salary for her sobriety leave but not sure whether to pay her vacation time."

"Why wouldn't you?"

"She's taking advantage of me, don't you think?"

"You want my opinion?"

"Sure."

"Pay her for both."

"Why? Because she's an old friend? Because she's worked for me a couple of years? Because she needs the job?"

"No . . . well, yes and no. I'm not suggesting that you act out of sentiment exactly. What I am saying is, be more generous than you have to. That's the right thing to do, don't you think?"

"Even in business?"

"Even in business."

"You don't think I'll look like a fool to her? That she'll think I'm a softie and take even more advantage of me?" Lexie asked in a doubtful voice.

"Don't worry about looking like a fool when you're doing the right thing. But if she's mean enough, or stupid enough, to take advantage of you, then -- and only then -- do whatever you have to do. But give her a chance."

Lexie smiled. "Well, Mother Theresa, I'll think about it." She looked at her watch. "I think it's time for pea shoots and tendrils. Ummm."

Though it was against prison-spa rules, Lexie left her cell phone on after lights out. She'd fallen into the deep, dreamless sleep of the thoroughly exhausted when it played *Nine to Five.*

"Hello?" she answered, her eyes still shut.

"Lexie, it's me," Rolie said. "Where are you?"

"I'm in Arizona at a spa. Only it's not as nice as it sounds."

"Were you asleep?"

"I was. Still am. What time is it?"

"One in the morning here. I have news."

"It couldn't have waited till tomorrow?"

"No."

Lexie sighed. "News about what?"

"Your old boyfriend Steve."

Lexie switched on a bedside lamp and sat up. "What about Steve?"

"His girlfriend, Vicki Grinderman, was found dead this morning."

"What?"

"You heard me."

"Dead? You're kidding. Where? How?"

"In her bedroom in Le Cavalière. Haven't heard how she died, but there are rumors she was beaten or strangled or something. Don't know whether she was raped or not."

"You said she was found today. When was she killed?"

"Don't know. The last time she was seen was Saturday night. A friend saw her and Steve eating dinner at Hartley's."

"So?"

"What's interesting is they had a screaming argument. Vicki was throwing things around, yelling names, the whole nine yards." Rolie chuckled.

"Why are you laughing?"

"Never have a public argument with somebody just before they're killed."

"It isn't a laughing matter, Rolie. I can't imagine Steve screaming or having an argument in public."

"I didn't say he was screaming, but she was, that's for sure."

"How was she found? . . . Who found her?"

"Her mother. She went over to Vicki's house this morning because the family couldn't get hold of her and she didn't show up at work. She saw what no mother should see."

"Poor woman."

"Steve's probably sitting under the hot lights as we speak."

"He's a suspect?"

"If he was the last person to see her, he is."

"If he's not the killer, and I'm assuming he isn't, then he wasn't the last to see her."

"Don't know the answer to that."

"Steve would never kill anybody. Not in a million years."

"Maybe he liked rough sex and she didn't."

"Oh, for God's sake, Rolie. Get your mind out of the sewer."

"I never liked the guy."

"Why?"

"Not sure."

"Bob said the same thing, but he couldn't give me a reason either."

"Maybe he's just too good to be true, Lexie."

"I don't know what you mean."

"Everybody likes him. Even the people he builds houses for like him. That's not normal."

"But you don't like him. Bob doesn't either, so you've just made the case against your own argument. Maybe you're jealous of him."

"Me?" Rolie laughed. "I'm not jealous of anybody. I just don't want you to get involved with a guy like Steve. He might be after your money, you know."

"Why do you even think he's after me at all, Rolie? We're not seeing each other."

"You had dinner at Club Soda with him. Then he was at your house last week."

"How do you know that?"

He affected a Halloween laugh. "I have my sources."

"If your sources were worth listening to, you'd know he's not after me as a woman, let alone my money, Rolie. That should be obvious. He was romancing Vicki."

"When he wasn't killing her." She could hear Rolie slurping a drink. "When are you going to be back, Sis?"

"Don't call me Sis."

"I repeat -- ."

"I was planning on Friday, but I'll have to change that so I can attend the girl's funeral. Do you know when it's going to be?"

"No, but why bother? You didn't even know her, did you?"

"No. But I know the Judge and it would be rude not to pay my respects to the family."

"When you get back, can we talk about the smelter then?"

"Oh, for Pete's sake, Rolie. I'm on vacation, you call me late at night after I've gone to sleep, you've just told me about a murder, and now you want to schedule a business meeting?"

"Just asking."

"I'll call you when I get back."

Despite her sore muscles and extreme fatigue, Lexie had a hard time going back to sleep. She desperately needed the rest but sleep wouldn't come until almost dawn. An hour later she woke in a sweat from a dream of trying to run uphill, with heavy, sore legs, from a masked pursuer who seemed intent on pushing her off the mountain.

25

Comforter in Chief

Monday, February 2, 2009

As Treasurer, Deacon, and the most prominent member of The Three Rivers Congregation of the New Covenant, Bob Passwatter felt it was his duty to comfort Judge Paul Grinderman, also a faithful member of the church, on his tragic loss. He and Clarissa drove to the Grindermans' house on Cherry Lane early in the evening of the day Lydia had found her daughter's body. Clarissa was carrying a chicken-and-broccoli casserole; Bob was carrying his Bible.

Paul had tried to put off the Passwatters, saying they weren't in any shape to receive visitors, but Bob was having none of it. He knew he was needed. So after somber greetings at the door, Lydia, her face ravaged by grief, led Clarissa to the family room, where some of her female friends and relatives were gathered, and the Judge led Bob to his study, where they each took a leather club chair. Bob kept firm hold of his Bible.

"Paul, I want you to know how deeply sad Clarissa and I are for your loss."

"Thank you."

"Vicki's in a better place now. All her suffering is over."

The Judge looked slightly worried. "I hope so."

"What do you mean?"

"I'm not sure she was a believer. She was into New Age stuff I couldn't stomach -- serpent gods, mother earth, crystals and amulets, goddesses of this and that."

"You didn't talk to her about that?"

"Of course I did. So did Lydia."

Bob looked very stern. "Our highest duty to our children is to introduce them to the Lord."

The Judge, who thought he'd been a pretty good parent and wasn't in the mood just then to question how well he'd done his duty by Vicki, stayed silent.

"Paul, I can only imagine how you're feeling."

"I don't think you can, Bob. Not until you've been in my shoes."

Bob was taken aback. "Oh, but I assure you I can put myself in your place. My heart grieves for you."

"Pardon me if I'm skeptical, not about you personally, just in general. Every day the scum of the world parades before my bench. I listen to lies all day long, not just from defendants and witnesses, but from prosecutors and defense lawyers as well. Lies fly around my courtroom like overfed crows defecating on my head. The defendants don't grieve for their victims, so I'm a little cynical about how much one person really appreciates another person's pain."

"You have any idea who did it?"

"I don't. I can't help wondering, though, if it's somebody I've sentenced before and has gotten out of prison. Over the years, I've looked into the empty faces of thousands of heartless miscreants. Any one of them might have murdered my daughter."

"You think it's someone who's getting revenge on you?"

"I hope not, Bob, but it's a possibility."

"How'd the murderer get into her house?"

"Lydia says the front door was locked because she had to use her key to get in. Once the cops got there to secure the scene, she had to leave and we haven't been told much yet."

"So your daughter might have known her killer and let him in."

"Too early to know."

"Was anything stolen?" Bob twisted his class ring. "What I'm getting at is, if she didn't let the guy in, did she surprise a robber or something?"

"Doesn't look like it. The TV was still on in the living room, and her purse was on the daybed. If anything was taken it might be the underwear she was wearing."

"She was naked?"

Paul put his hand over his eyes. "Can't talk about that."

"So she was naked, wasn't she? That means she was raped."

"As I said . . . ."

"I know, I know. You can't talk about it. But missing underwear makes me think."

"Think of what?"

"You've heard about the Panty Raider, as my assistant calls him?"

Paul nodded.

"Well, it sounds to me like he's stepped up his game."

"Could be. I'm sure the police will consider that."

"I hear your daughter had an argument Saturday night with Steve Wright at Hartley's."

"Word gets around fast, doesn't it?"

"What was the argument about, do you know?"

"No."

"They were dating?"

"That's an old-fashioned word, Bob. They went to dinner on Saturday nights."

"I never liked that guy."

The Judge looked startled. "I never had reason not to like him. What do you have against him?"

"We had a little dispute years ago about his uncle's trust fund."

"Well, the detective tells me Steve has been very cooperative."

"Does he have an alibi?"

"Until the time of Vicki's death is narrowed down, nobody has an alibi."

Bob was indignant. "Well, I do. You do. Everybody who's innocent does."

"I didn't mean to insult you, Bob," the Judge said, repressing his exasperation at having an obvious point misinterpreted.

"Has he lawyered up?"

"He has in the sense that he hired Duke Simmons, the best in northeast Indiana, but not in the sense of clamming up. As I said, he's reportedly cooperating in every possible way."

"Is Steve the only suspect?"

"I don't think he's a suspect, Bob. At most he's a person of interest. He dropped her off at her door Saturday night, and no one saw or heard from her after that, so he might know something. For now, I just think of him as a potential witness to something that might help solve the mystery."

Bob snorted. "Dropped her off! Is that what he claims?"

Paul shot his friend a quizzical look. "You seem pretty sure he's our guy."

"As I said, I never liked him."

"Well, as a judge, I'm keeping my mind open. Much as I would like to know who did what, I'm not going to leap to unjust conclusions and smear a good man. Let's all wait for the evidence."

"You're a better man than I am, Paul. I'd be all over Steve Wright."

The Judge couldn't keep the asperity out of his voice. "That's the difference between people trained in the law and laymen. We wait for the evidence and then draw our conclusions with as little bias as possible."

"Do you know how your precious daughter died?"

"Lydia has her ideas, given what she saw, but the cops said not to talk about it."

"Your daughter's famous in my office now, that's for sure. I think that's all the girls talked about this afternoon."

"What a sickening thought." Paul closed his eyes a few seconds. "Until we get the Coroner's report, we aren't going to know for sure when or how she died. The last time Cricket heard from her sister was Saturday morning. The last person known to see her alive was Steve Wright Saturday night and Lydia didn't find her until Monday morning, so it could have happened any time in between."

There was a long silence. "Such iniquity." Bob shook his head. "Would you allow me to set up a memorial fund for Vicki? I'm thinking ten thousand."

"Very generous of you, Bob, but let's talk about it some

other time."

"It's hard to believe how bad some men are, isn't it?"

"As I said," the Judge said, getting to his feet to signal that this bereavement call was over, "I find it easier to believe than you do. At this point, I wouldn't trust the Pope."

Bob got to his feet too. "Would you like me to pray with you, Paul?"

The Judge placed his hand on Bob's shoulder, gently but firmly guiding him to the door of the study. "Ordinarily, yes, but not tonight. I appreciate whatever prayers you want to offer, but right now I want to get back to my wife." Before the Judge opened the door, he offered his hand. "Thank you for coming over, Bob. You're a good friend."

26

Suspect and Cad

Tuesday, February 3, 2009

Steve's world was coming apart. No matter how the police couched it, he knew they viewed him as a suspect in the murder of Vicki Grinderman. He knew he wasn't the killer, of course, but the guilt of having left her alone at the door hounded him. If he'd gone in with her, she might still be alive. He'd been troubled enough about her state of mind to return in his car to watch the front of the house for a few minutes, but he'd had no suspicion whatsoever that a killer might be lurking inside. Or did the killer enter the house later, perhaps after she went to bed? The police had told him very little. He desperately, futilely wanted to run the clock backwards to protect her if he could.

Now he had the duty, he knew, to talk to Vicki's father, so he was on his way to the Judge's chambers for what he expected to be a very uncomfortable meeting.

"Thank you for meeting me here, Steve. I'm taking a few days' leave, but this is the best place for us to talk."

"Judge, I can't tell you how deeply sad I am about what happened."

"I appreciate your courage in coming here."

"It would take more courage for me to stay away. I know what you might be thinking."

"My mind is open."

"Then you're a better man than most. I want you to know from me personally I had nothing to do with . . . with whatever happened to her."

"I hear the police have questioned you."

"For hours. I went in voluntarily. I gave them fingerprints and DNA, signed release forms for my cell phone records, gave them permission to search anything they want, and am going to take a lie detector test next week, with my own polygraph examiner present. They photographed me naked from the waist up."

"Why?"

"Don't know, but if there's any blood or . . . or something as a basis of comparison, my DNA results should prove my innocence."

"Are you acting on the advice of Duke Simmons?"

"I'm acting on my innocence. I've nothing to hide, but I know it's unwise not be represented by legal counsel because, no matter what the cops say, I'm a suspect."

"You were very careful Sunday night, when I called you, to say you didn't go in the house with her. You dropped her off at the door, you said."

"I did."

"Some people might think you were setting up an alibi before anyone even knew Vicki had been murdered."

"I told you the truth."

"I have a very delicate question to ask."

"Ask away."

"Do you know what lingerie she was wearing Saturday night?"

Steve blinked, embarrassed. "That is delicate, but no, I don't know. We didn't . . . ." He trailed off, reluctant to finish the sentence.

"You said the reason you didn't go in was that you had an early day on Sunday. Was that the truth?"

"Yes, to get ready for my Super Bowl party, but if we hadn't had a bad argument at dinner, I would have gone in for a few minutes. You have no idea how many times I've wanted to rewind the film so instead of leaving her at the door I went in to be sure she was okay."

"Are you thinking the man was already inside the house?"

"I have no idea, but I suppose somebody could have been waiting for her. There was no car parked on her street, and her house was completely dark when we got there. She didn't turn on any lights, only the television by the time I pulled away, but that fact could mean anything. Do you know when or how the killer got in?"

"No. Tell me, Steve, if you would: what did you two have an argument about?"

"First, we argued about the trip I'm taking with friends later this month to Arizona for spring training. She was angry that it was men only. She thought I should take her to Cozumel instead. Then she wanted to talk about getting married."

"And you didn't?"

"Not there. Not then."

"Were you ever intending to marry her?"

Steve, embarrassed, shook his head. "I told her in the

beginning of our relationship that I was too sore from the divorce from Matty to think about marriage. In fact, that night I was planning to tell her that . . . ."

"That . . . what? What were you planning to tell her?"

"That we'd taken our relationship about as far as it could go."

"Pardon me for being so personal, but did you love her?"

Steve looked away.

"You didn't love her."

"I liked her a lot. I thought love would happen, but it didn't. We just didn't have enough in common."

"She was twenty-six, the age when a woman thinks about marriage. No woman ever believes that a long relationship won't lead to marriage, Steve. You must know that."

"I do now." Unexpectedly, Steve felt his eyes grow watery. "I feel like a total cad."

"For what it's worth, I think you might have been a cad all right, but for the moment I don't think you're a murderer. I'm a good judge of character and I've listened to thousands of stories -- mostly false, self-serving stories -- in my career. When I hear a lie, it reverberates in my head like a war drum. Your story doesn't do that. It sounds right because it doesn't make you a hero. And coming from me, it's a lot for me to place you way down on the suspect list because, frankly, I don't trust anybody right now."

"I'm still on your suspect list?"

"Not really. But for the cops you might be, at least until they get the DNA results back."

"What would the DNA results be compared to? Was there blood or . . . ?" Again, he couldn't bring himself to complete the thought.

"From the crime scene, it's plausible to surmise she bit her assailant and might have been raped."

"Oh, God, Judge, I'm so sorry."

"So am I."

An awkward pause followed. "I'm going to put up a reward for information leading to a conviction, if that's okay with you."

"Very generous of you. Bob Passwatter told me last night that he's starting a memorial fund. Maybe the two of you should coordinate your efforts."

"Anybody else and I'd be happy to do that."

The Judge looked startled. "You have a problem with him?"

"I do. If I may be frank, I hate his guts."

"Really?"

"No, I don't actually hate him. But I don't like him. I *really* don't like him."

"He doesn't much like you either. What's that all about?"

"My uncle's trust fund, sixteen years ago."

"He said something about that."

"Did he tell you anything else about it, Judge? Did he give you any details?"

"No."

"A hundred thousand dollars, which is the amount left to us in Ben's will, turned out to be less than half that by the time Bob took his hands out of the pot. My brother and I could never get to the bottom of it, and we didn't have the money to hire an auditor or a lawyer."

"What was his explanation?"

"Incoherent, full of jargon that Frank and I didn't understand. As I remember, Bob threw around phrases like transfer fees, death taxes, legal tangles, competing interests, deficient documentation, procedural problems, stuff like that."

"Have you ever said a word about this to anybody else?"

"No."

"Well, good. Bob would sue you for slander before you could get your breath. His entire career is built on his reputation for perfect honesty."

"I wouldn't have said a word if you hadn't mentioned his name. Anyway, you'll understand, I hope, if I don't confer with him, but I'm going to go ahead with posting a twenty-thousand-dollar reward if you have no objections."

"No objections. In fact, it's generous of you."

"And would it be okay for me to attend the visitation and the funeral?"

"I think you have to, given the rumors swirling around."

"I'm not worried about rumors. Well, not a lot anyway, though I'm just as dependent on my reputation for honesty as Bob. But, compared to what happened to you, my concern seems trivial and I don't want to offend you and your family. I would like to pay my last respects, but not if it poses a problem."

The Judge stood up and held out his hand. "No problem at all. As I said, it was brave of you to meet me like this. I wish you luck."

Part Two

"When trouble arises and things look bad, there is
always one individual who perceives a solution
and is willing to take command.
Very often, that individual is crazy."
Dave Barry (from Dave Barry Turns 50)

"Woe to you when all men speak well of you,
for that is how their fathers treated the false prophets."
Jesus speaking, Luke 6: 26

27

Nice Lady Like You

Tuesday, February 3, 2009

Late Tuesday afternoon, when Lexie and Jessica reached the Indianapolis airport, they were surprised to see Drago standing at the gate, holding a sign that read "Miss Royce." He was dressed like a country-and-western star ready for the limelight.

"What are you doing here, Drago?"

"Rolie sent me down, said to drive you home."

"Why?"

"Just to be nice?" he said in a tone suggesting he wasn't really sure himself.

"He didn't need to do that. I have a ticket to fly to Fort Wayne, where my car is parked."

"No worries about that. I picked up that sweet ride of yours at the airport and drove it down in case you didn't want to ride in the Rolls."

"How'd you do that? I have the keys."

"Mom found your second set." He dangled them in front of her, then eyed the e-ticket she was holding. "Is that the ticket for the last leg to the Fort?"

She nodded.

"Well, you can lose that right now, Mizz Royce," he said, gently removing it from her fingers and tearing it in half without waiting for her assent.

She looked at Jessica. "I don't think I'm left with a choice." She looked back at Drago with the faintest of smiles. "I'll let you drive. Can you drop Jessica in Carmel? It's on our way north."

"Whatever you say. You're the boss."

She made a little noise signaling that she didn't exactly feel like the boss.

After they dropped Jessica at her house, Lexie, sitting in the front passenger seat, dozed off awhile. When she awoke, it took her a second to figure out where she was. It was dark, the kind of deep, thick winter dark on the prairie that made a girl long for the lights of home. "Sorry. That was rude of me."

"Not at all."

She looked over at Drago, then tried to peek at the speedometer. "How fast are you driving? I feel like I'm in a rocket."

He chuckled. "Speed of light."

"I'd prefer the speed limit, if you don't mind."

"Okay," he said amiably, though he didn't actually seem to drop his speed. "None of my business, of course, but how come you're back so early?"

"I'm going to go to Vicki Grinderman's visitation and funeral."

"I hear her body hasn't even been released yet, so you could have waited awhile."

"I also want to talk to Steve. Rolie said he's the main

suspect, so he's got to be feeling pretty bad. He may need a good word from a friend."

"Speaking of Steve, you know if he has a thing about women's underwear?"

"Good heavens, Drago, where did that question come from?"

"Rolie. He said there's talk the girl's killer took some of her pretty underwear."

"Where'd he hear that kind of talk?"

"Don't know for sure, but he had a word with Vicki's sister, Cricket, so maybe that's where he heard it first."

"I don't know that much about Steve." *Unlike many high school sweethearts, we never slept together, so I am completely in the dark about his bedroom habits.* "But if you want my opinion, he's not that kind of guy. He's as normal as men get."

"You never know what people do behind closed doors. Know that." Drago started to sing in imitation of Hank Thompson, "'And when we get behind closed doors, then she lets her hair hang down and she makes me glad I'm a man . . . .'"

"Exactly," she said, truncating his performance, which was disturbingly intimate. "Good voice, by the way. But feeling like a man and stealing women's underwear are two entirely different things, don't you think?"

"Couldn't agree with you more. Rolie's hoping it's Steve, though."

"Why?"

"He hates the guy."

"Again, why?"

"I spoke out of turn. Rolie doesn't exactly hate him. He just doesn't want him around. You ever considered, Mizz

Royce, that if you get serious with some guy and marry him, Rolie won't inherit all your money? He thinks Steve is the man who might get you to do that."

Lexie's stomach lurched. The point was obvious, yet she hadn't ever let herself acknowledge it. "How do you know what's in my will?"

His mother had found a copy and read it, pleased to discover she was being left a hefty pension in honor of her long service to the Royces. But he couldn't admit that. "You must of told Rolie. Where else would I hear it?"

"I've never discussed my affairs with my half-brother, but I suppose it's a natural supposition that he's my heir."

"I'm not prying into your affairs, know that. My point is that you wanna look out for yourself."

"How do you suggest I do that?"

"Well, for one, a guy going around killing girls who live by themselves and stealing their underwear -- you might want to think about beefing up your security. Put some cameras in or something. Get a guard dog. Put in a fence and an electric gate across your driveway."

"I haven't told many people this, Drago, but I'm one of the Panty Raider's victims. It apparently happened one afternoon while I was attending a bridal shower in Sycamore Hills. I don't know if it's the same guy as killed Vicki, but it makes me think."

"Mom told me. She said the house hadn't even been broken into, so far as she could see, and nothing else was stolen."

"That's true. Any other words of wisdom?"

"Wisdom! You making fun of me?"

"No, definitely not. Sorry if it sounded like that. I'm all

ears."

"Keep an eye out for that ex-husband of yours. Mom says she's seen him out on the street a few times, pretending to be a runner."

"He is a runner."

"I ran track. I was in the Mastodon Stomp last year, so was the Hawk, blowing like a whale before we got to the end of a 5K. I know a real runner when I see one, and he ain't no real runner."

"Until he does something that's really threatening, the police say their hands are tied."

"Cops!"

"Please don't say you think of them as pigs. I can't bear the cliché."

"I don't. I just think they don't know what they doin' half the time. If as boys they spent time on the streets, then as men they'd know what they were dealin' with, do a better job."

Lexie laughed. "Be a criminal first, then apply to the police academy?"

Drago laughed too. "I hear you. But I'm not done. Don't let anybody borrow this handsome wagon," he said, patting the steering wheel.

"No? Why?"

"Stuff can be done you don't know nothin' about till it's too late."

"Like what?"

"Brake lines tampered with, sugar in the gas tank, oil drained out, tire valves removed. All kinds of things. How about hidden tracking devices, guys knowing your route but you don't know it? So keep it in the garage when you're at home. Careful where you park it when you're out and about. Keep it locked. Don't skimp on service. When you take it in for an oil change, have the service guy check out everything."

"You're scaring me."

"Don't mean to do that, Mizz Royce. Just be careful is all I'm saying."

"Why are you telling me all this?"

"Nice lady like you, living alone, rich as all get out . . . ." He glanced at her, his face serious. "Lot a people might want a piece of you. You always been good to me and my Mom. I don't want you to get hurt, that's all."

"You think someone in particular wants to hurt me?"

He sighed. "As I said, you're in a position . . . you're the kind of woman needs to be careful."

"Maybe I should hire you as my bodyguard."

"May-be." He laughed. "Now there's a thought." He laughed again, this time so hard -- something he never did -- that Lexie wondered what was hidden under all that merriment.

28

A Man of Singular Courage

Wednesday, February 4, 2009

Bob Passwatter had never met Xiu-Xiu's sister, but he was glad to do a favor for his beautiful but unattainable assistant. He straightened his tie and slicked back his hair as if preparing for a first date.

Tiffany Jean was shorter and thinner than her sister, finer-boned, with penetrating eyes. Clad in flowing silk garments under a python jacket and wearing a musky perfume, she had an air about her -- elegant but seductive -- that knocked him out. When she shook his hand and then held it a long time, a bolt of electricity shot through him all the way to the parts that, at least in the office, were mostly dormant.

"Mr. Passwatter, I'm honored to meet you. I've heard so much about you. You're my idol, you know." Her eyes were the eyes of a demonic angel with a secret message that would change his life if he was willing to act on it.

"Me?"

"You." Still holding his hand, she gazed at him as if she were about to eat him up. He wished she would. The *frisson* passing through him like a bolt of lightning numbed his mind while electrifying his body.

"Why? How do you even know about me?" He gently pulled his hand away and sat down in one of the visitor's chairs. The way she looked at him, he felt like a Calvin Klein model, young and sexy but with brains.

"I'm an engineer working on a master's in business," she said, taking the other chair. When she crossed her legs, her split skirt fell open, revealing slim, satiny legs. Bob had a hard time keeping his eyes on her face. "I've read all about your financial empire. Maybe you don't know it, but your business model is the envy of the world."

Bob was struggling to hold onto his composure, his humility. The envy of the world! No man could beat him in the matter of pride, but he'd never allowed himself to imagine he was the envy of the world before. Perhaps he should include a quote from her in his personal note for *Columbia Magazine,* pretending to be embarrassed by it. She was so effusive in her praise that, for once, he was prepared to downplay his success. "I do my best. All I want is for my global family to be prosperous, the way God intended." He wished he smoked cigars so he could fiddle with something, look manly and important, distract himself from her fierce but erotic gaze.

"That's why I'm here. My fiancé is a client of yours."

"Xiu-Xiu mentioned that. Ferrell Hawke, I believe."

"He's a good man, but he's not good with money and sometimes . . . well, sometimes he's a little short-sighted in that department."

"I think I know what you mean. He gave me a very hard time when he started with us. And, as you know, he's demanding that I release half his principal, which is strictly against the rules. Don't let him know, but I won't even take his calls now."

"I'm here to ask that you don't let him withdraw any of his money."

Bob felt his blood pressure drop. The fact was that his financial empire had always been dependent on a bull market. But now that the bears had come out of hibernation and were rampaging across the landscape, creating havoc with global markets, he had to keep moving money around just to stay afloat. His clients' paper returns of a steady ten percent were once less than he actually made from his investments, enabling him to live like a king off the margin, but now the returns were wildly overstated. A ten percent annual gain wasn't possible after the market crashed. Since there weren't enough new investors to cover his obligations to the old ones, he didn't want a dollar to be withdrawn from any account.

"Are you a co-owner of the account now, Miss Chow?"

"Tiffany Jean, please. No, I'm not a co-owner yet. But I will be once we're married."

"You're getting married?"

"No date yet, Mr. Passwatter -- ."

He cut her off. "Bob, please. Call me Bob. I feel like we're old friends already."

"Bob."

In her luscious mouth, his name sounded like an endearment. He wanted to skip all the preliminaries, take her in his arms, and ravish her. With great effort, he willed his mind to go blank like a frozen computer screen. "Tell me what's on your mind."

"I don't want Ferrell to do something rash. That nest

egg needs to stay where it is. It's all that stands between me and the poor house."

"No worries there, my dear. I don't make exceptions for anyone."

"None at all?"

"Well . . . ." What exception did this lovely creature want from him? Once again, the computer screen came alive.

"There's one exception I'd like you to make, Bob. For me."

"What's that?" he asked, his voice cracking like a schoolboy's.

"I'd like the dividends on Ferrell's account to be deposited into a bank account I control, one that Ferrell knows nothing about. Let him think the dividends are staying here, of course. I can't let him know what we're doing."

"But if what you're concerned about is keeping the nest egg intact, then it's best to keep the returns here, adding to his equity."

She let her head drop and her voice tremble. "I didn't want to have to tell you this."

"You can tell me anything, Tiffany."

"I'm sick, Bob." Her voice trembled. "I'm between jobs, without health insurance, and I need to start an expensive course of chemotherapy or I'll die."

"No! You have cancer?"

"I do."

"Like your mother?"

"Yes. I haven't told anybody, even Xiu-Xiu. I don't want to worry anybody."

"You're so young. Is it genetic?"

"That's what I'm told. It's a very rare, very aggressive

thing that only Asians are afflicted with." She removed a lacy handkerchief from her Brahmin bag and dabbed at her eyes. "I'm scared to death, Bob."

"Why won't Ferrell pay for the treatment? He earns a good salary, doesn't he?"

"Do you know how much he spends on himself? There's no money at the end of the month to help me out." She pushed up the sleeve on her python jacket and held out her arm to show him the bruises. "He does this to me sometimes."

"He doesn't!"

"He does. He's a selfish man, sometimes mean, but I love him. It's the curse of my life to fall in love with a man like Ferrell. And even if I decide someday to leave because I just can't take the abuse any longer, I can't do it now. Not when I'm so sick. I'm sure, as a man of God, you understand that, Bob. Right now, I'm as vulnerable as a woman gets, and I need help from a good, brave man. You're the only man in the whole world who can help me."

Images of the help he could give her flashed through his mind so vividly he was afraid she could see them flickering across his forehead like an old silent movie.

"Bob, I don't want you to do something that's difficult."

"Nothing's too difficult for me."

"Or that would cause trouble. I know from Xiu-Xiu that your ethics are of the highest order."

"They are. But ethical questions are complex and the right answer isn't always the obvious one."

"So true. Should we live by some silly old manmade accounting rules, or act like the good Samaritan, as God intended?"

Marveling at her moral sensitivity, he comforted himself that in that department he was top-flight.

"Remember, even Xiu-Xiu doesn't know I'm sick."

Bob nodded solemnly. The fewer people who knew what they were about to do, the better for everyone.

"May I give you a hug, Bob? I'm so grateful."

He didn't hesitate. Rising to his full height, he pulled her close to him. Though he wanted desperately to kiss her, he limited himself to a discreet sniff of her hair, which smelled -- well, which smelled like spice and woodsmoke, the way he imagined the air in Hong Kong to smell.

"Do you think you can help me?" she whispered.

She was so close, he wondered if she could feel his heart hammering. "I can and I will."

"Thank you, Bob. How soon can I open my account?"

"Tell me where to wire the money."

"Tower Bank, right downstairs."

"Why don't you go shopping for an hour, come back, the money will be ready."

"You're my hero, Bob, a man of singular courage."

By the time Tiffany Jean wafted out of Robert Passwatter's office, she was elated. She winked at her sister. "Six-thirty at Club Soda?" she mouthed. Xiu-Xiu nodded.

Attempting to look as if the earth hadn't moved, Bob stood in his doorway, watching Tiffany Jean glide through the reception area to the elevator. He was shaken to his core, not by the perfidy he was about to commit on the dastardly Ferrell Hawke, but by his desire for the Chinese goddess who had just called on him for help. He knew he'd be honored in heaven for smoothing the rocky path of this brave, graceful woman, but his mind couldn't get past her vague hints that there might be other pleasures awaiting him here on earth.

29

Forgiveness

Wednesday, February 4, 2009

Wednesday evening, Steve took a seat in the bar at Baker Street, angled so he could watch the door. He was surprised and gratified that Lexie wanted to talk to him, but he realized that she probably chose the safety of a crowded public place just in case he really was the murderer.

Despite the clouds hanging over him -- Vicki's death, the suspicion that had fallen on him as a result, the harsh news from his bank, the sluggish housing market and gloomy economy thwarting all his development plans -- his heart skipped a beat when Lexie paused in the door from the reception area, surveying the room. She was pretty and sensible. She wore simple elegant clothes, nothing like the flashy, girlish outfits Vicki had been partial to. She had a life of her own. A palm reader was not in her future, nor were ugly public scenes. Her world would not end on December 21, 2012. How comforting it would have been to have had Lexie as his companion all these years. Crawling out from under the suspicions and burdens that had fallen on him like an anvil would be so much easier.

But at least he had her as a friend. This time he held out his arms, inviting a hug, which she returned. "I was surprised to hear from you, Lexie."

"Really?" She smiled as he helped her off with her sheared beaver jacket. "What kind of surprise are we talking? Great, I'm glad she called, or oh crap."

"Great, of course. I hope it means you're not afraid of me."

She looked shocked. "Why would I be?"

"Some people are a little standoffish these days. They're probably thinking dark thoughts about me."

"Unfortunately, that's to be expected, I suppose. Everybody in our crowd seems to know about the fit Vicki threw at dinner. But, you watch, your friends will rally around."

"You look rested. What's the secret?"

"I'm actually not rested. Jessica and I went to Rancho Salud for a week. You ever hear of it?"

"No."

"I wish I hadn't. It's in the Red Rock country around Sedona. Anyway, we went there for a week of R&R that turned out to be the worst experience of our lives. We were prepared for facials, massages, mineral baths, gourmet food, and a little light yoga, but instead we did the Bataan death march every day and ate way too few calories from foods we'd never heard of. We got lectured on eating locally grown pesticide-free, organic, genetically unmodified, fibrous tubers and bitter greens until we actually wanted to shop at Scott's and buy every processed food known to man. I haven't had a Twinkie since I was about four years old, but at Rancho Salud I fantasized about them."

"So you're not unhappy to be back."

"Well, just a little. We were going to spend the remainder of our trip at the Phoenician, but when Rolie told me about Vicki and the suspicion you're facing, we decided to come back early. I don't want to slight the Judge, who's an old friend of my father's, and I don't want you to feel abandoned."

"That's very nice of you."

"I'm very sorry, by the way, about what happened to your friend."

"So am I. I keep rewinding the clock in my head. If I'd gone in with Vicki instead of just walking her to the door, maybe she'd have been all right."

"You just dropped her off?"

"Not a gentlemanly thing to do, I know."

"Why didn't you go in? Or is that too personal?"

"We'd had a big fight at dinner, as you heard. She wanted to get married and I didn't. She was screaming and crying, making no sense at all, and I just wanted to get away from the hysteria. In fact, I was planning to break up with her that night but I never got a chance to say anything. Her actions, however, kind of put 'paid' to the relationship without my having to say a word. Ironic, huh?"

"I'd say somebody else put *paid* to everything about the poor girl."

"You're right."

"Didn't you tell me at Club Soda you'd been seeing Vicki for a couple of years?"

Steve nodded.

"That's a long relationship, as things go these days."

"Far too long. I misled her without meaning to."

"You don't think it was reasonable for her to think

marriage was in the offing whether you said anything or not?"

He looked guilty. "Her father asked the same thing. But I didn't lead her on, I swear, because I was never in love with her and never even hinted at marriage. We never conducted ourselves as a couple. In fact, I told her that because of the bitter divorce I experienced, I didn't think I'd ever marry again. But there's no getting around it: in her eyes, I was a cad."

"You must be carrying one big steaming load of guilt around, Steve."

"You said it. I'm a walking, breathing honey-wagon."

Lexie patted his hand. "I don't think you're guilty of anything like murder, just so you know. Neither does Jessica or anybody else I've talked to."

"Is that true?"

She paused. "Well, not entirely. Rolie and Bob hope you're guilty."

"I know why Bob does, but why Rolie?"

"Drago said something interesting on that subject."

"Drago?"

"Phyllis' son, remember. Rolie's chauffeur."

"How did it come up with him?"

"He drove me home from the Indy airport. He spent a lot of time warning me to be careful, as if I'm in great danger from somebody. His theory is that so long as I stay unmarried, Rolie gets all my money if I die."

"And how do I come into that picture?"

"I'm embarrassing myself here, even just repeating what Rolie thinks. He's afraid I'll marry you."

"He knows the future better than we do?" He shook his

head. “I can’t tell you how sick I am of people who think they know the future. Vicki believed that life would end or be transformed on December 21, 2012. She believed a palm reader’s prediction that we’d get married and honeymoon somewhere far away. Now Rolie knows what will happen to us. By the way, do you want to have dinner or . . . ?”

“Dinner. I’m famished.”

“A booth just opened up. Maybe we can snag it.”

Over dinner, Steve worked up the courage to say something else that was on his mind. “I have an apology to make.”

“To me?”

“To you. Apologies don’t come easy to me, so it’s a big deal. Savor it, Lexie.”

“I’m all ears.”

“At Club Soda, I said some things I wish I hadn’t said. All these years, I’ve been angry that we broke up. In my view, going steady all through high school the way we did, you led me to assume we’d stay together, even through college.”

Lexie tipped her head. “I sort of understand that.”

“Now I’m accused of having led Vicki on. Jean too.”

“Ah.” She nodded. “For a good man, that’s almost the equivalent of a crime as horrible as murder.”

“Suddenly the shoe is on the other foot.”

“So now I’m not a heart-breaker?” she teased.

He smiled. “You’re a heart-breaker, all right. I’m not letting you off the hook entirely. It’s just that I’m one too. At Club Soda I thought you should ask my forgiveness for breaking up with me, but you never did.”

Lexie felt tears well in her eyes. She reached for his hand. “Then I ask your forgiveness here and now. I wish I had made a different decision all those years ago."

He held her hand in both of his. "Accepted. I need it too for being such an ass all these years, so I'm apologizing here and now."

"Also accepted."

When he was paying the check, Steve broached a delicate subject. "What do you think about going to the funeral together? I hate to show up alone. I'll look like the guilty guy, pretending to be grieving but secretly gloating at my cleverness."

"You can join my little group -- Phyllis, Drago, Lucy, and Matilda. If you and I go alone, we'll look like a couple, which wouldn't be wise, given the circumstances."

"Rolie's not going to show up?"

"He might but he never reveals his plans, you know."

"That boy's going to get himself killed one of these days."

"What do you mean?"

"The drug scene has changed so much, so much more violent than when he was in high school, I doubt he can hold his own."

"Drug scene? He takes drugs?"

Steve gave her a long look. "I think I just spoke out of turn."

"Well, now you're going to have explain yourself."

"He's been dealing since he was a teenager."

"Dealing what?"

"Marijuana."

"How do you know that?"

"It's common knowledge."

"How come I never heard about it?"

Steve shook his head.

"Dad suspected he was doing something under the table because once his allowance was cut off, he never asked for a dime, yet he seemed to have plenty of money for clothes and parties. Dad probably assumed somebody else was paying, at least for the partying."

"The Bosnian thug who was found crushed at your Scrapyard was in a very ruthless gang, mostly guns but drugs too. Dave tells me that the police are worried about somebody getting revenge."

"Dave Powers? He's not in gangs or guns or drugs, is he? I thought his bailiwick was property crime."

"True, but like most cops he knows the whole crime scene in Fort Wayne. We've been good friends ever since high school, so we catch up on things often. In fact, he's one of the foursome going to Arizona later this month for spring training and golf."

"You mentioned revenge. Revenge on whom?"

"Your brother."

Lexie looked shocked. "My brother? Why? Somebody thinks Rolie killed the guy?"

"Either that or he told someone else to."

"I can't believe that." She drained the water from her glass. "I don't mean I think you're lying, just . . . ."

"I know what you mean. Dave said the police are afraid of a gang war."

"A gang war! It gets worse and worse."

"I wouldn't have mentioned it except I thought you knew. A lot more than scrap gets sold at your Yard."

"It's going to take awhile for me to digest this, Steve."

"If Rolie has any brains, he'll get out while he can."

"He has brains but he's lazy and greedy and doesn't seem to have a lot of scruples."

Before they parted to go their separate ways, they made a date for a week from Saturday night at Catablu on Broadway, an old favorite that they heard was closing soon.

30

Loosen Your Wallet

Friday, February 6, 2009

On Friday night, after Vicki Grinderman's visitation at D. O. McComb and Sons, which she attended alone, Lexie got on I-469 on her way to a bar near New Haven, a small city southeast of Fort Wayne. Rolie had asked her to meet him at Sue-A-Side, a biker bar along the Lincoln Highway.

"How's that spelled?"

Rolie spelled it out for her. "Sue, the owner, has a great sense of humor."

"I can tell."

Lexie wanted nothing to do with a late night meeting at a biker bar with a loathsome name, but she was tired of Rolie's nagging. He talked her ear off about his new Fat Boy and his plan to join the Rude Dudes, a motorcycle club. He was meeting a couple of guys at Sue-A-Side to talk about a Fourth of July trip, so she'd be doing him a favor if he could kill two birds with one stone -- an unfortunate metaphor, she thought.

"I can pick you up, give you a ride, if you want."

"No thanks, Rolie. I'll meet you there."

The parking lot in back of the bar was packed with choppers and bikes of every description, looking like the showroom of a dealership. She had no idea so many people rode motorcycles in the winter and was especially surprised that Rolie, who hated discomfort of every kind, would do it. Having no idea what his ride looked like, she couldn't tell if he'd already arrived.

She entered through the back door, passing through a narrow knotty-pine hallway flanked by restrooms marked "Biker" and "Biker Chick." The skeleton painted on the women's restroom door had a rose in its teeth. The skeleton on the men's was peeing out of a handgun. She shuddered.

The bar was dark and aromatic, the walls covered with neon beer signs and posters of heavy metal bands. The alcove for pool tables teemed with raucous competitors, the overhead big-screen televisions were tuned to sports channels with the sound off. Over the bar, a video of Guns N' Roses was playing *Welcome to the Jungle* with the sound amped up. The place, paneled in knotty pine and floored in linoleum, looked like it had been built in the Fifties and lived rough ever after.

Not knowing exactly what she was getting into, she'd worn an old cloth coat over a dark pant suit, a beret that covered her ears, and simple jewelry so that the message she flashed was "Nothing to look at here." Still, she was seriously misplaced in the sea of tattooed men and big-haired women, most of them in leather and denim -- and, despite the season, sometimes not much of that.

The many eyes turned her way were discomfiting. Wanting to disappear from the limelight as quickly as possible, she pulled out an empty bar-height chair at the horseshoe bar. With disgust, she realized the back of the heavy oak chair was sticky and the bar was none too clean. Afraid to hook her old Prada over the back for fear of its being stolen, Lexie kept it in her lap, hugging it as if it were the life jacket that would save her when the plane hit the water. Indeed, she felt like a passenger in a jet falling out of the sky with smoking engines. What was she thinking, agreeing to this?

Though it was the coldest part of the winter, the bartender, a skinny guy with a skimpy goatee and a long ponytail, was wearing only a sleeveless vest and jeans. Maybe the tattoos kept his arms warm. Standing at an angle as if ready to run a race, he asked her out of the corner of his mouth what she was having. "Gin and tonic, please." She didn't call Tanqueray, as she would normally do; no doubt the bartender would simply boost the price without actually giving her anything more than the cheap swill he had.

When he returned with her drink, he asked, keeping his eyes on the room behind her, "You meeting somebody?"

"My brother, Rolland Royce. He said he comes in here sometimes."

"Rolie? I know who you mean. I'll send him over soon as I see him."

The minutes ticked by. She didn't know what to do with her eyes. She checked her watch. He'd said 9 and she'd arrived a few minutes early. Every time she dared to look around, she caught a big guy wearing a leather cap and vest staring at her. Suddenly, the bartender set another gin and tonic in front of her, saying Murph wanted to treat her.

"Who?"

"Murph. That guy you been looking at."

"I haven't . . . . " She caught herself. Why explain

anything to a bartender? She kept her eyes on the Guns N' Roses video, not registering what was flashing across the screen. Should she wait a few more minutes or not? She was furious at having allowed herself to be talked into driving in the dark to a place she'd never been before and would never set foot in again.

Suddenly, the couple next to her got up and left. The big guy with the leather cap and vest abruptly took the vacated chair next to her. "Mind if I join you, Miss Royce?"

She kept her eyes on her drink. "How do you know my name?"

"Enjoying your cocktail?"

Cocktail! Such a pretentious word in this knotty-pine anteroom to Hell. She glanced at him, noticing his silver death's head earring for the first time, then back at the gin and tonic she hadn't touched. "Are you Murph?"

"I am."

"Do you have a last name?"

"Murphy."

"Well, thank you, Murphy, but I'm just about to leave."

"Perhaps you'd stay a few minutes, keep me company."

"I'm not here to meet people . . . other than my brother."

He laughed. "I can tell."

"You never told me how you know my name."

"Rolie told me what you look like. No other lady here fits the description."

Frankly, I don't see any other ladies here, bud. "Where's Rolie? Why isn't he here?"

"He couldn't make it tonight, sent me to talk to you."

"Talk to me! About what?"

"Your family business."

"I don't talk about that with strangers."

"You should." His tone was perfectly even, but still she sensed a threat. He held out a pack of Camels with an inquiring look.

"No thanks."

He lit a cigarette and blew smoke at her.

She waved her hand. "Why should I discuss family matters with you? Who *are* you, by the way? I've never heard Rolie mention you."

"Not important who I am. I'm just here to deliver a message."

"What message?"

"Loosen up your wallet."

"What?"

"I think you heard me, sister."

"What does 'loosen up your wallet' mean?"

"Rolie said you'd know."

"It sounds like a threat."

Again, he laughed. "Sounds that way to me too."

She started pushing her chair away from the bar, but he suddenly put his hand on the back of it so she couldn't move. "I want to leave."

"What's the hurry?"

"I shouldn't have come here."

He looked around the room, then back at her. "We aren't good enough for you?"

Retorts filled her mouth but she knew better than to let any of them fly out. She tried to catch the bartender's eye, but he avoided her importunate signal. Suddenly, she felt herself in very great danger with no easy way out. "Tell Rolie I'll talk to him tomorrow at the Yard."

"That's all the answer you've got?"

She pushed back again, this time harder because Murph was still gripping the back of her chair, but she had no way of foreseeing that he would abruptly let go. Her chair teetered backward. She flailed, doing her best to right herself, but there was nothing she could do to reverse the backward momentum. She fell over, hitting her head on the floor. Rolling to her side, she lay there a second, humiliated and angry. When she tried to get to her knees, she winced. Her wrist was sore, her knee wrenched. Glancing upwards, she saw Murph smiling at her, not moving an inch other than to kick her purse away. A few yards away a thin middle-aged woman, her arms crossed on her chest, watched with disapproval but made no move to help either, though she exchanged a glance with Murph.

Lexie felt like a sick elephant in a herd that killed its sick. Was she going to get out alive? Would anybody help? Murph's eyes were dancing with amusement.

She finally struggled to her feet, found her purse, and turned to leave. A few people were staring and laughing. The indignity of her fall almost outweighed her fright. Before she started for the door, the bartender suddenly deigned to notice her. "You trying to leave without paying? Here's your bill, lady," he said, shoving a damp piece of paper across the bar. "It's eleven fifty."

Eleven fifty! For one filthy drink? She wanted to tell him to put it on Rolie's tab, but this was no place for a dispute about a bill. Lexie frantically scrambled around in her purse. She shouldn't be paying anything; somebody should be calling the cops. But she was too frightened to protest. All she wanted was to get out of there. When she found a twenty, she threw it on the bar and began limping to the hallway to the parking lot. At the door she stopped and turned around to be sure no one was following her. Once outside, she half-ran, half-limped in pain to her car, started the engine, and squealed onto the Lincoln Highway.

Back on 469 to Fort Wayne, Lexie realized that in her current emotional state she shouldn't be driving at all, but what choice did she have? Her right knee was throbbing so hard she was scared she couldn't press the brake if she had to. In her distinctive bright red car, she felt like a rolling beacon at the very moment she wanted to be invisible. She couldn't wait to get home.

Halfway to her exit, she spotted a posse of bikers in her rear-view mirror. Was it just a random coincidence, or was Murph, with his buddies, following her?

The thunder of the bikes filled her ears as the posse drew near and then, riding two by two, moved to the left lane to pass by. There were at least two dozen leather-clad monsters, all flattened over their handlebars, their dark space-age helmets facing straight ahead. No one even glanced at her. Thinking she'd just been paranoid, she breathed a little easier.

But then she noticed the last biker had slowed to keep pace with her. He turned his head in her direction, and though she couldn't see a face through the dark shield on his helmet, she had a feeling it was Murph. He stuck out his arm and waggled his gloved thumb up and down, up and down, finally holding it down, like a Roman emperor condemning a gladiator. After a mile of that performance -- an eternity to Lexie -- he roared away.

She shivered. The highway was very dark, the sky was

nothing but a blanket of low clouds, and it was starting to snow. She was alone and frightened.

31

The Equalizer

Friday, February 6, 2009

Still shaken by her encounter with Murph and his posse, Lexie ran upstairs to her bedroom when she arrived home. She had just showered and pulled on the sweat suit she wore in lieu of pajamas when her doorbell rang insistently. Her watch read 10:45. Who in the world approached a woman's door this late? She slipped on some sneakers, picked up her gun and her cell phone, and limped down the stairs. By the time she reached the front door, the bell was silent. She pulled aside the curtain on one of the glass side panels but saw no one on the porch. She checked the door. It was securely locked. Then she fastened the chain lock, which she usually ignored.

She was walking toward the kitchen when she heard pounding on her back door, but by the time she reached it, the pounding had stopped. Again she checked the door, and again she found it securely locked.

She sat down in a chair in the kitchen, infuriated at being frightened by some joker. She debated whether to call 911, Dave Powers, or Steve Wright. She punched in Steve's number. "It's Lexie. Are you at home?"

"Yes. What's up?"

"I hope I didn't wake you."

"It's okay."

"Someone just rang my front door bell, then pounded on my back door." Just then she looked up and saw a figure standing outside one of the long windows on either side of her breakfast nook. She screamed.

She was so panicked, it took her a second to return her attention to the phone.

"Lexie, Lexie!"

"I'm here," she said shakily.

"My God, what's wrong?"

"Someone's outside. I just saw him through the kitchen window."

"Can you see who it is?"

She got up and walked over. "I think it's Ferrell."

"I'm on my way. Hang tight till I get there. Leave your phone on so I can hear you."

"Okay."

Ferrell was running in place in the snow. He signaled her to go round to the front.

Keeping the chain on, she opened the front door a few inches. "What do you want, Ferrell?"

"I want to come in and talk."

"At this time of night?"

"You're awake, so what's the difference?"

"About what?"

"Money."

"Are you drunk?"

"No. I've had a few shots of Macallan, but that's all."

She raised her gun. "See this?"

He nodded as if it were no big deal to find his ex-wife holding a gun on him. "I'm freezing out here. In case you haven't noticed, it's snowing. Have a heart."

She undid the chain and opened the door, still holding the gun. "Keep your distance. Have a seat in the living room."

"Why don't you put that gun away?"

"I don't think so, Ferrell. Take your shoes off."

"Why?"

"So you don't track snow all over my wood floors."

"You're going to have to shoot me first. I'm not taking anything off."

She watched with dismay as he tracked dirty snow through the hallway to the living room, then sat down, wet with melting snow, on her velvet sofa.

He smiled derisively. "You didn't shoot me, so I'm wondering . . . ."

"Don't push me. Just tell me what's on your mind."

"As I said, money. You have a lot and I don't."

"I earned it, and I don't owe you a thing."

"We were married for almost ten years. I didn't get my fair share." He smiled as if they were discussing nothing more incendiary than the latest Mike Nichols movie. "If you paid me ten dollars for every time I was called Mr. Royce, I'd be as rich as Croesus."

"That was settled years ago. You thought seven million was fair then. And you didn't earn a penny of it."

"Taxes, lawyers' fees, market losses, most of it's gone."

"That's not my fault."

"The Lake James cabin needs a lot of work, and I can't

sell it unless I take care of all the problems, with money I don't have."

"Again . . . ."

"Yeah, yeah, it's not your fault. It isn't mine either."

Well, then, whose fault is it? "You must have something left."

"Your friend Bob Passwatter won't let me withdraw any of the principal I invested with him."

"If you invested with him, then you must have had at least a million in your pocket at the time."

He waggled his head, unwilling to admit she was right.

"You can't live off the returns from a million dollars?"

"He won't pay those out either. They're reinvested."

"You want me to talk to him?"

"No. I'll do it myself."

"I don't understand, Ferrell, what your problem is. You have a good job, don't you? Professors make a lot of money these days, with great benefits. Men with wives and kids live on those salaries."

"My girlfriend is high maintenance."

"Well, there's your answer. Find one who isn't."

"You always were callous, Lexie. Your way or the highway."

"Things might go better if we avoid harsh words."

"I speak my mind, you know that. You have a bottle of water? I'm getting dehydrated."

"I'm not losing sight of you for a second, so you'll have to stay thirsty."

"Have it your way. At the time of the divorce, you were already negotiating a deal to franchise your businesses, weren't you? You hid that information, I suspect."

"I'm not getting into that. It's over, Ferrell."

"My guess is, you were secretly negotiating the sale of your company to that conglomerate that paid you so much money but held off till I was out of the way."

She shook her head. Words were useless.

He looked around the room, admiring the coffered ceiling, the rich moldings, the hardwood floors, the wood-burning fireplace. The furniture was fine too, the proportions of the room impressive. "This house of yours -- what'd you pay for it?"

"For heaven's sake, Ferrell, it's none of your business how I spend my money now."

"How about deeding it to me, free and clear of all liens and mortgages."

Out of injured pride, Lexie was about to retort that there were no liens or mortgages, but the house needed everything done to it, very expensive repairs, replacements, or upgrades to tuckpointing, roof, windows, kitchen and bathrooms, security system, furnace and water heater, plumbing, and electrical, even reinforcement of joists where a maid's staircase had been removed years before.

But it gave her an idea. Why not give him the house while pretending it was all his idea so he wouldn't guess how unhappy he'd be if his wish came true? She'd rid herself of a burden for which she had little enthusiasm. For that ploy to work, however, she had to pretend some reluctance so he'd believe he'd outmaneuvered her. "That's the most shameless proposition I ever heard."

"I think the word you're looking for is effrontery."

"Thank you, Professor Hawke. Your vocabulary is impressive."

"You give me the house, the furniture and appliances, and a kicker to pay taxes and utilities for a few years, I'll back off."

She pretended to shrink from the hard look he threw at her. "You're not asking for much, are you?"

He glanced toward the back of the house. "You know how easy it is to break into this house? You really should lock your doors, you know. All of them. First thing I'll do when I move in here is put in better locks and a few cameras, arm the security system."

Lexie's stomach lurched. The conversation had taken a turn. "You were the one who entered this house a couple weeks ago?"

"That's for you to figure out."

"How'd you do it?"

He shook his head.

"You stole my underwear?"

He stared at her appraisingly. "Whatever you say."

"You set my car on fire in Indianapolis?"

A faintly startled look appeared on his face. "That's also for you to figure out."

"So if I don't give you the house, I'm in for it. I can expect endless mayhem."

"I'm not threatening anything. I'm making a proposition that's fair to both of us."

She pretended to be thinking about his proposition. "There'll have to be some kind of condition . . . say, the title reverts to me if you ever ask me for another dime." She wasn't even sure that was legal, but he probably didn't know either.

"Sure. All I want is this house."

"I'll have Marty Solomon call you."

"So you'll do it?"

"I didn't say that, but I'll give it some hard thought if it means the end of midnight visits like this."

"Well, think hard."

"There'll be a few other conditions, just so you know."

"Like what?"

"The sale is 'as is,' with no kickers."

She was spared the inevitable argument, for just then, the doorbell rang. She sprang out of her chair and, wincing, limped to the front door. Steve was on the porch.

"Thank God you're here."

"What's going on?"

She was still holding her Smith & Wesson. "Ferrell's in the living room."

"Is that thing loaded?"

"Of course."

"Why'd you let him in? I told you I was on my way."

She shook her head, unable to explain.

He strode into the living room and without hesitating walked over to Ferrell, grabbed him by the front of his jacket, and jerked him to his feet. "You son-of-a-bitch. What are you doing, skulking around at night?"

Ferrell pulled away and shook himself. Though he was taller than Steve, he didn't work construction for a living and instinctively knew he wasn't likely to win a contest with this guy. "I'll call the cops if you dare to touch me again."

"I'll call 'em myself if you don't leave right now."

Ferrell looked over Steve's head at Lexie. "Are we done, darling?"

"Darling, my ass." Without warning, Steve punched

him in the gut. Ferrell grunted and fell back onto the sofa, but Steve immediately pulled him to his feet and roughly pointed him toward the door. "Get out now. I've got twice as many cop friends as you do, you two-bit wuss-bag, and if you don't want to be arrested for stalking, you'll leave and never return." He brandished his cell phone. "And I heard every last word of the extortionate demand you just made on Lexie, so if I decide to make trouble for you, it'll blow the Richter scale. Got that?"

At the door, Ferrell, still full of bravado, gave Lexie a teasing look. "Be a good girl and wipe up the floors now that they're mine."

Steve, breathing hard, gave him a shove, then slammed the door and locked it. He turned to Lexie. "Do you have any idea how much I hate that plummy British accent?"

She laughed shakily. "I used to like it. By the way, what's a wuss-bag?"

"Australian slang for really pathetic wuss."

"Oh, Steve-o, I love it."

Steve pushed the curtain aside. "Wuss-bag's reached the sidewalk but I don't see his car anywhere."

"It must be parked somewhere near here."

"Is he a jogger?"

She nodded. "To hear him tell it, he's a great athlete, the best at everything -- jogging, tennis, pickup basketball, you name it. He's so accomplished, practically a professional, that he can't find anyone good enough for a decent golf game."

"I'll bet he cheats on every hole. He's not in that great a shape, I can tell you that. Deep down, he's weak and cowardly, the kind of guy who thinks the world owes him because he's so superior."

"Very astute, Steve. He's been bitter all his life about getting cheated out of an aristocratic title and the money and land to sustain it."

"You really want to give him this house?"

"I never thought about it until tonight, but I do. I'd rather build something new and modern than gut this place and live in a mess for a couple of years. I don't know why I didn't think of that before. Start fresh, you know? Perhaps you could recommend an accomplished builder."

He smiled for the first time that night. "I think I need a drink."

"I do too. I haven't even told you yet about what Rolie did to me tonight."

"By the way, are you limping?"

"That's what I want to tell you about."

"I'm all ears, but I'd rather talk somewhere else. Why don't you come home with me tonight? Pack up a little bag and let's get out of here. It's not safe, and I don't want to leave you alone."

"You have a guest room?"

He smiled teasingly. "I've never been asked that before, but if that's your pleasure, yes. I have two, so you can choose."

"It's a deal."

32

New Projects

Saturday, February 7, 2009

Lexie woke up Saturday morning to the smell of coffee and frying bacon. Without changing from the sweats she'd slept in, she made her way from the biggest guest room to Steve's kitchen. "Are you making breakfast?"

"I am. Still limping, I see. How's your wrist?"

"Better."

"How do you like your eggs?"

"Poached with Hollandaise sauce."

"Oh, sure. Eggs Benedict coming right up." He frowned playfully. "I meant, scrambled or over easy."

"Scrambled."

"Do you actually poach your eggs and make Hollandaise?"

"No," she laughed. "I just thought I'd test you. Where's the juice?"

"In the fridge. Help yourself. I have orange juice, no pulp." He laughed. "Or you can have orange juice, no pulp -- take your pick. You might want to check the expiration date. Pour yourself some coffee. You want cream?"

"No, the blacker the better."

"Good. I don't have any cream."

"I'm impressed that as a single guy you have fresh eggs and bacon in the house. I almost never eat breakfast, so this is a treat."

"I think the toast is done."

"I'll butter it. You do have butter, I suppose."

"Right here," he said, pushing the tub toward the toaster.

"What time is it, by the way?"

"Eight thirty," Steve said, glancing at the digital clock on the stove.

"I've got to eat and run then. Vicki's funeral service starts at eleven, doesn't it?"

He nodded as he scooped eggs onto her plate. When they were on their second cup of coffee, Steve said, "I've been thinking. Last night you were in real danger, first from your brother, then your ex-husband. Just in case you're ever in a situation again where you're threatened and can't speak freely, you need a code word or phrase so I know that something bad is going on and you need help."

"Like 'help?'" she said, smiling.

"I'm serious. A phrase that sounds innocuous and natural but isn't so common you'd use it in everyday conversation and leave me puzzled."

After tossing around possibilities, some frivolous and silly, some unnatural and eccentric, they finally agreed on "for old times' sake."

"You think we'll see Rolie at the funeral?" Steve asked. "I'd like a word with him." He punched the air. "I've kind of gotten into the mode of punching the other men in your life, so what's one more?"

"Once upon a time, Rolie dated Cricket, Vicki's sister,

and they still talk from time to time, so I imagine he'll show up, but I don't want to get into it with him at a funeral. Do you think I should call Dave and tell him what happened last night? He said to call him any time if I felt threatened."

"I'll give him a call, see if we can meet with him. Maybe not this afternoon, since it's the weekend, but next week if you're available."

"Depends on the day. Tuesday I'm flying to New York to meet with a literary agent. She wants me to write a book for women entrepreneurs." She made an approving noise. "These eggs are delicious, Steve. Cooked in butter, just the way I like them."

"Thanks." He smiled. "Writing a book sounds like work."

"It does, but I need some real work. I haven't had this much free time since I was five, and I don't like it. Fortunately, now I have two projects: a new house, and a book."

"And maybe, with the house you're going to build, I can get the Tonkel Road project off the drawing boards."

She raised her arm. "I call shotgun."

"What?"

"Since I'm going to build my house in your new development, I want to name the streets."

"You already have an idea about that?"

"Elysian Fields is a name from Greek mythology. I assume you know that."

"I do, but how do *you* know that?"

"Jean told me. She looked it up on Wikipedia. So why not continue with that theme? Use the names of Greek gods and goddesses. I've always wanted to live on Athena Lane."

"Always? Since childhood you've been thinking of

that?" he asked teasingly, but with severe doubt in his voice.

"Wild exaggeration, but I do like the name. She's the goddess of wisdom and warfare."

"You consider yourself wise, do you?"

"No. More like the victim of warfare, but I'm hoping to be the victor, like Athena -- for which I'll need wisdom. I spent more than ten years in business warfare and now I seem to be at war with everybody but you -- Rolie, Ferrell, Jean, even Matilda and Bob in a way."

"Is there a god of negotiation?" He pointed to his chest. "That's me."

"Negotiation is a promising word. So you'll consider it, Steve-o? I not only get to design my own house, but name the street too."

He looked at his watch, then smiled at her. "We'd better get you back to Forest Park if you're going to get to the church on time."

"That's not an answer, Steve."

"I know."

33

Madman

Monday, February 9, 2009

On a cold Monday morning, the sky heavy with the threat of more snow, Lexie arrived at the Scrapyard to meet Rolie. She assumed the heavily chromed, tricked-out Harley-Davidson parked between Nate's dirty Dodge Ram and Trude's relatively clean Suzuki Equator was her brother's new ride. He strode out of the office to meet her. "Wannna ride the Fat Boy?"

"Sounds like a vulgar pickup line."

He smirked. "I'll remember that. Might get me somewhere."

"You look like you've put on a little weight, Rolie."

He patted his expansive waistline. "I suppose I could stand to lose ten pounds."

Or fifty. Suddenly, she felt something soft pressing against her right ankle. It was a skinny calico, one of the many yard cats the Royces had always tolerated to control the rat population, but as soon as Lexie made a move to pet him, he fled.

"Smart boy, that cat; get the hell out of here." She

returned her attention to Rolie. "That looks like an expensive machine."

"It is. The best investment I ever made."

"Investment? What's the payback?"

"You can't imagine how many new people I've met. It gets the girls' attention, let me tell you."

"You think your plaything will appreciate, do you? That's what a good investment does, you know."

He frowned. If she could take digs at him, he could dig back. "Did you notice who Cricket's friend Tiffany took to the funeral?"

"Who's Tiffany?"

"The Chinese girl with Ferrell."

"Oh. I saw them. I didn't know that was his girlfriend."

"Tiffany's about twenty-four, same as Cricket. How much younger than you does that make her, Sis?"

Lexie grimaced, remembering what Ferrell had said about his high-maintenance girlfriend. "She looks expensive." But it was too cold to discuss Rolie's failure to distinguish between a wise investment and a costly indulgence or Ferrell's odd choice of a girlfriend. She nodded in the direction of the office. "I take it Nate's in there?"

"He's somewhere out in the Yard."

"In that case, I'll stay outside."

"You afraid of me?"

"Given what happened Friday night, I think it's prudent to stay where I can run."

"There'd be no reason to be afraid if you'd do the right thing."

"Which is what?"

"Put some of those millions of yours into this enterprise

so it can flourish."

"Is that what Murph meant by loosening my wallet?"

"That's what he meant. What'd you think of him, by the way?"

She was nonplussed at the question, as if he'd introduced her to an eligible bachelor and was waiting for her assessment. "About what you intended me to think. After delivering a threat, he and his leathery friends followed me home on their bikes."

"I heard about that." He laughed. "I didn't tell them to follow you. But that's Murph, always thinking for himself, amping stuff up to the next level."

"Why did you stand me up in a place like that? I've never been in a scarier bar."

"Something came up."

"I don't think so. I think you're too cowardly to deliver your own message."

"I'm here, aren't I? Reason doesn't seem to work with you, Sis, so it's your own fault if I have to resort to intimidation."

"Reason works very well with me, but your business proposal isn't reasonable and your math sucks. The way you run the Yard, I'd just be shoveling cash into a furnace."

He suddenly took his ringing cell phone out of his jacket pocket and studied it as if any random message might be more important than this conversation. "We're not talking furnaces. We're talking smelters."

"Don't get smart with me, Rolie. And why don't you look at me when we're talking?"

He looked up from his phone with a contemptuous smile. "Always have to be the center of attention, don't you,

Sis?"

She fought with her rage, but since she had the upper hand, it was a battle she could win if she kept her head. "Unless there's a change in management, unless you stop selling drugs here, unless this Yard stops taking stolen property -- I'm not lending you a dime or investing anything. In fact, unless things change, I'm going to sell my interest while I can."

He grabbed her arm. His eyes were cold, his face dark. "You'll do no such thing. You're in this till you die."

She tried to twist away as he tightened his grip. If she hadn't been wearing a thick coat, bruises would be forming. "You're hurting me."

"You don't know the meaning of hurt yet."

"Let go or I'll scream."

"Go ahead," he said, looking around the Yard. "These men work for me. They do whatever I say."

"Let go," she shouted.

"You owe me, Sis. Time to pay the bill."

Just as she renewed her efforts to twist away, Drago whipped into a parking space next to where they were standing. He leaped out of his Jeep with an inquiring look on his face. "Nice to see you, Mizz Royce." He stared at Rolie's grip on her arm. "Something going on here?"

"None of your business," Rolie said, releasing Lexie.

Drago stared at his boss. "I heard this fine lady yelling as I rolled into the Yard."

"So what?"

"I don't like to hear a lady yelling. Ain't right."

Lexie backed up the few steps to her car, rubbing her arm, her eyes fixed on Rolie. Once in her car, she lowered the window. "You're working for a madman, Drago. If he can threaten his own sister, think what he can do to you. Get out while you can."

Rolie turned on his heel and strode into the office, but Drago stood where he was, rooted to the ground, his face thoughtful, watching Mizz Royce drive away until she was long out of sight.

34

Triumph

Monday, February 9, 2009

Sitting in his office between classes on the IPFW campus Monday evening, Ferrell Hawke was going over his utility bills and writing out checks. For several minutes, he eyed Tiffany's VISA envelope as it were a ticking time bomb that would explode in his face. Finally, he slit it open with his Waterford crystal paper knife, removed the bill, and laid it flat. He couldn't believe his eyes.

True, the personal charges were hefty: over three thousand at Pappas Furs on January 18, then a day later almost five hundred at H&M and another five hundred at Macy's. But since then, she hadn't spent a penny on frivolous personal items. All the charges were made at Scott's Maplecrest, a nearby Walgreens, a parking lot downtown, a Lassus Handy Dandy on Dupont, a Hallmark's in Northcrest Shopping Center, and Andrew Davis in Covington Plaza: groceries, birth control pills, parking (for what?), gasoline, and a birthday card and high-end birthday present for him.

January 19 was the last frivolous personal charge. He flipped a few pages on his calendar. That was a Monday, the day he'd gotten so angry when he discovered the fur coat tucked into the back of the coat closet. Though Tiffany had tearfully promised to stop spending so wildly, it had only taken her a few hours to break her promise at H&M and Macy's, but after that she seemed to have reformed her ways.

So! This time he'd scared her into going straight. He smiled at the bill. Maybe the prospect of moving into the house on Forest Park Boulevard had something to do with Tiffany's new attitude. Of course, it wasn't a done deal yet, but scaring Lexie seemed to have worked just as well as it had with Tiffany. After all, it had taken only the weekend for Lexie to make up her mind to give him the house. Tomorrow he was meeting with Marty Solomon to work out the details.

He stood up, slipped on an old tweed sport jacket with leather elbow patches and a well-worn odor, uselessly slicked back the shock of hair that fell boyishly over his forehead, and picked up his notes. He felt triumphant. Women were almost more trouble than they were worth, but he knew how to handle them.

35

Madame Butterfly

Monday, February 9, 2009

Monday afternoon, Bob Passwatter called his wife to tell her not to hold dinner for him. He was meeting a potential investor in his office, a man so important he couldn't disclose his identity to anyone, not even Clarissa. "He and I will catch a bite afterward, maybe at the old Oyster Bar on Calhoun."

"What time will you be home, Bob?"

"Not sure, darling. But don't wait up. It could be a long night."

Around six-thirty, he knocked on the door of the townhouse Tiffany shared with Ferrell Hawke. He expected to feel guilty, but instead he was as excited as a schoolboy. He'd often felt lust before, but it never led him anywhere. If things went the way he hoped, however, he would finally be embarking on his first affair. He was rather glad now that he hadn't pursued Xiu-Xiu beyond making a few suggestive hints, for her younger sister was much more seductive, and somehow banging two sisters seemed like a greater sin than banging just one. The word "affair" scrolled through his brain like the banner on a cable news show. He was about to become a man of the world, valued not just for his financial acumen but his irresistible masculinity as well.

Tiffany stayed hidden by the front door, pulling him into the house as if they were spies in a French movie. After setting his gift bottle of wine on a table, she allowed him to hold her in his arms a few seconds but turned her face away so his kiss landed on her temple.

"Ferrell will be back when his class is over, around nine, so don't let me lose track of the time."

"I thought you said he'd gone to a conference somewhere."

"No. He's teaching a night class."

Though he was momentarily confused -- had she lied or had he misunderstood about where Ferrell was supposed to be? -- and disappointed by the brevity of the encounter that lay ahead of him, he was still excited. "You look beautiful, Tiffany," he said, shrugging off his coat.

She giggled as she turned around so he could admire the big pink heart and rhinestone applique on the back of her jacket. "I should. You can't believe how much a Twisted Heart track suit costs."

"I think you could be wearing a gunny sack and look gorgeous." He had a hard time unlocking his gaze from her firm, round breasts, so different from Clarissa's, but when he finally took in his surroundings, he was dismayed. The space he was in, presumably the living room, was small and drab, so unlike the exotic girl standing a few feet away. He'd expected the house to look like a set from *Madame Butterfly*.

"I hope you like moo-shu pork and garlic chicken."

He gave her a teasing look. "Garlic isn't good for romance, you know."

"It is if we both eat it." She walked behind him, put her hands on his shoulders, and said, "It's getting hot in here, Bob. Let me take your jacket."

He trembled at her touch. He trembled again when she removed her jacket, revealing a very low-necked pink camisole. She didn't appear to be wearing a bra, yet her breasts were high on her chest, round as apples. The scene was so charged he didn't care about food, but Tiffany insisted she was famished and couldn't wait to taste the wine he'd brought.

With much touching of hands, she taught him how to eat with chopsticks. She told him sad stories about her parents' former lives in the Hunan province of China. She toasted every remark he made as if it were the most intelligent thing she'd ever heard, and though he downed glass after glass of vino, she seemed never to have to refill hers. Finally he asked how her chemo was going.

"Thanks to you, I start next week. I'm just hoping I don't lose my hair."

"I'll buy you whatever wigs you want."

"You're so good to me, *nánpéngyou*."

"Nappy what?"

She put her hand over her eyes as if embarrassed. "Napping," she corrected, mispronouncing it only slightly less egregiously than Bob. "It means boyfriend," she whispered.

"How's it spelled?"

"In our letters, or in Chinese characters?"

"Our letters." He reached for her hand. "Actually, I don't care how it's spelled. It's the most beautiful word I ever heard. I didn't know you spoke Chinese."

"Mandarin," she said modestly.

"I'm impressed. I've never heard Mandarin spoken before. Such a musical language."

"I'll teach you."

"I want you to teach me something all right, something only you can teach me, but not Mandarin." He reached across the table, intending to pull her face toward his, but she suddenly leapt out of her chair. "Oh, my God, Napp-ing, it's almost eight-thirty. You have to get out of here before Ferrell gets back." She ran to the living room, retrieved his coat and suit jacket, and pushed him toward the back door. "Go out this way so if he's coming down the street he won't see you."

She followed him out to the snowy patio and threw her arms around his neck. "Thank you, thank you, Bob. You've saved my life."

He slogged through snow up to his calves, then walked an extra block to circle back on his car, glowing with the idea of saving a woman's life, aching with frustrated desire, and wishing he'd worn boots. He doubted that his precious Berluti loafers would survive.

Unfortunately, he arrived home well before Clarissa normally went to bed. She was reading in the family room but hurried to the door from the garage.

"You're home early, Bob."

"I didn't expect things to go so . . . so fast." He couldn't help frowning at her flannel pajamas, her terry robe and slippers. She wasn't wearing a bra either, he could tell, but the contrast with Tiffany was dispiriting. Why was gravity so hard on women?

"Is that a good or bad omen for the new investor?"

"Good, I think. I always reel them in, you know that."

She kissed him, then made a face. "Whew! What in the

world did you eat at the Oyster Bar?"

"Garlic chicken."

"I didn't know they served that."

"It was a special."

"Don't I smell wine too?"

"We split a bottle."

"That's not like you." She looked down as he stomped his feet on the rug. "What did you do to your shoes? Your pant legs are wet to the knees." She laughed. "Did somebody throw you in a snow drift?"

He backed away, wishing he felt like laughing. "Something like that."

36

Don't Call Me Shirley

Monday, February 9, 2009

Monday night, Lexie finished packing for her trip the next day to New York. Steve was waiting downstairs, ready to drive her to his house in Autumn Ridge, where she was still occupying the guest bedroom. Once Marty Solomon worked out the details of deeding the Forest Park house to Ferrell, she would begin packing up personal items, some to be sent to Steve's house, some to storage. She was happy to leave behind all the furniture except the Empire desk and Klismos chair that had once belonged to her mother. They had moved with her everywhere she ever lived. Having been only three years old when her mother was killed in an automobile accident, she could no longer remember her mother's face, but at least she had something to remind her that she hadn't always been an orphan.

When she appeared at the head of the stairway with her roll-on, Steve ran up the steps. "Let me get that."

"It's not heavy," she said.

"That's not the point, Lexie."

"I think I'll take my Burberry in case New York isn't

quite the frozen ice chest that Fort Wayne is." She rummaged in the front hall closet, finding the coat in a clear plastic bag. "Ah, I see Phyllis sent it out for cleaning."

"It doesn't look warm at all. Does it have a lining?"

"It does. It's warmer than it looks, but I can take the lining out if there's a thaw and I need to throw on something lightweight."

"Why do people always say they have a Burberry rather than just a trench coat?"

She laughed lightly. She tore off the plastic and held up the coat for his inspection. "Because a Burberry is expensive and distinctive. Notice the left storm flap? The special buttons? The D-ring on the back?"

"I'm afraid those details go right over my head, but I'm a practical man and that light color isn't practical when mud's splashing around, is it?"

"Women aren't practical about their clothes, you know that."

"I do now. But let's save the small talk for home. If we don't get going, you're not going to get enough sleep before your six o'clock flight."

But Lexie was rooted to the spot, staring at the coat. "I just realized something."

"What?"

"This coat. It looks just like the one the guy is wearing in the security tape Dave Powers showed me. The guy the Indianapolis police think torched my car was wearing a coat like this one, a little too light-colored and feminine for a man. He was also wearing a Colts billcap like the one Drago was wearing today at the Yard. Plus, remember the black

Cherokee that passed us on I-69 and then ended up in the ditch? Drago drives one just like it."

"You don't think Drago was the arsonist, do you?"

"I don't want to think that, but I didn't tell Phyllis to send this coat to the cleaners. Why did it need cleaning? Because it smelled like gasoline?"

"I thought you said the guy on the tape looked like an old white man."

"He did, but he walked like a young guy with an attitude -- the way Drago walks sometimes. What we could see of the man's face didn't look entirely natural, like he was wearing a mask or heavy makeup."

"So you're thinking it wasn't Ferrell."

"You said to keep an open mind, and besides the guy in the tape looks shorter than Ferrell."

"So now you're thinking it was Drago," he said, picking up the roll-on and walking out the front door."

She set the alarm, then joined him on the porch and locked the door. "I still have an open mind, but the coincidences are stunning, don't you think?"

"Why would Drago want to destroy your car?"

"I don't think he would. But Rolie . . . well, Rolie's another matter. Every time I turn around, he's trying to scare me."

"I think we need to talk to Dave the minute you get back from New York. I'm taking you to the airport, and I'm picking you up. You're staying with me until your new house is built, and you're arming the damn security system at all times."

As Steve held the passenger door open, Lexie smiled and

saluted. "Surely you are right."

He grinned. "And don't call me Shirley."

37

That Midwestern Upbringing

Tuesday, February 10, 2009

Arriving mid-morning on Tuesday at LaGuardia, Lexie was grateful she had the means to book a limousine to the Hôtel Plaza Athénée on east 64th at Madison Avenue. The day was blustery and the taxi lines long. A limo conferred the added benefit of not having to answer the annoying question all New York City taxi drivers asked their passengers about which bridge they wanted to take to Manhattan. She never knew the answer. With enough money, she discovered, she didn't have to answer trick questions in hostile territory. Money took the edge off the misery of travel.

Situated on a tree-lined street of impressive townhouses, the hotel, brightened by red awnings, was elegant on the outside and breathtakingly luxurious on the inside. Her suite had a glass-enclosed atrium terrace that gave her a spectacular view of the New York skyline. She couldn't wait to see it at night.

She showered and changed into a fitted black Armani suit and spritzed on a little of her favorite daytime scent, Jo Malone nectarine blossom and honey cologne. For the big-city edge, she put on a pair of Genevieve Jones diamond earrings shaped like safety pins. Anywhere else, $1,200 safety pin earrings just looked stupid, but not in the city that sat at the navel of the artistic universe. After she donned her Burberry, she slung on a green Chanel "cross-body pouch" in crackled patent calfskin, $3,200 retail. The little purse was ridiculously inadequate to carry all the stuff she normally carried, but it was a challenge for purse snatchers to get it off her body and, since it was weirdly colorful and didn't match anything else she was wearing, it was New York chic.

Her meeting with Bettina Lazare, the fiftyish literary guru who owned her eponymous agency, The Lazare Group, took place in an office minimally furnished with expensive, hard-edged furniture, set off by black-and-white photos of New York City. Except for a wall of books, it reminded Lexie of Miranda Preistly's office in *The Devil Wears Prada.* If Lexie really was a writer at heart, wanted nothing more than to get published, was short on money, and needed the right entrée to the literary world, she would have been overawed by the setting.

Bettina herself was no less intimidating. A pretty, plump woman wearing a massive red amber necklace, she draped her *avoirdupois* in the best garments Donna Karan could concoct for rich women with weight issues. Her short hairdo was so complicated Lexie couldn't imagine how it had been cut or waxed into place.

Altogether, Bettina and her office projected an air of self-importance that must be very intimidating to an unknown author, but Lexie had dealt with intimidating men all her life, and if she didn't get a book contract, oh, well. She'd find something else to do. She nevertheless adopted an attitude of deference and respect. *Let's see how this scene plays out.*

After a few pleasantries about Lexie's trip from Fort Wayne and what she thought of the Plaza Athénée, they got down to business. "We aren't fixed on a self-help book, just so you know, Alexandra. Do you cook? Celebrity cookbooks are all the rage. We can get you on Rachael Ray and The View and you can demonstrate some easy dish from your childhood."

Lexie laughed. "Not without burning the set down or cutting a finger off. I've worked all my life, long hours, so my knowledge of the domestic arts is minuscule." *And at the moment I have no interest in learning.*

Frowning, Bettina tapped *Money* magazine, open to an article about Lexie and other women entrepreneurs. "I read that you work out religiously, and you look very fit. Would an exercise book interest you, perhaps a DVD to go with it?"

"The only thing I do religiously is go to church, so no, I'm far from an expert on exercise routines, and I'm not a size two, so I'd photograph badly, don't you think?"

"Well, there's that. So . . . ." Bettina sighed. "Do you have any interest in writing your memoirs perhaps?"

"I'm only thirty-three. It's been an interesting life so far" -- *and it's a little too interesting for comfort at the moment* -- "but I'd be embarrassed to pretend I'm colorful or wise enough to write a book about myself that other people would want to read." *Even most of my best friends find my money more interesting than anything else about me.*

Bettina looked up brightly. "Then we'll stick with the book for women entrepreneurs, should we? You're a nationally recognized expert, and you'd be doing other women a great favor by guiding them. We have a ghostwriter to help."

Lexie was taken aback. "A ghostwriter?"

"Yes, it's standard procedure for celebrities like you. You prepare an outline, and he'll do the necessary research, organize the material, edit it, put it into good English, prepare the captions and sidebars, that sort of thing. In fact, if you don't want to write anything down, you can just talk into a tape recorder. It'll make it much easier for you, and the book will end up in a format our readers like."

"I'll have to think about that."

Bettina looked startled, her eyes opening wide without lifting her forehead even a centimeter. "You don't want help?"

When Lexie didn't immediately answer, Bettina said consolingly, "There's no shame, Alexandra. Ghostwriters -- call them co-authors or research assistants, if you prefer -- are everywhere these days. Popular writers like Tom Clancy and James Patterson use them all the time to inflate their production and keep their readers happy. So do artists. Have you ever heard of Jeff Koons?"

Lexie smiled. "News of the art world isn't embargoed west of the Hudson, you know." She waited for a laugh, but there was none. "Yes, I've heard of Jeff Koons. The American artist of kitsch who admits there's no hidden meaning in his work."

Bettina frowned. "Kitsch? That's a matter of opinion, of course. His work may only be kitsch to you, but to the rest of the world it's pioneering and worth a lot of money. Anyway, he has an army of assistants and he's proud of the fact that he no longer puts a brush to canvas. Collectors clamor for his work anyway, just as they do for Rembrandt's because the concept is important, not the execution. The same is true of some very popular authors and almost all celebrities. You don't even have to credit the guy. He'll stay anonymous. The book will look like your baby and no one else's."

"But I want a project I can sink my teeth into, Bettina. I'm bored out of my mind. I've been studying or working since I was five, and when I sold my businesses, I mentally gave myself a year's sabbatical, but that expired months ago. Now I need something absorbing in my life, something where the time passes without my noticing it. I'm not a professional writer, of course, but my college professors used to say my papers were 'workmanlike,' so I think I can write decent prose. It might need a little editing, I understand that, but I want the book to sound like me. And I know how I want to organize my book, I know what I want to say."

"But it's customary for a celebrity expert to use a ghostwriter."

"Getting credit for something I didn't do is not customary with me, and if I'm really an expert, then I have to write my own book."

Bettina sat back, annoyed. "It's that Midwestern upbringing, isn't it?"

"What do you mean?"

"You're all about being 'real.'"

"You make being real sound like a character fault."

Bettina sat forward, her arms crossed on her desk, her eyes hard. "What's the difference between reality and illusion, Alexandra? Tell me that."

Lexie was nonplussed. "I should think everything."

Bettina shook her head. "No. There is no difference if

we say there's no difference. We have to package the product cleverly, of course, but we're experts at doing that." This time she shot Lexie a smile that not only didn't move her forehead but didn't even reach her eyes. "You're an expert at creating a business, I'm an expert at selling books. The average woman who's going to pick up your book won't know or care who really wrote it. She'll admire your photo on the book jacket and hope if she does what you tell her to do, she'll magically end up looking like you and be just as rich and famous. She'll thumb through the table of contents, read a page or two of prose so simple she'll think she understands your business principles, and be hooked. You make money, I make money, the publisher makes money, everybody's happy."

The image of Myrtle Lodger appeared before Lexie's mind's eye. That poor woman needed real help, not a slick book she couldn't afford. Not an easy-read book that promised magic.

Lexie finally broke the awkward silence. "I'm afraid we've wasted each other's time."

"No, we haven't," Bettina said firmly. "You prepare an outline, I'll look it over, and then we'll talk some more."

38

Assemblages

Tuesday, February 10, 2009

When Lexie walked out of the high-rise office building to Fifth Avenue, she looked at her cell phone, wishing she could call Steve to tell him about her meeting with Bettina Lazare, but she knew he was taking a lie detector test in an hour or so. This was no time for a depressing story about ghostwriters.

Instead, she took a taxi to the Metropolitan Museum of Modern Art, where she spent an hour wandering through an exhibit called *Wunderkammer: A Century of Curiosities.* Joseph Cornell's enigmatic assemblages -- collages in three-dimensions -- had always intrigued her, especially the one featuring a cockatoo, suspended in mid-air, surrounded by sticks and corks, a metal tube resembling a bullet, and other found objects. Though she liked very little outsider art and Cornell's shadow boxes made no rational sense, something about them resonated anyway, stirring fantasy and memory. If she ever adopted a hobby, she would try assembling strange objects in shadow boxes.

She returned to Madison Avenue in the Sixties to eat a

late lunch at *Veneto*, an Italian wine bar offering an expansive wine list and a select chef's menu called *I Primi*, a phrase she wasn't sure she understood. "Primi" probably meant "first," but first what? The waiter, his speech heavily accented, treated her with great disdain.

"What is *I Primi*?" she asked.

He corrected her pronunciation. "First courses. Little dishes. You say here appetizers, I believe."

"And what is a *Frittata Arrotolata*?"

"An omelet roll with spinach." His tone was that of a nursery school teacher explaining to a toddler which crayon was red.

Lexie wanted to ask about a few other dishes but was too weary to go on. She handed her menu to the waiter. "Sounds perfect. I'll have that, and a glass of Prosecco."

Fortunately, she was seated at a little bistro table near a window on the street, so instead of regretting that her purse was too small to hold her Kindle, she watched people. Chic secretaries taking a quick afternoon break -- to do what? Well-dressed matrons carrying bags of designer clothes. Serious men with facial hair, professors maybe, or art gallery owners or music executives. Model-worthy, cocky young men who looked way too prosperous for their age. Old men and women, dressed in yesterday's styles, looking like they'd lived in the same rent-control apartment since the Civil War. Rich college students posing as down-at-heel revolutionaries. Dark-haired women holding hands, dressed in the fashions of other countries. An Hasidic Jew with his long side curls and distinctive black hat striding a few steps ahead of a sturdy man in a hard hat lugging a huge coil of yellow cable.

So many people, from so many corners of the globe,

flowing up and down the street, choreographed like schools of fish so as not to bump into each other, not knowing each other at all but mysteriously appearing on the same street at the same moment in time. The only thing they might have in common was that God had made them all in his image, breathed life into them, though many would deny it. What did it mean, to be made in God's image? It was Joseph Cornell's world, right there on Madison Avenue: A transient assemblage of strangers who would never exchange a word, not even look at each others' faces if they could help it, but who were nevertheless supernaturally connected.

The sheer number of the strangers hurrying by, the barrier of the big glass window separating her from the life on the street, the curtness of the waiter, the disappointment of her meeting with Bettina Lazare -- altogether, they made Lexie feel more alone than ever.

She ate her delicious lunch, sipped her sparkling wine, paid her bill, and slowly walked back to her hotel room for a few moments of naptime oblivion.

39

Hand-Shucked

Tuesday, February 10, 2009

After her nap, Lexie went in search of the fitness center. After showering and once again changing clothes, she spent an hour in the hotel's Bar Seine lounge, nursing a Crystal Cosmopolitan, wishing she had someone to talk to, wondering why she wasn't hungry.

Back in her room, she walked out to her private atrium to admire the city's soaring skyline, so unlike anything in Fort Wayne. One Summit Square was at 27 stories the tallest building, and the Lincoln Tower, the first skyscraper built in Indiana, was only 23 stories -- Lilliputian by New York standards.

She looked straight up. It had begun to snow. The atrium made her think about the house she wanted to build. She'd love an open-air atrium right in the middle of the house, like the palazzos or villas or whatever they were called where the rich and powerful lived in *Rome,* the best two-season HBO series she'd ever watched.

Her house, her new house . . . still nothing but a vague idea, so new that nothing much had formed in her mind yet.

What would it look like? How big should it be? Should she design it for herself as if she'd never marry again, or for a husband too? How about children?

Her house was still nothing but a dream, but Steve was real, a known quantity. He was handsome. He was smart and kind, and so physically attractive it was all she could do to stay in the guest bedroom. Last night, just as they were parting for the night, he asked her if she was still comfortable sleeping in the guest wing.

"Yes, of course."

"But it's so far away from me."

"I know," she whispered.

"Then why not join me, Lexie?"

She hesitated. "You said you'd never marry again."

"I said I *might* not."

"I don't know what that means."

"Why does it matter?"

"Because if I sleep with you, I'll begin to think I love you. I'll start planning an imaginary future that you might not want to share. That's what happens to women in bed."

"Is that so terrible?"

"For some women, perhaps not, but I've gone through one very unhappy relationship. I'm not risking a broken heart again, Steve. The next time I sleep with a man, it's for keeps."

"Your body clock is ticking." The words were out of his mouth before he realized he'd made the same sarcastic remark to Vicki.

She let her hurt show. "Women are different from men, Steve. What's wrong with that?"

"Nothing. I should have said, you want somebody to

grow old with."

She laughed shakily. "I want somebody to be young with first. I want a man I can count on. I want a man who's kind and makes me laugh."

He nodded thoughtfully. Saying nothing, he turned to go to his wing of the house. He didn't seem angry, but she didn't know what his silence meant.

Still he was her best friend, and she needed him. She had to hear his voice.

"Steve, it's Lexie. Are you at home? Have I called at a bad time?"

"I'm downstairs watching a movie. Hold on while I pause it." Coming back on the line, he imitated John Candy's voice. "'Chanice, I'll be honest with you. If I could think of an excuse that you'd buy, I'd use it.'"

"Are you watching *Uncle Buck?*"

"Don't tell me you recognize the line, Lexie."

Lexie did her best imitation of John Candy. "'Honey, I have some bad news.'"

"'You ever hear of a tuneup?'"

"'You ever hear of a ritual killing?'"

They both laughed. "Don't forget *Planes, Trains, and Automobiles,*" Lexie said. "That scene where the men are driving the wrong way on the Interstate and Candy thinks everybody else is drunk or crazy? My favorite."

"And what about *What About Bob?*"

"That's another one I like. I used to identify with Dr. Leo Marvin, arrogant as he is, but now it's Bob Wiley. I feel like I'm taking little tiny baby steps into the next phase of my life."

"Where are you calling from, Lexie? The hotel?"

"I'm in my gorgeous suite, standing in a glass-enclosed atrium, staring at the fantastic skyline and watching it snow. I think you'd love it here. But only for a few days."

"Why only a few days?"

"I'm looking at a hundred Towers of Babel, only they reach even higher than the original ziggurat and are electrified, all lit up like Roman candles. It's a very pagan place. You can feel it on the street. People here worship every idol you can imagine -- money, food, clothes, success, looks, socialist heaven. It wouldn't shock me if the City built another Coliseum and started feeding Christians to lions."

"That'll happen in D.C. first, don't you think? I've only been to New York once," Steve said, "and I stayed in some flea bag near Times Square, so maybe I should get out there again, see what the fuss is all about."

"The right hotel in the right location changes everything about this very strange, unfriendly city. To tell you the truth, it doesn't feel like it's even in America. Not the America I know, anyway. English is the language you hear least often. And the prices! I stopped at a little fruit stand. Do you know what a navel orange cost me?"

"A dollar?"

"Two fifty."

"Not a good place to be poor, is it? Anyway, how did your meeting with the literary agent go?"

"She wants me to make an outline and then hand everything over to a ghostwriter."

"And you don't, I suppose. I can hear it in your voice."

Lexie walked over to an armchair and sat down, still facing the brilliantly lit skyline. "I don't. I want a real project." She affected Bettina's authoritative, clipped voice.

"Do you know what the difference is between reality and illusion?"

He gave a puzzled laugh. "What?"

"That's how Bettina Lazare -- or as I shall henceforth call her, Lettina Bizarre -- sounds. She asked me that question today."

"And what did you answer?"

"I said I thought there was all the difference in the world, but, leaning forward with crossed arms and hard eyes -- she has an enormous, expensively draped bosom by the way -- she assured me there is no difference if she says so. That's why a ghostwritten book is as good as any other. Better, maybe."

"So how did you leave it?"

"She wants an outline. I didn't say yes or no."

"Well, at least did you eat at some great restaurant?"

"Late this afternoon I did, but tonight I wasn't hungry, so all I did was to go to the hotel lounge for an hour, where I sipped a very expensive Crystal Cosmopolitan. Now I'm drinking an eight dollar bottle of water thoughtfully set out for me when I returned to find my bed turned down and Belgian chocolates on my pillow."

"Wish I could have been there to keep you company."

"So do I. I didn't have a soul to talk to. So now I'm talking your ear off."

"Actually, my ear's just fine."

"What I really called about was the lie detector test. Were you nervous?"

"Yes and no. I've never taken one before, of course. Facing the unknown and doing anything for the first time is nerve-wracking. But since I'm innocent, I wasn't nervous in that sense."

"So you passed with flying colors."

"I did."

"What about the DNA tests?"

"Duke Simmons had a sample of my DNA run separately, but since we don't have a basis of comparison yet and the government's tests are still being run, there's no conclusive answer . . . though, of course, I know I'm not the culprit."

"So officially you're in limbo."

"What's the difference between limbo and hell?"

"Not as much as between reality and illusion, I suppose."

"I wish you were here, Lexie. I'm getting used to your company. Movie night for two is better than for just one lonely bachelor eating peanuts and drinking beer."

"Speaking of food, Ms. Lazare asked if I wanted to do a celebrity cookbook. Isn't that hilarious?"

"I didn't know you cooked."

"I don't. Phyllis leaves dinner in the oven for me when I'm at home, and that's good enough."

"Remind me when you're getting back."

"My ticket says 9:30 tomorrow night. I was going to spend tomorrow shopping, first on Fifth Avenue . . . well, let's be honest, just at Bergdorf Goodman. Then I was going to return to Madison Avenue to see if my favorite bookshop is still open, then duck into a few of the odd little boutiques offering unique clothing, but . . . ."

"But what?"

"But maybe I'll rebook. I'd rather be home."

"You would?"

"I would."

"Is this home now?"

She tried to keep her voice light. "It's beginning to feel that way."

"Do you like *Groundhog Day*?"

"Love it."

"Popcorn?"

"Hand-shucked, piled high and fluffy," she giggled.

"Mike's Hard Lemonade, so cold it's almost frozen?"

"I'll bet it's perfect with hand-shucked popcorn bathed in butter and salt."

"Just let me know when you're getting in."

"I'll -- ."

"Sorry to interrupt, but I just had a thought, Lexie. Why don't you book your return to Indianapolis, without making a connection to Fort Wayne? I'll meet you at the airport. I haven't eaten at P.F. Chang's in ages, and I have a hankering for Chinese food. Maybe Jessica and Ed are available."

"It gets better and better. I'll call you back in fifteen minutes."

Lexie booked a first-class seat on a mid-morning flight out of LaGuardia. She was more excited to return to the gray and frozen Midwest than she had been about the prospect of shopping all day on glamorous Madison Avenue.

40

You Did What You Had to Do

Wednesday, February 11, 2009

The night of Lexie's return to Fort Wayne, Phyllis and her son were once more ensconced in her old yellow bungalow in Huntertown, this time feasting on Drago's second favorite meal, pot roast with carrots, onions, and potatoes, smothered in beef gravy. After eating dinner and lighting a cigar, Drago asked, "So what's on your mind, Mom?"

"This morning, Mizz Royce asked me why I sent her trench coat to the cleaners."

"Where were you?"

"At Mr. Wright's house in Autumn Ridge. That's where she's bunking at the moment."

"Is she really going to give the Forest Park house to the Hawk?"

"How did you know about that?"

"Lucy's a friend of Tiffany's, remember?"

"I never understood what those two have in common."

"They're both young and beautiful. They were classmates at Carroll. They love clothes. Tiffany wants to open a boutique and wants Lucy to work for her."

"But Tiffany's an engineer, isn't she? Why is she thinking about a boutique? She's so educated."

He cocked his head. "And Lucy's just a clerk in her parents' liquor store, is that it?"

"Don't get mad at me. I'm just saying."

"Lucy's smarter than you think. She could sell dirt to a farmer. Know that. She just never cared for school -- no more than I did." He had no desire to argue with his mother about his choice of a wife. "Are you going to be working at Autumn Ridge now?"

Phyllis removed her glasses and rubbed the bridge of her nose. "That's what I understand. I'm not sure Mr. Wright really thinks I'm necessary, but so long as Mizz Royce is around, I'll have a job." She ran her hands through her hair. "I'm too old to find something else to do."

He smiled. "Too old? You ain't even fifty yet."

"There are days I feel twice that."

"You think Mizz Royce and Mr. Wright got something going on?"

"All her clothes and makeup are in the guest wing, and she appears to sleep there, so unless she's slipping across the house at night, or he's coming to her room, I'd say not. In my presence, they never touch each other, don't act like a couple."

"Then why is Mizz Royce staying there?"

"She had a late night visit from her ex that scared her. Besides, she'll be moving out of the old house soon." She gestured her bewilderment. "I don't know, Drago. I don't know why she doesn't rent some place on her own. I don't know how rich people think."

"Rolie's going to blow his top if he hears about those

two being in the same house, even if they're living like a priest and a nun." He rolled the ash off his cigar. "So what'd you tell her about the coat?"

"I just said it hadn't been cleaned in awhile and I saw a spot on one sleeve."

"She believed you?"

"Maybe. She asked if you'd been in Indianapolis on January 17, the night of the big blizzard. She and Mr. Wright saw a black Jeep Cherokee in the ditch along I-69. Just like yours, she said."

He closed his eyes, remembering something. "She asked me the same thing one day outside the Yard but then sort of laughed and dismissed the idea, said she didn't think I'd ever drive as crazy as the guy in the Jeep did. You have any idea why she's asking these things?"

"I do. A few hours later, I was in the kitchen, preparing a casserole from a recipe she gave me off the Food Network when she mentioned that she'd been at the police station a few weeks ago and viewed a security tape from the garage where her car was parked when it was burned. She said the guy on the tape was wearing a coat that looked a lot like hers."

Drago looked thoughtful. "What else did she say about the guy on the tape?"

"He looked like an old white guy but might have been wearing a mask or heavy makeup because he walked like a young guy with an attitude."

Drago made a sound that was almost a laugh. "Yeah, that's me."

"I'm not done. He was wearing a billcap that might be a vintage Colts cap."

"So that cap's gotta be put back in storage."

"Burn it."

"No way, Mom. I love that cap. I'll bring it over next time; you can put it back in my bedroom. . . . So what do you think I should do?"

"I leave that to you."

"You think I should talk to Mizz Royce?"

Phyllis barely heard him. "Something else to tell you. Mizz Royce said she's going to build a house in Mr. Wright's new development on Tonkel Road, the one called Elysian Fields."

"So?"

"I have something to tell you."

"About . . . ?"

"About Elysian Fields. That's where your father is."

Drago, who'd been lounging casually in his chair, sat straight up. "He's living rough out there? Camping out or something? You mean, he's been within a few miles of us all this time?"

"He's buried there, in the southeast corner, where the grove is."

For once, Drago had no words.

"You remember the last time you were here, I said I'd done worse than you did?"

Drago nodded.

"You didn't believe me."

"No, I didn't."

"When you were in the hospital, I killed Carver."

He stared at his mother in shock. "You?"

"Me."

"Why? How?"

"He wasn't sorry for what he'd done to you. I knew, soon as you got home, he'd be after you again. Carver had no patience with rambunctious little boys. I think he started hating that he was a husband and a father, regretting the choices he made."

"Was I that bad?"

She reached for his hand. "No, you weren't, son. You were lively and noisy, sometimes naughty the way boys are, but you were normal. Carver would come home from work and want the house quiet, but a six-year-old boy isn't quiet. He'd yell at you if you ran in front of the television or slammed a door or threw a ball or ran a toy truck into the wall. He'd get mad if you didn't want to eat everything on your plate. He got mad at me for not being a better mother. He'd just get mad for nothing at all."

"Did he come after you or something, you had to defend yourself?"

"Yes. Well, no, not exactly. He looked like he was going to hit me that night, but he'd done that before when he'd been drinking."

"Why wasn't he in jail for doing what he did to me?"

"Thanks to me, he made bail. Instead of pleading guilty, he was determined to have his day in court. But that's what made him the maddest. He didn't think the hospital should have reported him to the authorities in the first place, and he was sure I'd talked to them -- which I had. I was going to testify for the prosecution. So he was in a very foul mood the night before you were going to be released.

"His anger toward me wasn't what set me off, though. It was his attitude toward you. He didn't think he'd done wrong. Sparing the rod spoils the child and all that rot. He wasn't sorry. He didn't promise to do better. He didn't even pretend to understand that a boy can't be kept quiet and perfectly behaved. We had a fight so bad about what he was going to expect from you once you came home the next day that I knew if I didn't kill him, he'd kill you. So, God help me, I took matters into my own hands."

"What else could you have done?"

"I don't know. Gotten him to go to counseling or something, I suppose. But he wouldn't."

"How'd you do it, Mom?"

"Shot him with his own gun. In the back of the head as he walked toward the kitchen."

"You said he's buried out on Tonkel Road."

"It was farmland back in those days. Ruth helped me get his body into the trunk of his car. There was a little dirt path partway into the cornfield, so we backed in as far as we could. Fortunately the field wasn't wet, but we got cut up pretty good from the corn -- the leaves cut like knives, in case you didn't know -- and though Carver wasn't a big man, he was heavy enough Ruth and I had to put him down every few yards and catch our breath. It took us an hour to carry him to the grove, more time to dig a grave, which neither of us had ever done before, of course. It was way past midnight by the time we could get out of there. You can't believe how dark it is in a grove at the edge of a cornfield at night."

"Aunt Ruth helped you? I can't see her carrying a dead body."

"Well, I hope you can't see me doing it either, but it had to be done."

"What happened to the car you hauled him in?"

"I drove his old car to Pontiac and abandoned it near the

prison, where he'd served some time, then rode back with Ruth. I threw the gun in the river and sold the shovel at a garage sale when we moved here. I had the carpet replaced in the living room before I sold the house."

"Who knows about this?"

"Just Ruth and me. I told Pete, Carver's boss, that he simply left without telling me where he was going. Carver was a steady worker, but he was so hot-headed, so full of anger, Pete could easily believe that Carver would do something impulsive like that."

"And the cops . . . ?"

"Never questioned me until he failed to show up for trial."

"Why not?"

"I never reported him missing. The cops were curious, of course, but I was prepared with a story -- that he was temperamental and just left, I wasn't sure why. The reason I didn't tell the police right away, I said, was that it was an embarrassing personal story for a woman. My husband left me. Besides, he was over 21, he could do what he wanted. I said I didn't know where he was, but maybe he was just staying with a friend so he could get mentally prepared for his trial. If he had really disappeared and nobody could find him, then my best guess was he was afraid of losing and didn't want to go back to jail. If I ever heard from him, I'd let somebody know."

"They believed you?"

"I don't know, but the clincher was a fact they couldn't dispute. I was the one on the hook for the forfeited bond; I'd pledged the house and a savings account we had. What the cops didn't know was that old Isaac Royce quietly stepped in to pay what I owed, even though I'd only been working for the Royces about five years by then. If he hadn't, you and I would have been living on the street."

"I never knew that. Did old man Royce know what you'd done?"

She looked briefly away. "I never told him, of course, but he was a perceptive man. He probably suspected something was awry, but I'm sure he didn't suspect I'd go so far as to kill Carver." She looked at him with sad eyes. "I hoped I'd never have to tell you any of this."

Drago lit another cigar. "So now what happens?"

"If that grove gets taken down, they'll find Carver and the questions will start. Mizz Royce wants that back corner of the land because it's got a creek at one edge and is on a little rise, so I imagine something will happen to the grove. She might want to keep that big oak, of course, but the cottonwoods and scrub will have to go. She has no idea that she's chosen the very spot where Carver was supposed to spend eternity."

"Can he be identified if they find him?"

Phyllis looked pained. "He always wore a heavy silver rope chain, and I forgot to take it off him. Maybe somebody remembers that. I wrapped him in an old quilt; maybe that can be traced to me. Otherwise, I don't know how the Coroner would know who he is -- or was -- but I suppose there are ways."

"So he's got to be dug up before somebody else finds him."

Phyllis covered her eyes. "Ruth says she won't help."

"That's okay. We don't need her. The ground's still frozen, so there isn't going to be any work out there for awhile. Am I right?"

"Probably."

"We have some time to think about this."

Phyllis began to cry. "I'm so sorry, Drago. I did a horrible thing. I took your father away, which I had no right to do."

He got up, pulled his mother to her feet, and hugged her. He was startled to notice how rounded her back was, as if she was carrying the weight of the world on her shoulders. "Don't cry, Mom. You did what you had to do." *And you did it for me.*

"What are we going to do now, Drago?"

He shook his head. "I'll think of something."

41

Game of Headless Chicken

Thursday, February 12, 2009

Rolie had taken the passenger seat in the Rolls because on this trip to Angola he had some instructions for Drago, which he didn't want to shout from the back seat. But first, he called Lexie and put her on the speaker for Drago's benefit.

"Have you thought any more about the smelter, Sis?"

"I told you, I'm not putting money into the Yard. Don't ask me again."

"I think you should reconsider. By the way, what were you doing at the police station today?"

Drago glanced at the phone. Had she gone there with her suspicions about him?

A long pause followed. "How do you know I was there, Rolland?"

"I have my sources. You know that."

Sources! Drago thought. *So the tracking device on the MINI-Cooper is being put to good use.*

There was a pause before Lexie spoke again. "It's time you tell me what they are."

"What would Sun Tzu say about that -- revealing my sources?"

"Are you referring to your favorite book, *The Art of War?*"

"I am, Sis."

"I don't know what the man would say."

Rolie spoke in a sing-song voice, a bad imitation of Chinese. "Use spies for every sort of business. Don't let the other side know."

"Are those direct quotes?"

"No, but they're close enough."

"Are the two of us at war then? Is that what you're saying?"

"I'm telling you, I won't give up till one of us dies."

Another long pause. "Is that a threat, Rolland?"

"Take it any way you want. So what were you doing at the police station?"

"It's none of your business."

"Give me a hint."

"Is Drago there with you?"

Rolie smiled at his driver. "Right beside me. We're rolling north on I-69."

"You have me on speaker?"

"Drago's listening to every word."

"Drago," she said.

"Yes, ma'am."

"I hate to ask you this, but were you at the Conrad Hotel on January 17? Were you wearing my trench coat? Did you set my car on fire? Was that your Jeep in the ditch on I-69 that night?"

Drago stared straight ahead. He knew this might

be coming, but still he wasn't prepared for Mizz Royce's bluntness. He avoided Rolie's face. "No, it wasn't, Mizz Royce."

"You swear on your mother's honor?"

He winced. "Swear."

"I'll take you at your word."

Drago looked at his boss, then at the phone. "What'd you say to the cops, Mizz Royce?"

"Not a thing about you, Drago. Or you either, Rolie. I told them about Ferrell threatening me. So the two of you can relax."

Rolie suppressed a guffaw. "Well, you did the right thing, Sis. Ladies don't hang their dirty underwear out to dry where everybody can see it."

"Real ladies don't have dirty underwear." There was a pause. "But besides that, Rolie, who hangs dirty underwear out to dry?"

Drago laughed. "She got you there, boss."

Rolie sneered at the phone. "I hear you're living with Steve Wright now."

"'Living with Steve' implies a situation that isn't true. I'm just staying at his house for a little while. Until I get a new house built, I don't have anywhere else to live."

"You can live with me, Sis."

She snorted. "Like that would ever happen." There was a pause before she came back on the line. "You said you're driving north on I-69."

"So?"

"So where are you going this time of night?"

"Business."

"What kind of business?"

"Collecting a debt, that's all."

"Don't we have people who do that for the Yard?"

He snorted. "Sometimes you just gotta take matters into your own hands."

"Are your hands clean or dirty, Rolie?"

"None of your business."

"Well, since you called, may I remind you that Matilda's birthday is next week. We should plan something. Or at least you should."

"You do anything you want with my mother. Far as I'm concerned, the less I see of her, the better."

Drago frowned. Disrespecting one's mother was the worst sin a man could commit. And saying so in front of others was uncalled for.

"She loves you, Rolie. She's proud of you."

"She made me live with that mean old father of yours."

"He was your father too, in case you've forgotten."

"I forget nothing," he snapped, abruptly ending the conversation.

The two men rode awhile in silence. Finally, they exited from the Interstate and eventually took a right onto a country road winding alongside a railroad track. The narrow shoulder was gravel, dropping off into a deep ditch that in the summer ran with water but was now filled with snow and slush. The road had apparently been plowed by someone with a sense of humor, a cowboy who kept the plow blade elevated a few inches above the blacktop, just for the hell of it. Driving in the icy ruts, even at the wuss-speed of thirty miles an hour, took all of Drago's concentration.

After a long silence, Rolie said, "I want a tracker put in her cell phone."

"Whose phone?"

"What do you mean, whose phone?" Rolie shook his iPhone. "Lexie's."

"The tracker in her car isn't enough? Seems to me it worked pretty well, you knowing she was at the police station."

"Why are you keeping your eye on the rear view mirror, Drago?"

"A pickup pulled out from a driveway we passed a mile back."

"So?"

"It's acting crazy."

Rolie wasn't to be distracted. "Your mother could take my sister's phone, pretend it was misplaced, slip it to you long enough to alter it, then pretend to find it again."

Drago shot a furious look at his boss. "Don't bring my mother into this."

"I could buy Lexie a fancy new phone, you could do what you have to do, then I'd give it to her as a present."

"For what?"

"Valentine's is coming up."

Drago shook his head. "That's sick, boss. Brothers don't give sisters Valentine's presents. Know that."

"Just thinking."

Drago was too distracted to protest further. The pickup, carrying a gun rack like the antlers on a buck, was following close behind, dropping back, then speeding up within yards of his back bumper, then dropping back again. Several times it flashed its headlights and honked the horn. Probably just a bunch of teenagers acting the fool, but teenagers were dangerous and Rolie would explode if anything happened to the Rolls. Disgusted, Drago looked for a straight stretch of road so the pickup could pass, and when he found one, he pulled to the right as far as he dared to signal the way was clear. The pickup pulled into the left lane and then slowed to keep pace with them.

Drago lowered his window and, as the pickup pulled alongside, shouted, "Fools, what you doin'?" He pointed his right index finger at them as if it were a gun.

Too late, Drago realized his mistake. The bulbous-nosed guy in the passenger seat grinned at him. He was flashing a gold tooth and holding a real gun. Drago recognized Fazel, the brother of the Bosnian thug who'd been crushed at Summit City Metals. In slow motion, Drago watched Fazel pull the slide and turn the Luger sideways like a gang-banger. The muzzle was pointed straight at Drago, not a yard away.

Drago instinctively floored the Rolls, saving him from death. The first shot took out the side window behind his head. Then Drago stomped on the brake, fishtailing the Rolls and throwing Rolie forward, right into the line of fire of the second shot, which penetrated the windshield at an angle on his side of the car. The pickup then pulled further ahead, still in the left lane, Fazel hanging out the passenger window, laughing and waving the gun.

When Rolie screamed and slumped into the passenger door, Drago tried to see if he'd been hit by flying glass or by a bullet, but he couldn't tell. Maybe the pussy was just being dramatic. When Drago tried to brush glass shards out of his own hair, he felt something sticky. Blood! He frantically patted his head but could find no wound. He looked again at Rolie. Blood was spattered everywhere on that side of the car, ruining the upholstery.

For miles, the pickup played a game of headless chicken, weaving back and forth, slip-sliding perilously close to the ditches on either side, slowing down, then speeding up, blocking Drago's every attempt to escape. Fifteen long minutes passed before he managed to find a way back to I-69. He roared south toward Exit 116, so he could get his boss to the emergency room at Dupont North.

Drago was sick with anger and embarrassment. They'd ridden right into an ambush and he'd made it worse, rolling down his window, shouting at the fools, and pointing his finger. Who was the fool now? He'd never thought of himself like that before.

Every time he glanced at Rolie's limp body, he wondered if the man was alive or not. He reached over to shake his boss, but there was no response. If Rolie didn't regain consciousness by the time the cops arrived at the hospital, he'd be the one answering the questions, and he'd better be ready with a story. A really good story. But what?

42

The Wrong Crowd

Thursday, February 12, 2009

The night Rolie called his sister from the Rolls, she and Steve were in the downstairs media room with Dave Powers and his wife, Sheila, playing pool. Before the call, their subjects of conversation were casual, but after the call, all they could talk about was Rolland's naked hostility and greed. "Well," Lexie said to Dave as she flipped the phone shut. "I won't be erasing that conversation, will I?"

"I don't like that part about how he won't give up getting money from you until one of you is dead," Dave said.

"And how do you think he knows I was at the police station today?"

Dave shook his head. "I think you'd better start assuming somebody's following you and see if you can figure out who it is, or at least what he's driving."

"Rolland said he's collecting a debt somewhere in the vicinity of Angola."

Steve snorted. "Sure, but not a debt for the Scrapyard, not this time of night, and not that way."

"Drugs?" Lexie asked.

"That's my guess."

"Do you really think it was Drago who set your car on fire in Indianapolis?" Sheila asked.

"I think it's likely, but I don't want to get him in trouble before we have more proof. I've known him since he was born, and he's not a bad kid. His mother raised me, after all, so Phyllis and Drago are practically family. He just got in with the wrong crowd."

Steve smiled grimly. "By crowd, you mean your brother."

"My *half*-brother. If Drago did anything, he didn't do it on his own. Rolland's the guiltier party."

A half hour later, Dave and Sheila were just getting up to leave when Lexie's phone rang again.

She listened in shock for a few seconds. "At Dupont North? . . . We'll be right there."

She hung up and looked first at Steve, then at Dave. "That was Drago. Rolie's been shot. He's already been taken to surgery."

43

I've Got Blood on My Hands

Thursday, February 12, 2009

Drago knew he didn't have to say anything to the police and saying anything at all was dangerous, especially since he and his boss hadn't had a chance to coordinate their stories. When Rolie woke up -- assuming he woke up -- he might tell a completely different tale from the one Drago could make up off the cuff. Then he'd be caught in contradictions and lies. Telling the truth was out of the question, too. But silence would make him appear guilty.

He did his best.

"Where did this happen?" The detective who was sitting with Drago in a corner of the reception area was dressed in jeans and a nylon windbreaker, looking very serious. He'd already asked a lot of other questions about the two men -- names, addresses, that sort of thing -- and despite the innocuous nature of the preliminary questions, Drago was beginning to sweat. He knew what was coming.

"On a country road off of Exit 148."

"If we took you back there, would you know exactly where it happened?"

"I doubt it." He wanted to appear helpful. "I'd try, though."

"About what time did the shooting happen?"

"I wasn't looking at the clock."

"Let's narrow it down. Before or after eight?"

"After, I'd say. Before nine."

"Tell me what happened."

"Some dudes in a pickup pulled alongside and just started shooting."

"Tell me about the pickup."

"It was dark." He pictured the gun rack. "Can't remember anything special about it. It was moving too fast for me to see a license plate."

"Did you recognize anybody?"

Drago pictured Fazel with his gold tooth. "As I said, it was dark, things happened fast. I couldn't see any faces."

"Can you describe the gun?"

"No."

"Let's narrow it down. A shotgun? An assault rifle? A handgun?"

Drago pictured the Luger. "Couldn't see it well enough, but probably not a rifle."

"You said neither you nor Mr. Royce lives in Angola. So what were you doing up there?"

Drago hesitated. "Rolie wanted to look at farmland. He's thinking of buying some."

"You were looking at farmland at night in the winter?"

"*He* was. I was just driving." Drago knew how stupid he sounded.

"Why were *you* driving?"

"That's what I do for him. I told you, he owns Summit

City Metals. He's rich, doesn't like to drive himself."

"How come you drove all the way back to Fort Wayne instead of taking him to the nearest emergency room?"

"I didn't know where a closer one was."

"Anything else you want to tell me?"

Drago shook his head. "I told you all I know."

"Sure you did." The detective closed his little notebook. "Well, you need to come to the police station tomorrow."

"Why?"

"Just talk to us. We'll have some more questions by then."

Drago was relieved to see Lexie and Steve approach. He stood up.

"Drago, are you all right?" Lexie asked, patting his arm. "My goodness, you've got glass in your hair, blood on your cheek."

"I'm okay." He didn't like being pitied. "How's Rolie doin'?"

"We haven't heard anything yet. By the way, this is Dave Powers and his wife Sheila. I think you and Steve have met."

Drago stood up, nodded at Steve and Sheila but didn't offer to shake hands with Dave Powers, explaining, "I've got blood on my hands." He watched Dave turn around to catch up with the detective heading for the door. When they stopped just inside the building to talk, Drago nodded in their direction. "Is Mr. Powers a cop?"

"He is," Steve said. "He's an old friend from high school, just happened to be at our house when Rolie called."

"You told him about the call?"

"Lexie had him on speaker, so Dave heard the whole thing. He's the cop who showed Lexie the security tape from Indianapolis."

Drago's heart sank. He remembered what his mother said about the man on the tape walking like a young guy with an attitude, but he was so nervous he didn't know if he could walk any other way without looking like he was faking it. He didn't want to walk out until the detective left -- Officer Powers too. All he wanted to do was get home to Lucy.

"I know this is upsetting for you, Drago," Lexie said, "but would you sit down a few minutes and tell us what happened?"

Drago reluctantly took his seat again and told them what he'd told the plainclothes detective.

When he was done, Lexie patted his hand. "What did you tell him about the debt Rolland said he was collecting?"

Drago shook his head. "Rolie said that?"

Lexie nodded. "We heard him. You must have too."

"I don't remember him saying that," Drago said stubbornly. "We took a drive because he was looking at farmland."

Lexie looked at him with a question in her eyes. "Farmland? At night? In the winter?"

Drago could see no way out of the foolish story he'd already told the detective. "That's what Rolie told me."

It was well after midnight before Lexie and Steve, joined by Matilda, could visit Rolland in the intensive-care unit. They were told by the surgeon that the chest wound had been repaired and the surgery was a success. "He's a lucky man," the surgeon said. "If the bullet had penetrated his chest a centimeter to the left, he probably wouldn't be alive."

Steve and Lexie drove the short distance back to Autumn

Ridge, leaving a tearful Matilda in the guest chair, determined to stay the night with her precious son.

44

This Is Your Lucky Night

Wednesday, April 1, 2009

Drago, his mother, and his aunt Ruth arrived at Elysian Fields near midnight on April Fool's Day, the Jeep loaded with flashlights, a metal detector, turf-cutting and trenching spades, trowels, gloves, an ax, duct tape, rope, a brush, plastic sheeting, and a tarp. Some grading had already begun on the site, but at midnight the earth-moving machines were idle of course. A rough dirt road had been cut in the direction of the grove, making it possible to pull the Jeep within a few yards of the spot where Ruth, taking her bearings from an outcropping of rock and the oak tree, thought Carver was buried. The sky happened to be clear but there was only a sliver of moon to provide light.

The women held flashlights while Drago ran the metal detector over the ground until it growled. He hoped that meant he had located the heavy silver chain his mother said Carver was still wearing when he was buried. Then he began digging through heavy, wet clay and hacking through tree roots, sweating and cursing all the while. Finally, he reached what looked like a moldy quilt and then a thick rope of tarnished metal. He put the spade down and pulled on heavy gloves. Like an archaeologist, he first used a trowel to move dirt, then when he felt something hard, a brush, and finally his hands, delicately flicking dirt aside until he uncovered a skull. The skull was facing away from him. He could see a hole in the back of it.

He sat back on his haunches and looked at his mother, who had covered her mouth with her hand. Ruth had her arm around Phyllis' shoulders. From what Drago could see of their faces, both women looked stricken; suddenly, they sank to their knees. "God forgive me," Phyllis murmured.

Still on his haunches, Drago gazed at the skull, searching his heart for some semblance of filial emotion but found none. He searched his memory for the face that went with the skull, but again he found nothing. No fond memories came flooding back, no regret at Carver's final destiny. In an old album he'd once been shown a photograph of Carver sitting on his haunches, just the way Drago was now doing, embracing the three-year-old boy standing in front of him. Had Carver felt love that day for his son? If he had, was it just for a moment? How could love be so fleeting?

He stood and shed his jacket, for despite the cold wind, he was sweating. This was a terrible job, exposing his father's remains so as not to expose his mother to judgment, but he would do it. Unlike his mother, he felt no need to seek or extend forgiveness.

It took several more hours of the dirtiest work Drago had ever done to uncover the skeleton and put the bones onto a plastic sheet. When one of the flashlights went out, he didn't have enough light left to be sure he found every bone, but he was getting tired and more and more disgusted with the task. If he missed a few bones so what? Finally, he called it quits.

It was almost four in the morning before the four of them -- three living, one dead -- were back on Gump Road, heading toward Phyllis' house in Huntertown, where Drago would deliver his mother and Ruth before heading to the Scrapyard to dispose of Carver's skeleton, now duct-taped in plastic sheeting, roped in a tarp, and fitted into a gigantic cardboard box. The car smelled like dirt and mold and something else, something unnameable.

They were only a couple miles from Phyllis' home when Drago saw the flashing lights of a police car in his rear view mirror. He swore under his breath, "What the hell!" He pulled into a driveway far enough that the patrol car could pull in behind him, rolled down his window, and waited to hear what was wrong.

"Evening," the patrolman said, approaching with his hand on his holstered gun. He was a guy in his fifties with a brush cut and a stocky build. Though he looked strong enough to wrestle alligators, his face was friendly.

"Evening, officer."

"Shut off the engine, please."

"Yes, sir."

The officer shone his flashlight into the car. When he saw the women, he nodded. "Who's with you?"

"My mother and aunt. Did I do something wrong?"

"Whose Jeep is this?"

"Mine."

"You have a tail light out, son."

"I didn't realize that."

"You want to show me your license, insurance, and

registration?"

"Yes, sir. My license is in my wallet, but the other two things are in the glove compartment."

"Why don't you step out and show me the license while your mother retrieves the other documents." Though the tone was polite, the statement wasn't a request but an order.

"Yes, sir."

While the officer was examining his license, Drago, out of the corner of his eye, watched his mother open the glove compartment, feel around, hesitate a second, then pull out a leatherette envelope containing his owner's manual. Had she touched the gun and realized she should pretend it wasn't there? "Are the insurance and registration cards in here?" she asked, holding out the envelope and slamming the glove compartment shut.

"Yeah," he said, taking a deep breath.

After the officer examined the documents, he looked at Drago. "Pendragon's a very unusual name. Are you the guy I saw at Dupont North a couple months ago?"

"I don't know who you saw. Am I?"

"Your boss got shot, isn't that right?"

Drago nodded.

"I talked to you a few minutes before the detective got there. Remember?"

"There was a lot going on -- ."

The officer cut him off. "Your papers look okay. Anything in this car I should know about? Guns, drugs, paraphernalia, anything like that?"

"No," Phyllis said. "My son's just taking us home. We live in Huntertown."

"Family night out, huh?"

Phyllis nodded. "We had a late dinner."

The officer looked at his watch. "At four in the morning?"

"It was at our" -- pointing to herself and Ruth in the back seat -- "sister's house in New Haven. We got to talking. The time got away from us."

The officer looked at Drago. "Mind if I have a look in the back?"

"For nothing but a tail light? Is that necessary?" Despite the cold, he was sweating again.

"Any reason you don't want to open up the back?"

"No. No reason." Drago reluctantly followed the police officer to the back. He fiddled with the door as if he'd forgotten how to open it. "Got a bunch of stuff in here."

The officer looked at the spades and trowels. "You a landscaper?"

"No. Did some gardening, that's all."

"Well, let me give you a tip. Clean those tools if you want them to work like they should." He stuck his head further into the Jeep, then quickly pulled back. "Whew! What were you doing? Burying a pet dog?"

Drago did his best to sound casual. "Course not. I'm taking my tools to Mom's house so I can grub out some old bushes for her. I'll clean the tools after I'm done." He tried to chuckle. "You know how it is, a mother who works all day and lives alone, her son the only man in her life." He hoped the officer had a soft spot for mothers.

The officer reached in and picked up the metal detector. "Got a hobby, son? I thought people only used these on beaches."

"You'd be surprised what's underground . . . what you can find in a cornfield." At the thought of what had been underground only a few hours ago, he was hit by the impulse to swivel his eyes toward the cardboard box sitting behind the equipment, tucked up against the back seat. What kind of story should he make up about what was in the box and why it shouldn't be opened? He hadn't thought of a thing when, suddenly, the officer turned and walked a couple of yards toward the patrol car, all the while speaking into his shoulder. "Where? . . . . Injuries? . . . . I'm on my way."

The officer hastily returned to the Jeep. "It's your lucky night, son. You can close that up. I've got to run to an accident at Union Chapel and Tonkel, so no ticket tonight." He touched Drago's arm. "Be a good citizen, get that tail light replaced tomorrow, hear me? And while you're at it, for the sake of your mother, you might want to clean those tools and fumigate the car. Smells like death in there."

Drago stood in the driveway, watching the officer throw his car into reverse until he reached Gump Road, then slam the car into drive, and roar away in the direction of Tonkel Road, lights flashing and siren screaming.

Drago wanted to scream himself. *What do you mean, for the sake of my mother? Everything I did tonight I did for her sake.*

45

Tiffany's Asian Bazaar

Friday, June 5, 2009

One more week, and Tiffany would open her new boutique in Covington Plaza. *Tiffany's Asian Bazaar* -- the red letters rendered in a fake Chinese font, the "i's" dotted with the yin-yang symbol in black and white -- had already been painted across the bottom of the show window, where a couple of headless mannequins were standing in awkward poses, waiting to be clad in something more than the chunky rough-cut jade necklaces draped around their truncated necks. Tomorrow Trent -- formerly Vicki's best friend, now her sister Cricket's -- would dress them in Cheongsam dresses and silk Happi coats, place white jade birds in their upraised hands, and set up a peony floor screen behind them.

The shop was attractively stocked with porcelain garden stools, glass bonsai trees, jade and ivory carvings, porcelain tea sets, cloisonne beads and knicknacks, Buddha heads, wall plaques, paper lanterns, silk kimonos, and a rosewood dining table with eight Ming style chairs.

It was seven o'clock Friday evening when Tiffany, Cricket, Lucy, and Trent called it a day. Seated in the rosewood Ming chairs at one end of the table, they were drinking cheap champagne and giggling about what fun it was to open a smart Asian shop.

"If this was my place,"Trent said, getting up to adjust one of the chunky necklaces for the tenth time, "I'd call it *The Pink Lantern.*" Turning dramatically to face the girls, he held up his half-empty champagne flute. "Remember when we used to drink Bloody Marys at Vicki's on Friday nights?"

"I like champagne better, even though it gives me a headache," Lucy said.

"Where's that handsome husband of yours tonight, Lucy?"Trent asked.

"Drago's working at the Scrapyard now, but" -- checking her watch -- "he promised to be home by eight-thirty and we're going out to dinner."

"Has Rolie recovered from being shot?"

Cricket spoke up before Lucy could respond. "I talked to him yesterday. He said he's still in a lot of pain."

"Milking it," Lucy said. "That's what Drago says." She wanted to return to the subject of Vicki. "Cricket, tell me again about the palm reader. I wish I'd been there."

This was Cricket's favorite story, and she had told it many times. Her sister's death had caused great grief, of course, but now that she was the only child in her parents' life, she was the center of their attention, a circumstance she enjoyed to the hilt. She also enjoyed replacing Vicki in their circle of friends; Trent was now her private sherpa, willing to do anything for her. Telling stories about Vicki caused less and less pain with each recital, especially when Trent was present to make it feel like performance art. Cricket got up, removed a few necklaces from one of the mannequins, and draped them around her neck. "Mama Bee came in late, draped in layers of gauzy stuff, wearing pounds and pounds of ethnic necklaces." Then she walked over to Lucy and took her hands. "First, she told us that she learned to read palms in India. Then she said the left hand is what the gods gave us, the right hand is what we do with it. All of us had our palms read before Vicki, who was last. Mama Bee examined Vicki's hand over and over, even using a little flashlight because the lines in her hand were so faint -- ."

"Because she had an air hand," Trent interrupted. "Mine is water, Cricket's is fire."

"That's right," Cricket said, taking her seat again. "She said Vicki was a romantic and always had been, was in love and had been in love in all her past lives."

"She was very experienced in the romance department," Trent added.

"How did Mama Bee know about Vicki's past lives?" Lucy asked.

Cricket was patient. "Because that's the art of palm reading."

"Karmic past," Trent explained. "What goes around comes around, you know."

"I know what karma means," Lucy said, "but I still don't understand how anybody can know the past unless they lived it, especially just by looking at a hand."

Cricket resumed. "Well, I can't explain it any better than I already have. Then Mama Bee said Vicki was smart -- ."

"Not exactly," Trent said. "She said Vicki had a thirst for knowledge, especially about the occult."

"That's right," Cricket continued. "She said she was going to open a boutique -- ."

"A *New Age* boutique," Trent said.

"What is this, Trent?" Lucy laughed. "Were you taking notes or something?"

"I have a photographic memory."

Cricket smiled a little tentatively and took a deep breath. "Trent does. He really does. Anyway, then Mama Bee told Vicki a big change was coming in her life."

"What kind of change?" Lucy asked. Though she knew the answer, she never tired of hearing it.

"The big change involved a man, Mama Bee said, and a surprise trip to a faraway place."

"So, Cricket, what did Vicki think that meant?"

"Marriage to Steve Wright and a honeymoon on St. Kitts, of course."

"She must have been thrilled."

"She was, but then Mama Bee looked at the Girdle of Venus . . . it was the Girdle of Venus wasn't it, Trent?"

He nodded.

"She said there'd be some kind of difficulty -- ."

"Obstacle," Trent said. "She'd face some kind of obstacle. Mama Bee was very specific about that."

Cricket nodded, holding up a finger of explication. "But she would overcome it because she was good at manipulating people."

"Which we all agreed with," Trent added. "Don't forget, Cricket, that Mama Bee said Vicki would become famous as a result of overcoming the obstacle."

"Which she has, now that her face is on billboards advertising a big reward for information about her death."

"That last part bothers me," Lucy said. "Everything came true in a way. A big change involving a man: death at the hands of her killer. A trip to a faraway place: the spirit world. An obstacle: encountering the killer alone. And fame: the billboard advertising a reward for information leading to a conviction in her murder. But Mama Bee missed the crucial fact -- Vicki didn't manipulate her way out of the problem, or she'd still be alive."

"Maybe she couldn't," Tiffany mused. "The obstacle was just too big to overcome."

"Maybe she didn't recognize the obstacle," Lucy said.

"What do you mean, Lucy?" Trent asked. "There must have been at least a moment before Vicki died when she knew what was going to happen."

"But it must have been too late by then, don't you think?" Tiffany asked stubbornly.

"Knowing my sister as I did," Cricket said, "I'm sure she did know what was coming because she was very intuitive, very attuned to higher vibrations. I'm also sure she tried her best to manipulate the man."

"But all of you are missing the point," Tiffany insisted. "Vicki didn't manipulate her way around the obstacle, so with regard to the most important part of Vicki's future, the palm reader was dead wrong."

Lucy clapped her hand over her mouth. "You didn't say that, Tiffany."

"Sorry. It just came out wrong."

"You know the regret of my life?" Cricket asked, looking at each of her friends in turn and waiting for someone to ask.

Trent volunteered, though he knew the answer. "What, Cricket?"

"That Mama Bee didn't have her crystal ball with her. She called it the space-time dimension. With her crystal ball, she could have seen the future. Then Vicki would have known what to be on the lookout for."

Trent shook his finger at Tiffany. "You know what you should do at the opening? Invite Mama Bee so all your new customers can have five minutes with her."

"I don't know about that. Mama Bee was wrong about the most important event in Vicki's life."

"But she was right about most of the things that happened to Vicki. Think of it as a public service. It'll be a big attraction."

Tiffany squirmed. "I'll think about it. I'd rather have a *feng shui* expert come."

"Not practical," Trent said, irritated that his marketing idea had been rejected. "What could such an expert possibly say in five minutes that would help anybody?"

About as much as the palm reader did. "Anyway," Tiffany resumed, "I don't want to argue and I hate talking about the past. What I want to know is who did it to Vicki so we all know who to be on the lookout for."

"Well, Dad said it wasn't Steve Wright. The DNA results are back and they don't match either blood or semen. But Dad said an Internet search showed that a dozen registered sex offenders live within two miles of her house, including one guy who just got out of prison, so they're being questioned and asked to volunteer DNA samples if they hadn't already given them when they were arrested." Cricket shivered. "The thing you won't believe is most of the offenders are old, over forty. Can you imagine -- being raped by an old guy?"

"For heaven's sake, Cricket!" Tiffany exclaimed. "Who wants to be raped by anybody, young or old? And then strangled!" She looked at her watch and jumped up. "Sorry to make an early night of it, but my financial guy is coming in a few minutes, so you have to get out of here."

"La-de-da, Tiffany!" Lucy stood up. "You have a financial guy?"

"How else did you think I found the money for the shop?"

"How about your boyfriend?"

Tiffany waved her hand dismissively. "He's rich but cheap."

"But he bought you that new mansion on Forest Park."

Tiffany wasn't about to disclose the truth about that transaction. "And that's where all his money has gone." She made a double whisk broom of her hands. "Now scat, girls. I've got to clean off my desk in back so he thinks I'm organized and reliable."

Trent laughed, a little too loudly. "Well, good luck with that. What's his name?"

"Why do you want to know?"

"Just in case I ever need a financial guy."

"His name's a secret, Trent. If I told you, I might as well shout it from the rooftop."

Trent pretended to pout, though he was proud of being the most popular gossip in his circle. "Me? You know I'd never tell one soul -- not one."

Lucy put her hands on his back and pushed him out the door. "We all know you wouldn't tell *one* person but you would tell twenty." Lucy, Cricket, and Trent made their laughing way to the parking lot just as the bell rang on the back service door of the shop.

* * * * *

Tiffany let the bell ring again and again until she saw her friends get in Trent's car and drive away. Then she locked the front door and spent a few seconds before a full-length mirror, adjusting her bra and tucking in a wisp of hair that had escaped from the bun she'd secured with miniature ivory chopsticks. Men liked taking a pretty bra off and letting a woman's hair down. When the bell rang for the sixth time, she ran to the back of the shop and pushed the heavy metal door outward, again pulling Bob in as if they were making a spy movie.

"Napp-ing," she whispered, taking his briefcase and setting it near her desk. She generously let him hold her in his arms for almost a minute. "When it gets dark I'll take you to the front so you can see the progress."

"I don't care about the progress of the store."

Tiffany pouted. "My beautiful shop. I owe it all to you."

"Just teasing. Of course I care about the shop, and I'm glad I can take care of you. But it's your beauty I want to admire. May I?" he asked, tugging at one of the sticks in her hair.

"Take them out."

After he removed the sticks, she shook her head and gave him a flirtatious look. "I have champagne."

"Later." He let the sticks fall to the floor and ran his fingers through her silky hair. "You smell so good. What are you wearing?"

"*Organza Indecence* by Givenchy," she murmured, butchering a French accent.

He threw his head back to smile at her. "Indecent! I like that."

She laughed, pushing her hand down his trousers.

"Something else is indecent, I see."

"That's me," he panted.

She backed up. "Let's take it slow this time. We have an hour."

"I don't know if I can take it slow, darling girl." He knew what she meant, though. The first time he'd come to the shop, he'd been in a hurry and it had not gone well, so why not try something different this time? Why not try acting like a sophisticated man who knew his way around a bed?

He tried conjuring up the atmosphere of a Shanghai brothel, which wasn't hard, for the Chinese wedding bed was draped in gauze and the pink lanterns glowed seductively. Still, as he watched Tiffany undress herself, then him, he knew he was losing steam. The more she did to excite him, the less desire he felt. Once they were rolling around on the Chinese wedding bed, he was completely limp. Bob sweated and strained and tried to picture that brothel again but he simply had no mo-jo, none at all.

Nothing was working the way it should. Twice now, he'd failed. He couldn't believe it: he never failed at anything. For the risk he was taking, both with his financial empire and his marriage, he deserved this luscious reward, and it lay right here, within his grasp. He wanted it so much. But Tiffany might as well be in China as on this beautifully carved bed for all he enjoyed the moment.

When he finally left the shop, having taken the guided tour without registering anything he saw or hearing a word Tiffany said, and then drinking a glass of the worst champagne he'd ever tasted, he was subdued and humiliated. He felt like a dried-up husk of a man, old and useless. And really, really angry with God. Why give a man his most precious organ if it wasn't going to salute a goddess when by magic she appeared in his life, ready for the taking?

46

Suckered Again

Friday, June 5, 2009

Ferrell was so frustrated he wanted to destroy something. At Tiffany's insistence, he was trying to install closet fixtures in a storage room adjoining the master bedroom closet in the house on Forest Park. Tiffany needed the closet expansion for all her clothes and shoes. Though he was an engineer, he could not interpret the badly translated instructions for assembly, and he kept misplacing screws and tools. He was a klutz in the presence of the material world.

Without consulting him, Tiffany had had a huge safe installed at the back of the closet without, apparently, considering the layout of the hanging poles and shelves she ordered, and now nothing appeared to fit the rough plan she had drawn for him. He had measured over and over and even cut himself on the metal tape measure when he engaged the rewind mechanism. He had earlier cut himself with a box cutter as he opened package after package of rails and rail covers. Furthermore, the rough wooden floor was slightly concave in front of the safe, and every time he went near it, the floor creaked alarmingly. He was afraid the safe would fall through to the kitchen. Why hadn't the safe installer noticed the problem?

When he heard the alarm beep twice as the door from the garage was opened, he knew Tiffany was home. At last! She was so damn preoccupied with the boutique in Covington Plaza she seemed to have forgotten about him and was almost never home when he arrived after teaching his night classes. He sat down in a corner of the closet, waiting for her to come upstairs, but after five minutes, he realized she wasn't coming up. So he went down, fuming.

He found her in the kitchen, opening a bottle of wine. "It's about time, Tiffany."

She smiled at him. "Yonja. You look like you've been working."

"More than you know. That bloody closet plan of yours sucks."

"Maybe you should hire a handy man." She walked over to him and caressed his cheek. "A big-time professor like you shouldn't be fixing up a closet."

Was she making fun of him, a big-time professor? An engineer who couldn't put a closet together? A man too cheap to hire an installer? "I'm perfectly capable of doing the work, Tiffany, but some things take four hands and you weren't here."

"So it isn't ready yet?"

"No." *It hasn't even been started.*

"How about a glass of wine?"

"No."

"Macallan?"

He sat down in a chair. "Okay."

"Ice?"

"Neat."

When she handed him a cut-glass tumbler half-full of scotch, he drew her onto his lap. It was hard to stay mad at her. He put his nose in her hair, then her neck. "Where've you been? Who've you been with? You smell like aftershave."

She drew her head away and laughed. "Trent was at the shop with Lucy and Cricket. I think he uses a whole bottle of scent every time he showers." She suddenly grabbed his wrist. "Did you cut your fingers?"

"Yes, my little princess. On the measuring tape and box cutter."

She laughed. "My big, smart engineer cuts himself on a measuring tape."

"It's not funny, Tiffany."

"It's a little funny."

"You've been at the shop all day?"

"Of course. Working like a dog."

"What's this praise for a dog? Don't your people eat dogs?"

She made a face. "My people were civilized when yours were running around in blue paint, worshiping trees and losing to the Romans."

He scoffed. "Your version of history is a little self-congratulatory, so I'd stick with engineering if I were you." He sipped his scotch. "Have your parents taken a look yet at what their money is buying?"

"No. I'm going to surprise them."

"I thought they were saving their money to expand their take-out shop."

"They were, but they want to see me happy."

"Is Xiu-Xiu lending you money too?"

Tiffany got off his lap and took a chair kitty-cornered from his. "No. She's very selfish, you know. She only thinks about herself."

"I don't understand why you're giving up a professional career to run a silly bazaar."

"Yonja! It's not a silly bazaar. It's beautiful. You should see it."

He stood up. "Before I pass out, I want you to go upstairs with me and show me how your plan is supposed to work now that the safe has been installed."

"If you promise not to do any more work after that, okay."

He pulled her to her feet. "I promise. I need a payoff for my hard work."

"Let me refresh our drinks first, okay?"

He smiled. "You do that, but don't keep me waiting. I'm knackered."

By the time she entered the closet, he was growing angry again. He was holding a bundle of track rails to be mounted on the walls for hanging shelving units. "Where the hell do these go now?"

"What do you mean?"

"Where the safe is means there isn't room for the units to be hung on either side." He looked at the floor. "And you'll notice the floor is sagging."

"No, it isn't."

"Why do we need a safe anyway?"

"For jewelry and papers. You know that."

"It should have been put in a corner." He stepped in front of the safe and stomped up and down, still holding the track rails. "See how weak the floor is? The safe is too heavy."

Suddenly, with a great cracking sound, the floor gave way beneath him. Ferrell tried to throw himself backward and then grab something solid but events moved too fast. He found himself falling through the floor right into the kitchen, track rails flying everywhere. The noise of his own screams, the clash of metal hitting metal and ceramic tile, the roar of breaking wood filled his ears. Lying on the kitchen table in the breakfast nook, writhing in pain, covered in plaster dust and wood fragments, he was so stunned he couldn't speak.

He looked up at Tiffany, peering through the hole in the kitchen ceiling.

"Are you okay, Yonja?"

"No," he grunted.

"You shouldn't have stomped."

Ferrell gritted his teeth and sucked in a big breath. "I need help," he roared.

"Open your mouth. I'll pour some scotch down."

"Oh, God, you stupid cow, stop horsing around." He was screaming now. "I think I broke my back. You're going to pay for this."

"I'll be right down. You want me to call 911?"

"No. If you value your life, get down here."

Another great cracking sound filled his ears, and as debris began raining down again, Ferrell suddenly realized that the safe might follow him to the kitchen. Fortunately, he hadn't broken his back. He rolled off the table and crawled toward the middle of the room just before the safe plummeted to the floor, transforming the kitchen into a demolition site. He was so angry that when Tiffany arrived in the kitchen and knelt to help him to his feet, he signaled his pain, humiliation, and fury by grabbing her arms in a viselike grip.

She cried out in pain and tried to jerk away.

He gripped her arms all the harder. "Shut up. I'm the one who paid the price for that ridiculous closet of yours. Now it's your turn."

It wasn't until a few days later that Ferrell learned from an inspector that he'd fallen through the space where, many years earlier, the old maid's staircase had been removed without the installation of supporting joists.

Once again, both Lexie and Tiffany had suckered him.

47

A Gentleman's Game

Saturday, June 27, 2009

At seven-thirty in the morning on the last Saturday in June -- a hot, sunny day, unusually still, without a cloud in the sky -- Steve Wright and Dave Powers were milling around with other golfers outside the Clubhouse at the Autumn Ridge Golf Club. It was the second day of the tournament Bob Passwatter was sponsoring to fund a scholarship in Vicki Grinderman's memory. Given their standings as a result of the opening rounds on Friday, Steve and Dave were now playing against Bob Passwatter and Ferrell Hawke.

"What should I know about Passwatter and Hawke?" Dave asked.

"Passwatter is a financial genius, or at least that's what he wants the world to think. My guess is, he cheats at everything. Hawke is an engineering professor. He fancies himself a great athlete, but I'll be surprised if he has the discipline and power to be a good golfer."

"You think the professor cheats too?"

"He will if his performance doesn't match the view he has of himself." Steve turned his head aside. "Warning. The professor's approaching."

"You guys ready to battle the Hawk? I'm Ferrell Hawke, by the way," he said, extending his hand to Dave.

"Dave Powers."

"I noticed you yesterday. I take it you work for Steve."

Dave shook his head. "No. I'm a detective."

"Private?"

"Again, no. Police Department."

"Oh, well, somebody's got to do it. It must make it hard to pay the entry fee though. Two fifty! I had to think twice about it myself."

Dave smiled. "I can manage."

Ferrell winked conspiratorially. "I'll bet. Confiscate a pound or two of heroin off some poor Mexican drug dealer who can't speak English or produce his papers, then turn around and sell it on the street . . . . I know what you guys are up to."

Dave wasn't easily rattled. "We're going to talk a little smack, are we? This is supposed to be a friendly game for charity. By the way, what's that accent?"

"British. The Queen's English. Some call it BBC English. You probably call it upper-crust."

"Actually, I don't, but is there a lower-crust English?"

"Yeah. Yours. You can't hear yourself, of course, but the American accent, like Cockney and Aussie, grates on the nerves of the educated."

"Clever observation. It goes both ways for us." Dave pointed at Ferrell's chest. "I've never seen a shirt that stylish out here."

"UKKO polo in Palace Blue. Again, upper-crust British."

You've made your point, you jerk. "So what are you doing

in our country, Ferrell?"

"I'm a professor of engineering at IPFW." Ferrell extracted a TaylorMade R9 TP iron and began some practice swings. "Did you see my hole-in-one yesterday?"

"I heard about it," Steve said, watching Ferrell smashing imaginary balls. *That's a great iron, but you don't have a smooth, athletic swing to go with it.* "Very lucky."

"Oh-ho! The little green monster is out and about. Luck had nothing to do with it, old chap. It was brilliant, and it wasn't my first. So what's the best score either of you ever shot?"

Steve was annoyed. "What are we, in fourth grade?"

"I think it's a fair question. I hate wasting my time with amateurs. Mine was a sixty-nine at St. Andrews in 2004."

"Without cheating, I take it."

Ferrell smirked. "A man who mentions cheating has to be watched." He held out his rule book. "I have the rules right here, so you two better watch your p's and q's."

"So what's your handicap?" Steve asked, wishing he could grab the son-of-a-bitch by the collar again and march him to his car.

"Thirteen."

"Isn't that a little high if you're that good?"

Ferrell was saved from having to give an explanation by the arrival of Bob, who was carrying a Louis Vuitton golf bag filled with Ping golf clubs. The John Lobb golf shoes and Romeo 2 Oakley sunglasses did nothing for Bob's Lily Pulitzer socks, green plaid golf trousers, and seagrass kangol. He looked like he was making a sappy Robert Redford movie. "You're late, old chap."

Bob briefly removed his cap and wiped his head with a

towel. "As the sponsor, I have things to do. Everybody wants a piece of me."

"We were just talking about handicaps, Bob."

"Mine's a seventeen. It'd be lower if I had the time to play more often."

"Well, it certainly looks like you have the right equipment."

"Anything I do, I do well." He reached into his golf bag and held up a ball. "Titleist Pro V, monogrammed. I like to know I'm carrying the best balls ever made."

Dave couldn't help laughing. "Don't we all?"

Bob replaced the ball and pulled out a Bushnell PinSeeker. "My eyes aren't the best, so I'm going to use this, if you don't mind."

"May I see that?" Dave asked. After a few seconds, he said, "You're not supposed to use things like that in tournament play."

"Well, I did yesterday and nobody complained. Besides, as the sponsor, I think I'm entitled to set the rules myself."

Steve pointed to Bob's very expensive golf bag. "You could buy a Porsche with the money you've got sunk into this equipment."

"I have a Porsche."

"Well, there you go. So what kind of money do you think you'll raise for the memorial fund, Bob?" Steve asked.

"The whole amount I promised the Judge: ten thousand."

"So you get credit for a ten thousand dollar memorial fund you didn't pay for?"

Bob bristled. "You have no idea how much work it was, or how much it cost me, to put this tournament together, to put the billboards up."

"What did you spend on all those billboards advertising this tournament, showing you in full golf regalia, swinging a club as if you were Sam Sneed? I've seen half a dozen of them at least."

"You have a few billboards up too."

"Yeah, but I'm not on them. Mine advertise a reward for information leading to a conviction in the murder of Vicki Grinderman, picturing only her, not me. My name isn't even mentioned on them."

"Then you missed a business opportunity, my friend. Never let a good deed be done in secret, not in this economy anyway." He pointed his finger at Steve. "It's fitting, I think, that you of all people paid two hundred fifty dollars to play."

Steve cocked his head, pretending he didn't understand. "How's it fitting?"

"You were Vicki's fiancé -- ."

"We weren't engaged."

"And I hear you haven't been entirely cleared, so it's blood money, isn't it? Isn't that what the reward's about too? A diversion?"

Now Dave was getting annoyed. "Where'd you hear that?"

"Around town. It's still the hottest talk going. People don't believe Steve had nothing to do with that poor girl's demise."

"Very stupid talk." Dave held out his hand to Bob. "By the way, we haven't met yet. Dave Powers."

"Robert Passwatter. Call me Bob."

"Very kind of you, Bob. But I'd watch the accusations, if I were you. I'm with the Fort Wayne Police Department, and in light of the DNA tests eliminating Steve, I know just how stupid that particular rumor is. We call that slander."

Bob took a step back. "I didn't say I believed it. Steve should know what's being said about him. That's what friends do for friends."

With friends like you, who needs enemies? "Steve knows. But I'm glad to hear you don't believe it and won't repeat it again. So," Dave said, "let's flip for who keeps score the first nine holes."

"We'll go last," Bob said.

Of course. Then you can figure out how much you have to cheat to win. "Very generous, Bob," Dave said wryly, "but we're going to flip." He took out a silver dollar. "What's your call?"

"Heads we go last," Ferrell said.

Dave flipped the coin and turned it over on his hand. "Sorry, tails. So you go first."

Ferrell grabbed the coin. "Is there a head on this plug?"

Dave pocketed the coin with amusement. Ferrell was a sore loser.

As they drove to the first tee, Dave said to Steve, "I think we'd better keep an eye on these braggarts. I'll bet the score we keep won't match theirs."

Steve and Dave had played with cheats before, but none like Bob and Ferrell. On the first hole, Bob pretended he didn't have to finish the putt and simply declared he'd done it, though he was seven feet from the cup. Dave reminded him that in tournament play he couldn't do that. Bob retorted that as the sponsor of the tournament, he'd do what he wanted, but in fact he didn't do it again.

On the second tee, after a few practice swings, Ferrell stepped up, swung, and missed but did not count his whiff as a stroke. Steve reminded him to count the whiff but Ferrell indignantly protested that though it might have looked like he was teeing off, he was really still just practicing.

When Ferrell landed in high grass, he kicked the ball to a better lie before pretending to find it. When Dave said it looked as if he'd kicked the ball, Ferrell hotly denied it.

Bob finished the third hole with a Maxfli rather than the monogrammed Titleist he started with. Steve reminded him that that little trick cost him the entire hole. Bob said he was dead wrong, claiming that the Maxfli was his, a leftover from a game he played the week before, and he'd pulled it out by mistake.

On the fifth hole, Dave stealthily counted the clubs in both Bob's and Ferrell's bags; Ferrell had fifteen, one over the limit. Dave decided not to call him on it -- a two-stroke penalty for each hole -- until the entire round was over.

On the seventh hole, Ferrell asked Dave what club he used. Dave retorted that Ferrell had to record a penalty against himself just for asking. Ferrell denied that such a rule existed.

"Let's have a look at the rule book you were waving around," Dave said.

Ferrell was furious. "I can't be held accountable for a rule I've never heard of and that makes no sense." He was scornful. "It was obviously just a friendly question, since I have no real interest in an amateur's answer."

The next nine holes when Dave and Steve were keeping score were played no cleaner. Bob and Ferrell furtively changed the lie of their balls whenever they were in tall grass or sand. Instead of measuring the right distance from water hazards, they simply dropped their balls wherever they pleased. More than once, they ended a hole with a ball different from the one they started with. But, at least this time, for the last nine holes, the official scorecard was accurate.

Then came the clincher. Dave and Steve waited with bemusement until their opponents had signed their scorecards. Then Steve pointed out that Bob hadn't added his score correctly, though by signing he'd affirmed it was correct. That disqualified him altogether. Bob protested that he was tired and had simply made an understandable error and as the sponsor couldn't be disqualified. Dave then again made an elaborate point of counting Ferrell's fifteen clubs -- a two-stroke penalty for every hole.

"I had an extra iron, that's all, and I didn't even use it. So what does it matter?"

"You want me to show you the rules again?" Dave asked, reaching for the rule book.

"No, I don't, prick." Ferrell pulled out an iron and held it at a threatening angle. "You know what I want to do with this?"

Dave smiled. "I can guess. But in America, golf is a gentleman's game." He lowered his voice so no one else could hear. "We don't call each other prick here -- you ponce."

Ponce? He wasn't effeminate at all. In fact, he was the straightest man he knew. Ferrell fumed but lowered the club. A racial epithet was on the tip of his tongue but he was afraid to spit it out. He was the tallest man in the foursome, but not the strongest, so fighting with either Steve or Dave was sure to end in humiliation. He turned on his heel, picked up his overloaded golf bag, and walked to the parking lot to throw it into the trunk of his Aston Martin.

When he turned around, Bob was waiting for him. "You son of perdition, how stupid can you get, putting an extra iron in your bag!"

"And you can't add an effing golf score, which is a little odd for a self-proclaimed financial genius, a master of the universe. Monday I'm coming to your office and if you don't return my money, every last penny, right then and there, I'll sue your ugly socks off."

"You aren't going to sue anybody."

Ferrell felt his blood-pressure rising to the stratosphere. "I am. You owe me that prize, you ponce." *There! How do you like that? Now I'm not the ponce.*

Though they continued to argue and exchange insults for another five minutes, they parted without blows. Neither was a master of fisticuffs.

Primed for a fight he could win, Ferrell finally made his way back to The Grill Room to see if could get up a poker game. Nobody was better at poker than he was, and he needed to recover his entry fee.

48

Where Is Tiffany?

Sunday, June 28, 2009

Xiu-Xiu returned to her Old Fort apartment Sunday around noon, exhausted from the long flight from Hawaii to Los Angeles, then to Chicago, where she had a long layover, then on to Indianapolis, and finally to Fort Wayne. She'd had to buy an extra duffel bag just to hold the sundresses, shorts, sandals, lingerie, silk scarves, designer handbags, hand-painted sarongs, and Tahitian pearl necklaces she'd bought both for herself and Tiffany Jean.

She threw her cases into the bedroom, then made her way to the kitchen, where she saw the yellow light flashing on her phone. She had seventeen messages. She made herself a pitcher of iced tea, then sat down to listen to them. She was surprised to hear Ferrell's voice on the last message. "Xiu-Xiu, this is Ferrell, Saturday night, 11:30. Tiffany isn't home. I drove to the shop but she isn't there. I called your parents but they haven't seen her. Is she with you? Do you know where she is?" There was a pause and then a sigh. "I was at Autumn Ridge all day, playing in a golf tournament. This morning she said she'd be working in the shop, but she isn't there. Call me."

Xiu-Xiu decided to open the sliding door to the balcony for some fresh air, shower, change clothes, unpack, throw some things in the washing machine, and pick up Miss Lila before calling Ferrell. Maybe Tiffany had finally had enough and left the Hawk. It would serve him right. And now that her sister had the shop, she could support herself.

Finally, around seven, she returned from eating a lobster sandwich and watching ducks on the river at The Boardwalk. Pouring herself a glass of pinot grigio, and pulling Miss Lila onto her lap, she called Ferrell. "This is Xiu-Xiu. I got your message about Tiffany."

"Where've you been, for Christ's sake? Why didn't you call earlier?"

Xiu-Xiu bristled at his peremptory tone. "I just got back from ten days in Hawaii. I couldn't have called earlier."

"Well, so where is Tiffany?"

"I have no idea. Why don't you know?"

"I can't get hold of her. She's not answering her cell phone."

"Did you hit her again?"

"Hit her? What are you talking about?"

"She showed me the bruises. Maybe she left. Maybe she's hiding from you."

"I never touched her -- not in anger, I mean. I don't hit women."

"I told her to leave if you ever hit her again."

He couldn't keep from shouting. "How dare you tell her that! I told you I never hit her -- not ever."

"I don't know then why she'd leave you."

"Stop saying that. She hasn't left me. She better not

have left me."

"Slow down, Ferrell, and stop screaming. With that accent I can hardly understand you."

"What are you talking about? I'm not screaming and I speak the Queen's English, which is more than you do."

"You're getting off the subject. Tiffany has an office in the back of her shop. Did you go into her shop and look in the office?"

"No. I don't have a key."

"So how do you know she isn't there, Ferrell?"

"It was dark. I looked in the front window but nobody was there."

"You can't see the office from the front of the shop."

"Okay, okay. Do you have a key to the shop?"

"No. Our parents might. Ask them. Or hire a locksmith."

"What about her friends? You have their names and numbers?"

Xiu-Xiu decided to lie. "No. I'd know them if I saw them but they're not in my personal phone book. Check Tiffany's."

"Her purse is gone. So is her BlackBerry and her phone. She must have them with her."

"Look on her computer, Ferrell. She probably has a list of friends there."

"I don't have her password."

"You live with her and don't have her password?"

"So shoot me."

"Well, that's an idea, but other than that, I'm empty. My guess is she's run away for awhile and will come back when she's good and ready."

Unfortunately, for once in her life, Xiu-Xiu was wrong.

Just before going to bed at midnight, she opened the door to her office to get some cash for the next day. After turning on the light, it took a second to comprehend what she was seeing.

Her sister was lying on the floor, her arms flung out, staring blankly at the ceiling. She was naked except for a lacy thigh-high stocking encasing one leg. The other stocking was tied around her neck so tight that Xiu-Xiu wouldn't have known what the ligature was except that the lacy top of the stocking hung down on her chest. The face of her once beautiful sister was, in death, grotesque, the stuff of nightmares. One side of her face was bruised, as were her upper chest and both of her arms.

Xiu-Xiu stumbled backward and stepped on something -- Tiffany's black Brahmin purse. Then she noticed that her sister's red Cheongsam dress was draped neatly over the desk chair but her embroidered mules lay yards apart as if lost in a struggle. Xiu-Xiu could see no underwear.

Xiu-Xiu screamed and screamed. Choking back the urge to vomit, she knelt to feel for a pulse but instinctively knew from the condition of her sister's face that it was a useless gesture.

How long had her sister been on the floor? What had happened? Who had strangled her? What was Tiffany doing in her apartment? How did she get in? For that matter, how did the killer get in or know Tiffany was here? It looked like she'd removed her dress willingly, so did she know her attacker? What had gone so wrong?

The horror of having walked around the apartment for hours with no inkling that her dead sister lay in the office hit her like a hammer. Blissfully ignorant of just how close

Tiffany was, she'd told Ferrell that her sister was probably just in hiding and would return when she was ready. How could she not have felt the presence of death a few yards away?

Stumbling backward out of her office, she fell onto her sofa in the living room and stared into space. It must have been Ferrell. All that elaborate pretense on the phone about not knowing where his girlfriend was, calling people, going to the shop, pretending he didn't know what had happened! He was just setting up an alibi, wasn't he? She'd never liked the man, and she knew from Tiffany that he was capable of violence -- but murder? That much evil she wouldn't have guessed. Obviously, Tiffany hadn't guessed it either.

Then guilt assailed her like a cold east wind. The moment Tiffany showed her the bruises on her arms at Red Robin, as a good sister she should have insisted Tiffany leave Ferrell and stay in this apartment until she could get on her feet. Instead of buying so many guilt presents for Tiffany, she should have spent the money to take her to Hawaii, where she would have been safe.

Once again, trembling violently, Xiu-Xiu pulled Miss Lila onto her lap and picked up the phone, first to call the police, then Mr. Passwatter. When she could think of the right words for *mah mah* and *bah bah*, she would call them too. But let Ferrell find out however he might that the body had been discovered -- preferably in handcuffs.

49

An Awful Night

Sunday, June 28, 2009

To Xiu-Xiu's shock, her boss arrived before the police, wearing khakis and a polo shirt.

"How did you get here so fast, Mr. Passwatter? At this time of night?"

"God's looking out for us, my dear. I'm part of a street mission for the church and was delivering blankets to a woman's shelter a few blocks away." He extracted a big white handkerchief from his back pocket and wiped his forehead as if he'd run up the stairs instead of taking the elevator. "Did you check for a pulse?"

Xiu-Xiu nodded.

"Where is she?"

Xiu-Xiu pointed toward the office.

"Are you sure she's not still alive?" Without waiting for a response, he strode to the office door and opened it, walked in, knelt by the body, and felt for a pulse. Then he put his ear to her chest and finally started mouth-to-mouth resuscitation.

Xiu-Xiu stood in the doorway, horrified at having a

man -- her boss, no less -- see her sister's naked body, let alone touch it so intimately, even though his motives were obviously heroic. "Mr. Passwatter! Come out of there."

He looked up. "I took the Red Cross course, so it's worth a try, but I don't think it's going to work. She's really cold." He stayed in a kneeling position on the floor, looking around. "We need to cover her." Spying a knitted throw on an armchair, he ripped it off, unfolded it, and spread it over the body. "There. That's better. Now let's say a prayer."

"I don't think we're supposed to . . . contaminate . . . ."

Before she could finish the thought, the police were at her door. When one of them entered the room, Bob was on his feet, holding Tiffany's purse.

"What's going on here?"

"I'm just trying to help," Bob said. "I had to cover her and I was straightening up. The purse was right in the doorway and I almost walked on it when I came in." He bent down to pick up a shoe. "I checked her pulse, gave her mouth-to-mouth. Nothing."

The officer walked over and put his hand on Bob's shoulder. "This is a crime scene, sir."

"I know, I know."

"Then you know it shouldn't be disturbed. Put that down, please, don't touch anything else, and leave this room. Go sit down and wait, preferably on the balcony. We need to talk to you."

Bob bristled but retreated to the living room while a team of uniformed men and women processed the crime scene. A plainclothes detective debriefed him and Xiu-Xiu.

The last question the detective asked each of them was whether they had any idea what had happened.

Xiu-Xiu got up and again replayed Ferrell's message from Saturday night. She looked at the detective. "He's the only person who'd have a motive to harm Tiffany. He was often mad at her for spending so much money, and he'd hit her before. The first time she showed me the bruises, I told her to leave but she said she was a survivor and she'd stay with him until she was ready to leave. My theory is, she finally had enough of his abuse and left him. Maybe she was hiding out here, knowing I was on vacation, but Ferrell wasn't about to let her leave, so he followed her. They had an argument and then . . . ."

"But there's no sign of a break-in so she must have let him in. By the way, did she have a key to your apartment?"

"No. That's a puzzle. Only *mah mah* and *bah bah* do."

"We need to talk to them too."

"They don't even know yet. I don't know how to tell them." Xiu-Xiu began to cry.

Bob patted her shoulder. "I'll go with you. I won't let you face this alone."

"So," the detective said, turning his attention to Bob, "do you have anything to add to what Miss Chow has told us?"

"No. I wish I did. But I really didn't know Xiu-Xiu's sister. I'd met her once in my office, of course, but other than that . . . . Well, what I'm saying is, Ferrell isn't a bad guess, as far as I know. He's a very sore loser, as I found out Saturday at Autumn Ridge."

"Tell me about that."

"I sponsored a two-day golf tournament to raise money for a memorial scholarship in the name ofVicki Grinderman. Remember her?"

"Of course."

"Ferrell and I were partners in a foursome. Ironically, one of the men we were playing against, Steve Wright, is a suspect -- or at least was -- in Vicki's death, so don't write him off. Anyway, it wasn't a good outcome at the tournament, and Ferrell got so mad about the scorekeeping that we had an argument in the parking lot. I thought he was going to hit me with one of his clubs, so I walked away."

"The guy has a temper, is that what you're saying?"

"That's an understatement. Ferrell's a very sore loser. If Tiffany was really threatening to leave him, I can well imagine he might do something violent. And I can imagine why she'd want to leave. She had cancer, poor girl -- a very rare, aggressive cancer requiring treatment -- and Ferrell wouldn't give her the money for chemo."

Xiu-Xiu looked at her boss in shock. "She had cancer?"

Bob looked down. "I wasn't supposed to tell anyone but it doesn't matter now. She didn't want you and your parents to worry. The same kind of rare Asian cancer, she said, that your mother has. Do you know if she'd started treatment yet?"

"No." It was Xiu-Xiu's turn to look down, for it was she who'd made up the story about her mother's putative cancer so she could take an afternoon off from work when she wanted. She knew that Tiffany had gotten her hands on Ferrell's investment account with Bob's help, but she didn't know that Tiffany had pretended to need the money for cancer treatment. She needed time to think through the lies.

Bob looked at his silent assistant. "You need to stay somewhere tonight, my dear. I'm sure Clarissa would welcome you. Just let me call her first."

Xiu-Xiu shook her head. "Thanks, but I have to break

the news to my parents anyway, so as soon as the police are done, I'll drive over there and stay the night."

"Well, take the week off. Take all the time you need." Bob stood up and held out his hand to the detective. "You know where to find me, so call me if I can be of any further help. But I think you have two good suspects: Steve Wright and Ferrell Hawke."

Xiu-Xiu drove alone to her parents' house, where she spent an awful night. Ferrell's was worse.

50

Where Are the Drones?

Monday, June 29, 2009

Steve and Dave each collected a two-hundred-fifty dollar gift certificate to Andrew Davis, a high-end men's clothing store in Covington Plaza, as the prize for winning the charity golf tournament sponsored by Bob Passwatter. Steve wasted no time in taking advantage of it. Lexie had taught him a few things about the importance of his appearance. Besides, if he was going to secure the financing he needed and sell his concept for luxury living in a bad economy, he had to look like a confident, successful developer with superb taste.

Late Monday afternoon, Steve was finally done shopping. With Chris Lambert's help, he had selected two pairs of shoes: Donald Pliner loafers and Allen Edmonds wingtips. The Zanella flat-front slim trousers fit so well he ordered three pairs. He'd never heard of Eton shirts from Sweden, but he was so taken with the fabric and fit that he bought three casual shirts and two dressy ones, plus a couple of daringly colorful Italian sport shirts by Hickey Freeman. Until today, a cashmere sweater had never appeared in his closet; now there would be two. The graphic Yoder socks were so unusual he wasn't sure he could wear them, but when Chris said they were named for a Fort Wayne surgeon with a taste for distinctive footwear, he took another look and ended up buying half a dozen pairs. Handsome trousers required better belts, and fine shirts required better ties than he owned, so those joined the growing pile. He'd also been measured for a custom-made suit in a lightweight wool.

"You're one hell of a salesman, Chris. You sure you aren't Italian?"

"In my dreams. An Italian with a full head of hair and a swimmer's body."

"I came in here ready to cash in the gift certificate, maybe spend a little more, but," eying the huge assortment of clothes and accessories that were now his, "I think I've just spent as much as my first car cost." He picked up a sample bottle of Black Tie cologne and sprayed some into the air. "Is this guaranteed to make a man irresistible?"

Chris laughed. "It's always worked for me."

Just then, a clerk from another store stepped in to speak to him. "Did you hear about that poor girl who opened the Asian bazaar at the other end of the mall?"

"No."

"Her body was found in her sister's apartment last night."

Steve turned around. "I couldn't help overhearing that. You mean Tiffany Chow, Ferrell Hawke's girlfriend?"

"I don't know whose girlfriend she was."

"How did she die? When?"

"Sometime over the weekend, apparently. Her sister got back from vacation and found her, but I haven't heard yet how she died."

Suddenly someone was tugging at Steve's arm. He

turned around. "Jean! What are you doing here?"

"I came to buy Dwight a birthday present, but I'm glad to run into you."

"Did you hear about Ferrell's girlfriend?"

"The Asian girl I saw him with at Vicki's funeral? She's the sister of Bob Passwatter's Girl Friday, isn't she?"

Steve nodded. "Tiffany Chow."

"No, I haven't heard anything. What about her?"

The clerk repeated his announcement. "Yesterday her sister found her body."

"You're kidding." Jean put her hand over mouth. "Boy, that puts me out of the mood for shopping."

Jean, however, didn't leave until Steve did. She walked out with him, then asked, "Would you mind having a drink with me at Chop's, maybe an appetizer or something?"

"Lexie won't be back until tomorrow, so that's fine. I've got to eat anyway."

"I'll follow you over there."

The two booths in Chop's bar were often reserved by five o'clock, but they managed to snag the back booth. Its position and high back gave them privacy.

"I'm in shock, aren't you, Steve?"

"The death of someone as young as Tiffany is always shocking, especially if it wasn't natural."

"You think it was murder?"

"Well, that comes to mind, doesn't it?"

"First Vicki, then Tiffany," Jean said, studying the menu.

"You think their deaths are connected?"

Jean looked up. "Both young, female, single, pretty, good families. They knew each other."

"That doesn't make their deaths connected."

"Vicki was raped and strangled and her underwear was nowhere to be found. Nothing was taken from her house. Do you know whether that's the same for Tiffany?"

"I hadn't heard a thing about Tiffany until someone at Andrew Davis mentioned it a half hour ago. So, no, I don't know what happened to her."

"Did Ferrell ever date Vicki?"

Steve frowned. "Not that I ever heard. . . . And I never dated Tiffany."

Jean looked embarrassed. "I didn't mean anything by the question -- not about you anyway. . . . I just wondered if somehow they knew the same man, or made the same man mad enough to kill them. So, what's Lexie doing in Miami? I made all her reservations but she never said what she was doing there."

"She's investigating a sturgeon aquaculture operation."

"A what?"

"A high-tech water farm for very special fish imported from Eastern Europe."

"Why?"

"She doesn't like the stock market and figures if the Progressives stay in power and this socialist trend continues, it's going to be hard to make money in any of the traditional ways. So she's buying farmland in Benton and White Counties for wind turbines and looking at sturgeon farming in Florida. She's also investigating a synthetic fuel operation in Iowa."

"I sort of get wind and fuel, but why sturgeon?"

"For the caviar. The good stuff from Russia is selling for around two thousand a pound -- some ridiculous amount, anyway -- and some sturgeon is on the endangered species list, she said, so it might be worthwhile seeing if good caviar can be produced domestically."

"Lexie thinks of businesses I've never even heard of."

"You and me both, Jean. She's not averse to taking risks, that's for sure, but she spends a lot of time making sure she's more likely to win than lose." A surprising thought struck him just then. Those were exactly the characteristics that impelled Lexie to keep their relationship from rising to the next level. If he didn't signal his lifelong commitment soon, they'd part for the second time once her new house was finished.

"You two are still living together, aren't you?"

"In the same house while I'm building hers."

"Friends with benefits?"

He frowned. "No benefits. At least not the kind you're thinking of."

She smiled. "So, what kind of house is she building?"

"Big." He signaled their waitress and asked for a napkin. Then he drew the house as he described it to Jean. "When you reach the end of the cul de sac, the first thing you see is a huge open courtyard to one side of the house. That's her favorite feature. The gate to the courtyard faces the street. When you get inside, on your left is a row of rooms, including two office suites and a studio if she decides on a hobby. Against the back wall in a corner there's an outdoor kitchen with a barbecue grill and pizza oven. As you're standing in the courtyard, on your right is the main house with doors that slide into the walls so the outdoors is indoors, as she puts it. The courtyard contains a fountain and a table big enough for banquets. Then, behind the courtyard, there's a heated swimming pool and jacuzzi, plus a pool house and a screened pergola. On the opposite side of the house from the courtyard is an attached five-car garage with two upstairs apartments -- servants' quarters, maybe -- and a conservatory off the kitchen."

"And inside?"

"Media room, game and exercise rooms, library, master suite, four guest suites, formal dining room, humongous kitchen connecting to a family room -- and I'm not done."

"Are the foundations in?"

"No. I have a lot of site work to do first. We haven't even cleared her lot."

"I can't picture such a big house. Is Lexie going to live there alone?" Jean took the napkin and slipped it into her purse.

"I guess so, but I don't know what she's got planned."

"Will the rest of the development be as spectacular?"

"It has to be. Her house changes everything about Elysian Fields; I had to buy the rest of the section just to have room for everything. Every plot is now at least an acre and all of them are situated on the sprawling lake, each lot with its own dock. Lots of green space, a clubhouse, tennis courts, two swimming pools, walking and bike paths, and an 18-hole golf course. The model house, which is three times the size of the one I originally planned, is being decorated by Beth at Wild Hare, very tastefully but with the eye-catching quirks she's famous for."

"Who's going to buy the lots and build great houses on them? Who has the money in this economy?"

"Since the medical parks are being expanded on Dupont, I'm hoping for some doctors, but you'd be surprised who's making money right now. Creative risk-takers like Lexie.

They're in every field you can imagine and some that didn't exist ten years ago." He paused. "Speaking of money, I hear you're paying her back for Hazelden."

Jean was startled. "How do you know about that?"

"Lexie and I talk about things. She said you put the whole ninety thousand fee on the firm credit card."

Jean's face was momentarily defiant. "I didn't have a choice."

Steve cocked his head in doubt. "I don't mean to sound harsh, but I think you had a choice. You could have worked out a payment plan with Hazelden instead of forcing Lexie into one."

"I suppose so, but I wasn't thinking when I did it. Anyway, I am paying her back. She's deducting a certain amount from every paycheck."

"Even so, she paid you for the time you took to stay at Hazelden and she's paying your salary for the two weeks you're going to spend in London."

"Yes." Jean's voice was barely more than a whisper. "She's very generous, and I owe her a lot." She blew her nose.

"I notice you didn't order any wine tonight."

"I'm trying to stay on the wagon." She laughed shakily. "Sometimes I have to hold on for dear life. Like tonight."

"How are things with Dwight?"

"Same as ever. I think I want to get married but he isn't sure."

"Sounds like neither of you is positive."

"True. What about you?"

"Not something I'm ready to talk about, to tell you the truth."

Jean paused until the waitress had set their food before them. "I owe you an apology, Steve."

He gave her an inquiring look.

"For Club Soda. I made a scene, and I'm sorry. I'm really, really sorry."

"What was all that about me leading you on?"

"Forget I said it. I was wrong."

"It'll never come up again?"

She nodded.

"Well, that's that, Jean. We won't say another word about it."

For another hour, they ate and talked about lighter subjects. Mostly, Jean talked about the trip she and Dwight were going to take to London in September.

When they reached the parking lot, Rolie and a woman Steve had never seen before were just dismounting from his Harley-Davidson. Both were dressed in leather and denim, windblown and sweaty.

"Well, if it isn't Lexie's main man," Rolie said as he took off his helmet. He winked at Jean. "And her trusty assistant. Stepping out on my sister, are you?"

"Just had dinner," Steve said. "Lexie's out of town on business."

"Let me introduce you to Sorella."

Steve nodded at the woman, who was shaking out her long, stick-straight red hair and unzipping her jacket to reveal a butterfly tattoo on her neck and a very tight sleeveless t-shirt with the American flag outlined in rhinestones. She looked ten years older than Rolie, despite her obvious attempts to look ten years younger.

"Are you a biker now, Rolie?" Jean asked, eyeing his

leather chaps and his tricked-out ride.

"You bet. It's the most fun I've ever had."

"That must mean your chest wound is all healed up."

"Finally. I got shot in the winter, you know, and it took awhile to recover, but I'm a lucky man, according to the surgeon. You're looking at a living, breathing miracle." He put his head back and pointed to the sky. "Somebody up there is looking out for me."

"And who would that be?" Steve asked. "A drone with a laser?"

"Very funny. Tell Lexie hello when she gets back." He laughed. "Don't bother. I'll tell her myself."

Steve walked Jean to her car. "Why is the government wasting our tax money on drones in Afghanistan when they're needed here? Tell me that."

Jean laughed. "Because we all have our enemies lists, and if we could get our hands on drones, no one would be left to pay taxes. That's why."

51

Gamblers and Investors

Tuesday, June 30, 2009

Once again, late on the last day in June, Drago was waiting at the Indianapolis airport for Mizz Royce. She told him to meet her at the arrival gate for the Miami flight, but this time, without carrying a sign. Having found the flight was delayed a half hour, he bought a grande latte, extra shot, no foam, and sat down where he could keep an eye on the gangway door behind the check-in desk. He had time to think. Mostly he marveled at how things had worked out for him.

While Rolie was still in the hospital, recovering from the bullet wound, Mizz Royce had asked Drago to meet her at the Scrapyard on an ice-cold February afternoon when Nate was absent. They sat in Nate's little office with the door closed so Trude couldn't overhear them.

He was taken aback by how forthright his boss' sister was.

"It's time for us to be straight with each other, Drago."

"Yes, ma'am."

"It was you who destroyed my car at the Conrad Hotel,

wasn't it?"

He looked ashamed but said nothing.

"And it was Rolie who told you to do it, isn't that right?"

"Yes."

"Why?"

"He wouldn't tell me then, but I think I've figured out why. He wants to scare you into giving him money. If you won't give it to him, he'll make your life miserable." Drago shifted uncomfortably. "Hate to say it, but Rolie's all about money."

"Why did you do such a nasty thing to me?"

"I'm really sorry I did, but at the time I thought I had to. He was my boss and I didn't want him to fire me."

"Are you all about money too?"

"I guess you could say that."

"I don't think so."

Drago looked startled.

Mizz Royce took her time explaining herself. "You have a wife. You love her, don't you? You support her."

He nodded.

"You have a mother. You love her too."

He nodded again.

"Rolie doesn't have a wife and doesn't love his mother, so he can be all about money if he wants to, but you can't."

"Never thought of it that way."

"I don't suppose you love Rolie, but you're so loyal you'll do whatever he asks and won't give his secrets away." She laughed humorlessly. "Looking at farmland at night when it's all covered with snow! Give me a break."

Drago didn't know what to say.

"The debt Rolie was collecting that night was a drug

debt, wasn't it?"

"I think so."

"You *think* so?"

"It was a drug debt."

"And the guy who shot Rolie from the pickup -- the guy whose face you couldn't describe, riding in a pickup you couldn't describe, pointing a gun you couldn't describe -- had something to do with drugs. Am I right?"

Drago nodded. "Drugs and revenge."

"Revenge? Does that mean the shooter was connected to the man found in the crushed car that morning you went car shopping with me?"

"Is that a guess?"

"A little more than a guess."

"The shooter was Fazel, Kadim's brother."

"Kadim?"

"He was the dealer we had a problem with. Fazel was his enforcer."

"So you've told lies to the police to protect my brother."

He nodded. "Protect myself too."

"You do the dirty work, you protect Rolie at the risk of your own freedom, but he makes most of the money, I suspect."

"You suspect right."

"You're smarter than that, Drago. And you're better than that."

"I have to make a living." *Though I am thoroughly sick of the mayhem that follows Rolie around like a storm cloud.*

"That's what I want to talk to you about. You can make an honest living here."

"How?"

"Rolie's going to be out of commission for awhile, and I want some eyes and ears who are loyal to the Yard and to me. My proposition is this: You're going to follow Nate around and learn every aspect of the scrap business, from the office to the crusher to the warehouses. You're going to report to me. I want the loads screened so no stolen property gets in. No drugs will be sold on the premises. All money is accounted for, none skimmed off. And I want a drive-through recycling window set up, fast and honest, for householders, regular Joes and their wives, who want to bring in their tin cans and old electronics, stuff that's trash to them but valuable to us."

"Nate would allow me to follow him around, be that nosy?"

"Nate works for me. He'll allow it if he wants to keep his job. I not only want this operation run by the book, but I want somebody who's creative, who thinks of ways to get more business. If this Yard doesn't start growing again, it'll die. As it should, by the way. If we can't compete, then we don't deserve to survive."

"Why do you trust me?"

"I have no reason to trust you, do I?" She gave him a long, appraising look that would have made him squirm if he wasn't in his P. Diddy persona. "Some instinct tells me you can turn your life around, Drago. I could be wrong, of course, and if it turns out I've been a fool, that won't be the first time. But if I'm a fool and you mess up, then you're unemployed or back on the street, taking daily chances with death. So, do you have any interest in my proposition?"

"I do. But I can't see how Nate or Rolie is going to like it."

"They're not your worry. They're mine. But I can't

make everything easy for you. I'm not promising you a rose garden. You'll probably have some tough relationships to work out, but if you can't do that, then you don't have a future here anyway. Or anywhere else, for that matter."

When he talked it over with his mother, she said God was giving him a second chance through Miss Royce and persuaded him to meet with Pastor Luther. As a result, Drago was a changed man -- not a perfect man, but a somewhat better one.

Now, it was four and a half months later, and he loved the Yard as if he'd grown up in it. Nate spoke in riddles, swore constantly, and tried to ditch him, but even so Drago had learned a lot, mostly by swallowing his pride: ask questions, no matter how dumb they sounded or how irritated Nate got; stick to Nate like a shadow, however hard Nate tried to shake him; take the criticism without being defensive. Instead of turning Trude's hostility back on her, he'd set out to charm her. He still hated paperwork, but at least now, thanks to Trude, he understood it. He understood the employees too, especially the ones with criminal records, and knew better than Nate how to distinguish the trustworthy from the unrepentant. He'd gotten to know every truck driver on a first-name basis and could identify the honest ones. He liked working outside, with machinery and guys who weren't afraid of hard manual work. Every day was different.

The lessons he'd learned at the Yard were so obvious he couldn't believe he hadn't learned them long ago, if only by doing everything the reverse of the way Rolie did things. First, make yourself likable. Next, be persistent. Then, learn everything there was know to about an operation while acknowledging that there was always someone smarter than you, in this case, Mizz Royce. Finally, be satisfied with respect instead of trying to make others jealous. Someday, God willing, he would be the Scrapyard King.

The side benefit of being at the Yard was a little darker. He didn't allow himself to think about it much, but familiarity with every nook and cranny meant he could be sure his father's remains would never be found. His mother could face the future with more peace than she ever had before.

Suddenly, he was awakened from his reverie. An attendant had thrown the metal door open to the gangway, and passengers were beginning to emerge from the plane. Mizz Royce was among the first. He stood up and walked to the aisle to intercept her. "Good to see you, Mizz Royce. Want me to carry that tote?"

"Sure. Sorry to keep you waiting."

"Not your fault. How was the ride?"

"I'm thinking of buying some time on a charter jet, that's how it was."

"That bad, huh?"

When they were finally rolling north on I-69, Drago mentioned the death of Tiffany Chow. "Lucy's very upset, you know. Two friends in five months, both murdered -- or anyway that's the rumor about Tiffany. Lucy's superstitious, sure that a third friend will die soon, and she doesn't want it to be her or Cricket."

"I talked on the phone yesterday with Bob Passwatter. He got to Xiu-Xiu's apartment before the police did and tried to revive her. He said the girl was beaten and strangled and left naked except for one stocking and that Ferrell told Xiu-Xiu she'd left sometime on Saturday and he couldn't find her, even at her new shop. Bob says that if the police have any sense, they'll give Ferrell a hard look because he'd been violent with her before and she was spending a lot of money, which made him mad."

"So the Hawk's in trouble?"

"The Hawk?"

"That's what Lucy said Tiffany called him."

"Really."

He glanced at Mizz Royce. "So. Do you agree with Mr. Passwatter? About the Hawk, I mean."

"Bob thought Steve was Vicki's killer, so his batting average is zero and all I know is what he told me." Lexie looked off into space. "I suppose Ferrell is a logical suspect, but I shudder to think I was once married to a man who might have killed me. There was one time I thought he was about ten seconds from actually doing it, but he didn't. According to Bob, he's just making things worse for himself."

"How is that?"

"Bob said Ferrell is refusing to cooperate and hired the same lawyer Steve did, Duke Simmons. But whereas Steve gave the police everything they asked for, Ferrell is refusing even to talk, let alone give a DNA sample. Steve might have heard from Dave Powers if there's enough evidence against Ferrell to get a court order for a DNA sample and search of his house. I'll ask him tonight."

"That makes the Hawk look pretty bad, doesn't it?"

"He's a very proud man, and I can just imagine, even if he's innocent, that he would stand on his rights and be indignant that anyone would even think of him as a person of interest. I think he's in a world of hurt."

"Well, we can't solve that puzzle, Mizz Royce, but have

you heard the government might start buying clunkers and then trashing them?"

"Yes, I wanted to talk to you about that. It might start in August."

"You think somebody should start making the rounds of the car dealers, make sure the clunkers come to us?"

"I do. I think that somebody is sitting right here, named Pendragon Bott."

He smiled. "That's what I was thinking too. I'll bet the paperwork is going to be a bitch."

"But Trude's up to it, don't you think?"

"She loves paper, that woman. Know that. And she loves me, so it'll get done."

"Trude loves you, Drago? How'd you manage that?"

"She's partial to Dunkin' Donuts. Maple Frosted Coffee Rolls and Coollatas get her motor running, so I make sure she has them every morning. She also collects pigs. They're all over her desk. You know what her favorite sweatshirt is?"

"Didn't know she had a favorite."

"Two pigs, one labeled 'IRS,' the other 'Taxpayer,' are standing in an alley. The IRS pig is holding a gun on the other one, saying 'Pork It Over.'"

Lexie laughed. "The tax man might want to think twice about visiting her."

"For sure. So every once in a while I surprise Trude with some little pig thing. Lucy likes shopping, so she helps out with that."

"How about Nate?"

"He just wants me to act like a puppy. In fact, he calls me Pup."

"You? Acting like a puppy? Being called Pup? Very

hard to picture."

"You'd be surprised what I can do when I put my mind to it."

"No, I wouldn't. And what about Rolie?"

"He hardly ever shows up at the Yard, doesn't talk to me much anymore."

"How does that feel?"

He paused. "Bad, at first. I got used to him. Sometimes I miss the old life, but if I didn't make a clean break of it, I was afraid I might slip backwards, so I don't seek him out. But when I have the time and Lucy's doing something else anyway, I drive him in the Rolls a few places. Now that the weather's good, he mostly rides that Fat Boy with Sorella hangin' on the back, but when he wants to go to a casino at night, he likes me to drive him. Sometimes she goes along."

"I knew he liked Las Vegas, but I didn't know he hung out at the casinos."

"Once he made me drive all the way to the Horseshoe Casino in Hammond but I didn't like it there, said I wouldn't go again. So he sticks with the Blue Chip in Michigan City."

"What's his game?"

"Craps and roulette."

"Does he win?"

"He says he does. Sorry to say it, but with Rolie you never know. If he was sober when he came out, I might believe him."

"Do you gamble?"

"No. Oh, I tried blackjack a few times, but I don't like losing, so now I wait in the car, watch the people, take a nap, listen to books on tape." He made a sound resembling a laugh. "But you could say I'm a gambler in a way. I'm working for you, ain't I? I'm learning a whole new business, ain't I? I was in so far over my head at first, I didn't think I'd make it, but everyday gets a little better."

"You're thinking of it the wrong way, Drago. You're not a gambler. You're an investor now. No guarantee of success, of course, but if you know what you're doing, if you work at it with single-minded focus and play by the rules, if you provide a better service than anyone else at a fair price, you're more likely to come out a winner than a loser."

"An investor," he said, trying out the words.

"But save your money."

"Why?"

"Because if things go well, I might let you buy in. Then you'll be a capitalist-owner. A capitalist running pig, as the Communists used to call us."

"A capitalist running pig. Trude would like that. I'll have a sweatshirt made up for her."

"And best of all, Pup, you won't end up dead in a crushed car or shot by somebody in a pickup on a country road at night. And you won't spend the rest of your life rotting in a prison cell as somebody's bitch."

He winced at the thought of being somebody's bitch but brightened the more he thought about what she said about his not being a gambler.

"Me, Drago Bott, an investor. A capitalist." He actually smiled. "I like that."

52

Worst Case

Wednesday, July 1, 2009

For the third day in a row, Ferrell found himself in the office of Duke Simmons, who Ferrell thought resembled an overweight, somewhat disheveled mortician more than a famous criminal defense lawyer. The office's grandeur was obliterated by the sheer amount of paper present in stacks of boxes, files covering every available surface, overloaded bookshelves, and overflowing cabinet drawers. Obviously, Duke was a fisherman; a four-foot muskie and a five-foot northern pike glared from the walls.

"Mind if I smoke?" Duke asked, without waiting for an answer. "Let's go over again what you said to the police Sunday night before you said you wanted a lawyer."

"I got home about nine-thirty after the golf tournament at Autumn Ridge. I'd played poker for a few hours. Tiffany wasn't home."

"How do you know that?"

"Her car wasn't in the garage. I looked in every room for her."

"Sure about that? Every room, I mean?"

"Not every room. Not in the extra bedrooms or the basement or attic."

"So your answer wasn't accurate. From now on, don't exaggerate. Be precise. Think about the accuracy of your answers."

Ferrell bristled at the correction.

Duke pointed his cigar at him. "Don't be defensive either." He rolled the ash of his cigar. "Then what?"

"I tried calling her cell but there was no answer."

"How many times?"

"A couple. Then I called her parents, but they didn't know where she was."

"What time was that?"

"I don't know. Ten, maybe. Then I left a message on her sister's phone."

"Did you leave the house Saturday night after you got home?"

"Yes. I drove to the shop and looked in the front window. There were no lights on and she didn't answer the knock on the door. I went around to the back and rang the bell, but again, no answer."

"Anybody see you doing that?"

"There weren't many people around that time of night, and I wasn't thinking about who saw me, so the answer is I don't know."

"Why did you just look in and ring bells? Why not go in?"

"I don't have a key."

"Why was that?"

"She didn't have a key to my campus office either. We just weren't like that."

Duke frowned. "When was the last time you saw Tiffany?"

"Saturday morning when I got out of bed, around six. She was asleep."

"Did you wake her up before you left?"

"No."

"Did you report her missing?"

"No."

"Why not?"

"Because I didn't think she was missing. I was sure she'd call or be back soon."

"You told the cops all this Sunday night?"

"Some of it."

"Is there any life insurance I should know about?"

"A month after she moved in with me, Tiffany demanded that I get a life insurance policy naming her as the beneficiary, so I took one out on her too, naming me as the beneficiary."

"How much?"

"One million each."

Duke whistled. "Was she earning money at the time?"

"No."

"And, of course, you didn't have any kids. So why a million?"

"Nice round number, that's all. At least in Tiffany's mind. Since that's the amount she demanded on my life, I demanded the same on hers."

"You told the cops about the insurance yet?"

"No."

"You have any debts?"

Ferrell sighed. "Yes. My car, her car, real estate taxes and the mortgage on the Lake James Cabin, repairs to the

Forest Park house, the boat up at the lake, some back taxes on income, credit cards . . . ."

"Give me a round number."

"A quarter million?"

Duke whistled again. "But you're not sure. It could be higher."

Ferrell nodded.

"That's not good." Duke picked up some papers. "The court is likely to seek a motion to compel you to provide a DNA sample and fingerprints and a search warrant for your car, house, computer, cell phone, records of all kinds. That could happen any day. Frankly, I'm surprised it hasn't happened already. The cops will show up when you least expect it."

Ferrell was livid. "What's the DNA sample for? Was Tiffany raped or something?"

"We don't know."

"Why do they have to search my house and my car? They think I killed her at home and put her body in the trunk of my Aston Martin to dump it in her sister's apartment?"

"In their minds, that's a possibility."

"Bollocks! I didn't do anything to her, so why should I cooperate?"

"You don't have a choice now."

"Can't you block the search warrant?"

"It'll be served without notice. Besides, if you want to start fighting everything, it's going to cost you."

"Appeal everything."

"Then you're going to have to put up cash to go along with a lien on your house."

"I have money, but it's invested with Bob Passwatter and

I signed papers agreeing not to withdraw the principal for seven years."

"I'll need to see that agreement. Chances are, you can get at your account in exigent circumstances so long as you pay a hefty penalty." He pointed his pen at Ferrell. "You need to make some notes, boy, because finding those papers fast is important. The circumstances don't look good for you, so if you're charged with murder, you're going to need some bail money, lots of it and fast."

"Charged? With what? There's no evidence I killed her."

"The circumstances are against you. She was your girlfriend, she lived with you, you were the last to see her, you don't have witnesses for where you were during significant periods between Saturday night and Sunday, and, as you confessed to me yesterday, you have a history of domestic violence."

"Put it that way, I sound like the killer. But I'm not, and I didn't have a motive."

"Not an essential component to a prosecution, but in fact motive won't be a problem. The prosecutor will find out about her spending habits, your debt, and the insurance policy. And since she appeared to have undressed voluntarily, she was either with you or entertaining a lover in her sister's apartment. If it wasn't you, then the cops will claim you found out that she was fooling around, followed her there, and killed her in a jealous rage."

"That scenario makes no sense. I can poke holes all day in it."

"The prosecution can poke holes in your story too. When we get the Coroner's report, we'll know what time period you need an alibi for, but even if cell phone records show you called Tiffany's parents and her sister from your house and spent an hour or so checking out her shop, there's a lot of time unaccounted for with no corroborating witnesses. Even if some other guy's semen is found in her, that doesn't mean he was the murderer. The sex might have been consensual. Then, later, let's say, you found out about the infidelity, followed her to her sister's apartment where she'd run for cover, and killed her. That's one of the ways the cops might see it."

"Why would she have let me in the apartment if she was having sex with another man and I found out about it?"

"Maybe she let you in because he'd left before you got there. Maybe no man had been there and she thought you'd come after her to make up."

"Whose lawyer are you anyway?"

"Yours, Ferrell. Make no mistake about that. And you'd be terrible on the stand. You're arrogant, defensive, and easily angered. What color are your eyes?"

"Hazel. Why?"

"Right now, your eyes are actually black. Your face is flushed and dark, a study in defiance. No sign of remorse. So taking the stand in your own defense is likely to be a no-go. But juries don't like a defendant who won't tell them what happened. They're not supposed to hold silence against a defendant, but they do."

Ferrell was scornful. "I'm innocent, so of course I'm angry, and I have nothing to be remorseful about."

"That attitude doesn't work with juries. Half a dozen questions on cross-examination and you'll be so angry that the jury can easily imagine you strangling your girlfriend in a fit of rage because she was, as you called her, a spendthrift or because you thought she was having an affair."

"I admit getting mad at her for wasting money, but I wouldn't have killed her for that, and I had no reason to think she was having an affair."

"Where did she get the money to open that shop in Covington Plaza?"

"From her parents."

"You know that for a fact?"

"That's what she said."

"So you don't know it for a fact. You're an engineer, man. You must understand the difference between a fact you've verified and hearsay. Not to belabor the point, but once again you just answered a question you don't really know the answer to." Before Ferrell could protest, Duke continued. "Were you underwriting the expense of the shop?"

"No. She stopped racking up credit card bills in January after we had a row about her spending. In fact, she stopped asking me for money altogether."

"So let's say she didn't get the money from her parents and you know you didn't give her any. Then where did she get the money for the shop?"

"I have no idea."

"Do you know if she had a bank account somewhere?"

"No."

"So could the money have come from a lover?"

"Anything's possible, I suppose, but she didn't have a lover. She was too busy with school and the shop."

"She never came home late, never smelled like another man. Is that what you're saying?"

Ferrell was startled.

"Remember something?"

"Maybe."

"What do you remember?"

"That night I fell through the closet floor to the kitchen, she'd come home late and smelled like aftershave. When I asked about it, she said it was from the gay guy those girls hung out with."

Duke almost smiled. "When was the last time you had sex with her?"

Ferrell squirmed. "The last time we had a shag was at least a couple weeks ago."

"Shag?"

"Sex."

"You can't use words like that in front of a jury -- if you end up in front of one, that is. Not all Americans are fond of Brits. Anyway, back to the subject. Why so long since you 'shagged,' as you put it?"

"We were fighting all the time. She was always tired."

"Was that the pattern from the start of your relationship?"

"No."

"When did it change?"

Ferrell closed his eyes. "When she started putting the shop together, maybe a little before that."

"I hit a nerve, didn't I? I want to see her credit card bills, her course registrations, all her business papers for her new venture, everything about her. Unless, of course, the cops seize them first." He pointed again at Ferrell. "Write that down too."

"You say I look defiant. How's an innocent man supposed to look?"

"Everybody's different, but you don't have a poker face."

Again, Ferrell bristled.

"And don't tell me you're great at poker. You brag a lot, which won't endear you to a jury. You give everything away on your face. And what you haven't said to me is as telling as what you have said. For instance, you haven't said a word about being sorry your girlfriend is dead. You don't look like a man in mourning."

"This is business, not a bereavement call. I'm grieving privately."

"I'm telling you all this, Ferrell, so you know how a case can be built against you. It'll be the worst case, believe me. Are you on medication?"

"Why?"

"I need to know."

"Tegretol."

"For what?"

"Bipolar. Manic-depression."

"You've been taking it regularly?"

"Yes."

"You've faithfully renewed the prescription every thirty days. Is that what your prescription records would show?"

Ferrell frowned. "No. The stupid doctors don't know what they're doing, so sometimes I take it, sometimes I don't. Sometimes I cut the pills in half."

"What was your mood Saturday night and Sunday?"

"I started out Saturday in a really good mood because I expected to win the golf tournament. But by late that evening, I was in a really foul mood because I lost at golf, thanks to Bob Passwatter, the wanker, who couldn't even add a golf score correctly, and then I lost five hundred at poker to some prat because he was cheating."

"Ah, now we get the truth about poker. So, let me guess. In a matter of hours you went from manic to depressive. You weren't taking the Tegretol as prescribed."

"No. But that's not relevant."

"It could be, Ferrell. The prosecution will find an expert to testify that in your depressive moods, you're violent, and you were in a depressive mood when you killed Tiffany."

"I'll take a lie detector test."

"Too early. We'll do one privately first, if I'm convinced it's the right thing to do, but it's risky and my job is to diminish the risks to your freedom as much as I can."

Ferrell was indignant. "I'll ace that test. I didn't kill Tiffany."

"I know you're getting pissed off with me, but you need to know the worst case that can be made against you if you're going to make sound decisions about your defense. And we don't know the worst case yet because the facts aren't all in. When was Tiffany killed? Where were you at the time? Can your whereabouts be corroborated? Was she killed where she was found or somewhere else? Was her body moved? Was she raped? Was she having an affair? Was she robbed? Or was anything taken from her sister's apartment? And given the circumstances -- whatever the facts turn out to be, however innocent you are -- your defense is not going to be cheap."

"You don't believe I'm innocent, do you?"

"You blink a lot when you're asked questions."

"What does that mean?"

"Some might take it as a sign of guilt."

"Shit, Duke, if you don't believe me, what hope do I have?"

"I don't have to believe you, my friend. I just have to defend you." He pointed his cigar at Ferrell. "Which I'm very good at, by the way. Don't forget that."

Ferrell was so furious he wished he actually had killed Tiffany. Even in death, she was costing him a fortune and now he had to wonder if the cow had been unfaithful as well. He was even more furious when he stormed into the suite occupied by Passwatter Global Investments and was told Bob had left early to celebrate the Fourth at an undisclosed location and wouldn't be back for at least a week.

53

Happy Talk

Friday, July 3, 2009

The day before the Fourth, Bob and his two sons, Bob Junior and Les, finished playing golf at the Wawashkamo Golf Club on Mackinac Island Friday in time to join Clarissa, their two daughters-in-law, Stephie and Gloria, and their granddaughter Kennedy Ann for afternoon tea in the Parlor of the Grand Hotel. Bob was very high on life. The chamber music recital soothed the soul. The little finger sandwiches and scones weren't satisfying fare for a big man who'd just played eighteen holes of golf, but the champagne and sherry gave the touch of East Coast sophistication he relished.

He gazed at his family with pride. They were good-looking, healthy, and prosperous, but not as prosperous as he was. He was proud that he could afford a private jet to fly them to St. Ignace and offer them the stellar accommodations of his magnificent log cabin, all eight thousand square feet of it. He was proud of beating his sons at golf, though they joked about his cheating. Tonight they would barbecue t-bones and salmon on the grill, roast marshmallows in the fire pit, and then play gin rummy until lights out.

Tomorrow would be an even bigger day. The men would spend the morning fishing, while the women spent the day preparing mountains of food -- fried chicken, old-fashioned potato salad, and half a dozen cream pies. They'd end with a festive picnic on the beach and then watch fireworks.

But there was a shadow over Bob's life. In the office on the second floor of the Alpine Cottage behind the Lodge sat a little pile of demand letters -- unreasonable, unexpected demands he had no way of satisfying.

Alexandra Royce intended to withdraw ten million dollars to invest in various operations in Florida, Indiana, and Iowa and to pay for her new house.

Ferrell Hawke's attorney was demanding the release of his entire account to pay defense fees and hire experts now that he was a person of interest in Tiffany's death. That account was seriously deficient because of the money he'd diverted to Tiffany, and if he was forced to comply, his forgery of Ferrell's name might be discovered unless he paid out the full amount Ferrell thought he was owed, which meant that he would have paid out twice the dividends Ferrell was actually owed. The threat of a lawsuit infuriated him. Even if he could delay the payout to Ferrell, it might cost more than it was worth. Furthermore, if enough threads were pulled from that twisted skein, his affair with Tiffany might be revealed, thus imperiling not only his investment house but his marriage as well.

Both Rolland Royce and Matilda were also demanding the return of their entire accounts. Matilda claimed she needed the money for expensive injections and physical therapy to relieve an inflammation of the spine. She also claimed that she had to buy a condo in Florida because her doctors ordered her to go south in the winter to ease her pain. Since she planned to spend a lot of time in Florida, she'd move the balance of her account to a Naples investment house that her friends recommended.

Rolland gave no reasons for his demand.

It was nothing less than a run on his investment house. If he moved enough money around, he could cover the demands of Alexandra, Ferrell, Matilda and Rolland, but he wouldn't have enough left to cover all his other clients' accounts or live the way he wanted. It would put him in serious jeopardy with the SEC if that nosy but largely ineffectual agency ever discovered what he was up to and how he did it.

And it was all Alexandra's fault, he could see that. Everyone demanding money was connected to her. He pictured her as Medusa, her head sprouting writhing serpents instead of hair, her beautiful face so fierce that men who gazed on it were turned into stone. He squinted off into space, picturing a slide in his Classical Mythology class at Columbia. Medusa ended up as a symbol on Athena's shield. Is that how Alexandra Royce saw herself? Athena? The goddess of war? Smarter and stronger than men?

What had he ever done to that woman to deserve her fury? Who did she think she was? If his clients got wind that as brilliant a businesswoman as Alexandra Royce was pulling her money out of Passwatter Global Investments and had convinced her family to do the same, then he was done. He'd be exposed as a fraud, broke and humiliated. He might even end up in prison teaching accounting to his fellow inmates.

He knew Alexandra's brother, Rolie, hated her. Perhaps there was a way to talk some sense into him. Surely he wasn't his sister's puppet. He'd given no good reason for the withdrawal. Maybe together, as men of the world, they could quiet the squall blowing up around him.

"Dad," Les said, passing his hand across Bob's eyes. "Where'd you go?"

Bob smiled at his son. "I'm right here. I'm just tired, that's all."

"Not too tired to cheat," Bob Junior said, laughing. "You're good at that. Do you ever bother to take a putt?"

"How many balls does it take a financial genius to complete a hole?" Les asked.

Bob's face darkened. His sons had always teased him about the way he played golf, but today he was in no mood for it. "I don't cheat. I'm creative. And at my expense you just got to play on the oldest course in Michigan."

Clarissa patted his hand. "It's okay."

Bob pulled his hand away. "And may I remind all of you who's paying the bill here? Twenty-five dollars apiece for this spread, I believe. Let's see," he said, pretending to count the people around his table, "seven. If I can still multiply, that's a hundred and seventy-five dollars for tea, not counting taxes, tip, and admission fee. Don't I always pay the bill?"

Les saluted. "That's why we love you."

"It better not be the only reason."

Clarissa patted his hand again. "Of course it isn't, dear."

He picked up a tiered serving piece. "Now, who wants another scone? Eat up. Drink up. I want to get my money's worth. And let's have some happy talk. Somebody tell me a funny story."

54

He'll Ride Your Ass

Friday, July 3, 2009

Rolie knew there was a private back room at Sue-A-Side but Sue had invited him into it only once before.

He studied her as if she were a reptile long thought to be extinct. Somewhere in her fifties, Sue was very thin with a sunken chest. He'd heard that she was once a chain smoker but had quit. Now she chewed gum as if it was all that kept her alive. She had deeply set gray eyes, a gravelly voice, freckles overlaying a vampire pallor, and a wet cough, but he could tell from her high cheekbones and full lips she had once been pretty. She still had a presence about her that meant no one messed with her.

Despite her frail look, she was an active owner, constantly patrolling the bar, watching every order the waitresses took, every dollar the bartenders took in and every drink they poured. All her employees were required to call her Mrs. Doody, but if she had a husband, no one had ever seen him. Customers who got out of hand according to her unwritten rules received no warning at all; they were simply escorted out, and the worst were warned never to return. They didn't dare. She knew almost everybody by first and last names and what they drank, and though she was polite with everybody, her steely eyes invited no small talk, no confidences. She didn't mind a noisy, lively, even rowdy, scene but she hated cops and prided herself on running a cop-free establishment. There were loaded guns under the bar and in her office.

"Have a seat," she said, gesturing toward an old, very distressed leather sofa. He obeyed, sinking so far down on broken springs he was afraid he couldn't get back up. She took a nearby chair that allowed her to look down on him.

"You want a beer or would you prefer bourbon? I prefer bourbon myself."

"Beer. So, Sue, what's new with you?"

"I think I made a mistake, Rolie."

"How's that?"

"Covering your gambling debts."

"I'm going to pay you back."

"Yes, of course you will, Rolie. But when?"

"Give me another month."

She glanced at a calendar tacked to her knotty pine wall. "I don't think so. I might be dead by then. Or you will."

"What?"

"You heard me. I'll give you a week."

"I have plenty of money, you know that. But I can't get my hands on it that fast. My lawyer sent a demand letter to the investment house where my money's stashed, but he says it could take awhile for an answer. You know how -- ."

She cut him off without raising her voice. It was her look that scared him. "Stop whining. Your problem is not my problem. Your problem is your problem. I didn't get where I am letting cocky young men like you get the best of me."

"I never thought of myself as cocky, but young -- I like that."

"You are young. Wet behind the ears."

He playfully dipped a finger into his beer and wiped the back of his ear. "That's me. Wet behind the ears."

"Do you know the meaning of the word 'contract?'"

"What are you talking about?" he asked, watching in fascination as she spit out one wad of gum and inserted a fresh stick. He'd never seen her without gum. She probably owned a chewing gum company.

"I was willing to help you out of a jam because I know you have an interest in Summit City Metals. I lent you money. You agreed to pay me back. That's a contract."

"But it's not in writing."

"It's written here," she said, first drawing a finger across her forehead, then across her heart.

"A lot of good that'll do you in court."

"I never go to court to collect a debt. But I do collect them, in full."

Rolie felt himself beginning to sweat. Time for a new tactic. Even though she looked like ninety pounds of stringy hair, freckles, and mucus, he'd do anything to change her mind, even . . . even that. "Couldn't we work something out? I like to party, you like to party."

She produced a sound that was probably meant to be a laugh but sounded like a sack of slimy rocks being shaken. "Oldest trick in the book. Doesn't work with me. Owning a joint like this one, I party every night of the week. I can also have any man I want, and you're not it."

He was actually insulted. Who was Sue Doody to refuse

him? The old bat was at least twenty-five years older than he was, looking and sounding as if she'd been run over by a train multiple times, so how could she not be flattered by his veiled proposition?

"That's harsh."

"You don't know harsh, Rolie. I suspect nobody in your life has ever been harsh to you. You've been coddled from the cradle on. That's why you're a marshmallow."

"I'm not a marshmallow!"

"Good. Then you're going to do the right thing. Murph will be visiting you a week from now, at that famous Yard of yours, noon sharp." She looked at the wall calendar. "Friday, July 10. He'll be expecting cash."

"Murph's my friend," he protested.

"You think?"

"I ride with him. In fact, he taught me to ride. He helped me out with my sister one time, right here in your bar. Remember?"

"You'll see whose friend Murph is if you don't have that cash next Friday, Rolie. He and I are both very serious about money. He'll ride your ass all the way to your grave if he doesn't ride back here with a fistful of cash."

"Come on, Sue. That's not lady-like language."

In the back of her throat, she shook another bag of slimy rocks. "No, it isn't."

"Let me take you to the Blue Chip for a big weekend. Let's see if we can't win back every penny I owe you and more. I'm more fun than I look."

"And I'm less." She sipped her bourbon. "I prefer the money."

Rolie rubbed his chin. He was now sporting a two-day

stubble as a sign of his toughness but it itched like hell. In fact, he felt itchy all over. "Not at the Yard. Tell Murph to come to my house. I'll give you the address."

"I have the address."

"You do? My home address?"

"Unlisted phone number, social security number, your mother's maiden name, even your spending habits. Want me to go on?"

Rolie didn't want her to go on. He was so wobbly when he walked out the back door of Sue-A-Side, he wasn't sure he could get his magnificent machine home in one piece.

55

A Happy Fourth

Saturday, July 4, 2009

The Fourth of July meant very different things to Lexie's circle.

***Drago was surprised by the hog roast his wife, Lucy, had planned at their little house in Huntertown a few blocks from his mother. She invited Trude Weide, Nate Grabbendorf and his wife, and all the employees at the Yard, plus Lucy's parents, Phyllis and Aunt Ruth, and the neighbors who lived on the block so there would be no complaints about noise and street parking.

"Are we paying for this?" he asked as he stood in the backyard, watching the hog man setting up his roaster near the alley and one of the neighbors arranging folding tables and chairs in the yard. The equipment for a cornhole game -- the Midwestern version of bocce ball -- was lying in the yard, and a badminton net had been strung between two trees. Croquet wickets and stakes had been set up in one neighbor's yard and horseshoe stakes in the other. A plastic bin of assorted fireworks sat on the corner of his small patio.

His boombox and speakers had been arranged on a cedar table, and red, white, and blue paper lanterns had been strung up everywhere. His mother and aunt were inside preparing food in gigantic quantities: cole slaw, jello towers in red, white, and blue, pasta salad, baked beans, cornbread, brownies, and gallons of lemonade.

"Of course we're paying for this."

"Why?"

"So someday everybody wants you to be the Scrapyard King." He would have kissed her if they'd been alone.

He'd never attended a hog roast before, let alone hosted one, but he found the whole party unexpectedly exhilarating. After the feast but before it was completely dark, Lucy put a Ray Charles CD on the boombox, amping up *America the Beautiful,* then insisted that everyone face the flag hanging on the side of the house and recite the pledge of allegiance. It was the Fourth of July, after all. Then she announced she was pregnant. When Drago got over his shock, he actually put his arm around his wife's waist, very briefly, and whispered, "Is it a boy?"

She giggled. "It'll be a surprise." She'd wait to tell him it was twins.

Public displays of affection weren't part of Drago's gig, so he affected his most casual attitude, as if hog roasts and surprise babies were an everyday occurrence, but he'd never felt more like a man. He did his best not to swagger or even smile too much.

At the end of the evening, after Nate set off an hour of fireworks and the kids had worked their way through the sparklers, Trude, preparing to leave in her Suzuki pickup, hugged Drago. "Thank you."

"I put on this roast just for you, Trude, knowing how you like hogs."

She chuckled. "I'm going to have to teach you the difference between a hog and a pig."

"Didn't know there was a difference."

"You have a lot to learn." Her voice was gruff. "But when I'm done with you, Pup, you're going to be as good a boss as Isaac." She patted his cheek. "Now there was a man. Someday I'll tell you about him."

⋆⋆⋆Bob Passwatter did his best to stay upbeat and keep the dark clouds at bay. He helped Kennedy Ann with her sparklers. He sprayed anyone, whether they asked or not, with bug spray. He ate two pieces of fried chicken. He complimented his daughters-in-law on the chocolate cream pie.

But when at last his family climbed the 93 wooden steps to the log cabin up above the beach, he stayed behind, saying he wasn't sleepy, he'd be up in awhile. He stared out at Lake Michigan, that vast, rough inland sea, wishing he'd been an Ojibwe chief two hundred years ago, camping on the beach with his family, worried about nothing more than catching the next fish, killing the next bear, or moving the whole damn tribe south to winter grounds.

He couldn't drift far enough away from the present, though. He just didn't have the requisite imagination. He weighed the costs and benefits of continuing to live. He pictured the Luger in his office in the Alpine Cottage and wondered if he should play Russian roulette with himself. What would God think about that?

His thoughts then turned to Tiffany. Poor girl didn't

deserve to die. Where was she now? Would Ferrell, that son of perdition, be arrested for her murder?

***Rolie, who lived on a ten-acre spread on State Line Road, part of a farm his father had purchased long before he was born, celebrated the Fourth with Sorella. They took a ride on his Harley-Davidson up to Auburn, where they spent a couple of hours in the Auburn Cord Duesenberg Museum. He bought two diecast model cars, a 1936 Cord 810 and a 1934 Duesenberg Model J, for his collection.

Back home, the two of them splashed around in his swimming pool awhile, drinking a lot of beer. Still in his swim trunks, from the comfort of his lounge chair, he shot a couple of rabbits. Then Rolie grilled some hamburgers and drank more beer. After two calls from his mother, neither of which he answered, he turned off his phone.

"Are you nervous about something, Rolie?" Sorella asked, rubbing suntan lotion on herself. "You're so jumpy."

"Nah. Nothing makes me nervous."

"Why didn't you invite Murph and the gang?"

"You really want to know?"

"Yeah."

"Well, I'm not going to tell you, but we aren't going to be seeing much more of them, so get used to it and don't ask any more questions."

"Are you going to set off some fireworks?"

"No."

"But I like fireworks."

"Maybe next year. You want to put some of that lotion on my back?"

At the end of the night, very drunk, he sobbed into

Sorella's chest without telling her why.

★★★Independence Day meant nothing to Ferrell, who spent the day alone, searching every inch of the house for the papers that Duke Simmons said he had to find. Finally, he ordered a large sausage pizza and, after downing half a bottle of Macallan while watching a boring BBC news program on the telly, fell into a disturbed sleep on the water-spotted velvet sofa in the living room.

Unfortunately, when he was more than half in the bag, the cops showed up with the search warrant. After the search, he was taken to the police station for an unpleasant interview.

★★★But Steve and Lexie's day was happier even than Drago's.

They grilled a pork tenderloin, jacket potatoes wrapped in tinfoil, and fresh corn in the husk and ate their dinner on the screened porch. Then they stepped outside to watch the fireworks set off by their Autumn Ridge neighbors.

It was almost midnight when they retired to the media room. It was Lexie's turn to pick the movie, and she had chosen *My Best Friend's Wedding.* When they came to the scene where Julia Roberts and Dermot Mulroney are on a sight-seeing boat passing under a Chicago bridge and Mulroney says, "Kimmy says, if you love someone, you say it. You say it, right then, out loud. Otherwise the moment just passes you by," Lexie signaled Steve to pause the movie.

"What?" Steve asked.

"That's the crux of the movie, right there. It breaks my heart, that scene."

"You're kidding."

"No. I'm not kidding. If you don't get together when you have the chance -- if you let the moment pass -- then it's all over, no matter what silly promises you make about marrying each other if neither is married by a certain age. It's too late."

"You believe that?"

"I do . . . I think."

"Are you talking about us?"

"I don't know. Am I?"

"Are you thinking we let the moment pass fifteen years ago and now it's too late?"

She tried to blink back the tears. "Maybe."

"Well, I don't." He got up and said he'd be right back. He ran upstairs and was back in five minutes. "Okay, I'm going to give you a test."

"On what?"

"On your view of the passing of the right moment."

She gave him a puzzled look and shook her head without saying anything.

He sat down and handed her a ring box.

"What's this?" she asked warily.

"Open it."

Inside was a platinum ring set with a three-carat square diamond in an Art Deco style. "Is this what I think it is?"

"Well, if you think it's a ring, it is," he laughed. "I designed it with some help at Freeman Jewelers." He slid toward her and took her hand. "Do you like it?"

"I do. It's lovely."

"Those are very promising words. Because I love you. I may be saying it fifteen years late, but I love you."

"I love you too."

"Will you marry me, Lexie?"

"Really?"

"No, this is just an elaborate joke." He ruffled her hair. "Yes, really."

She leaned into him and whispered that she would.

"Does the ring fit?"

She slipped it on and held out her hand, wiggling it back and forth to catch the light. "Perfectly."

"So you'll keep it?"

She smiled. "Yes. And I'll keep you."

"Is there something you want to change about the ring?"

"Not a thing. It's as if you knew what was in my head." She gave him a kiss. "But what made you so sure I'd say yes? After all, if I'd declined, you'd be stuck with an expensive ring you custom-designed for the wrong woman."

"It's that house I'm building for you. It's meant for a family, not for a woman living alone. The double office suites gave the game away."

"That's it?"

"And that book by Dr. Crabb you left lying around. *The Marriage Builder.* I thought that might be a hint, so I read it."

"Anything else?"

"Letting me name the streets in Elysian Fields. I took that as a sign of the respect a woman is supposed to have for her husband."

"Am I that obvious?"

"I wouldn't say you're obvious, Lexie, far from it, but I'm beginning to figure you out. I think it's going to take me at least fifty years, though, so I hope you're in this for the long haul, because I am." They kissed again.

"Me too. I promise. I'm definitely in it for the long

haul."

"One thing scares me, though."

"What?"

"Your choosing exactly that movie, stopping it at exactly that bridge scene, saying exactly what you did. Was that a test?"

"Not consciously." She smiled. "But I can see how you'd see it that way."

"Consciously or not, you tested me. And I could have failed, isn't that right?"

"You would have passed with a few words. The right words. Believe me, I didn't have a ring in mind. I wasn't expecting that."

"So, at least for tonight, I was one step ahead of you."

"More than one step, Steve-o."

That night, Lexie moved out of the guest bedroom.

56

Shooting Rabbits

Tuesday, July 7, 2009

When Bob called to talk about the closing of his investment account, Rolie at first refused, saying there was nothing to discuss. But Bob was persistent, saying there was a lot to discuss. He hinted that maybe Rolie could hang onto his money if his sister could be dealt with. That intrigued Rolie. Dealt with how? Bob said he'd even drive out to State Line Road so Rolie wouldn't be inconvenienced.

"I'll be out by the pool. Park in the driveway and walk around to the back."

"Just the two of us, Rolie."

"Sorella will be at work anyway, so I'll be alone."

Tuesday was a scorching hot, blindingly sunny day, the kind of day Bob hated. The moment he got out of his air-conditioned Porsche and walked to the back of the house, he felt like he'd just walked into a furnace. His dress shirt was pitted out before he reached the swimming pool, where Rolie was sitting under an umbrella, dressed only in swim trunks, drinking a beer.

To show who had the power, Rolie stayed seated, his

sunglasses firmly on his nose, without offering to shake hands. "Have a seat, Bob. God, you make me sweat just looking at you."

Bob wiped his forehead and neck, determined to be civilized. "Why the two-day stubble?"

"A new look to go with the Harley. What do you think?"

"I guess it's good to experiment when you're young. How was your Fourth? Did you celebrate?"

"No, I didn't, Bob. Did you?"

"Of course. Up at Eagle Pass, our lodge in the UP. I spent the day before the Fourth on Mackinac Island, playing golf with my sons on the oldest continuously played Scottish links course in Michigan, then had an elegant tea to the accompaniment of chamber music at the Grand Hotel with the whole family. On the Fourth, my sons and I fished, then picnicked with the women on the beach and watched fireworks. It was everything a man could want."

"Sounds boring as hell."

Bob was stung. "And your life isn't?"

"It's definitely not boring."

"I was surprised to get your letter saying you want to close your investment account."

"Why?"

"You didn't give a reason."

"I don't have to. I've met all the terms, haven't I? What more do you need?"

"It's a very bad move on your part."

"Why?"

"You're young. You inherited that money. You're not good at making money on your own and you're going to need every penny when you're old." *Though if you don't lose the equivalent of a hefty fourth-grader, you won't see old age.*

"I need every penny now."

"For what?"

"Don't want to say."

"Did you know your sister is demanding ten million dollars from her account?"

"For what?"

"Not to invest in the Yard, that's for sure. Not to buy that smelter you want. I suppose I shouldn't be telling a client's secrets, but since Alexandra is your sister, I think you're entitled to know. She's building a mansion in Steve Wright's development out on Tonkel Road."

"I know that."

"Do you know what it's costing?"

"No."

"Millions. She's also investing in all kinds of new businesses -- wind turbines, synthetic fuel, fish farming, you name it."

"So?"

"In this market, no investment house wants to pay out ten million in one lump sum. And then there's your demand and your mother's and even Alexandra's ex-husband's. It's stupid for you guys to pull out. I'm making you more money than you can possibly make anywhere else." Bob wiped his neck and forehead again. "Sorry to bother you, but could you get me some ice water? I'm burning up here."

When Rolie returned with a bucket of ice water, Bob dipped his handkerchief in it, wrung it out, then draped the cold wet cloth around his neck. "That's better."

"Talk all you want, Bob, but . . . ." Without any warning, in the middle of his sentence, Rolie picked up his shotgun, took aim, and popped a rabbit. "Damn pests. I hate them. Almost as much as I hate my sister."

Bob stared at the rabbit as it flopped around. "But you wouldn't shoot her, would you?" Bob chuckled to show it was a rhetorical question.

"Don't tempt me, Bob."

"I heard from your mother that Alexandra and Steve Wright are engaged now. She'll be cutting you out of her will."

"Yeah, Ma told me the same thing. I told her I was surprised."

"Why?"

"A week or so ago I saw Steve and Jean walking out of Chop's. Lexie was out of town that night. Jean's had a thing for Steve ever since high school. They pretended it was just dinner, but I know better. He's cheating on her."

"Does Alexandra know that?"

"I haven't told her yet."

"Why not? Don't you think she'd want to know?"

"I'm waiting for the right moment."

Bob stared at the rabbit, which was now still. "Maybe now is the right moment. If she doesn't marry Steve, she might stop the construction of that house. And if she doesn't marry Steve, you'll stay in her will and get all her money. And if she withdraws her demand, or at least part of it, I'll arrange your payout immediately. However you help, I'll make sure you're rewarded."

Rolie pushed his sunglasses down on his nose and grinned at Bob. "But the only way she withdraws her entire demand is if she's in the same condition as that rabbit. Isn't that right?"

"I didn't say that. I didn't even think such a thing."

Rolie scoffed. "Everybody's a saint but me! I'm surprised you're not wearing a halo, Bob."

"All I'm saying is, the solution's in your hands. You can keep your own investment account if you get creative."

Rolie didn't answer. He'd been considering the solution for months. The uncreative but final solution. It wasn't that hard to kill a woman if he thought of her as a rabbit.

"You still haven't told me why you need so much money, Rolie. I've been your investment advisor ever since Isaac died, God rest his soul, and your secrets are safe with me."

Rolie scoffed. "Safe! You just told me Lexie's."

"That's different. You and I have a special relationship. Now tell me why you need all that money."

Rolie took so long to respond that Bob wondered if he was going to say anything. Finally, Rolie pushed his sunglasses back into place and pointed his face in the direction of the dead rabbit. "I like to gamble. Usually, I win, but lately my luck's been bad. Really bad. I owe someone a shitload of money. And she's a witch."

"Are you talking about your sister?"

"No. Different woman altogether. I thought this woman was my friend, but she isn't."

"Is she threatening you?"

"Yeah. I've got to come up with the money by Friday or I'm toast."

"Friday! That's no time at all. My house isn't a bank, you know."

Suddenly, Rolie picked up his shotgun and shot another rabbit.

"For Pete's sake, Rolie, will you quit shooting animals?"

"You got a soft spot for all of God's creatures, do you?"

"Who doesn't?"

"I don't. Most people don't. If that rabbit is one of God's creatures, then I am too. Right? Yet I'm getting a visit Friday by a guy named Murph who doesn't give a shit what I am. He'd just as soon shoot me as look at me. I thought he was my friend, but it turns out he's the woman's enforcer."

"Can we put a name to this witch who's threatening you?"

"Might as well tell you so if somebody finds me dead, you know who did it. Sue Doody. She owns a biker bar on the Lincoln Highway."

"Never heard of her."

"You wouldn't."

"What time on Friday is this Murph paying you a visit?"

"Noon sharp."

"I don't want to see you get hurt, Rolie."

"Then we'd better come up with a plan."

57

Best Wishes

Wednesday, July 8, 2009

Wednesday evening, Matilda was already seated at a dining table in the Sycamore Hills Clubhouse. When she spotted Lexie, she rose and waited for her to approach. "Thank you for coming, my dear." She air-kissed her step-daughter. "It's so good to see you. I ordered you a Tanqueray and tonic. I hope that's still your cocktail of choice."

"It is, thank you. I came down a few hours early so that while I was on this side of town I could shop at Susan's. I have a couple of baby showers to attend this month and needed some fresh looks."

"Give me your hand so I can see that ring of yours." She wiggled Lexie's hand back and forth to catch the light. "My, my, that's a diamond you can't miss."

"Matilda! It's half the size of yours."

"Good. That means Steve paid for it with his own money instead of yours. The important thing is, are you happy?"

Of course Steve paid for the ring. "Very. We're both happy."

"You have my best wishes. So have you set a date for the wedding?"

"No. We're thinking September."

Matilda looked shocked. "That doesn't give you much time to plan, does it?"

"It's not going to be a big wedding, so there won't be that much to plan. In fact, we're thinking of flying to Bermuda and getting married there."

"On the beach? Somehow, I can't see you with sand between your toes, a ring of baby's breath in your hair, having your vows blown back into your face by a stiff ocean breeze."

Lexie laughed. "I can't either. But a second wedding can't be a big, white church wedding, can it? It would look ridiculous. I would feel ridiculous, and so would Steve. So whatever we do, it's going to be a very small, private affair. We'll give a big party for friends and family when we get back from wherever we go."

"Do you like lobster?" Matilda asked, closing her menu and pushing it aside as their drinks were set in place.

"It's on the menu?"

"No. But I called ahead and it's available tonight for us. Just for us."

"How kind. I love lobster."

Matilda laid her hand on the waiter's arm. "Tell Chet we'll both have the lobster, with Duchess potatoes and grilled asparagus, please. Tell him not to overcook the asparagus. We'll start with Caesar salads." She turned back to Lexie. "So, my dear, are you keeping yourself busy these days?"

Lexie laughed. "You mean, other than building a new house, planning a wedding, helping to plan a class reunion, and flying around the country looking at companies to invest in?"

Matilda laughed too. "Other than that."

"Well, class reunion first. Linda Adler's in charge. Remember her?"

"Yes. Very serious girl."

"She's set our fifteenth class reunion for the Labor Day weekend. Jessica and Ed Singer and Steve and I have decided to underwrite a big fall festival with a barbecue and dance in Johnny Appleseed Park on Harry Baals Drive." Lexie laughed. "Can you believe we ever had a mayor named Harry Baals?"

"I don't like intra-family lawsuits, but that's one case where the son should have sued his parents."

I'm glad to hear that part about no intra-family lawsuits. "My part in the reunion is mostly just writing checks, but another project requires more of my time. I'm writing a book for a New York publishing house, a guide for women entrepreneurs."

"How's that going?"

"Dead slow. I probably need to hide myself away for a month to get a draft for the agent to read. I've been thinking about asking Bob to loan me his cabin in Michigan."

"Have you ever been to Eagle Pass Lodge?"

"No. Have you?"

"Yes. Years ago with Isaac. It's the creepiest place I've ever been."

"Creepy?"

"You'll find out for yourself if he lets you stay there."

"But I assume it's quiet. That's what I need -- a temporary refuge where I can find out if I have a book in me. I was a little high-handed with the literary agent when she told me a ghostwriter or co-author could write the whole thing for me. I got a bit huffy, told her I wanted to do it myself. Now

I have to find out if I can."

"It was too quiet and remote for me -- for your father too -- but I grant that the place is very luxurious in its way and the property is beautiful if a little wild for my taste. Basically, Eagle Pass Lodge is a place to sleep in the middle of a wild nature preserve. The quiet and isolation would be good for you, though. You wouldn't be tempted to do much of anything other than work on your book. But would you really spend a whole month there?"

"No. I couldn't, even if Bob would let me. But maybe I could work in a week here and there."

"How's Jean doing?"

"Fine."

"I hear she's back from Hazelden."

"Who told you she went there?"

"Her mother."

"I don't think Jean would want many people to know about her stay there, but yes, she's back, and she's on the wagon."

"Her mother says Jean is taking your engagement very badly. I'm sure you know that."

Lexie couldn't conceal her surprise. "What do you mean?"

"She cries constantly. She told her mother you stole Steve from her out of spite."

"That's insane."

"Jean hasn't said anything to you?"

"No. I was in the office today and saw no sign of any resentment. Jean seemed completely normal, cheerful even. She congratulated me when I told her about the engagement, but she hasn't made a big deal of it since."

"What woman reveals her heartbreak to another?"

"You think she's . . . ?"

"Dissembling? Yes, I'd say Jean is dissembling with you but being honest with her mother. She needs her job, so she's not going to tell you the truth. But you might want to keep an eye on her. She's not done fantasizing about Steve and she might not give up easily. And, who knows? Maybe Steve feels the same way Jean does, but you're a much better catch than Jean."

"Matilda!"

Matilda laid her hand on her arm as if to console her step-daughter. "Being a rich woman makes it very hard to trust men. I know that personally. As Isaac's widow, I've had a few chances to remarry, but if I look hard enough, I always find some bad motive lurking in the background. Mostly the bad motives are about money. Grace has had the same experience I have. That's why, much as she loves men, she's never remarried."

Lexie was stung to the core. "But Steve wanted me years ago before I had any money. He's willing to sign a pre-nup."

"It's very convenient, for him, isn't it? High-school sweethearts, both of you divorced and now marriageable at the same time. When your car is destroyed in Indianapolis, he's right there to drive you home. When he's under suspicion for Vicki Grinderman's murder, he runs to you for cover. When your violent ex-husband starts stalking you, Steve offers you the protection of his home. When he can't find the money to develop his Tonkel Road property, you're right there, needing a new house."

"Is that how people see our engagement? Convenient for Steve?"

"Or you buying a husband. How else should they see it? The rumor is that you've bailed Steve out by investing in his development."

"That's ridiculous. I bought a big lot, of course, and he's building my house, but I haven't invested in Elysian Fields the way you mean."

"I told Jean's mother I didn't think you would. After all, you won't even invest in Summit City Metals, which is a family business, so why would you invest in an old boyfriend's business?"

"Matilda, I'm tired of being nagged about the Yard. What do you understand about running a scrap business? Can you read a business plan? Can you critique your son's proposal?"

Matilda was unruffled. "No. I left all that to Isaac and now I'm leaving it to Rolland."

"Well, then, you have no idea whether the Yard is being run well and is a sound investment or not. I'm doing my best to make it profitable with a new consumer recycling center and getting in on the Cash-for-Clunkers program -- which as a taxpayer I find just stupid -- but until the operation gets cleaned up and Rolie either learns the business or stays the hell out of it, I'm not investing another penny. In fact, if things don't turn around in a year, I'm selling my shares."

"That's not a Christian thing to do, Lexie, abandoning your family."

"It's not Christian to waste the resources God gives us, so don't lecture me about the Christian thing. Bob does a good enough job of that, saying I wouldn't have enemies if I were a nicer person. And your son's threats are downright evil."

"What threats?"

"When I told him I might sell out, he said I was in this till

I die. He lured me to a dangerous biker bar, where a friend of his threatened me physically. Speaking of my torched car in Indianapolis, Rolie was the maniac who arranged it. And somehow, for months now, he always knows where I've been. I could go on and on."

"That can't be true."

Lexie sighed. "It is true. You don't know the half about your own son."

"Tell me."

"From high school on he's been dealing drugs, a very dangerous business, so dirty I don't want it anywhere near the Scrapyard. He's been warned to get out of the drug business before he gets killed, but is he smart enough to listen? I wonder." Lexie folded her napkin and placed it beside her plate. "Tell me, Matilda, when he was shot near Angola in February, what did you think had happened? Why was he shot?"

"No one ever told me."

"It wasn't a car-jacking and it wasn't random. He'd previously arranged to have another drug dealer killed and it was a revenge shooting."

"That's slander."

"The truth isn't slander, and unless you tell someone, the secret stays with us and the cops."

"The cops?"

"They know more about your son than you do. It's only a matter of time."

"Until what?"

"Until he gets himself into trouble he can't get out of."

"I don't believe it."

"I'm disappointed in you, Matilda. You invite me to a

nice dinner with no hint that the real purpose is to warn me off Steve and manipulate me into funding your lifestyle."

"You're being paranoid." She patted Lexie's hand. "I'm just telling you the same things your mother would if she were here. Don't marry the wrong man and stay loyal to your family."

"I've been in a lot of tough negotiations, Matilda, but I've never seen anyone quite as unflappable as you. In my experience, the only people who never let their emotions drive them off course are those who are monomaniacal about their goals. And your goal is my money, isn't it?" Lexie stood up. "I could forgive you for that, but bringing my mother into it pushed you right to the line of the unforgivable. I can't imagine a real mother saying the things you just did."

She held back the tears until she reached her car. When she regained rational thought, she realized her step-mother's purpose was to sow the seeds of doubt about marrying Steve. Unfortunately, they landed on fertile ground. Her half-brother and step-mother didn't love her. Jean didn't. Ferrell hadn't either. Even Bob was more concerned about Matilda's and Rolland's welfare than hers. All any of them seemed to want was her money. So why would Steve be any different?

Despite Lexie's best efforts, the wild seeds of doubt began taking root in the deepest, loamiest reaches of her mind.

* * * * *

Along with the doubt came more fear. A few miles before Lexie reached the Dupont exit from the Interstate on her return from Sycamore Hills, her cell phone rang. Unwilling to glance at the screen while driving, she simply answered. She wished she hadn't. It was Rolie.

"So you had dinner with Ma."

"She called you already?"

"No. You're almost home."

"How do you know that?"

"I've got my sources."

She glanced in her rear view mirror. "Are you following me?"

"That's for you to find out. So, did she talk any sense into you?"

"About what?"

"Steve."

"She thinks he's after my money. I can guess where she got that notion."

"You know he's running around on you, don't you?"

"He's not."

"He and Jean? They still got it going on."

"Matilda hinted at that, but Steve and Jean never had anything going on."

"You are so blind, Sis. That night you were in Miami? They had dinner at Chop's. I caught them sneaking out. They looked pretty lovey-dovey, holding hands, whispering. Check with Sorella if you don't believe me."

"One dinner doesn't make an affair."

"You're in denial. I know you. Poor little rich girls like you want to be loved for something other than their money. Well, you never will be."

"You're sick. I'm hanging up."

"Be careful when you drive into the garage."

"What do you mean?"

"I'm dead serious." Then abruptly he was gone.

When she reached Steve's house, she had her eyes on the garage instead of the cement, so she felt the bumps under her tires before she saw what was causing them. When she clicked on her brights, she saw the problem: dozens of rabbit corpses, strewn like a fur carpet on the driveway, all the way to the garage.

Part Three

"Two things are infinite: the universe and human stupidity;
and I'm not sure about the universe."
Albert Einstein

Do you see a man wise in his own eyes?
There is more hope for a fool than for him.
Proverbs 26:12

58

Favors and Prayers

Thursday, July 9, 2009

Early the next morning, Lexie wasted no time waylaying Bob in his office.

"He's got an appointment in five minutes," Chelsea said, rolling back her chair to halt Lexie's progress.

"Where's Xiu-Xiu?"

"She just stepped out for a minute."

Lexie held up an open hand. "Don't bother to get up. I can open his door by myself. And five minutes is all it will take."

Before Bob could rise out of his chair, Lexie took a seat. "I need a favor from you."

"Well, hello to you too."

"Sorry to be so abrupt but Chelsea said you only have a few minutes before your next appointment and I'm in a bit of a panic."

"You know you're my favorite woman in the world and I'll do anything I can for you. So what's the favor?"

"I need to hide out for awhile, somewhere peaceful and quiet. Somewhere remote."

"Why?"

"Two days ago I'd have said just to have a place to start writing a book that a New York publisher has proposed."

"And today?"

"To get away from Rolie."

"Why?"

"He threatened me again last night, and I'm really afraid. He and his mother are telling me not to marry Steve. I think Rolie's following me -- or having me followed -- because everywhere I go, he knows exactly where I am. He warned me to be careful going into the garage. And, what do you know? When I got home last night, there were dead rabbits lying all over Steve's driveway."

"What do rabbits have to do with Rolie?"

"He shoots them every chance he gets. If you've ever been out to his house, you know."

Bob blinked. "I might have heard something about his eternal war with them."

"Steve had a fit when he saw his driveway. He called our friend Dave at the police department."

"Very unwise of him. Don't get the police involved in a family feud."

"It's not a feud, Bob. It's war and I didn't start it, I don't want any part of it, and it's dangerous."

"You said his mother told you not to marry Steve."

"That's right. She's off her rocker."

"What did she say exactly?"

"Both Matilda and Rolie claim that Steve's been seeing Jean behind my back."

"I heard that too."

"You?"

"It's common knowledge."

"It can't be because it's not true."

"Have you asked Steve?"

"Yes. Last night I told him about the warnings from my step-mother and half-brother and he laughed. When I was in Miami on business, he and Jean met by chance while they were shopping and she asked him to have a drink with her. She wanted the chance to apologize to him, that's all. They went their separate ways in the parking lot."

"For what? What did Jean want to apologize for?"

"That's personal between the two of them, and I know all about it, but my point is, they're not seeing each other."

He didn't respond.

"You don't believe me, Bob."

"How do you know they went their separate ways?"

"Because Steve said so and I believe him."

He steepled his hands and pursed his lips. "I suppose it only matters what you believe."

"Oh, dear God."

"Do you want me to pray with you?"

"Not now. I'm way too rattled. I'd like to leave tomorrow to get away from all this. Matilda told me about Eagle Pass Lodge, how beautiful and quiet it is. Is there any chance you'd let me stay there a few days?"

At that moment, Chelsea poked her head in. "Mr. Cartwell is here to see you."

"Tell him I'm running ten minutes late."

When the door was once again closed, before Bob could say anything, Lexie spoke up. "I realize that in the circumstances I'm asking a lot of you."

He hesitated a fraction of a second. "We'll talk about

your intended withdrawal when you get back. But I'm not petty and you have to look out for yourself. 'A prudent man sees danger and takes refuge, but the simple keep going and suffer for it.' That's from Proverbs."

"Very appropriate."

"You're not a simple woman, Alexandra, and your father was like a brother to me. Of course you can stay at the Lodge. Clarissa and I and the family were there over the Fourth and we have no immediate plans to return. Besides, this weekend I'm going to be in Cincinnati chairing a panel for the National Association of Professional Financial Planners." He opened a desk drawer. "I have a set of keys right here. I'll call ahead to my agent so he's there to meet you, air out the place, make sure it's clean and everything's working, stock the place with food and drink. How long do you think you'll stay?"

"I don't know, Bob. Not longer than a week."

"Stay as long as you like. I'm honored to have you as a guest at Eagle Pass."

"One more favor."

"What's that?"

"Please don't tell Rolland where I'll be. I talked about Eagle Pass Lodge with Matilda last night, but since that was before you offered the place and I'd made any definite plans, Rolland can only guess where I am even if he talks to his mother. And I plan to turn off my cell phone."

"You'll be the first person who doesn't mind not being able to use a cell phone up there. Hardly any of them work in the UP."

"I'm so ready for this, Bob, I wish I could leave right now."

"Why don't you?"

"I have to pack. I have some things to do in the office this afternoon to make sure it functions without me. I have to buy a map. I just have things to do."

Bob smiled. "That's a woman for you. Clarissa can't go shopping without packing a bag for emergencies. So when do you think you'll leave? I need to warn Stewie."

"Who's that?"

"My agent. Stewie Kramer and his wife, Alice, take care of the Lodge."

"I plan to leave tomorrow morning. How long will the drive take?"

"About six hours, plus whatever time you take for gassing up, eating lunch, that kind of thing."

Lexie rose, the keys to Eagle Pass Lodge in her hand. "Thank you, Bob. You're a good friend."

"Stay safe."

59

Eagle Pass Lodge

Friday, July 10, 2009

Lexie reached Eagle Pass Lodge late Friday afternoon. Stewie Kramer, a short, bald man in his fifties wearing khakis and a polo shirt and sporting an anchor tattoo on his forearm, was waiting in the courtyard to greet her, carry her luggage up the stairs to the main floor, turn on lights, and show her what doors the keys opened.

Lexie looked at the Lodge. "I didn't realize quite how big this place is."

"Eight thousand square feet," Stewie said with an air of pride. "And this dark green building on your left is a little over half that."

"What is it? It looks like Heidi's cottage on steroids."

"It's called The Alpine Cottage, a copy of a famous lodge in Austria. The ground floor, which has no windows, is for storage of a boat, snowmobiles, golf carts, dune buggies, and bicycles plus other sports equipment of all kinds. There's room for three cars but that space is empty at the moment. You can pull your car in there when we're done. Up above are guest apartments and an office. Mr. Passwatter offered to let Alice and me live in one of the apartments, but we prefer our little cottage -- a real cottage -- in St. Ignace."

When they reached the entry hall to the main lodge, he put down her cases. "First, if it's okay with you, I'll give you the inside tour so you know how the Lodge is laid out. Then we'll double back on a few things so you know how they work. Then we'll tour the outside and finally The Alpine Cottage. There's a lot to take in."

"Lead the way."

"This place is very famous." He pointed to a framed magazine cover on the entry hall wall. "Eagle Pass Lodge was featured in *Log Home Living* a couple years ago. Mr. Passwatter is very proud of that fact. There are nine bathrooms in the house. The first one we come to is this guest half-bath." He turned on the light and stood back to let her enter. "Very distinctive. You'll notice the sink is a beautiful amethyst geode, polished so it won't cut your hands."

"The soap dish. Is that what I think it is?"

"A bear paw. Notice the stuffed eagle above the mirror."

She smiled. "He looks like he's daring someone to pee in his territory."

"He's the only eagle in the house. The other bathrooms have owls or crows."

"Oh, well, that's a comfort. It's not kosher to kill eagles, is it?"

"I don't know how Mr. Passwatter got his hands on this guy, but he didn't kill him and he'd never do anything illegal."

He led her to the great room. "The furniture is all custom-made, very distinctive."

Lexie looked at a giant chair beside the massive fireplace.

"Is that chair made of tree trunks?"

"It is. The trunks of saplings so the legs are proportional. You'll notice the rest of the furniture except for the sofas is made of antlers, drift wood, twigs, and saplings, highly polished, of course. Very tasteful, wouldn't you say?"

She choked back a laugh. Antlers and drift wood and saplings were poking out everywhere. "You wouldn't want to stumble around in the dark with a snootful, would you, Stewie? You might stab yourself and bleed out before anyone could reach you."

Stewie smiled. "I don't think Mr. Passwatter ever gets a snootful, as you put it. You'll notice the stuffed civet on one side of the mantel, the albino jackrabbit on the other." He pointed to the wood floor. "The rugs are bear and pony hides."

"Oh, my gosh, that bear in the corner is taller than I am!"

"It's just a little black bear, actually, not a grizzly. We don't have grizzlies here."

"But there are black bears here, is that what you're saying?"

"Quite a few of them, but they mostly stay to themselves. They live in the woods, fish on the beach, rarely eat meat. An occasional moose, but that's about it."

"*Mostly*? They mostly stay to themselves? They *rarely* eat meat?"

"So long as you don't feed them or leave food outside, they won't bother you. He does look rather fierce, though, doesn't he? Quite a fine specimen I'd say. The fireplace wall is faced with local river rock and you'll notice there is no stack of firewood because in this room all you have to do is flick the switch on the wall. The fireplace is gas-fired, so no need to remember your Girl Scout training."

"As if I had any. Are the lampshades what I think they are?"

"Animal skins and shells." He pointed toward the fourteen-foot ceiling. "You'll notice all the animal heads. Deer, moose, elk, bear. Those fish are pike and carp, among the biggest ever caught in Lake Michigan."

"Did Bob shoot all the animals I see on the walls, catch all those fish?"

"I don't think so. But he loves nature."

"I like nature too. But I've never experienced it quite like this -- peering at me from dead eyes."

Stewie looked at a moose head as if seeing it for the first time. "Well, in the circumstances, it's better than peering at you with living eyes, wouldn't you say? I take it you're a city girl, Miss Royce."

"To tell you the truth, I never thought of myself that way before, but I do now."

He led her along the window wall. "As you can see, the dining room is very special. The floor-to-ceiling windows provide a great lake view. The table is a giant round slab of wood cut from the base of a tree with the bark still on. The chairs, you'll notice, have hooves."

"Real hooves?"

"Yes. We have lots of deer in these parts."

"Well, a few less now." She counted the chairs. "Eight less, to be exact. I hope one of them is the deer that killed my mother."

"Killed how? Car accident?"

"Yes. I don't weep when I watch *Bambi*, I'll tell you that."

"I don't either. People have entirely the wrong idea about deer. They're not sweet and passive, and if their hooves hit you in the chest? You're dead. In the rutting season, the bucks are especially wild. They'll even attack a full-grown man, thinking he's a rival." He seemed to catch himself. "But I don't want to scare you. We've never had a deer attack here. You leave them alone, they leave you alone."

"They're more afraid of me than . . . ."

"Exactly," he said.

Another twenty minutes and they had covered the first floor. "Now let me take you up to the bedrooms. I'll let you see the master suite, but you'll be staying in a guest bedroom down the hall. When you reach this landing, you'll notice Scrofa." He rubbed Scrofa's snout. "He's a Russian wild boar, imported to the Americas by sportsmen."

"Scrofa?"

"*Sus scrofa*. That's the genus, I believe. Or is it the species? I forget. Anyway, Scrofa's completely harmless now, but hunting wild boar isn't a sport for the faint-hearted, believe me. Well, let's take a look at your bedroom. We've put you at the end of this corridor in the bedroom with a sleeping porch facing the lake, and of course it has its own bathroom." He turned on the light. "You'll see it's wood-paneled and the four posters on the bed are birch trees. Cured, of course, and shellacked. Watch the roots. They're easy to stumble over in the night."

"I have never seen a stranger room."

"The word I'd use is 'unique.' Now, let me take you down to the veranda."

He let her take in the lake view before explaining what she was seeing. "This veranda is seventy feet long. There's a barbecue at one end, a little screened porch at the other, and a dozen rocking chairs in between. You'll notice the lawn is fairly deep with a sharp drop-off. There's no fence to warn you that you're about to fall off the bluff, so keep your eye on those evergreens marking the edge and you'll be okay." He pointed to the screened porch. "There are a lot of night critters here, so once it's dark, most people -- well, at least the women -- retreat to the screened porch."

"What night critters?"

"Bats, skunks, raccoons, possums, cougars, coyotes, wolves, civets. Of course, if you have a fire in the fire pit, the animals will stay away. Let's walk down there and take a look." He invited her to sit on a limestone slab canted into the ground. "It's very cozy at night to build a fire here."

"But the woods are only a yard away. That's where the critters live, right?"

"Yes, but as I said, once you have a fire going, you're safe. I've arranged the wood for your first fire so all you have to do is light it, but there's plenty of firewood in that pile. Alice stocked the refrigerator with hot dogs and the pantry with the makings of s'mores, so I hope you'll give it a try."

"How do you get down to the beach?"

"Let me show you." He walked to the opposite side of the property and around a hedge. "See this cigar-store Indian? And this totem? You can see them from the veranda. They mark the head of the stairway. It's 93 steps down to the beach, by the way, interrupted every twenty feet or so with landings outfitted with benches. Take your time coming up. Even young people like you get out of breath. We don't want you having a heart attack. Most people don't go down there at night, of course. It's very dark."

"And the bears are fishing, I suppose."

"Don't let the bears ruin your vacation, Miss Royce. You won't see one while you're here, I guarantee you that. Just relax and enjoy the unspoiled nature. That's the main attraction up here. If you want to fish, by the way, there's equipment in The Alpine Cottage."

"Good to know." *But I've never fished in my life.*

"Are you expecting guests?"

"No. It's just me. I came up here for the peace and quiet."

"Well, you're going to get it here. You're a hundred feet from the neighbors on either side, so it's going to be very quiet."

"So nobody will hear me scream."

"What?"

"Never mind. Just a city girl's wild imagination. I feel like I just walked into Hiawatha's territory."

"Wrong place, wrong century. We're in Ojibwe territory. You might want to visit the museum in St. Ignace if you get the chance. Now, let me show you how to start a fire in the fireplaces and operate the jacuzzi, the barbecue grill, the televisions, and the generator in case there's a power outage. We get some big storms, you know."

"You do?"

"Spectacular lightning and thunder. In fact, a storm is predicted for tonight."

"Oh, great."

"Don't worry. That's why I'm going to show you how to operate the generator, and there's a whole bin of candles and matches in the pantry. Here's my card in case you need me. I'm going to show you a lot of stuff, just as a precaution because I don't actually expect you to remember everything. I'm on call twenty-four hours, and I don't want you to hesitate for a second to call me if something isn't working. That's what I'm here for. My wife will come by tomorrow around ten to clean up the kitchen and bathroom, make your bed, do your laundry, get your grocery list, so you just rest. Let us take care of you. That's what Mr. Passwatter told us to do. You're a very special guest."

"That was kind of him."

"He told me you're writing a book." He made a little half bow. "We're honored to have an author as a guest."

She laughed. "The honor is premature, Stewie. I'm not an author yet. This week I'm going to find out if I have a book in my head." *And a marriage in my future.* "By the way, will my cell phone work up here? I was going to leave it in my briefcase, but I'm starting to think I might need it an emergency."

"Most cell phones don't work up here, but there's a land line in the kitchen. If you want to use your cell, you can drive into St. Ignace, where the service is better. Before I leave, let me show you the cottage."

Back in the courtyard, he opened a door to the cottage, flipped a bank of light switches, and led her through a passage to the room where the bicycles were stored. He walked over to an old blue Schwinn. "This is the one Mrs. Passwatter uses, so if you want a little exercise, you might want to try this one out first."

"Where does that staircase in the corner go?"

"Mr. Passwatter's office. Around the back of the cottage you'll find an outside staircase to a veranda that runs across the whole back side. There's an outside door to the office up there. Would you like a tour of the upstairs?"

"Sure. Why not?"

Their first stop was Bob's office. Stewie unlocked the door and ushered Lexie in. "You'll notice how neat it is, everything in its place. I was a Chief Petty Officer when I retired from the Navy, so I think I'm pretty well organized, but I could take some lessons from Mr. Passwatter."

"This is quite a setup for a vacation home."

"Poor man. When the family comes to visit, there isn't a day goes by that Mr. Passwatter isn't up here, working away in his private sanctuary for at least a few hours. No one ever joins him in this office. As you can see, there's a whole bank of computers, a big safe, a fax machine, several printers, everything you'd expect to see in an office."

"Where does that door go?"

"An interior closet. It's always locked. Mr. Passwatter once told Alice that's where the big guns are kept -- deer-hunting, I believe -- and the family stores costumes and props in there."

"Costumes and props? For what?"

"I understand they put on little skits and puppet shows for their granddaughter, and I know they sometimes dress up on holidays, like Halloween and Christmas. Anyway, this office seems to be the price of being rich and successful. You never get away from work. Me? I don't envy Mr. Passwatter a bit. I'd rather be me, living my modest little life, a cozy home and a good wife, without his worries and responsibilities. How about you?"

"A modest little life sounds good to me."

60

Scrofa

Friday, July 10, 2009

For the rest of the afternoon and evening, now all alone, Lexie felt like she'd stepped into a parallel universe. It was going to take awhile to get used to the place, so many rooms, so much bizarre furniture, so many dead animals with their eyes following her everywhere she went. The smell of the place was strange too, damp and very earthy. She wished she'd brought some scented candles. Still, she enjoyed the novelty of having the luxurious lodge all to herself with nothing on her schedule but writing a book.

She thought about the note she'd left for Steve after he went to work. "Steve -- I need a few days to myself to think about the book and other things. Bob is letting me use Eagle Pass Lodge near St. Ignace. Don't worry if you can't reach me -- I don't know yet if cell phones work up there. I'll be safe, and I'll be back. -- Lexie." If he'd left a note like that for her, she'd be puzzled, maybe even angry. It was downright rude not to warn him well ahead of time that she was leaving for a few days. And what did "other things" mean? This trip was the craziest thing she'd ever done. But she couldn't make herself pick up the wall phone in the kitchen to call him.

Before supper, she decided to descend to the beach and dip her toe in. Only a few yards of sand allowed her to walk between the rocks under the bluff and the lapping waves of Lake Michigan. Off in the distance she could see freighters, one after the other, carrying cargo she could only guess at.

Because she was facing west, she didn't notice the stranger approaching from the east with his German Shepherd until the dog barked. Upon hearing the bark, Lexie whirled around. The stranger was carrying something that looked like a weapon. Meeting a stranger on this lonely, deserted stretch of beach was alarming enough, but the sound of the German Shepherd and the sight of the weapon caused her heart to race with fear. She considered running to the stairway, but she'd have to run past the stranger, and if he meant harm, she didn't have a chance. But if he was just a friendly neighbor, it would look foolish, even rude.

"Evening," she said warily. The weapon, she saw with relief, was only a policeman's flashlight and the dog, who was on a long lead, didn't lunge at her.

"Evening. Hope we didn't scare you, Miss."

"Not at all." She put her hand on her heart. "Well, just a little. Do you live nearby?"

"About half a mile down. I'm Will Berry."

"Lexie Royce," she said.

"I haven't seen you here before."

"I'm a guest at the Lodge, just trying to get the lay of the land."

"Well, it's a nice beach, but don't stay down here too long. There's a storm coming, you know. Bruno and I are going to head back soon ourselves. He looks tough, but he's scared to death of thunder and lightning."

"May I pet him?"

"He doesn't like his head touched, but if you extend your hand under his chin, he'll realize you mean no harm."

She did as she was told. "Hello, Bruno. You're a handsome fellow." She laughed lightly. "I wish you were my roommate tonight."

"He's a very special dog, you know. He was a K-9 officer until a couple of years ago, trained to find cadavers."

"You're kidding!"

"No. He was very good at it."

"Are you a policeman too?"

"Was. I retired a year ago. Bruno and I never worked together while we were officers, but when I heard about him, I had to give him a cushy retirement. The old boy richly deserves it." Will Berry cast an eye at the sky. "Well, Bruno and I are creatures of habit, so if we're going to complete our usual walk before the storm hits, we've got to get going."

"Actually, I was just on my way up too. Good night." The climb back up the bluff was as enervating as anything she'd ever experienced. Twice she took advantage of the benches to rest.

Before it got really dark, Lexie stepped off the veranda and walked to the fire pit with a bag of marshmallows, a couple of willow sticks, and a split of Prosecco. It was very strange, sitting by herself on a limestone slab, no one to talk to, nothing to do but experience the moment. As the sun set into the lake, the moon rose out of the woods, and the stars became visible one by one, she marveled at the vastness of the universe, the power of the waves below. Strangely, sitting under a vast sky near a huge inland sea, surrounded by enormous trees and swarms of unseen animals, evoked more awe of the Creator than being in church.

She was so lost in thought that she hardly noticed the gradual drop in temperature, the rising of the wind, the increasing noise of the waves crashing against the bluff. Sitting with her back to the woods a few yards away, she stared at the fire as it consumed log after log in honeycomb bites and crackling explosions.

At the sound of a rustling in the trees and bushes behind her, she was jolted out of her reverie. Some big animal was moving about. For a minute, the sounds moved closer, then stopped, then moved closer still. Was the animal stalking her? What was it? Was it gazing at her with hunger or curiosity? She was frozen, afraid to turn around. But a sudden explosion of sound brought her to her feet, armed only with a willow stick and a scream. The animal that burst onto the lawn paused to stare at her a few seconds, then bounded across to the woods on the other side of the property. She laughed hysterically. It was a deer, not a bear. Still, it was time to go in.

She was mixing a gin and tonic in the kitchen when the wall phone rang. She stared at it, unsure whether to answer. If only it had caller ID. Somebody was probably trying to reach the Passwatters . . . but why would that be? Or maybe it was Stewie. On the fourth ring, she picked up.

"Alexandra. It's Bob."

"Hi."

"I know it's late, and I'm about to go to bed, but I wanted to be sure everything's all right at the Lodge."

"You're in Cincinnati?"

"Got here around noon."

"How's the conference?"

"Tedious, but I'll liven it up tomorrow. So. Are you enjoying yourself? Is Stewie taking good care of you?"

"Everything's great, thanks. I'm just making myself a drink to take out to the veranda. A storm's blowing up, so I thought I'd watch it awhile."

"Wish Clarissa and I were there with you. This hotel room is stuffy, but what can you do? I can't even open a window."

"Well, this place definitely isn't stuffy."

"Have fun. Anything you need, just call Stewie."

"I'll do that, Bob. And thanks again."

Sitting on the veranda, she discovered, wasn't peaceful. The bats were flying cargo runs up and down, back and forth. The idea that a mammal could fly -- equipped with sonar and an appetite for insects and darkness, no less -- was just creepy. It made her shiver.

Then the promised storm blew up. First, the lightning flickered above the clouds like a laser-and-fog show teasing the fans of a rock concert into a frenzy. Suddenly, shadowy figures near the stairway to the beach caught her eye. Were those men standing there, looking her way? Were they moving, or was it a trick of the light? She stood up, alarmed, ready to run into the house, but then, without warning, lightning split the clouds, illuminating the darkness in blinding fluorescent flashes. The shadowy figures were revealed as nothing more than the cigar-store Indian and totem pole. Though she was alone, with no one to laugh at her, she was embarrassed at herself. Her overheated imagination was running away with her.

More flashes of lightning split the clouds. The thunder

rumbled across the sky and vibrated through her chest. The wind bent the pines as if they were made of rubber, and the rain splattered in fat drops, gradually building in volume until it was sheeting sideways in pellets that stung her face. Wrapping herself in an oilskin she'd found in the house, she retreated to a back corner of the screened porch until even there she was drenched. Finally she retreated to the house, where she watched the biblical display of power, hoping the lights wouldn't go out. It was a forlorn hope. Ten minutes into the storm, a bolt of lightning struck somewhere near the bluff and the Lodge went completely dark. She sat, paralyzed, in the Great Room, wondering if she could even find her way to the kitchen pantry where the candles and flashlights were stored. She could remember nothing whatsoever about the generator. Of course, the kitchen phone probably wouldn't be working, so she couldn't call Stewie for help.

To her great relief, the lights finally flickered on, and with the light, rational thought returned. She had to get hold of herself, stop being afraid. The stranger and his dog on the beach weren't serial killers. The animal crashing around in the woods near the fire pit wasn't a bear. The bats didn't make a nest in her hair. The figures standing at the stairway to the beach weren't there to scalp her. The storm didn't blow her away and the lightning didn't strike her. The lights came back on.

It was after midnight by the time she mounted the stairs, patted Scrofa's head on the landing, and made her way through the long corridor to her bedroom. She hadn't touched her computer or Kindle, watched any of the DVDs she'd brought, tested her cell phone, or made any decisions at all. She'd been a slug. Doing nothing felt good in its way

-- an unfamiliar guilty pleasure.

And though she knew Scrofa was harmless, he nevertheless figured in a particularly vivid nightmare about a man in drag being unmasked as a ferocious animal, his curved tusks dripping blood the same color as his porcine eyes. When she woke from the nightmare, she looked at her watch. Six in the morning. She never woke that early.

Before she got out of bed, she closed her eyes again, trying desperately to recall the threatening figure and the mask it was wearing. Was the mask Rolie's face? Or Steve's? Or Drago's? Or Nate's? Or Dwight's? Or Murph's? Or Ferrell's? The face of anyone she knew? Or a stranger's -- perhaps some intuition about the identity of the Panty Raider? What did the feminine costume mean? Perhaps it meant there was really a scary woman behind the mask -- Jean maybe, or Matilda. But the harder she tried to reconstruct the mask and the costume, to locate one identifying detail, the further the image receded into the depths of her brain.

As she walked down the stairs to the kitchen, she wished she had a dog like Bruno to keep her company. Somewhere she'd once heard someone say that the more he saw of humans, the more he liked dogs. How wise!

She made herself a pot of coffee and took a cup out to the veranda. As the sun rose over the lake, she felt a little less afraid and a little more hopeful with every second. She would stop imagining boogeymen around every corner. She would embrace the isolation and strange beauty of Eagle Pass Lodge. She would outline the book she wanted to write and review a few more prospectuses and annual reports. She would examine her heart. And she would call Steve.

She still didn't know if she'd write a book or how she'd

make it up with Steve, but she did know one thing. When she returned to Fort Wayne, she would visit an animal shelter to find a dog who needed her as much as she needed him. There would be one creature in her life who was loyal without knowing a thing about her bank account.

61

Trolls Do It Under the Bridge

Saturday, July 11, 2009

After Alice had come and gone, it was almost lunchtime, so Lexie returned to her bedroom suite to hang up the clothes she'd tossed on the bed and take a shower. Then she'd drive into St. Ignace for a lunch of fried whitefish at a restaurant on the water, poke around the shops a little, and see if her cell phone worked.

She discovered that Alice had put her clothes away, some in the dresser, some in the closet, but when she stepped out of the shower and prepared to put on underwear, she could find none in the dresser. No bras, no panties. She checked the suitcase tucked into the closet, but it was empty. She checked the drawer in the bedside table; nothing. She checked the hook on the back of the bathroom door, but the only thing hanging there was her sweat suit.

"The Panty Raider's here?" she asked aloud and then instantly realized how silly that thought was. Alice must have assumed all her underwear needed to be laundered. Or else Phyllis had simply forgotten to pack any. It wasn't a big deal to buy some new things in St. Ignace, but she hated putting on underwear she'd already worn. She was reminded of Rolie's taunt about not hanging out her dirty underwear for all the world to see. Well, the world wouldn't see it, of course, but she'd know she was wearing it.

After she was seated on the deck of a restaurant and had ordered lunch, she checked her cell. It worked, so she called Steve. "I just wanted you to know I'm fine, sitting in the sun, about to eat some fish."

"I was surprised to find your note."

"I'm sorry. I panicked yesterday."

"The dead rabbits in the driveway?"

"They horrified me."

"Are you sure that's the only reason you left without a word in advance?"

"It's the main reason."

"What's the un-main reason?"

"According to Bob, everybody knows you and Jean still have a thing for each other. Both Matilda and Rolie also made a big point about how no man could love anything about me other than my money. So I wanted to get away to think."

"We talked about this when you got home from your dinner with Matilda. All I can do is repeat what I told you before: I never had a thing with Jean. Never. I'm not responsible for what she imagines we did in the past or might do in the future. And as for your money .... Well, you know how I feel about that. I'm proud of your business skills."

"Thank you."

"And I'm not going to lie. It's nice to marry a woman with some money of her own so if the economy really goes to hell and never recovers, or if I break my back in a freak accident, there's a safety net to catch both of us, but I'd marry you even if you were poor as dirt. In fact, if you were poor as dirt, in some ways that would be good for my ego because people expect me as the man to be the big bread-winner -- which I would be with almost any other woman in the country."

"I never thought of it that way."

"But love trumps pride, so here I am, humbly ready to marry you any time you're ready."

"Me too. The doubts are really about my worth as a woman, not about your character."

"I don't understand that, but I'll let it go for now."

"Why don't you come up tomorrow? I can see the ferries plying back and forth between St. Ignace, where I'm sitting, and Mackinac Island, which I can see and want to visit. I'm thinking of going there tomorrow, but it'd be more fun to face the fudge and horse manure as a couple."

"The what?"

"Fudge and horse manure. Mackinac Island is famous for fresh and abundant handmade fudge. And no cars are allowed, only horses and bikes, so manure is fresh and abundant too, I hear."

He laughed. "You make it sound so enticing."

"You'll never believe, by the way, what Phyllis forgot to pack for me."

"A windbreaker?"

"My underwear."

"I take it that's a good excuse to go shopping."

"Actually, I needed no excuse for that. I've given myself the day off just to acclimate myself. I'm going to try one of the pasties the UP is known for and I already found underwear and a troll t-shirt."

"Did you say troll?"

"That's what the people up here in the UP call anyone who lives below the Bridge. I bought a t-shirt to sleep in that says, 'Trolls do it below the Bridge,' meaning of course the famous Mackinac Bridge. Which, by the way, is just as spectacular in real life as in the photos."

"Not to change the subject, but I have some news you might be interested in. Ferrell's in jail and can't make bail."

"The Prosecutor really thinks Ferrell killed his girlfriend?"

"He must. I've heard that Tiffany wasn't raped, nothing was taken from her sister's apartment, and as you know Ferrell has a history of domestic violence. Turns out, he's in debt, big time, and the life insurance policy will bail him out nicely. So if there's someone out there who had a better opportunity or a better motive to kill her, that man hasn't been identified."

"Her murder was so much like Vicki's: a pretty girl, all alone, late at night, bruised and strangled, left naked. The Prosecutor doesn't think Ferrell killed Vicki too, does he?"

"I have no idea, but the differences between the two murders are considerable, so there may be two different killers. Vicki was raped, Tiffany wasn't. Vicki's home was broken into, but the apartment Tiffany was in wasn't broken into. Blood and semen were present with Vicki but not with Tiffany."

"In other words, the murder of Vicki was essentially sexual but the murder of Tiffany wasn't."

"Put it another way: The point of the crime against Vicki was rape, with murder the afterthought, probably to keep her from identifying the killer, whereas the point of the crime against Tiffany was murder. I'm just speculating, of course, but If I'm right, then Ferrell might have killed Tiffany because he was mad at her, but unless he's a lot worse person than we think, he had nothing to do with Vicki."

"You're starting to break up, Steve. I only have one bar left on this phone."

"Is there a phone at the Lodge?"

"Yes. Let me find the number. I wrote it down somewhere." But as she dug in her purse, her phone went dead. Oh, well, she'd call him later from the Lodge's land line.

62

Pervert

Saturday, July 11, 2009

Saturday around five in the afternoon, Drago reached Rolie's ranch house on State Line Road. He'd picked up the Rolls on Friday morning, taken it to the dealership, The British Embassy, for an oil change and tire rotation, and was returning it to his imperious friend as the kind of favor friends do for friends -- except the favors were never mutual.

Rolie's driveway from State Line Road was long, curving around to the back of the house, ending in a large parking pad at the two-car garage, not far from the pool area.

Drago stopped beside his own Jeep, which he'd left for Rolie's convenience. The Harley-Davidson was sitting under a canvas cover near a far corner of the garage. Leaving the motor running, Drago got out, rang the bell on the back door, and waited. Then he rang again. No answer. Then he knocked. Frustrated, he walked to the sliding doors off the family room, pushed through the boxwood, and peered in but saw no one. The big-screen television was dark and the house seemed preternaturally still. He walked around the house to the front door and rang that bell. No answer. He returned to the back door and rang one more time, just in case. Nothing.

Disgusted, he returned to the Rolls, clicked the button for the garage door and prepared to put the car in the garage, though Rolie had commanded him never to do that. He didn't trust anyone but himself to garage the machine. His girlfriend's old Buick Regal was parked on the right, nearest the interior door to the house, so Drago prepared to ease into the narrow space on the left of the Buick.

As Drago was nosing the Rolls in, something caught his eye almost dead ahead. He stopped, put the car in park, and stared. Something was hanging from a beam. It had the rough shape of a person -- a mannequin or maybe an inflatable pool bumper. Leaving the engine running, he got out of the car and walked into the garage to get a better look.

But it wasn't a mannequin or pool bumper. It was Rolie.

Drago wasn't a novice in the world of dead bodies, but he was dumbfounded. He walked within a foot of the body and reached out a thumb and index finger to pinch the hem of Rolie's swim trunks, rotating him a quarter turn so he could see the face. He was pretty sure from the fat belly it was his friend, but once he saw the face with its oddly stubbled chin, there was no doubt. Drago stared at his dead friend for a minute or two, his mind completely devoid of thought. Then he looked down and saw a little three-legged stool, lying on its side in the mess made by a dying body. Rolie must have stood there to tie the rope and then kicked over the stool.

So Rolie had hanged himself! He couldn't believe it. What had gone so wrong that the Scrapyard Prince would want to end his own life?

He was backing up, not sure what to do with the Rolls, when he noticed that the interior door to the house was open. Out of curiosity, he decided to enter the house. Didn't suicides usually leave a note? If there was one, he wanted to read it. Using his knuckles, he pushed the door wide and walked into the kitchen. It was a mess. There were dishes and pots on the stove, cereal boxes and potato chip sacks scattered across the counters, coffee grounds and a milk carton in the sink, and a chair turned over. He walked through to the family room, detoured into the dining room, and finally reached the bedroom corridor, where the distinctive rotten-potato smell he detected in the garage was even stronger. He peeked into a bathroom and a bedroom, both neat, then reached a closed door at the end of the corridor. Covering his hand with the bottom of his work shirt, he tried the knob.

Inside was a horror. A dresser drawer had been thrown on the floor, a lamp knocked over, and the sheets half torn off the bed. A blackout curtain was hanging by one ring from the rod, and a pair of women's shorts was lying in the doorway to the bathroom. A woman lay across the mattress, naked. He crept close enough to see that her wrists had been tied to the bedposts and she'd been strangled with a rope. He recognized the butterfly tattoo on her neck and a hank of stick-straight red hair. Though the woman's face was covered by a pillow, he knew it was Sorella. Had Rolie killed her in a fit of rage, or had she died in a sex act that went too far, after which a remorseful Rolie took his own life?

As Drago was backing out of the room, he noticed something scattered on the floor. Photographs. Five of them. He knelt down to take a closer look, careful not to touch them. The images were shocking and disgusting: a pussy-wussy man wearing women's lingerie, a different set of underwear and a different background in each picture. Mr. Pussy-wussy had photographed himself by facing into a mirror, which caught a little bit of the room he was standing in, his own hands, and his torso. The flash from the camera obscured his face. Who was the man? Where was he standing? What was he doing? Whose underwear was he wearing?

The torso wasn't familiar to him. It wasn't Rolie's because the man in the picture wasn't fat. Sometimes the men at the Yard took their shirts off when the day was exceptionally hot, but he wasn't interested in other men's bodies and couldn't put a name to these pictures. Drago tried to picture the men who worked out at the Parkview YMCA, where he had a membership, and the men who ran the Mastodon Stomp, but nothing clicked. All he could say for sure was that the man in the photographs was white and athletic, in good shape, though definitely not in the right shape to model women's lingerie. The man seemed to have no hair on his body.

Why did Rolie and Sorella have these photographs of a pervert in their bedroom? He knew some people did strange things behind closed doors, but looking at this pervert would surely turn normal people off sex. So what purpose did these pictures serve?

With a deep sigh, Drago returned to the garage, taking one more look around for a suicide note but finding nothing. He cut the motor on the Rolls and spent a brief minute contemplating what to do. Six months ago, he'd have hightailed it out of there, but he was a different man now. He'd left the past behind him. He had responsibilities. He had a respectable job with a decent future. He had a wife and was about to become a father. His mother was pleased he had a real job. He was innocent; running away might make him look guilty. He could account for where he'd been every minute since he picked up the Rolls Friday morning, when Rolie and Sorella were very much alive, and there were plenty of witnesses to corroborate his whereabouts. And he wanted to know what had happened to his friend.

He called 911 on his cell phone, explaining what he'd seen and giving the dispatcher directions to Rolie's house. While he waited for the Sheriff, he got a call from his mother.

"Drago, I have bad news. I took Mr. Wright a sandwich and a thermos of lemonade out to Elysian Fields. The grading crew found bones today."

"Bones?"

"You know what I'm talking about."

"Shit. . . . Now what?"

"I don't know. The place was swarming with officers and dogs."

"I need a minute to think."

Then he called Lucy to tell her about Rolie but not about the bones.

63

Let's Talk About the Deceased

Saturday, July 11, 2009

Drago was asked to sit out by the pool while the Sheriff's investigative team pored over the house, the Rolls, the grounds, looking for clues. While the team was doing its work, a deputy he'd never seen before asked him questions and took notes. After an hour of questions about how he happened to be at the deceased's house driving the deceased's car, the deputy said, "Let's talk about the deceased. Does he have a job?"

"He's the part-owner of Summit City Metals and Scrapyard, but he rarely goes there. Nate Grabbendorf runs it. I work there."

"Who are the other owners?"

"His mother and sister."

"Tell me about them."

"Matilda -- that's his mother -- was married to Rolie's father. I think she's living on the southwest side of Fort Wayne now. Mizz Royce -- Alexandra Royce -- is his sister. My mom is her housekeeper."

"Where would I find your mother and the deceased's

sister?"

"My mom lives in Huntertown, a few blocks from where I live. Her name is Phyllis Whitlow. Mizz Royce lives in Autumn Ridge with Steve Wright -- you know, Wright Construction. But she may not be home."

"How do you know that?"

"I took the Rolls yesterday morning and on the way to the dealer took a peek at the read-out on a tracking device Rolie put on his sister's MINI-Cooper. She was in Michigan, headed north on I-75. I don't know where she was going."

The deputy looked startled. "Did you say he put a tracking device on his sister's car?"

Drago nodded.

"Why?"

"Don't know."

"Who put it on there?"

Drago hesitated. Rolie couldn't dispute the lie, and it was his idea, after all. "He did, I suppose."

"Did Miss Royce know about it?"

"I don't know." *But I sort of warned her to have the service guy look the car over so it could be found.*

"You said the woman in the bedroom is Sorella. She had a pillow over her face, so how'd you identify her? Did you lift up the pillow?"

"No. She's been living out here for awhile. I recognized the butterfly tattoo on her neck. She has red hair."

"Does she have a last name?"

"Probably, but I never heard it."

"Where'd the two deceased meet?"

Stop saying "deceased," would you? My friend had a name. He was alive once. "You mean Rolie and Sorella?"

The deputy nodded.

"Probably at Sue-A-Side."

"What's that? How do you spell it? Just like it sounds?"

"Don't know about the spelling. It's a bar on the Lincoln Highway outside of New Haven. It's where bikers hang out. Hang on." Drago dug into his jeans pocket. "I have a matchbook from there."

The deputy looked at the matchbook and then wrote down the name in his notes. "You ever go there?"

"No. Rolie handed me this once."

The deputy pointed to the covered motorcycle. "Is that the bike the deceased rode?"

"That's it. Rolie just started riding a few months ago."

"You have any names of people he hung out with at Sue-A-Side?"

"The only ones he mentioned were Sue, the owner, and Murph."

"What about them?"

"He said Sue's a tough character. Murph was his friend, except . . . ."

"Except what?"

"Yesterday, when I picked up the Rolls, he said Murph would be paying him a visit around noon -- noon, yesterday, I mean, not noon today -- so he and Sorella might take my Jeep so they wouldn't be here. Rolie was sort of joking around, but he sounded worried, like he didn't want to run into Murph, no way, no how."

"You have any idea what he'd be worried about?"

"Money. He was always worried about money."

"You think he owed this guy money? This Murph was coming to collect or something?"

"Could be."

"Collecting a drug debt?"

Drago tried to look puzzled. *I got out of that business months ago, and Rolie said he did too, but what do I know for sure?* "Not that I know of."

"If the deceased owned a big place like Summit City Metals, why was he worried about money?"

"Rolie lived large, but the Yard hasn't been doing very well ever since his dad died, so the money isn't what it used to be. Rolie liked his toys and he liked to gamble. Every year he went to Las Vegas, and once in awhile he had me drive him to casinos around the State."

"What's this Murph look like?"

"I only saw him once. Big white guy, goatee, silver earring, wearing a leather vest, no shirt, and a leather cap." Drago suddenly saw Mr. Pussy-wussy posing in fancy lingerie. "Murph didn't have hair on his chest, which reminds me of something. Have you seen those pictures in the bedroom where Sorella was?"

"Yes. Why?"

"Go in and look at 'em again. The guy in those pictures is hairless too."

"Stay here."

"I'm not going anywhere."

When the deputy returned, he nodded at Drago. "Good observation. Do you know if Murph is a cross-dresser, a transvestite or something?"

"You mean, a guy who wears women's underwear?"

The deputy nodded.

"No. I never even knew people did that -- not for sure -- till I saw those pictures. But have you heard about the murder of Vicki Grinderman?"

"Yes."

"She was one of my wife's friends. The story is she was found naked and some of her underwear was missing. I once talked about that with Mizz Royce after the Panty Raider, as the girls call him, took Mizz Royce's underwear from her house. You don't suppose the guy who killed my wife's friend killed Rolie and Sorella too, do you?"

"Are we talking about Murph?"

"Maybe. I don't know. Just thinking out loud. Can't be too many guys in the world like that, right?"

64

Dogs and Bones

Saturday, July 11, 2009

The rest of Saturday afternoon and evening was for Lexie a time of delicious anticipation. Steve was joining her. She'd done a foolish and hurtful thing, leaving that cryptic, vaguely threatening note for him, saying she had "other things" to think about. But he had forgiven her. She'd never make that mistake again. Living with him for months, like friendly roommates, allowed her to see his true character without the distorting fog of a sexual relationship. He did love her. And she loved him. He was easy to live with. She could imagine living with him forever.

Instead of starting an outline for her book, she decided to start planning a wedding and honeymoon, but doing Internet research was too difficult in the UP, so she switched to her Kindle, which she took down to the beach. She had read Joel Rosenberg's book about the End Times, *The Ezekiel Option*. Now it was time to start *The Copper Scroll*.

She was alternately reading and gazing out at the vastness of Lake Michigan when she suddenly remembered she'd never called Steve back with directions and the Lodge's phone number. So she ran back up the stairs and, panting, went to the kitchen wall phone and punched in his cell number. "Steve, I'm sorry, I just remembered you don't have directions from St. Ignace."

"It's okay. I haven't started yet. You sound like you're out of breath."

"I just ran up 93 steps from the beach. Anybody who lived here full-time wouldn't need to work out in a gym -- though there is a gym on the ground floor. When are you starting?"

"Unfortunately, it's going to be late. My guys were clearing that grove on the edge of your lot when they found a couple of bones that look like they might be human near a piece of cloth that might or might not be part of an old quilt. The cloth is so moldy the original color is impossible to determine, but some stitching is intact and the cloth has layers. The site's been shut down all day, investigators swarming over it like ants. In fact, that's where I still am."

"Human bones?"

"Could be animal, but one of them looks suspiciously like a fibula."

"That property was once a farm, so maybe it's where the family buried their dead back in the 1800s."

"Then I'd expect to find whole skeletons and wooden coffins and maybe a few old grave markers, not a fibula, maybe some toe bones, and a piece of quilt. Besides, it's too close to the creek to be a good burial site."

"So will testing be done?"

"I don't know. The piece of quilt is intriguing, don't you think? If that's what it is. Even if we'd found an animal bone, we'd have a mystery. People don't usually bury their dead animals in a quilt."

"But they might bury a beloved dead dog that way."

"I suppose."

"Speaking of dogs, when I get back to Fort Wayne, I'm going to adopt one."

"What kind?"

"I'm thinking a German Shepherd. I saw one on the beach yesterday. He's named Bruno. Very well-behaved but with intimidating eyes. He let me pet him, but I had the feeling that if I threatened his owner, who's a neighbor up here, he'd gladly disembowel me."

"Are you going to buy a pure-bred?"

"I could, I suppose, but maybe I'll check the shelters first."

"That's a happy project."

"So what time do you think you'll start?"

"Don't know yet. When I'm done here, I've got to go home and pack, check my e-mails, gas up the Expedition, get a bite to eat, so my best guess is I won't be on the road till ten or so. That puts me in St. Ignace about what time?"

"Four or five in the morning if you don't take long breaks."

"Well, I won't be doing that, but four or five in the morning is awkward for you. Maybe I should wait to start until morning. Otherwise, I'll be waking you up."

"No. Start as soon as you can. When you pull into the property, you'll see two buildings. The bigger one straight ahead is the Lodge. Go up the stairs and ring the bell -- unless I'm sitting on the steps waiting for you." She heard masculine voices in the background.

"Hold on a minute."

He came back on the line a few minutes later. "I'm told the second cadaver dog also made a hit on what looks like a shallow grave where the ground has been disturbed and where we found the bones. I'm told these dogs don't get confused between humans and animals. So we've got something serious here. Sorry to cut this short, Lexie, but I've got to talk to the investigator again, so I'm probably going to be here awhile. I'll call you at ten to let you know where I am. Now, what's that phone number at the Lodge? And how about the directions?"

65

I Don't Know How to Say This Gently

Saturday, July 11, 2009

Just as he'd promised, Steve called promptly at ten. "I'm already on the road, still on 69, but I got an earlier start than I thought."

"I can't wait until you get here."

"I have some bad news, Lexie. You might want to sit down."

"About what? The bones on my property?"

"No. Are you sitting down?"

"Hold on. I'll pull a chair over. . . . Okay, I'm sitting. You're scaring me."

"I don't know how to say this gently."

"Just say it."

"Rolie was found dead this evening."

She caught her breath and repeated the words as if that would make them comprehensible. "Rolie . . . was found . . . dead . . . this evening."

"Drago found the body when he returned the Rolls after having it serviced. Rolie was hanging in a corner of the garage."

"I can't believe it. Hanging?"

"Yes."

"Does that mean he killed himself?"

"Don't know, but that's the working theory. His girlfriend was found dead in the bedroom. She'd been tied to the bed and strangled."

"When did they die?"

"Sometime between Friday morning, when Drago picked up the Rolls, and this evening, when he delivered it."

"Did Rolie leave a note or something?"

"Yes. It was in the pocket of his swim trunks."

"What did it say?"

"It was addressed to you."

"To me?"

"To Alexandra."

"He never called me that. Rolie never called me anything other than Lexie. Sometimes he called me Sis, which I hated."

"Hold on a second. I'm coming to a junction. . . . Okay, I'm on the right road. I haven't seen the note and I don't have a copy. I only know what Dave was able to tell me. A friend of his was one of the Sheriff's men called over there, so Dave went over unofficially. The note apparently apologizes for harassing you and confesses to the murders of Vicki and Tiffany."

"You're kidding."

"As I said, I haven't seen the note yet, so I'm just telling you what I've been told."

"Does Matilda know about -- ?"

"Probably, but I didn't call her."

"He really murdered Vicki and Tiffany?"

"Surprising, huh?"

Lexie shivered. "My own brother. Why would he do that?"

"I'm just thinking out loud here, but Vicki was my girlfriend and now I'm your fiancé. All along, Rolie was warning you off me, thinking if we got together he'd be out of your will. Tiffany was your ex-husband's girlfriend. Both girls, in a way, were connected to you through the men they were dating. Rolie tried to get me into trouble and Ferrell too, in the process making you look bad, as if to say that any man connected romantically with you was a homicidal maniac."

"But Vicki was killed before you and I . . . ."

"But in Rolie's mind, we already were an item. That call he made to you in Arizona about her death -- he was warning you to stay away from me, wasn't he?"

"You're right."

"And Rolie has been harassing you for months. Maybe you were next."

She shivered again. "That's a horrible thought."

"He wanted your money. The only way for him to get it was to kill you before you changed your will."

"Drago sort of warned me about that."

"Bad as the whole thing is, I'm trying to find the positive. If you were next, at least he had the conscience not to go through with it. And now there won't be any more bikers threatening you, or phone calls in the night, or dead rabbits in my driveway."

"Poor Matilda! I suppose you'll just get up here and have to turn around because I really can't stay on vacation after this. I'll have to go back and help her make arrangements for

. . . ."

"For a funeral. I realize that."

Lexie finally broke the silence. "I suppose the tears will come, but it's such a shock that at the moment I just feel numb."

"That's to be expected. But I also think you can relax now. I hate to put it that way, but it's a fact."

"Where's Drago, by the way? He must be in shock too. Poor man, finding his old friend like that."

"He was still being questioned at Rolie's house when Dave called."

"But he's not a suspect, of course."

"If the theory of a murder-suicide pans out, no."

"There's no question about that, is there?"

"Not that I know of."

"Well, hurry, Steve. I don't like being alone tonight, that's for sure."

"Make yourself a stiff drink and . . . ."

"By the way, what happened at the site after we hung up this afternoon?"

"The Sheriff is going to make another visit Monday, but after that we can resume work."

"I mean, who do the bones belong to?"

"No idea whatsoever. It'll take weeks, if not months, to figure that out -- if the bones can even be identified. What's strange is that somebody recently removed the body -- well, the skeleton -- leaving a few bits behind. We know that to be true because the grave, if you want to call it that, was obviously disturbed. When you remove compacted soil, its volume increases so the amount removed doesn't fit back in the excavation. Whoever originally buried that body moved it -- well, most of it -- so it wouldn't be found."

"You don't think Rolie buried somebody out there, do you?"

"Not unless he was killing people when he was still a boy. One of the investigators said that whatever happened must have happened a long time ago, given the deteriorated state of that piece of cloth and the amount of tree roots and vegetation that had grown through the cloth and up over the place where the bones were found."

"I don't like thinking about bones and graves and . . . ." She trailed off, trying not to picture Rolie's hanging body.

"As I said, make yourself a stiff drink. I'll be there in a few hours. Love you."

"I love you too. Drive safely."

66

The Billboard

Saturday, July 11, 2009

It was ten o'clock Saturday night before Drago was back in his Jeep. Before he got to I-469, he stopped at a gas station to fill up, then pulled away from the pumps, idled near the exit, and called his mother.

"You think I should talk to Mr. Wright about the bones?"

"What would you say?"

"The truth?"

There was no response.

"Okay. The truth with a twist. Claim it was an accident, Mom. Dad threatened you, the two of you wrestled for the gun, it went off, you panicked. Ask Mr. Wright to stay quiet about it, then pray for mercy."

"Maybe. But Mr. Wright isn't here."

"Where is he?"

"He left an hour ago to join Mizz Royce at Mr. Passwatter's Lodge in the Upper Peninsula of Michigan."

"Where is that?"

"Straight up I-75 past the Mackinac Bridge. Ruth and I -- ."

He cut her off. "Tell me that story later. I'm punching up a map. Do you have directions, an address, anything?"

"Mizz Royce left them in Mr. Wright's office. I'm still at their house, getting ready to go home."

"Don't go yet. I'm going to stay on the line while you get them."

"You aren't driving up there tonight, are you?"

"I'm not going to put off what I have to do. I'll hold on while you get me whatever information you can."

Phyllis came back on the line a couple minutes later. "You have a paper and pencil?"

"Yeah. Go ahead."

"You go north on I-75 past the Mackinac Bridge. When you reach Route 2, go west about 15 miles to a private dirt road called Wolf Lair. It'll be on the left of the highway. This note says the sign for the private road is low to the ground, very hard to read. Then go right about two hundred feet, take a left into the driveway of Eagle Pass Lodge."

"The map says it's about a six-hour drive, so tell Lucy I won't be home tonight. If I get a chance, I'll call her, but I need to think, so don't nobody bother me for awhile. Okay?"

Drago had a lot on his mind. He couldn't concentrate. As soon as he started writing in his head an imaginary speech about the bones that had been found at Elysian Fields, he was distracted by images of bodies: Rolie hanging in the garage, Sorella tied to the bed, Mr. Pussy-wussy posing in women's underwear.

Then a lighted billboard caught his eye. He did a double-take, but he was moving too fast to be sure he saw what he thought he saw. He had to see the billboard again.

He abruptly swerved onto the shoulder, stopped, checked the traffic in his rear view mirror, and backed up half a mile until he could sit and stare at it.

67

Forgotten Speech

Sunday, July 12, 2009

Lexie woke up in the night, shivering. She had gone to sleep on the screened porch after watching the moon rise out of the woods and exhausting herself in a welter of thoughts and memories of Rolland. The temperature must have dropped at least ten degrees, but that isn't what woke her. Something was rustling around on the veranda. She almost screamed when she spotted the animal with the long snout and rat tail. It was ugly and primitive-looking: an opossum, walking in slow motion, carrying three babies on her back. Time to go in.

She glanced at the clock on the stove: three in the morning. Steve would be here soon. She'd pour herself a big glass of water and wait for him on the courtyard steps, but before she reached the door, the wall phone rang in the kitchen. Perhaps it was Steve letting her know where he was.

But it wasn't Steve. "Alexandra, it's Bob. Sorry to call at this ungodly hour, but I just realized I left my presentation for tomorrow -- well, actually, today, a few hours from now

-- in my office. I'm not a good off-the-cuff speaker, so unless I get that paper in my hands as fast as possible, I'm not going to be able to go back to sleep."

"The office here?"

"Yes. The office I'm talking about is the one in the Cottage behind the Lodge. I wrote the speech there over the Fourth and forgot to put it into my briefcase when we left. Did Stewie give you a tour of the Cottage? Do you have keys to it?"

"He did and I do."

"Would you be a darling and go up there now? The speech is lying on my desk, seven pages, double-spaced. You can't miss it. Then, if you would be so kind, you can fax it to me. I'll give you the number here at the hotel."

Glancing at the dark courtyard she would have to cross, she thought of the opossum and shivered. "You don't have it on your computer?"

"I must have deleted it. Of course, I wouldn't call you if I had any other way of getting access. I know I'm asking a lot, Alexandra. I'm going to owe you big time."

She sighed. "You owe me nothing, Bob. It's the least I can do."

"If Steve has arrived, make him go with you. I know Eagle Pass is kind of dark and scary for city girls."

"He isn't here yet."

"But he's on his way?"

"Unless he's run into trouble, he's probably about an hour away." She paused. "How did you know he was coming up?"

"I'm the good Samaritan, remember? I called him Saturday, practically ordered him to get his carcass up there so you wouldn't be alone. I know what it's like staying all by yourself in the woods. I did it once myself and said 'never again.'"

"Do you want me to call you once I've faxed your speech to be sure I sent the right thing?"

"That would be great. The office phone is fancier than the one in the kitchen. It has caller ID and three lines; just punch any one of them."

"Remind me where the light switch is."

"As you enter the Cottage from the courtyard, there's a bank of switches on the wall to your right. Turn them all on if that'll make you feel better. It'll light up the courtyard. When you get up the stairs to my office, the switch will be on the right again once you're inside."

"I'll go over to the Cottage right now. With luck, you'll have your speech in fifteen minutes."

"Thanks, Alexandra."

She drained the glass of water and set it down on the counter, found her keys and a flashlight, slipped on a hooded jacket, made her way to the door, and stepped outside. She paused on the porch, her ears alert, nervously scanning the ground for unwelcome critters, then trotted across the courtyard to the door of the Cottage. She flipped all the switches, which, as promised, lit up the courtyard and every room on the ground floor. When she reached the second-floor landing, before she could insert her key, she realized with surprise that the office door was slightly ajar. She slowly pushed it open, just a couple of inches, and peeked in. The hair rose on the back of her neck.

68

Flash

Sunday, July 12, 2009

One tiny detail he'd noticed on the billboard beside 469 bothered Drago. He'd seen it before, but where?

He'd driven a hundred miles, on his way to tell Mr. Wright about the bones, when in a flash he knew what the billboard detail meant, something he'd never have noticed had he not seen the pictures in Rolie's bedroom.

He knew who the man wearing the lingerie was. The way Mr. Pussy-wussy took his self-portraits, obscuring his face with the flash, he must have thought he couldn't be identified. But he'd overlooked something.

He found the card of the detective who'd interviewed him on State Line Road and placed a call. Though the officer wasn't half as excited as Drago thought he should be about his brilliant insight, he said he'd look into it.

69

Bull Durham

Sunday, July 12, 2009

Lexie couldn't believe her eyes. The office -- what she could see of it -- was a total mess. There were clothes festooned over the sofa. File drawers were open and paper scattered on the floor. A gaping briefcase sat on an armchair and a duffel bag had been thrown in a corner. Post-it notes in a colorful, wonky mosaic covered every surface. The door to the veranda at the back of the Cottage stood open, allowing a cool breeze to sweep through. And an unfamiliar sound emanated from a part of the room she couldn't see yet, the place where she knew the desk to be -- the clackety-clack of an old-fashioned adding machine.

She was frozen with fear. Someone must be inside, but who? Bob was in Cincinnati. Will Berry, the retired-cop neighbor -- had he broken in? But if he had, wouldn't Bruno be guarding the place? Or was Stewie Kramer not the good steward he appeared to be?

Believing she probably hadn't been heard climbing the stairs, she pivoted, ready to creep back down and disappear as if she'd never been there. Then she'd call 911. But before she could start down, a voice called out, "Alexandra, is that you?"

She could hear her own heartbeat pulsing in her ears. She recognized the voice. It was surreal to hear it.

"Come in, Alexandra. I know you're out there. No use pretending."

She pushed the door wider, and taking a step into the office, turned toward the noise of the adding machine. Bob was seated behind his desk, a blue button-down shirt open to the middle of his chest. He looked frazzled, pale and sweaty, his gray hair standing in tufts.

She fought down her shock. "I thought you were in Cincinnati, Bob. What are you doing here?"

He smirked. "Sit down."

She sat.

"My call to you Friday night fooled you, didn't it, Alexandra? You really thought I was in Cincinnati."

"Why would I doubt you?"

"And a few minutes ago, you really thought I was calling from that same stuffy hotel room hundreds of miles away."

She put her hand over her heart as if to slow it down. "I did." The thought that he'd been hiding in the Cottage since Friday made her physically sick. She fought down the urge to retch.

"I got here a few hours after you did."

"Really? Where's your car? I haven't seen it."

"Behind the Cottage."

"Why didn't you tell me you were here?"

He just glared at her. The silence lengthened.

"How are you going to get back to Cincinnati in time to make your presentation?"

He laughed. "You still don't get it, do you?"

"Get what? . . . . Oh." She too began to sweat. "There is no conference."

"Oh, there is. I'm just not speaking at it. If you'd checked, you'd have found that I wasn't lying about a conference."

"But why would I have checked? Why would I suspect you of lying?"

"You wouldn't, I suppose. I'm a Deacon, after all. 'A deacon must be above reproach, the husband of but one wife, temperate, self-controlled, respectable, hospitable, able to teach, not given to drunkenness, not violent but gentle, not quarrelsome, not a lover of money.' I'm above reproach. Paul-the-tentmaker would be proud of me."

Above reproach? Not a lover of money? "Why are you here, Bob?" she finally asked. She scanned the files scattered across his desk, some instinct telling her to pretend she believed he really was above reproach, that his unannounced presence was innocent and everything was normal. "I see you're working. Is there something I could help you with?"

"Money. It just doesn't add up." He glared at her. "You could explain to me why you're trying to destroy Passwatter Global Investments."

"But I'm not. What makes you think that?"

"Withdrawing your principal. Getting your brother, step-mother, and ex-husband to do the same."

"I didn't know they were doing that."

"And then you have the nerve to ask to stay here in my special retreat."

"I told you that in the circumstances I knew I was asking a lot of you."

Suddenly, she noticed the open closet door behind him. On one side was a gun rack. In the middle were costumes hanging on a rod. And on the right was a custom-built unit of drawers, one pulled out. Was she seeing what she thought she was seeing? Rows and rows of very neatly folded women's panties and bras in every shade imaginable. They were arranged in plastic dividers by rainbow shades -- red, orange, yellow, green, blue, indigo and violet, with special sections for white, nude, and black.

He caught the direction of her eyes. "Surprised?"

"Is that women's underwear?"

"Of course."

"Why does your wife keep her lingerie in your office?"

He snorted. "It's mine."

"Yours?"

He swiveled, rolled his chair to the open drawer, and let his hand hover over the bras. Finally, he selected a light blue Felina, size 34C, and held it up. "Recognize this?"

Lexie gasped. "It's mine." She hadn't seen it since Doreen's shower. "You're the Panty Raider!"

He handed it to her. "I wrote your name on the tag at the back. That's the way I keep track of who these lovely things belong to."

Glancing at the tag, she began to tremble. "Who else's lingerie is in there?"

"Dozens of women you don't know. Plus a few you do know. Vicki Grinderman, for example. Xiu-Xiu and her sister, Tiffany."

"But why?"

He sat back in his chair as if they were having a perfectly normal conversation. "Have you ever watched that old baseball movie, *Bull Durham*?"

Lexie nodded, unsure where this was going but full of

dread. She was hearing secrets that couldn't leave this room.

"One of my all-time favorites. Remember that scene where Nuke is persuaded by Annie to wear women's underwear when he pitches a game?"

"Yes."

"And it makes him feel so special he gets out of his bad groove and pitches a good game?"

She nodded.

Bob's voice became wistful. "The church of baseball! Love it."

Where's this going? Lexie wondered. *What kind of madman am I dealing with?*

"Anyway, it gave me the idea for a new hobby."

"A hobby? I don't understand."

"Women's lingerie. We men need to connect with our feminine side. And it gets us out of a bad groove."

"But you're a religious man. You just quoted from the Bible, so you must know better than that. It's just popular claptrap to think that cross-dressing makes a man whole."

"God makes mistakes, you know." He drained his tumbler of brown liquid.

"It isn't God who makes the mistakes, Bob." She looked around the room, trying to think of a way to get out without his following her. A brass drink cart was parked in a corner. "Is that scotch you're drinking?"

"Oban."

"Do you suppose I could have a little? I'm really thirsty."

"Of course. I could use a top-up myself." He stood up, and when he did, she realized he was not wearing trousers. She recognized the red thong she'd expected to find in her luggage. She felt faint. Catching her look, he unbuttoned his shirt to reveal his hairless chest and the matching red bra. "You have good taste, Alexandra. If you wore just a little bigger size, I could fasten this thing without tearing it."

"You stole my underwear -- when?"

"While you were sleeping. Did you know you talk in your sleep?"

She shook her head, unable to find words. When he reached the drink cart, she saw that he was wearing a pair of red stilettos she'd had in her closet only yesterday. The straps, unbuckled, hung open. His heels spilled over the back and his ugly toes, the nails yellow with fungus, splayed out the front, but his legs looked like they'd been waxed. He walked in her shoes as if it was the most natural thing in the world.

Without turning away from her for more than a few seconds, he picked up a bottle of Oban and another tumbler, then returned to his desk and poured a few jiggers for both of them. She sniffed it, as if she were the grateful guest of a generous, sophisticated host, though in fact she'd always hated the smell of scotch. The weird circumstances only made it worse. Pretending to sip the smoky liquid, she kept her eyes on Bob, hoping he'd drink enough to get drunk.

"I have to congratulate you, Bob."

He adopted a modest look. "For what?"

"For keeping your special hobby a secret all these years."

"It hasn't been easy."

"Tell me." Keep him talking.

"I plan really well. When I first started going into women's houses, I never entered one that wasn't within jogging distance of home; nobody notices a jogger."

"How did you get into my house?"

"You laid your keys on my desk once. Remember?"

"No."

"I took you out to lunch. One of the mailroom boys was instructed to take them to a hardware for copying. I had Xiu-Xiu's copied too. . . . Anyway, when I decided to go further afield, I parked a long ways away so my car wouldn't be spotted. I wore jogging clothes with visible print on something so if a camera ever caught me, the cops would be looking for a garment I'd discarded immediately afterwards. I never entered a house that wasn't empty. I always knew the woman whose lingerie I was borrowing."

Borrowing? "And you never got caught."

"Well, I did once, but not by the police, of course."

"Once?"

"Vicki came home earlier than she was supposed to."

Lexie shivered. "You were waiting for her?"

"No. I was in the house when she got home, but I wasn't *waiting* for her. I had no interest in seeing her."

"So then what? You killed her?"

"What choice did I have?" He asked the question as if it were entirely reasonable. "Once she found me in her bedroom, I had to do something because she recognized me. After we made love, I silenced her."

Lexie was almost at a loss for words. "Made love?"

"She just lay there like some Victorian maiden, too prim to acknowledge how much she was enjoying it, but, yes, we made love. The only way anybody would know it had been me was if she could still talk."

"I don't understand. If she was willingly having sex with you, why would she talk? Who would she tell?"

"My wife. Vicki was a spiteful bitch."

"She was?"

He squinted into space. "I didn't know her that well, actually, but I wasn't taking any chances. And my marriage was at stake."

"Your wife doesn't know about . . . about . . . ?"

"My little hobby?"

Which little hobby? Stealing keys and lingerie, breaking into houses, raping victims, or killing them? Lexie nodded.

"No. Clarissa wouldn't understand about the lingerie. And until Vicki, I'd never strayed from my marriage vows."

Raping a woman is the same as straying from your marriage vows? "Did you kill Tiffany too?"

"That was different." His tone turned angry. "The slut led me on. She said if I just made sure she had some of Ferrell's money . . . well, she implied she'd make me feel like a man. But underneath all that temptress facade, she was a black-hearted witch, stirring her secret cauldrons and mumbling her filthy curses. She could make a man wilt just looking at him."

Both of them jumped when the phone rang. As Bob turned to read the caller ID, Lexie dribbled her drink onto the rug. "S. Wright," he said, glaring at Lexie. The phone rang again. He opened a desk drawer, pulled out a Luger, and laid it on the desk, pointing it at her mid-section. "I'm going to put him on speaker, Alexandra. I'm not here. Tell him to come up to the office because you're faxing something to me. Don't act like anything's wrong." He tapped the gun. "Got that?"

70

Big Gold Ring

Sunday, July 12, 2009

After he got off the phone with the detective, Drago called his mother to get Mr. Wright's cell phone number, then punched in the number. "Mr. Wright, this is Drago Bott."

"Yes, Drago."

"I suppose you heard about what happened to Rolie, right?"

"Yes. Dave Powers called me."

"Did he tell you about the photographs laying by the bed where I found Sorella?"

"No."

"A man is taking pictures of himself in a mirror. He's wearing women's underwear."

"Rolie?"

"No. You can't see the man's face because of the flash, but you can see a ring on his right hand -- the hand holding the camera. A big gold ring, very flashy."

"Go on."

"That same ring is on Bob Passwatter's hand. I saw it on

one of those billboards advertising the golf tournament he put on for Mizz Grinderman. He's holding a golf club. The ring kind of stands out once you know it's important."

A long silence. "You sure about that?"

"I called the detective back, but he didn't seem very excited, so I thought I'd call you. Where are you, by the way?"

"I just reached the Mackinac Bridge. Why?"

"I'm not far behind you."

"Again, why?"

"I'd like to talk to you when I get up to the Lodge where Mizz Royce is, if that's okay with you."

"It can't wait?"

"No. You have any idea where Passwatter is?"

"Cincinnati, Lexie said, at a conference. He's chairing a panel for financial analysts. Why, Drago?"

"Doesn't sound right, does it? Did Rolie somehow get his hands on those pictures of Passwatter, or was Passwatter at Rolie's house?"

"You mean . . . ?"

"I mean, could he have killed Rolie and Sorella? If he did, how could he go to Cincinnati as if nothing happened? Is he that cold, you think?"

Just then, Drago heard -- he felt -- his right front tire blow out.

71

For Old Times' Sake

Sunday, July 12, 2009

Steve had been on the road over six hours, and though he liked to drive, he was tired and his head was foggy. He'd been up for more than twenty-four hours, working hard and driving hard. He'd run out of bottled water. Now he'd heard Drago's theory about Bob Passwatter. Much as he disliked the self-aggrandizing financial genius, he couldn't wrap his mind around the idea that he might have killed Rolie and Sorella and was perverted enough to photograph himself in women's underwear.

All Steve wanted was to sit somewhere without the scenery rushing by at seventy miles an hour, have a drink, talk to Lexie, and fall into bed.

Once he'd crossed the Mackinac Bridge and found Route 2 near St. Ignace, he checked the map on his dashboard and his odometer; supposedly, he only had fifteen miles to go. But fifteen turned into thirty without finding 10122 Wolf Lair. The profound darkness of the dense woods on either side of Route 2, the faintness of the highway stripes, the occasional nocturnal animals standing on the shoulders or darting across his path -- everything slowed him down. He couldn't spot the overgrown turnoffs to private driveways until he was almost past them, and the minuscule, unlighted address signs, some only a few feet off the ground, were virtually unreadable anyway.

He was frustrated. He hated to wake Lexie, but he was running out of options. Worse, he was running out of patience. He tried her cell phone, but as he'd been warned, there was no signal. Then, reluctantly, he tried the number she'd given him for the Lodge. When she hadn't picked up after half a dozen rings, he was afraid she wouldn't and he'd continue to wander around in the woods until dawn. He wanted to shout curses into the inky darkness.

But finally she answered.

"Lexie, sorry to wake you, but I'm lost."

"It's okay. I was up anyway."

"You were?"

"I'm in Bob's office. He left his speech here and asked me to fax it to Cincinnati."

"At four in the morning?"

"Yes."

"Is your voice trembling?"

"No."

"You sound different."

"No."

"Am I on speaker?"

"Yes."

"Why?"

Pause. "So I can keep working."

Usually, conversation with Lexie flowed like a stream, but tonight it was jerky, her voice trembly, her responses curt.

"You said you're lost, Steve."

"I'm on Route 2 but I can't find the turnoff to the Lodge. Instead of fifteen miles, I've traveled thirty since I got to St. Ignace. I've turned around and I'm heading back in a roughly eastern direction but I have no better idea now where to turn off than I did before. Is there some kind of landmark that would give me a clue where the Lodge is?"

"If you've gone thirty miles, you're west of the Lodge, so coming back, on your right, you'll see a pasty shop just before Wolf Lair."

"Pasty?" He pronounced it as she did, with a soft "a."

"It's a kind of filled pastry that's popular here."

"What's the name of the shop?"

"Hold on." The silence from her end was so long he wondered if the line had gone dead. "Wilkins Pasty Shop."

"Did you look it up or something?"

"Yes."

What was that pause about? If you don't know the name, what did you look up?

"Anyway, it's a little blue clapboard building that looks like a rambler somebody lives in, except for the sign in front. There's an old-fashioned white porch across the front. The next driveway is Wolf Lair." He heard her take a deep breath. "Soon as you get here, we'll have a shot of scotch for old times' sake."

Scotch? Steve thought. *You don't drink scotch.* Then it hit him. "Did you say for old times' sake?"

She tried to laugh. "You know what I mean. I can't wait to see you."

So Lexie was in danger. That must mean somebody was in the room, listening to the conversation, but who would it be? Ferrell was in jail. Rolie was dead. Bob was in Cincinnati. So it must be a stranger, but who?

Before Steve could think of a clever question that would elicit a clue, she abruptly said, "I have to go now, Steve." The line went dead.

72

Sneaky Devil

Sunday, July 12, 2009

Bob poured himself another scotch. "Despite what your boyfriend thinks, Rolie didn't hang himself, you know."

Lexie felt a bolt of electricity shoot from her neck to the bottom of her spine. "How do you know that?"

"The wall phone in the kitchen is handy." He patted his phone. "I listened in on your calls, so I know what Steve told you."

"I mean how do you know Rolie didn't hang himself."

He snickered. "Because I was there."

"You killed him?"

"Rolie never knew what was coming. He thought he and I were conspiring to kill you, but -- ."

"Kill me? You? You've been like a second father to me."

"But you're not acting like a daughter."

When was that a death sentence? "I knew Rolie wanted my money, but was he really willing to kill me? My own brother?"

"You're so naïve, Alexandra. Did you think he was just going to wait around for you to get married and change your will? Or I was going to let you pull your money out of my investment house?"

"So if he was going to kill me, why didn't you let him do it so you wouldn't have to?"

"The slug wasn't moving fast enough. I couldn't even be sure he had the guts to go through with it."

"Why did he need *all* my money?"

"He didn't need it all, but he had gambling debts. Big ones, enough to wipe him out. A guy named Murph was going to collect Friday noon -- ."

"I know Murph!"

Bob looked amused. "How the hell would you know a guy like that?" He tapped his fingers on his adding machine. "Never mind. I beat him to the punch. Rolie said Murph would show up at noon, so I waited until Drago left, then took care of things well before noon. If the cops suspect murder instead of suicide, I'll make sure they know about Murph and Sue Doody."

"Who?"

"Sue. The owner of Sue-A-Side. She was Rolie's lender."

"But why did you want Rolie dead?"

"The same reason you're going to die."

She began to tremble again.

"It'll take years to get your estates sorted out and the money stays with me until the market rebounds."

"Why did you kill Sorella?"

"Because she was a witness, and once I'd tied her to the bed, I couldn't resist."

"You raped her?"

"It wasn't rape. But she acted just like Vicki -- no help

at all." He looked off into space. "Funny thing is, I couldn't do it to Tiffany. I don't understand the power that witch had over me."

"You wrote Rolie's suicide note?"

"No. I made him write it before I hanged him. The handwriting is his."

"But you had him address it to 'Alexandra.' He never called me that."

"I didn't tell him what name to use."

"Only you call me Alexandra. So . . . so he was signaling me that he didn't write the note and the confession was false. He was even trying to signal that you made him write the note."

Bob looked thoughtful. "Sneaky devil."

"What kind of devil does that make you, Bob?"

He narrowed his eyes in anger.

"So, Bob, despite all your careful planning, you made a mistake."

"Well, the cops won't know that."

"But I do. So does Steve."

"Who'll be left to tell them?"

If she'd had any doubts about whether she was going to be allowed to live, they were utterly dashed. She thought longingly of the gun resting on her bedside table in the Lodge. Perhaps if she made a run for it, she could get down to the courtyard by the time Steve arrived, warn him about Bob and the Luger. She was nearer the door than Bob was and would be a few yards ahead. It might be enough of a lead since he had to get out of his chair and run around his desk, half-dressed, in stilettos that didn't fit, filled with enough scotch to slow his reflexes.

As if reading her mind, he let his hand rest on the Luger. "I know what you're thinking, Alexandra. I can see it on your face."

At the sight of his eyes, dark and hard as marbles, and his hand resting on but not gripping the gun, she impulsively leaned forward and swept her arms across the desk, pushing the gun, the adding machine, a lamp, files, and a big brass paperweight into his lap. Then she shot to her feet, turned, and sprinted toward the door to the bicycle room below.

But Bob was flummoxed only for a few seconds.

The shot hit the door just as she reached it. In her panic, she missed the first step and rolled down the stairs, hitting hips, elbows, and shoulders, losing her shoes, and coming to a hard stop. She screamed in pain. She was sure her ankle was broken.

In seconds, Bob was on top of her, pulling her back up the stairs, one hand on her hair, the other on the hood of her jacket. She screamed again in pain.

But more pain was coming. Back in the office, Bob dragged her into the corner near the open door to the veranda, where a rope was hanging from the ceiling. She hadn't noticed it before. "No!" she screamed, trying to wrench herself out of his hands. He pulled her to her feet and placed a noose around her neck, then made her stand on a little stool.

She couldn't believe she was going to die like this. If only Steve hadn't gotten lost.

73

Not Registered

Sunday, July 12, 2009

Drago was almost done changing his tire when his cell phone buzzed. He opened the passenger door and reached in to find his phone. "Yeah?"

"This is Ron Kenan, the deputy who interviewed you at the home of . . . ."

"Yeah, I remember you. I called you a few hours ago about Passwatter."

"You have any idea where he is?"

"I just heard he's at a conference in Cincinnati."

"His wife told us the same thing, at the Hilton Netherland where she thought he was giving a speech tomorrow, but he's not registered there."

"You sure about that?"

"Yes. I'd like to talk to you again, Mr. Bott."

"I'm way up north on I-75, near the Mackinac Bridge."

"Why?"

I'm not telling you about the bones, that's for damn sure. "Rolie's sister is staying in the UP this weekend -- at Passwatter's Lodge, as a matter of fact. I thought that once she heard about Rolie dying she might not be in a condition to drive herself home, so I'd get her and drive her back. I do that for her sometimes."

"Did you say Robert Passwatter's Lodge?"

"Yeah."

"Is he up there?"

"No idea. Never even thought about it."

"What town is the Lodge near?"

"St. Ignace, I think. Let me read you the address."

"I'm going to call the authorities there, tell them to take a look at the Lodge."

"Sounds good to me."

"Keep in touch, Mr. Bott."

"Will do."

Drago then immediately placed another call to Mr. Wright. "Did you know Passwatter is not in Cincinnati?"

"How do you know that?"

"From the deputy who questioned me at Rolie's place. Passwatter isn't registered at the hotel where his wife thinks he's spending the weekend at a conference."

"Why would he lie about that?"

"Don't know nothin' about that man, other than the underwear. Anyway, I gotta go. Wouldn't you know, I got a flat."

"Be forewarned, the turnoff for the Lodge is a bitch to find."

"Okay then." Drago returned to the tire. When all the nuts had been tightened and the hubcap replaced, he picked up his MagnaLight with its magnetic mount and placed it on the roof of his Jeep. He wished he'd had that light when he dug up his dad's bones because then there wouldn't have been any left for dogs to find and this trip wouldn't be necessary.

74

Drop Your Gun

Sunday, July 12, 2009

Finally, Steve found Wolf Lair. The dirt lane wound through brush and trees that clicked against his Expedition as he crept along. Ahead, the lane split to the left and right. Which way was the Lodge? Why hadn't anybody warned him about that? Spotting a light to his right, he took the right lane and found the Lodge. When he pulled into the courtyard, he found it lit up, just as Lexie had said it would be. She said she was in the Cottage, not the Lodge, but which building was it? On the left, as he remembered, the smaller one. He saw a light in the second-floor windows.

He removed his handgun from the case under the driver's seat, found the bullets in the back, and loaded it. Then he walked to the building on his left, cautiously opened the door, and stepped in. When he spotted the stairway in the corner, he crept over and looked up. The door at the top was closed but light was seeping under it. Lexie must be up there. If Bob wasn't in Cincinnati, could he be here? But what kind of danger would he pose?

He crept up the stairs, wondering if the door would

be locked. He paused, his ear close to the door, but heard nothing. Then he slowly depressed the lever door handle. When it clicked, he pushed it open as hard as he could.

The room was dark except for a bit of light coming from somewhere on the other side of the door. The first thing he saw was Lexie, standing in the corner near an open door on a stool, a rope around her neck. Her clothes were askew, her eyes black with fear. Strands of blond hair littered the carpet. What the hell? She rolled her eyes to a spot behind the door. But before Steve could think what to do, Bob stepped into his line of sight, a gun in his hand, a weird smile on his face. Steve was surprised to see the gun and revolted at the sight of the stilettos and red bra and thong.

"We've been expecting you, Mr. Wright."

"Drop your gun, Bob, I'll drop mine."

"Sure thing," Bob said, but he didn't drop the gun, instead pointing it at Lexie. "But I suggest you go first so your girlfriend gets to live a few minutes longer." When Steve hesitated, Bob fired a shot over Lexie's head, and Steve dropped his gun.

Lexie screamed. She was too panicked to cry, but when she realized she hadn't been hit, she said plaintively, "I can't stand here much longer. I think my ankle's broken. My leg is about to collapse."

Bob ignored her. Steve wanted to run to her, but that might be his death knell -- or, worse, Lexie's.

"Sit down, Steve. We have to talk."

"About what?"

"Slandering me. I never stole a dollar from you and Frank."

If I pretend to be compliant, maybe I can find a way to rescue

Lexie. "I believe you."

"Are you apologizing?"

"I am. Why don't you put that gun away?"

Bob laughed. "Not yet."

"Why are you wearing that stuff?"

"Your girlfriend's lingerie, you mean?"

Lexie's? You're wearing her underwear? He fought down the impulse to lunge over the desk and strangle the pervert. With Lexie whimpering in the corner, he could barely think straight. "How does a man famous for his piety wear . . . wear . . . ?"

Bob assumed the tone of a college professor explaining theories of literary interpretation to a class of bewildered students who liked to read until they enrolled in his class. "Two points of business wisdom I learned early, Steve. Pretend to be a believer so people assume you're honest and never question your ethics. Even the skeptics like to deal with a God-fearing man."

"Pretend?"

"Only an idiot *really* fears -- or trusts -- God. He's done nothing good for me. Everything I have, I got for myself the old-fashioned way."

"What way is that, Bob? Holding people hostage?"

"You've got a smart mouth. The second bit of business wisdom is this. Make it difficult to get into the club. People value only what is difficult to acquire. So in your case, don't make it easy for people to buy lots in your development. Make it a privilege."

Pretend this is a reasonable conversation. "That's quite a business model."

"I'd enjoy discussing it longer if the setting was just a

little different but I'm getting tired. I want you to get up and kick the stool from under your haughty fiancé."

"What?"

"Then I shoot you so it looks like a murder-suicide."

"Why would anyone believe that's what happened? What's my motive?"

"Alexandra came up here to get away from you when she broke off the engagement. She confided in me that she'd found out about your affair with Jean Arnold. Alexandra knew that your only reason for marrying her was to get hold of her fortune. Then, desperate for money and furious that you'd been publicly rejected, you followed her up here, and when she wouldn't change her mind, you killed her." Bob picked up the gun. "Now go over there and kick that stool."

Steve stared at Bob. *Are you really letting me get near Lexie?* He got up, turned to look at the love of his life, and smiled, mouthing the words "It's okay."

75

Pendragon

Sunday, July 12, 2009

With the help of his MagnaLight, Drago spotted the turn off on the left for Wolf Lair just as he was passing it. He made a squealing u-turn and entered the lane, turned right when it split, then left into a courtyard. He couldn't see Mizz Royce's MINI-Cooper, but Steve's Expedition was parked near the door to the building on his left.

He removed his gun from the glove compartment, went to the back of the Jeep to load it, picked up a flashlight, and walked to the courtyard door. He hesitated. The atmosphere was positively creepy. Something prevented him from opening the door to the building. Where were Mizz Royce and Mr.Wright? He decided to walk around a bit, scope out the territory.

When he got to the back of the building, the woods were so dense he couldn't have seen a thing without his flashlight. He almost bumped into a Porsche he didn't recognize. He tried the door and found it unlocked, then checked the glove compartment. No keys, but he found papers. The vehicle was registered to and insured by Passwatter Global

Investments. *So Passwatter really isn't in Cincinnati. He's here. But where exactly?*

He continued walking along the back of the building in the direction of a faint light on the second floor. When he came to the stairway to a long second-floor veranda, he stopped, straining to hear a sound or spot a figure in the lighted window above. Something flew above his head and he frantically swiped at the air. *What the hell is that?* God, why did people like the woods? He hated them.

He tested the bottom step. It didn't squeak. He mounted another step. Still no sound. Then a few more. He stood there a second, staring at the windows, the open door on the veranda. Then he heard the shot and a scream.

He raced up the stairs and crouched near the screen door. There was a body on the floor, a man. Mr. Wright? He thought so. Then he saw the woman standing on a stool, a noose around her neck. Mizz Royce, staring at something or someone he couldn't see from the veranda. Suddenly, Mizz Royce's legs gave out, the stool she was standing on fell over, and she grasped the rope, struggling to keep it from choking off her air.

He could wait no longer. He burst through the screen door and whirled to see where the shot had come from. He wasn't shocked to see Mr. Pussy-wussy standing near a door on the other side of the room, but Mr. Pussy-wussy was very shocked to see Drago. With the advantage of surprise, Drago grabbed Mizz Royce with one arm, lifting her just enough to stop the choking, simultaneously firing at the pervert who seemed frozen with shock. Drago's shot hit the door instead of the red bra he was aiming for, but his second shot found its target -- the pervert's ugly butt as it disappeared around the door. He heard the man clattering down the stairs, and though he longed to follow, he had other things to do. He got Mizz Royce out of the noose and carried her to a sofa. He didn't know what to do for her choking and gasping; he knelt to check Mr. Wright; he was alive but unconscious.

"Where's the damn phone?" he yelled. Spotting the desk, he raced over, punched a button to get a line out, then punched in 9-1-1. "This is Pendragon Bott. I have an emergency at Eagle Pass Lodge on Wolf Lair. Two people are down on the second floor of the smallest building. The shooter's on the run, and I'm going after him."

"No, no, sir, don't move. Stay on the line. What's happened?"

Drago bounced from one foot to another, impatient to get off the phone. He pictured finding Mr. Pussy-wussy and beating him to death before the authorities arrived. He wanted to leave his personal mark on the man who threatened the life of the woman who'd given him a second chance.

76

Feast

Sunday, July 12, 2009

Bob's lovely heels came off as soon as he entered the woods. He hadn't had time to grab the keys to his Porsche. If he were just wearing trousers, he'd have those damn keys in his pocket and be protected from the branches, pine needles, thorns and vines tearing his legs to pieces. He knew it was dangerous to leave a trail of blood in these woods. Though the pain in his buttock was escalating, he was too panicked to slow down. He could see nothing ahead of him, but he planned to stop crashing through the brush when he sensed from the downward slope that he was near the edge of the bluff. He had no idea how he'd reach the beach in one piece or what he'd do when he got there.

His concern about what he'd do when he reached the beach was wasted energy, for the mother black bear heard him coming and she wasn't happy about the invasion, the threat to her cubs. He didn't smell as good as a moose or a fish, but he was right there, ripe for the eating, and she was hungry. Plus he wasn't a bad change from honey, nuts, and berries.

She dragged the invader halfway down the bluff and then invited her cubs to the feast. They paid no attention to his screams.

Epilogue

Labor Day Weekend

Saturday, September 5, 2009

Labor Day weekend meant very different things to Lexie's circle.

★★★Lucy Bott spent Saturday at her parents' liquor store, which was overrun with customers stocking up for the holiday. Since liquor sales were banned on Sunday, people didn't want to be caught short Monday morning. Mostly Lucy sat on a stool at the cash register because, six months into her pregnancy, being on her feet was already tiring. A month ago she'd discussed with Drago whether to try to buy Tiffany's Asian Bazaar in Covington Plaza.

"I'd be good at running a shop," she said, "and we could buy the place cheap, stocked and everything."

Drago hesitated. "You don't want to stay home with the baby for a few years?"

She smiled. It was time to tell him. "Not 'baby.' Two

babies, Drago. We're having twins."

It took him a second to recover. "Twins?"

"Boys."

"Two boys? Wow, I'm good. Know that."

Lucy laughed. "We all know that."

But after discovering that Tiffany's shop was embroiled in the many investor lawsuits involving Passwatter Global Investments and might never be available, they decided it was much wiser for her to become more active in her parents' very successful business -- and to stop slipping Benjamins out of the till. She could even work part-time there after the twins were born by setting up a little nursery in the back of the store.

Meanwhile, after fighting off Mr. Passwatter and rescuing Mizz Royce and Mr. Wright, Drago had become famous. He'd been interviewed several times and then been offered a book deal, though he had no damn idea how to do a book, even working with a ghostwriter. Mizz Royce and Mr. Wright had given him a handsome reward for rescuing them: Mr. Wright's house in Autumn Ridge, which he and Lucy would move into as soon as Mizz Royce's house had been completed in Elysian Fields. He'd been promoted at the Scrapyard and given a small raise -- smaller than he thought he deserved, but still it was good.

There were only a few loose threads left in his life. One of them was the bones found in Elysian Fields. Neither Mr. Wright nor Mizz Royce was in any condition to talk the night Bob died, and after that Drago's new status as a hero made him reluctant to diminish it by bringing up something his mother had done many years ago. He'd wait to see if he ever had to explain the bones.

Someday, he'd be the Scrapyard King and Lucy would be the Liquor Store Queen.

***Clarissa Passwatter spent Labor Day weekend at Eagle Pass Lodge, without her sons and their families. But she wasn't alone.

She had received the news of her husband's death with greater calm than anyone could have expected. Several months before Bob tried to hang Lexie Royce and had shot Steve Wright, she'd been cleaning an attic space over the garage in Sycamore Hills when she stumbled upon a box of strange photographs. At first, she had no idea who the man was or why the pictures were in her house, but once she stopped denying the obvious, she knew. Her husband had a terrible secret. She considered confronting him, or turning the pictures over to the authorities, or at least urging Bob to talk to their pastor.

But she was afraid. The pictures of the dead women were the scariest things she'd ever seen. She knew who the women were, of course. If Bob could kill them, what would he do to her if she exposed his dark deeds? And the dire implications of her husband going to jail for murder made her sick, for Passwatter Global Investments would surely be destroyed. She was used to a certain style of life. Without Bob, who knew how she'd live?

After finding the pictures, she went straight to Marty Solomon to discuss her financial situation in case she sued for divorce. Fortunately, most of their personal assets had been put in her name, and since she never played any role in Passwatter Global Investments, she was likely to keep most of them no matter what happened, though no doubt she'd have to defend against lawsuits to recover investors' losses.

Then she got on the Internet to find out all she could about men who raped and killed women. The Green River and BTK killers -- Gary Ridgway and Dennis Rader -- were fascinating and somewhat comforting. Both men raped and killed many, many women but lived outwardly respectable lives, treating their clueless wives like -- well, like wives.

Believing she was relatively safe for the moment and knowing divorce was always a way out of her predicament, she decided to keep quiet and wait to see what happened. Of course, she took the precaution of sleeping in another part of the house, pleading a "female" problem. Every night, she locked the door to her bedroom.

What finally happened was surprising. A month after Bob was buried and the investigations into the deaths of Vicki Grinderman and Tiffany Chow were officially closed, a handsome younger man she didn't know knocked on her door. He was there to commiserate with her.

***Matilda Royce was devastated for a month after her precious son was found dead in his garage. She was even more devastated by the freezing of her account at Passwatter Global Investments.

"At least he didn't kill himself," she told Grace Venable. "I don't have that shame to deal with."

"He wasn't a very attentive son anyway, was he?" Grace asked in her inimitable directness.

"No. But he was the only child I had."

"Well, just get on with your life. That's the best advice I can offer."

"How? All my money was invested with Bob."

"But you have the income from the Scrapyard, don't you?"

"I do." She didn't admit that her step-daughter was paying her Rolland's salary on top of her share of the profits for another year or until the defrauded investors began recovering some of their assets, which ever came sooner.

"Why don't we buy houses next door to each other in Charleston? In my estimation, it's the loveliest city in the country, a lot nicer than any place in Florida, and the prices will never be better. A change of scenery will do you good. Then let's plan a river cruise in France."

They began making their plans.

★★★Ferrell Hawke had come within a hair's breadth of being indicted for Tiffany's murder. Every time he thought about it, he came close to exploding with anger at the injustice of it all. Worse, his account at Passwatter Global Investments was frozen, along with everybody else's, while the business was unwound and the lawsuits ground their way through the courts.

Fortunately, when the unpleasantness at Eagle Pass Lodge occurred in July, he was on summer break. And because the union protected him, he was not facing the loss of his job as a result of the suspicion he'd been under, the time he'd been in jail, or the notoriety he'd engendered.

So, once he'd been cleared, he flew to London to reunite with his family for a couple of weeks with the idea that he might return permanently to the country of his birth. Unexpectedly, he felt like a stranger there. The family home was cramped and ugly. His parents were bores. His brothers were much more successful than he was. Academic jobs were impossible to get and taxes were high. The constant threats to public safety posed by the IRA in his youth had been replaced by constant threats from the Muslim population.

Disappointed, he returned to the United States and once again stuck his head, this time voluntarily, in the barbed wire fence enclosing Fort Wayne. Then he had an idea. If he couldn't retrieve his fortune directly from Passwatter Global Investments, maybe he could retrieve it by romancing Bob's widow. Posing as a friend and fellow victim, he could at least find out if Clarissa was in possession of enough money to make it worth his while to court her.

Spending the weekend with Clarissa at Eagle Pass Lodge might yield the information he needed. Unexpectedly, he found himself mildly attracted to her. He'd never considered an older woman as a romantic object before. But he very much liked her quiet, humble ways -- so different from both Lexie's and Tiffany's -- and the luxury of Eagle Pass Lodge.

If things worked out, the name of the Lodge could be changed to Hawkemere. What a thrilling triumph that would be. Even without a name change, however, it was gratifying to sit on the veranda in a rocking chair beside the Widow Passwatter, sipping expensive wine and overlooking the woods where the man who had cost him a fortune and tried to frame him for murder had been eaten by bears.

***Attendance at the Fifteenth Reunion of the Carroll class of 1994 in Johnny Appleseed Park broke all records. The temperature was in the mid-70s, with only a slight breeze and occasional sun. The caterers had prepared a feast featuring prime rib and king crab legs. Danielle and The Hanson Brothers performed popular rock and blues in a giant tent outfitted with a huge dance floor and backed with an American flag. Danielle was asked over and over to sing *Here for the Party.*

"So, how are you coping, Lexie?" Jessica Singer asked, handing her friend a glass of wine. "Still having nightmares?"

"Not every night."

A teasing look on his face, Steve patted Lexie's back. "I think she's having them just so Henry will get up and lick her face." Henry was the four-month-old German Shepherd who slept on the floor of their bedroom. The day they'd recovered from their physical wounds, they adopted him from the City shelter on Hillegas Road.

Happy to be diverted from the subject of her near-death experience, Lexie's face lit up. "I've got Henry's pictures on my iPhone." She took it out of her purse and began scrolling. "See? He's just a bundle of baby fat, big paws, and wet kisses."

"Where's he going to stay while you're gone? Or is he going on the honeymoon?"

"No. Phyllis is taking him home with her, with instructions to limit the treats she gives him. She's volunteered to take him to puppy school."

From a discussion about dogs, the conversation eventually turned to Bermuda. "I've never been out of the country," Linda Adler said. "So I can't wait to get on that plane, wave goodbye to Indianapolis, and say hello to the beach. Are you as excited as I am about the wedding?"

"Of course. Jean has worked day and night on the preparations, and if she and Dwight weren't leaving for London that week, they'd be there too."

"How's your house coming along?" Ed asked.

"We're hoping to get in by Christmas," Steve said. "We'll be having a big party then, so set some time aside over the holidays."

"What's going on with Passwatter's estate?" Ed asked, turning his attention to Lexie. "You think you'll see any of your money?"

"The fight's just beginning and I'm told it could take years to get everything sorted out. Fortunately, I never invested all my money with him, so I'm okay."

"Did you ever suspect what lay behind all that piety?"

Lexie looked at Steve. Both shook their heads.

"I suspected he was dishonest," Steve said, "but I had no suspicion about the extent of it, and I don't know anybody who guessed he stole women's underwear."

"Or had an affair with Tiffany Chow," Lexie added.

"Or was a murderer and rapist."

"It makes you wonder about people, doesn't it?" Tad asked. "For weeks after I heard about what happened up there in the UP, I tried to guess the secrets that lay behind every face I saw."

"If only the bears hadn't eaten him and instead he simply died from the bullet from Drago's gun," Lexie said, suppressing a laugh, "Bob could have been stuffed and placed on the landing with Wild-Boar Scrofa. I'd have paid for it myself." Then the jokes began.

Author's Note

Margarite St. John is the pen name of Margaret Yoder and Johnine Brown, two sisters who were born in Iowa, live in Fort Wayne, Indiana, and vacation in Florida.

Margaret, the Storyteller, is a fan of true-crime stories. Formerly a school teacher with a B.A. in Education from Indiana Purdue at Fort Wayne (IPFW), she now leads a Bible study group. Married to a surgeon, Margaret has three children.

Johnine, the Scribe, is a retired attorney and college professor with a Ph.D. in English Literature and a J.D. from the University of Chicago. She has two children and five grandchildren.

We both love beautiful shoes and dogs -- even dogs who eat shoes. People seem to be surprised by our dark, irreverent sense of humor about everything. Our favorite fan comment is, "I couldn't put the book down."

Visit us on our web site at www.margaritestjohn.com or on our blog at www.margaritestjohn.blogspot.com. Our books are available for Kindle and other electronic devices and in paperback.

28173690R00262

Made in the USA
Lexington, KY
07 December 2013